TATTOOS & TEARS

Dark Truths

TATTOOS AND TEARS · BOOK EIGHT

AMIEE LOUISE

This book contains scenes of graphic violence, adult language, sexual situations, nudity, and adult content. It is recommended for readers over 18. Reader discretion is advised.

Dark Truths

Dark Truths

Tattoos and Tears Book 8

Hold Fast Publishing, LLC

"I looked for pieces of myself within every page. My story was mine and only mine to tell."

– Zeppelin Williams.

Prologue

Zeppelin

Never in my thirty years on this earth have I contemplated how I would die. I was too busy just living. I had my whole life ahead of me, and I was lucky to be alive, or so I was told. *Why would I burden myself with morbid, yet hypothetical thoughts of death?* However, in the weeks since I lost my best friend, I have thought about nothing more than how I would die on a near-daily basis. Would I get the generic Hollywood ending, whispering final words to those I love? Would I die in the arms of my soulmate, or slip away quietly in my sleep? Or would I leave this world the way I entered it, kicking and fucking screaming? One thing I was damn near certain of, I refused to go out quietly. I wanted my time on this earth to mean something; I wanted my death to be an exclamation mark, not a question mark.

But I'm an author, I have the ability to write my own ending, and I was determined to make it one to remember, like the one rare book that stays with you long after you've closed it. Every page would be dog-eared with wonder, smudged with ink from nights I couldn't bring myself to stop, and the words came much faster than sleep ever did.

I am snapped from my daydream as I stand at the floor-length window of Jax's mansion, looking out across the acres of lush green land that seemed to go on for miles. Air fills my lungs, and I feel my chest expand, the world rushing in with it. The events of the last week tear their way through my consciousness, making the stark reality feel almost too real. Just a week ago, my life was blissfully normal, or as normal as it could have been. I had fallen hopelessly in love with Jackson Chase. I had my cosy apartment, my overprotective best friend Rian, and my loyal canine companion Jericho. The stability of my writing career and both of my amazing, selfless grandparents, Jimmy and Pru.

Now, I was drowning in a nightmare, the moment when I opened an innocent box and came face to face with the severed head of my only friend, Rian St. James, playing in my mind on a constant loop. The metallic smell of blood and the acrid smell of rotting flesh permeating my nostrils, making my stomach roil, clinging to every one of my senses. I try desperately to erase the sight from my memory, but that image is forever burned into my retinas. I can't seem to come to terms with what happened and the sheer absurdity of it all. I clawed at the invisible walls closing in, my breath coming in ragged gasps, desperately seeking an escape from the suffocating weight of it all. *How could this be happening? Who would want to hurt him?* It had been a long time since I had experienced such a loss, but it never gets easier. It grips you tight and refuses to let go, driving you to utter despair.

Grief is like living two lives, splitting you in two, like two halves of one whole. One half is where you pretend that everything is alright, the other half is where your heart screams silently in agonising pain. It's like wearing a mask, and every so often, that mask slips. Grief comes in all shapes, sizes, and forms. I thought I had experienced genuine grief when I lost my father, Ronnie Williams, and my ex-boyfriend, Abel Creed, but nothing would ever compare to losing my best friend. The person who knew me inside and out, the person who knew every facet of me, just as I knew every facet of him. He understood me on a level that no one else ever has and probably never would. He knew my deepest, darkest secrets, and I knew his; he believed in me when no one else did, and I would miss him until the day I leave this mortal coil. The intense grief I felt overwhelmed me; it consumed my every waking thought and haunted my nightmares. I had lost a part of myself, and I would never get it back. It hurt to think of him suffering in his final moments. It hurt to think that he died alone, and it broke my heart to think of someone wanting to harm even a hair on his beautiful head. He didn't deserve to be just a number, another statistic, another unsolved murder; he deserved justice, and I was determined to get it for him, if it was the last thing I ever did for him.

As I look up into the concerned hazel eyes of Jax, the woodsy scents of musk and Diesel Only the Brave invade my nostrils, grounding me somehow. The pain of a thousand knives piercing my chest, threatening to choke me where I stand. My world was spinning wildly off its axis, and the gravity keeping my feet firmly rooted to the floor had abandoned me. I felt like I was free-falling, the crippling grief overwhelmed and dominating every part of my being. My world had crashed down around me, and there was fuck all I could do about it, other than ride out the storm and hope that Jax and I were strong enough to weather it.

For a long time, I carried parts of my story like a lead weight that I didn't want anyone else to see. The mistakes, the heartbreak, the moments that almost broke me. But every single piece of my journey shaped me; instead of running away from it, I embraced it. I owned my story, and my story mattered. As one chapter ended and another began, I would seek justice for Rian. He wasn't just a number, another statistic - he was flesh and blood, and I loved him. Along the way, I would find out some dark truths, and the past that I thought was firmly behind me would come back to haunt me. I would come face-to-face with some familiar faces, ghosts from the past, present, and future. The question at the forefront of my mind was, would I surrender to the darkness, or would I rise like a phoenix from the ashes and face those dark truths head-on?

I

Jax

Her eyes flutter open, and I study her carefully like a vulnerable, frightened animal about to bolt at the sight of trouble. I can see her mind playing catch-up, reminding her of the events of the past weeks. The small hitch of breath, as she sits upright in bed and frantically scans the room, her eyes landing on me. She is sitting on my king-size bed, her back pressed against the headboard, her blonde hair an adorable mess around her gorgeous face, her lithe body gloriously naked under the sheet that she so modestly clings to to cover her nudity. I cross one leg over the other, leaning back on the navy velvet chaise lounge in the corner of the room with my guitar at my feet. I place my dog-eared notebook and my pen down next to me, as I continue to regard her intently. Her breathing quickens as she realises I'm watching her, her mouth opening and closing as if her words are trapped in her throat. She swallows hard, and her tongue swipes over her dry lips, but she stays silent.

"Good morning, love."

I greet her cheerily with my usual boy-next-door grin, reserved only for her, trying desperately to gauge her ever-changing mood. Her complexion is pale, her face gaunt, and her silver eyes lacking their usual sparkle. She presses her lips together in a tight line, and I cock my head to the side.

"Would you like some breakfast?"

She shakes her head wordlessly. She's given me the same answer every day since she's been here. I'm so worried about her; she's not eating, she's barely sleeping, she's spoken less than thirty words to me, and she's crying all the time. I get that she's consumed by grief, but she's not coping with Rian's death at all. I've been keeping a watchful eye on her since she reluctantly agreed to move in with me temporarily, while the person who killed her best friend is on the loose. After she discovered Rian's severed head in a package that was delivered to her flat, the police were called immediately, and it was officially declared a murder investigation.

"When can I go home?"

Her voice is small, she's asked me the same question every day, and every day I give her the same answer.

"Not yet, sweetheart, it's not safe."

I use a soft, placating tone to my voice, and she drags the sheet from the bed, wrapping it tight around her body. She avoids all contact with me, sidestepping me so she doesn't have to come near me. She doesn't meet my concerned gaze as she goes into the bathroom, locking the door behind her. *Fuck my life.*

I don't know how much longer I can do this, watching her turn into a shell of her former self, it's soul-destroying and...fucking exhausting. I never know what mood she's going to be in from one moment to the next, and I'm constantly walking on eggshells. I want to support her, but she's pushing me away. It's been three long years since I've been in a long-term relationship, and I'm struggling to adjust and navigate life as a us, instead of an I. I run my hand through my long blonde hair, deep in thought, and lean back on the chaise lounge, my tattooed chest bare, as the bedroom door swings open. Thea rubs her eyes, wearing Scooby Doo pyjamas, with Jericho next to her, his tongue flopping out and his tail wagging wildly. Thea and Jericho have developed a close bond since Zeppelin moved in, Jericho taking on the role of her furry protector, following her around like a shadow. *It's actually quite adorable.*

"Daddy."

She mutters sleepily as she moves further into the room, letting out a long, dramatic yawn. Jericho matched her step for step, not taking his eyes off her.

"Good morning, Princess."

She holds out her arms for me to pick her up, and I lift her up, settling her in my lap. Jericho sits down proudly in front of me, watching her closely. As the morning sun filters through the floor-to-ceiling windows, it casts a warm glow on the room, and I can't help but smile at the heartwarming scene unfolding in front of me. My beautiful daughter, my world, the reason I'm still walking this earth, her infectious laugh fills the air, as she nestles herself in my lap. Her large, expressive eyes, sparkling with such wonder and innocence, were moments like this that I lived for. Jericho remained ever protective, a faithful guardian watching over his little princess. Even though he wasn't her dog, it gave me a sense of relief to know he was an extra level of protection for her. With one hand gently resting on Thea's back, I used the other to stroke Jericho's soft fur with my long, deft fingers, acknowledging his devotion and reassuring him that his family was now complete, even if it was only temporary. In this tranquil moment, the worries and pressures of fame and the outside world seemed distant and unimportant. It was just us in our own private sanctuary, and I felt blessed beyond measure to be surrounded by such love. I wish I could freeze this moment in time so I could go back and hold it in my memories forever.

The bathroom door swings open, and unexpectedly, the moment is lost. Zeppelin steps out in a perfume-filled haze, a bright pink, fluffy towel shielding her nudity. She doesn't meet my gaze, her eyes red-rimmed, she's been crying again, and it breaks my heart that she does it in the privacy of the bathroom. She doesn't confide in me; she's just clammed up, locked her feelings up tight. I set Thea down on her feet, and she looks up at me questioningly.

"Go and brush your teeth and get dressed, sweetheart. Daddy just needs to talk to Zeppelin, and I'll come and make you some breakfast."

I tell her softly, as she nods.

"Pancakes and bloobs'?"

She asks, smiling mischievously, and I roll my eyes with a smirk. *Fucking Brody*. She takes off a hundred miles an hour, closely followed by Jericho, until it's just me and Zeppelin in the room. I close the door behind Thea and approach Zeppelin cautiously, not wanting to intrude on her personal space. I couldn't ignore the obvious pain I saw in her turbulent silver eyes, and the air felt heavy with unspoken words, and I struggled to find the right things to say.

"Zeppelin."

I begin gently, and she finally meets my gaze.

"I can see that you're hurting, and I want you to know I'm here for you. You're not alone, sweetheart. Whenever you're ready to talk, I'm here for you. I'm not going anywhere."

She lets out a small, sad sigh, her vulnerability evident, as she wraps the towel tighter around herself.

"I can't."

She admits softly, her voice quivering with emotion. I take a step closer to the woman I had fallen so head over heels in love with. It was inevitable; she didn't make it easy to love her, but I couldn't help myself. They say opposites attract, and she couldn't be more opposite if she tried; that's what drew me to her. She was magnetic, stubborn, headstrong, and independent, but she made me feel whole again, and I'd always be grateful for her coming into my life.

"I'm scared, Jack."

She confesses, her voice barely a whisper. I swallow at her admission and encourage her wordlessly to continue.

"I'm scared of not being strong enough, I miss him...so much."

A dull ache settles in my chest, squeezing my heart in a vice-like grip, as if it, too, is mourning the loss. I reach out gently to touch her bare shoulder. She shivers as my fingers contact her skin, briefly closing her eyes, allowing herself to revel in my hands on her.

"It's ok to be scared, we all have moments of vulnerability, and that's ok, that's what makes us human. As for being strong enough, that's bullshit; you're the fucking strongest person I know, you've shown incredible strength in so many ways these past few weeks. Any other person would have crumbled under the strain, but you, you carried on, even when you thought you couldn't. I'm so fucking proud of you for that."

I tell her with such pride in my voice, as tears glisten in her eyes, but this time she doesn't look away. The look in her silver eyes makes my heart hurt for her.

"I wish I could believe that."

She murmurs, a glimmer of hope flickering in her expression, and I smile softly, offering her a sense of reassurance.

"Trust me, you're stronger than you think, you never have to face this alone. Whenever you're ready, I'll be here. I'm always here."

My voice softens, and for a split second, the weight of her emotions seems to lighten, as a fragile smile graces her lips.

"Thank you."

She whispers, her voice filled with gratitude, and I nod, acknowledging that I've said my part, and the rest is up to her.

"You don't have to thank me, but take all the time you need. I'm going to make Thea some breakfast; I'll be downstairs whenever you're ready."

With those words, I step out of the bedroom and make my way down the corridor to use the bathroom in Thea's room. I hope that someday Zeppelin will find the strength to confide in me unconditionally, knowing I'll always be here for her, no matter what.

2

Zeppelin

I wanted to believe that there was a version of me that could survive this, that could claw her way out of the wreckage and still recognise her reflection when she looked in the mirror. But the truth was, I didn't know who I was anymore. Grief had hollowed me out, and in its place was a desperate need for answers, for justice, for revenge. But after the heart-to-heart with Jax, I felt lighter somehow, and I clung onto the fact that maybe, just maybe, everything would be ok after all.

I make my way down the elaborate staircase; it never fails to amaze me that he lives here. A mixture of platinum discs and candid portraits of him and Thea at different stages of her life, along with various awards he's won with Rancid Vengeance, lined the stairs. It's ultra-modern but lived in, and I felt at home with him, Thea, and Jericho; it was like we were a family. I glided silently across the cool, polished marbled floor, the smooth texture sending a shiver up my spine. I made my way into the large kitchen; I didn't make my presence known, but it warmed my heart to see them all together. The mouth-watering smell of sizzling bacon and freshly cooked pancakes wafted through the air, filling the room with a tantalising scent that made my stomach rumble. I couldn't help but smile to myself, and those butterflies I write so frequently about were fluttering wildly in my stomach. The music filled the silence, and I froze as I allowed myself to take in the lyrics and the song. *"Journey Don't Stop Believin'" was playing loudly* through the state-of-the-art Bose sound system, as I was transported back to happier times.

Zeppelin

Past

As I sit at my dressing table, I stare at my reflection in the mirror and sweep the brush over my cheek. The rosy hue highlights my features and emphasises my natural beauty. I hum softly to Gladys Knight and The Pips Midnight Train to Georgia playing in the background. Jericho is lying quietly at my feet with his head resting on his front paws, looking up at me expectantly. He lets out a sigh, and I smile to myself.

"It's a hard life being a dog, isn't it, buddy?"

I muse as I concentrate on finishing applying my makeup, swiping mascara over my lashes. Jericho leaps up from his position at my feet, and his tail starts wagging, my lips quirking into a smile.

"The partaaaaayyy has arrived!"

Rian sings in his melodic voice, giving me a twirl and finishing with a theatrical kick of his leg. He's wearing black skinny jeans, which look like they have been spray-painted on. Today is his birthday, and he insisted that we go out to celebrate. He sets a bottle of pink Prosecco on my dressing table and produces two champagne flutes from a black leather bag. He quickly and deftly uncorks the Prosecco with a loud pop, pouring it expertly into the two glasses. He hands a glass to me with a beaming grin and a dramatic eye roll.

"If we're going out to party, then we need some decent music to get us in the mood! Come on, Zep!"

He lets out a loud sigh as he starts to scroll through my playlist with a look of pure disgust on his face. He spends a few minutes scrolling, as I take a sip of cool Prosecco, the bubbles bursting on my tongue. He clucks his tongue and flashes me a dazzling smile, his eyes dancing with mischief.

"Now, this is more like it!"

He starts to play Journey's " Don't Stop Believin' and turns up the volume. We both laugh at the memory; it's a song from my favourite musical, Rock of Ages. It was the first theatre show we saw together when I first moved here. He knew some of the people who were in the cast and managed to get us backstage. It was one of the best nights of my life, and I'll never forget it. He offers me his hand and pulls me up from my chair. He starts singing at the top of his voice and spinning me around. We dance and sing like loons for the remainder of the song. By the time the song ends, we're both breathless and giggling like children. At that moment, I promised myself I was going to go out, let my hair down, and have a fucking great time. It was going to be lots of booze, dancing, and good company.

The night continued in a blur of laughter and shared moments with Rian. With newfound energy, I decided to embrace the evening's spontaneity. We stumbled out of the lively club into the cool night air, our laughter echoing through the streets, our arms linked. The bustling city streets pulsed with electric energy, beckoning us with the promise of thrilling adventures awaiting discovery. In that moment, London wasn't just a city to me - it was a symbol of rebirth, a fresh start, a clean slate, and I decided to embrace it, as we wandered from one place to another, exploring the vibrant nightlife that the city had to offer. The neon lights illuminated the streets, casting a colourful glow on the faces of strangers passing by. The music from various clubs blended into our childlike excitement, drawing us further into its culture and scene.

At some point, we found ourselves on a rooftop overlooking the city skyline. The cool breeze tousled our hair as we looked out at the sea of lights stretching before us.

"The world is ours for the taking, baby girl! You and me against the world! WOOOO HOOOO!"

He said with a chuckle, and in that serene moment, surrounded by the hum of conversation and the distant city sounds, I felt an overwhelming sense of gratitude for the spontaneous decision to let loose and have a great time. I realised that this night had been a much-needed escape. It was a reminder that life could be unpredictable and beautiful, full of moments waiting to be embraced.

Zeppelin

Present

I was jolted back to the present by Jax singing at the top of his voice, doing air guitar, and Thea giggling at his over-the-top morning antics. She claps her hands and bounces in her seat excitedly. He was wearing loose grey jogging bottoms and a black t-shirt, which clung to his tattooed muscles, and I couldn't help but stare at him. He was just a dad trying to entertain his daughter, and it should have been a heart-warming moment, but I wanted it to stop. I couldn't listen to it any longer. I wanted to curl up in a ball and sob until I had no more tears left.

"Stop."

I mumbled as I put my hands over my ears to drown out the music and the painful memories it brought to the forefront of my mind. I could no longer bear the weight of those haunting memories that plagued my everyday existence. The music, with its driving rhythm and infectious beat, clawed at my raw emotions, threatening to drown me in grief.

"Please stop."

I pleaded, my voice barely audible and thick with emotion. The room felt like it was closing in on me, as hot tears cascaded down my cheeks. Jax was still oblivious to my meltdown, and he continued to spin Thea around the kitchen to the beat of the song. I could feel the raw ache in my chest, memories of happier times, reminding me what I had lost. My heartbeat quickened, and my chest began to tighten. *Please God no, not again.*

"JUST FUCKING STOP!"

I scream as Jax turns on his heel, his boy-next-door features marred with concern. A frown line jumps between his eyebrows as Thea looks up wide-eyed at him, questioning why I'm screaming at her daddy. Her hazel eyes brimming with tears and her bottom lip quivering, as she looks from me to Jax.

"STOP! STOP! STOP! PLEASE FUCKING STOP!"

He calls for Alexa to stop, halting the music almost immediately. The room fell into an eerie silence, and I sank to the floor under the weight of my grief. I was constantly exhausted, and I couldn't close my eyes without the image of Rian's gazeless stare playing on a loop in my head twenty-four seven. It breaks my heart to think he died alone, and I was struggling without him. He was my person; he was my best friend, the person who knew me better than I knew myself, the person who knew my deepest, darkest secrets and didn't judge me for them. He was the one person who understood me, and I would miss him forever. As I sob, gut-wrenching, wailing, hiccupping sobs, Jax sinks down to the floor beside me as the patio door swings open.

"Mornin'."

Lucas drawls, halting in his tracks, as he takes in the scene unfolding in front of him. He looks from me to Jax, and then to Thea. Her face lit up as her eyes landed on Lucas, her tears from a few moments ago forgotten.

"Hey, Thea!"

He croons, a beaming grin on his face. He is wearing running gear, consisting of a heather grey vest, long black basketball shorts, Nike trainers, and a grey beanie hat.

"Uncle Lukeyyyy!"

She squeals, and he swings her up in his arms, as Jax looks up, a stricken look on his face as they communicate wordlessly.

"Let's go and play some Mario Kart on the Switch!"

Lucas speaks enthusiastically, and she giggles, her tears suddenly forgotten. He takes her through the kitchen and out into her playroom, closing the door behind them. Jax pulls me into his lap, and I bury my face into his chest, my sobs turning to silent sniffles as he rocks me in his muscular arms. I bask in his warmth, taking in his unique scent. He makes me feel safe. These past few weeks, he's been my rock, and I would be forever grateful for his silent support.

"Tell me what to do, sweetheart. Tell me what I can do to make it better."

The raw emotion in his voice makes my heart slam against my rib cage as I bury my face deeper into his chest.

"It's going to be ok. Everything is gonna' be alright, I promise."

He soothes, as I cling tighter to him, feeling the warmth of his embrace. With each measured word, he speaks. I sob for my best friend; I sob for the life he once had that was cut far too short; I sob for the memories that we shared together, and I sob for the unconditional love and friendship we had over the years that would never be replaced. As I cling to Jax for dear life, I have never felt so alone, and that thought made me sob harder. I had entered the pits of hell, and I had no idea of how I would come back from this.

3

Jax

Watching the woman, I love to break down so completely, it shattered my already fragile heart. I had no idea how I could make it right; I wanted to shoulder the burden for her, I wanted to take her pain away, but I could feel her pulling away from me every second of every day she spent here with me. In the weeks that had passed, we had completed the U.K leg of our Rancid Vengeance tour, and tomorrow, we leave for the U.S. Despite asking her countless times, she refuses to come with me, and I had no clue how I was going to keep her safe in my absence. Three months was a long time to leave her unprotected, and I wasn't entirely comfortable with flying around the world without her.

After what seems like an age, her sobbing turns to silent sniffles, and she pulls away from me. She shifts her gaze to the floor, and I tip her chin up, forcing her to look at me.

"Look at me, sweetheart, we're going to get through this, I fucking promise you."

My voice thick with emotion, as another tear slips down her cheek.

"Please reconsider coming to America with us."

I ask apprehensively, knowing the answer before I've even finished my sentence. She shuffles backwards across the floor away from me.

"We've talked about this, Jack! I can't! Three months is a long time! I have to be here in case...something happens."

She hesitates for a few seconds, clinging desperately to any excuse she can think of, but I nod in agreement. *I had no idea what would happen, but fuck it, just go along with it, Chase.*

"I understand that, but that fucking psycho is still out there."

My tone clipped as I clenched my jaw at the terrifying thought.

"You're going to be here unprotected while I'm gone. I can't do that, Zeppelin, please. I left Ruby unprotected, and look what happened! I won't put myself through it again! I won't survive it, not this time! I've already lost one woman I loved; I won't lose another."

The frustration in my voice is evident as she puts her hand to her head and leans against the marble worktop, briefly squeezing her eyes shut.

"WHY DOES IT ALWAYS COME BACK TO HER? I'M NOT HER! I'LL NEVER BE HER! I'LL NEVER COMPARE TO THE WAY YOU FELT ABOUT HER!"

She screams, an exasperated tone to her voice, and I get to my feet, stalking across the kitchen towards her. I grab her arm and spin her around to face me, placing her hand on my warm chest, as she finally meets my eyes, brown on silver. She's inches away from me, and I can feel her breath gust out against my cheek.

"Do you feel that? My heart beats just for you now, you're the only woman I want. Ruby is in the past, you and me, we're the future, we're for keeps. The love I feel for you...it consumes me, it...it's everything I felt for her, times a million. You're it for me, Zeppelin, you're my second chance, you're my fucking reason. I didn't think I could love anyone else, until I met you."

I tell her sincerely, suddenly feeling like the biggest prick on planet earth.

"So, please, consider my offer, even if it's just for a few weeks. I know three months is a long time, but I can't leave you here; it goes against everything in me."

My voice soft, as her shoulders sag and she nods.

"I'll think about it."

She whispers, and I know it's just to placate me, but that had to be enough for now.

***

After Zeppelin's mini meltdown earlier, she retreated to her home office, shutting me and the world out. I had a feeling the next three months could make or break us, and I didn't want to be right. I was grateful for Lucas distracting Thea and shielding her from this whole mess. Thea is in her playroom with Jericho, and Lucas and I are sitting at the kitchen island drinking coffee.

"Wanna' talk about it?"

He asks as he takes a long sip of his coffee. I scrub my hands down my face and puff out my cheeks.

"I'm fucking exhausted, man. I don't know how much longer I can do this, Luke."

I hang my head limply in absolute defeat, resigned to the fact that our happy ending is becoming further out of my grasp.

"One question you gotta' ask yourself, brother, is she worth it? If the answer is straight up yes, then you know what you must do. If the answer is no, then as brutal as it will be, you have to cut your losses and walk away. But deep down, you and I both know what the answer is gonna be. Any fool with a pair of eyes can see that."

He states matter-of-factly with a casual shrug of his shoulders. I have no idea how he knows the right words to say and how to put into words how I'm feeling when I struggle to understand it myself. He is truly remarkable at reading people and empathising, even as he battles his own demons daily. I sometimes think it's to mask his own feelings, but I'm not entirely convinced.

"What book did you read that in?"

I tease, and he smirks.

"Mock me all you like, dude, but we both know I'm gonna' be right in the end."

I lean my elbows on the kitchen island and wrap my hands around my coffee mug, looking for the comfort I know I won't find in it.

"Come on, you replicated her office from her old apartment to make her feel more secure and at home, that's a pretty huge deal, man. She's grieving for her best friend, but we know all too well what that's like; we've lost people, too..."

He looks up to the ceiling, his eyes glistening with tears, as he stops himself from continuing his line of thought, and his mouth flattens into a straight line. The weight of his unspoken words hangs heavy in the air, a silence pregnant with emotions he can no longer put into words. His chest rising and falling, as he takes a deep, shuddering breath, trying to find the strength to carry on. I can't hide my surprise because Lucas never shows his emotions. He's usually so aloof and detached from every situation he finds himself in. Watching him unravel in front of me sets me on edge, as he lowers his gaze, his jaw clenching and unclenching. His voice, barely a pained whisper, breaks the silence.

“Slade and I have decided to call it a day; we’re not seeing each other anymore.”

He finally admits, trying to sound nonchalant, but the crack in his voice betrays him. I open my mouth to speak, and he shakes his head vehemently in warning. I wasn’t expecting him to say that, but I have the sense not to press the issue. I start to think that maybe, in another life, we all could have had the lives we always wanted, just not this one, and it was up to us whether we chose to accept that.

4

Zeppelin

I wasn't one of those needy girls who needed constant reassurance. I had been single for so long that I'd forgotten what it was like to rely on someone other than myself. But I was more than aware that I wasn't the first woman he loved, and even though I knew it was me he was going to come home to, and only me, in three long months. I couldn't help but feel insecure that I wasn't skinny enough, that I wasn't pretty enough; the women he and Rancid Vengeance surrounded themselves with were far superior to me. Jackson Chase was rock royalty compared to Abel Creed, and it showed in every aspect. Everything about his lifestyle screamed luxury and opulence, and I was just an ordinary, run-of-the-mill author with a normal working-class background.

As I turned over to his sleeping form, I took in his every feature, every sharp line of his jaw, every sculpted cut of his torso, the ridged bumps of his six-pack, down to the lean curve of his hips. He managed to look fit without looking overly muscular. His biceps were thick, but not too bulky. I wanted to commit every inch of him to memory because after tonight, I would have to make do with FaceTime calls for the next painful, gruelling three months. We would be in two different time zones, and this could be the ultimate test of our relationship. He shifts in his sleep, and I still for a moment.

"I can feel your eyes on me, sweetheart."

His voice is thick with sleep, and I can see him smirk in the dull moonlight. I cover my eyes with my hands, embarrassed at getting caught. He chuckles, and I groan audibly.

"I got caught perving!"

I admit, unable to hide the shame from my voice, and he quirks his eyebrow in clear amusement.

"Perving? What are we, fifteen years old?"

We both laugh; he's awake now, and he turns on his side, propping himself up on his elbow, his hair falling over his shoulder. I roll over onto my stomach, and he reaches over to stroke my cheek. I lean into his touch, humming in appreciation at the feel of his fingers running feather-light touches across my face.

"You're so beautiful."

He compliments, and I feel my cheeks flush. I place my hands over my face, hiding myself away from him.

"Don't hide that gorgeous face away from me, sweetheart."

He says with a chuckle as I feel the bed dip. Unexpectedly, I'm flipped onto my back, and he's on top of me, straddling me with my arms pinned on either side of my head. His erection is digging into my abdomen; I feel a familiar flutter deep within me, and my pussy floods with heat. I lift my hips up and grind myself against his cock, as he tightens his grip on my wrists. His cock grows harder, and my heartbeat starts to quicken. The look in his hazel eyes is smouldering, and he leans down, blanketing me with his hard, lean body. He kisses me on the lips in a searing-hot kiss, and I swear in that moment, I stop breathing. I deepen the kiss, not wanting it to end, and he swallows my moans, as I writhe beneath him. My pussy is aching for him to be inside me, my pulse is racing wildly, and I'm burning for him.

He frees my wrists and lowers himself until he's settled between my legs, my back arching.

"Jax."

I moan, lifting myself up to meet him, desperate to feel him pressed against me.

"What do you want, beautiful girl? Tell me."

He croons as I bite down savagely on my bottom lip. *Fuck, he's so much more experienced than me.* I feel inferior as I lie here, my whole body exposed to him. I shake that wayward thought away, as I focus on him and the pleasure that he can bestow upon me.

"Please, I want you, I want you to make me come, I want you to fuck me, Jax!"

My voice sounds breathy and needy, but I'm desperate for him. He plunges two fingers deep inside me, and I cry out at the feel of him deftly twisting his calloused fingers in and out of my soaking wet heat. He increases his pace with each measured and expert movement. He finger fucks me thoroughly, driving me towards my pending release.

"God, you look so beautiful, I want you to come for me."

He rasps, as his fingers continue their assault, moving deep within my slick channel.

"OH FUCK, JAX! OH GOD! PLEASE DON'T STOP!"

His eyes find mine, and I can't look away from him. With one swift movement of his fingers, my orgasm detonates, my mind feels like it is short-circuiting, as I scream out and we spend the rest of our last night together making slow, sensuous love under the covers. I lost count of how many orgasms he gave me so willingly, and I committed every inch of his body to memory, as it would be three long months without him. I had to hope with everything in me that he would come back to me.

***

I had begun to cherish the tranquillity of the early mornings. It was those precious few moments when life was as it had been before. I turned over in bed and stretched out like a cat, hearing the door closing. I smiled to myself, as I imagined Rian breezing in in his Ted Baker pyjamas and matching slippers, waving a brown paper bag in the air, announcing he had bought breakfast in his sing-song Welsh lilt. I ran my fingers idly across the cool sheets, unfamiliar sheets that felt alien to my touch.

I sat up slowly and scanned the room, my daydream just that, a figment of my imagination. I didn't want to be here; I wanted to be in my apartment in Notting Hill, I wanted to be sitting at my desk writing on my computer, overlooking Portobello Road Market with a steaming cup of coffee in my hand, listening to my eclectic Spotify playlist to accompany whatever book I was writing at the time. I wanted Jericho to be sitting at my feet, offering me some sort of comfort. But Jax insisted it wasn't safe for me there; it was my haven for five years, and it was something I could call my own.

I didn't want the lavish lifestyle that came with dating rock royalty; I wanted the simple life. I wanted a cheap Chinese takeaway; I wanted a glass of wine at our local pub. I wanted to step outside the gates without a camera shoved in my face. I felt all kinds of fucked up and out of sorts, to say the least. Jax had reluctantly gone on a three-month tour of the U.S and left me here under the protection of Rancid Vengeance's security team. He had asked Peyton of all people to check in on me, but after the way she reacted at the final of UK's Finest, I had politely declined the offer. I had a feeling she didn't like me much, but

Jax insisted she needed time to process the fact that he had moved on, that he had found love with someone who wasn't Ruby. Although she was a ghost in our relationship, pictures of her still hung on the walls. There were parts of her scattered around the house, from the picture of a monkey blowing a pink bubble in the bathroom to the Atticus poetry wall in one of the guest bedrooms. I still felt like a stranger here, a temporary house guest, and I wanted nothing more than to go back to the way it was before. I craved normality, even though Jax had thoughtfully replicated my home office from my flat in one of his many guest rooms, which I was grateful for, but it still wasn't the same.

I swing my legs out of bed, stripping my pyjamas off as I go, and I head into the bathroom, turn on the shower, and find my playlist. I tell the Bose showerproof sound system to play, and the room fills with *Blanco Brown Nobody's More Country.* I step into the walk-in shower cubicle, the seven jets pummelling every inch of my body, awakening my senses and boosting my mood for the day. I spend longer than my usual twenty minutes under the almost-too-hot shower spray, welcoming the sting of the water. My skin instantly turns a shade of pink, resembling a lobster. When I emerge from the shower, I feel refreshed and ready to face the day. I wrap my hair in a towel and move fluidly across to the sink, swiping the condensation from the mirror. I hum along to *Jolene by Dolly Parton* as I brush my teeth.

I pad back into the bedroom, drying my hair straight and pulling on a pair of black skinny, ripped jeans and a black-and-orange pineapple-printed shirt tied at my midriff. As I pick up my phone to check for messages, I hear a distinctly female voice. *Peyton Newbolt, fuck me, that's all I need. I'm not in the mood today.* She's made it quite clear what she thinks of me, and her reaction to me at the final of UK's Finest told me all I needed to know. I'd never be Ruby; I was a poor replacement, and the look in her eyes was forever embedded in my frontal lobe.

"I-I'm sorry, I-I-I can't."

Her words ring in my ears, as I try desperately to be as quiet as I can in the vain hope that she will realise I'm not here and just go the fuck away. I peek around the wall at the top of the stairs, aware I'm being childish by hiding from her.

"Hello? It's only me."

She calls out in a sing-song voice, as I straighten, pulling up my big girl pants and walking down the marble staircase barefoot. I see her standing in the open-plan foyer with an armful of shopping. She looks up at me, and I can't hide the disdain.

"If you've come here to be a complete bitch, you can turn around and leave because frankly, I'm really not in the fucking mood."

I state bluntly, and she lets out a sharp bark of laughter.

"I deserved that."

She says flatly, with a quirk of her perfectly plucked eyebrow, placing the bag at her feet. Her dark hair, with purple and turquoise highlights, is perfectly tousled on one side and braided on the shaved side of her head, secured with a purple bandana. Her small baby bump is visible beneath her galaxy-print dungarees. From what Jax had told me, she and Sam had hit a rough patch due to his bipolar disorder, but after a string of miscarriages, she had found out she was pregnant again.

"I can see why he likes you, you're feisty. He's got a type; he has a thing for feisty, tenacious women."

She muses as her shrewd blue eyes scan me carefully. Her photos do not do her justice; she is beautiful, she's one of those women who make you feel inferior somehow.

"Is there a reason you're here? Did Jack send you to check in? If he did, you'd have a wasted trip. I'm fine; you can shut the door on your way out."

I can't help the vitriol that spills from my mouth as I get to the bottom of the stairs and go to pass her. She nods slowly, biting down on her bottom lip and gently gripping my arm.

"For what it's worth, I am so sorry for the way I acted when we first met. It genuinely wasn't anything personal; it's been a long time since he's introduced us to a woman, and he's kept around for more than twenty-four hours."

She explains, and I nod in understanding, her apology sincere, but I can't help feeling jealous at her statement.

"Ruby was more like a sister to me, losing her was...unbearable...earth-shattering, fucking devastating. Not just to me, but to everyone she knew. She was magnetic; she would make friends in an empty room! She and Jax were so in love, but she was easy to love, ya know? I know it's probably not easy for you to hear, but it's been hard on all of us. All of us are in therapy because of what happened in Vegas. Thea is growing up without a mother, Jax is raising her as a single dad, and he got his happy ever after taken away from him. But you're his second chance, don't take that away from him."

Listening to the pure devastation in her voice makes my heart hurt for her. I had seen the news reports after the events that occurred at Sam and Peyton's wedding in Las Vegas. I can't imagine what they all must have gone through. Nine people in Rancid Vengeance's entourage died in the most horrific way on that day, including Ruby and Sam's mum, Lori Newbolt. Rumours were that it was Sam's sister, Savannah Newbolt, who was the mastermind behind the whole thing, along with the band's ex-manager and music mogul, John 'J.D' Dalton. I never asked Jax for the full details. I felt like it wasn't my business, but maybe one day he would trust me enough to tell me. Peyton breaks the awkward silence between us.

"He mentioned you recently lost your best friend, so surely you understand what it's like to lose someone you love?"

She cocks her head to the side, regarding me intently, and I swallow back the tennis ball-sized lump that has formed in my throat. I hum shakily, my eyes swimming with tears, unable to verbalise my thoughts and feelings without bursting into floods of uncontrollable sobs.

"I don't know you, but I'd like to, if you're willing to give me a second chance. I know I don't deserve it, but if you're going to be a part of the madness of the Rancid Vengeance family, then we at least should get along. I'm not a terrible person, believe it or not, depending on who you talk to! But I love every single one of those boys to absolute fucking death; their battles are my battles. Trust me when I say, in the beginning, he struggled; that's why he kept you to himself. I get it, I really do, more than you realise, being a part of this world."

She gestures around us, and the more she speaks, the more I understand what she and the other members of the Rancid Vengeance family went through.

"It's not easy, your life isn't your own, the press owns your fucking soul, and I can't stand it. But it comes with the territory, I guess. I miss being a nobody. I miss being able to go to the shops looking like shit. It's the little things, ya know? It's...exhausting."

She lets out a sigh of exasperation, and I smile warmly at her.

"I get it, more than most, I've dated a rock star before. It's not my first rodeo!"

I admit, sharing a little more than I'm comfortable with, but if we're going to get to know each other and eventually become friends, she deserves to know my story. She cocks her eyebrow, and her lips quirk into a smirk.

"It's always the quiet ones!"

She quips, and I let out a laugh.

"We were together for five years, it was my first serious relationship, it was a total whirlwind."

I trail off, as I remember mine and Abel's doomed romance.

"Aren't they all?"

She says with a sarcastic, wry chuckle, but I ignore her sceptical comment and continue.

"Abel was small-time compared to Jack, but I was young and naïve. I didn't quite fathom what I was getting myself into at the time. I was just a kid playing in the big leagues, and I got my fingers burned."

I explain wistfully, as her eyes widen and her forehead creases.

"*Christ,* you were with Abel Creed, from The Poison Puppets?"

She states incredulously, and I nod, pushing the unwanted memories of Abel to the back of my mind.

"Yeah, I was one of the sole survivors from the yacht accident."

I shift my gaze and idly play with an invisible thread on my shirt, as she reaches over to brush my arm.

"*Fuck,* I had no idea, I'm so sorry."

I shake my head and dismiss her with a nonchalant wave of my hand.

"It's fine, don't be. It's a terrible time in my life that I'd rather forget, but I guess we're more alike than we first thought."

I admit, with a shrug, standing in the opulent marble hallway of Jax's mansion, Peyton and I went from enemies to friends.

5

Zeppelin

I help Peyton with the shopping she kindly bought for me, and she follows me into the kitchen, as I set the bags down on the island.

"I still haven't got to grips with his fancy pants coffee machine!"

I laugh, pointing to the large, glossy black contraption sitting on the marbled worktop. She flashes me a smile, fills the machine with coffee grounds and water, and switches it on, making it look like the easiest thing in the world. It starts to make a rumbling sound, and I smirk.

"Are you sure it should be making that noise?"

I quip, and as she's about to answer, there is a sharp rap on the door. We look questioningly at each other.

"I'm not expecting anyone."

I tell her, as I go out into the hallway and cautiously open the door, aware that the grounds are heavily guarded. Whoever it was would have had to buzz the gate to be let in. I open the door and am greeted by two detectives wearing matching black suits.

"Miss Williams? I'm Detective Fellows, and this is Detective Maddox."

Detective Fellows introduces himself. He's of average height, well built, with a bald head, steel-blue eyes, and a dark Hercule Poirot moustache perfectly curled at the ends. The other detective, whom he introduced as Detective Maddox, is tall and lean, with dishevelled, mousy-brown hair and blue eyes with dark circles under them. His dark suit looks cheap, his shirt is untucked, and his tie is loose around his neck.

"Do you mind if we come in?"

I look from the Detectives to Peyton and nod my head politely, smiling awkwardly.

"Of course, come in."

I invite them inside, stepping out of the doorway to let them in, and I close the door behind them, unnerved by this unexpected visit.

"Apologies for the intrusion, but we'd like to ask you a few questions regarding the murder of Rian St James."

I try desperately to quell the tears I can feel burning behind my eyes at the mention of my best friend, catching me completely off guard.

"Would you like tea or coffee, Detectives?"

Peyton asks with a sickly-sweet tone to her voice, eyeing them warily, as both detectives nod curtly and reply.

"Coffee would be great, please. Mine's milk, two sugars; his is coffee, black, no sugar. Cheers darlin'."

Detective Fellows states with a forced smile on his face, he looks like he wants to be anywhere else but here right now.

Peyton nods and goes into the kitchen, busying herself making the coffee. I gesture for them to follow me into the living room and sit down on the large, sectional corner sofa. The detectives sit at the opposite end, turning to face me, and Detective Fellows takes out a notebook. I suddenly feel edgy and uncomfortable, wondering what the purpose of this unexpected visit is. Detective Maddox takes out an iPad, and after a few taps of the screen, he turns it towards me. The footage is grainy, but I recognise Rian straight away. He's walking confidently through the lobby of our apartment building, his arm wrapped around another tall man, wearing camouflage combat trousers, a V-neck black t-shirt, and black biker boots. His face is obscured by Rian's neck; it's impossible to tell who the man is as I watch the footage intently.

"Do you recognise this man?"

Detective Fellows asks, regarding me cautiously, and I study the video. I shake my head slowly as Rian and the mystery man walk across the lobby. Rian has a beaming grin on his handsome face, but the man's features are still hidden from view.

"Was Mr. St. James seeing anyone that you know of, Miss Williams?"

"Please call me Zeppelin."

I ask with a smile, and he nods curtly.

"No, Rian and I used to tell each other everything; we were best friends, I'd know if he was seeing someone."

I state adamantly and with more confidence than I feel.

"Is it possible that he was seeing someone, and he didn't want you to know?"

Detective Maddox counters.

"It's possible, but we knew each other inside out; it was impossible for us to keep things from each other."

I explain as Detective Fellows scribbles down my answers.

"And you definitely don't know this man, or who he might be?"

He probes.

"Can you rewind the footage so I can watch it again?"

I ask, as he swipes his finger across the screen, pulling the footage back to the beginning. I watch it closely, looking for any clues who this man might be, but I don't recognise anything about him. *What the fuck were you doing, Rian?* I whisper to myself as I continue to carefully scrutinise the video. My stomach was roiling at the thought that Rian kept the fact that he was seeing someone from me.

Why would he do that?

"Was Mr. St. James on any dating sites that you were aware of?"

Detective Fellows asks as he sets his pen down on top of his notebook.

"He was on Grindr, I think, but he'd just recently broken up with someone."

I reply honestly, as the detectives turn to look at each other.

"Do you know who it was that he broke up with?"

I nod.

"Yes, his name is Danny Debonair, he's a part of Rancid Vengeance's entourage, and he's their stylist. He and Rian were seeing each other on and off for a few months. It was getting serious until they broke up."

Detective Fellows writes down what I have just shared, and Detective Maddox shifts his gaze towards me.

"Do you know why they broke up?"

I shake my head.

"No, he didn't tell me the reason."

I answer honestly, and both detectives nod in unison, as Peyton brings the coffee in, handing the cups to each of them. They smile their thanks, and she looks at me questioningly. I shake my head slowly in response, and she leaves us to it.

"We understand you're in a relationship with Jackson Chase from Rancid Vengeance. Is that correct?"

Detective Fellows asks probingly.

"I don't understand why that's relevant."

I can't help the obvious snark in my voice. *How fucking dare they?*

"My best friend was murdered, so I don't see the significance of who I am and am not dating, *Detective.*"

I emphasise the word *detective,* and Detective Maddox looks at me with a quirk of his eyebrow.

"Is there anyone you can think of who might have a grudge against you or Mr. St. James?"

He asks and I am taken aback by that question. *Someone who could have a grudge against me, or Rian?* I visibly shudder at the thought, and I shake my head, suddenly feeling out of sorts.

"No, no one that I can think of, we kept to ourselves."

Then I start thinking of all the poison pen letters, but surely whoever is behind them couldn't really be capable of something like this? *Why would they go after Rian and not me? Oh God, this is all my fault.* I push those wayward thoughts to the back of my mind and decide not to say anything to Detective Fellows and Detective Maddox.

Before I know it, the detectives both rise to their feet at the same time.

"Thank you for your time, Miss Williams. This will be an ongoing investigation, and we'll be in touch."

I stand up and shake their hands in turn, as they both head to *the front door to leave. As I take a moment to process the revelations of the last twenty minutes, my mind starts racing. What if Rian knew his killer? What if it's someone we both know? What if I could have prevented it?* I must go back to my flat in Notting Hill. I need to be alone; I need to think about what this might mean for me, for Jax. I don't want to purposely put him in harm's way; he's been through enough, we both have. Peyton peeks her head around the door frame.

"What the fuck was that all about?"

She states abruptly, and I let out a bark of laughter.

"I'm fucked if I know! They were asking questions about Rian and if I knew if he was seeing anyone. I didn't, but what if I didn't know him as well as I thought I did, Peyton? What if he was hiding something from me?"

I muse, and she shakes her head.

"Listen to me, babe, there's no purpose of the phrase what if, I learned that the hard way. I spent far too long dwelling on what if, and it didn't get me anywhere. I lost a year of my life on what if, and if it taught me anything, it's insignificant...inconsequential...fucking pointless. If he was seeing someone and didn't tell you, I'm sure he had his reasons. I know you want answers, but sometimes you're better off not knowing. Do you need to call Jax?"

The concern was evident in her tone as she observed me closely. I shook my head, an idea forming in my mind.

"Actually, I need to go back to my apartment to grab some more stuff. I've been meaning to do it for a while, but I haven't got around to it."

I explain, trying to sound convincing, and she nods, regarding me intently, as she pulls her phone out of her pocket. She swipes the screen and puts the phone to her ear.

"Hey...yeah, it's me...I know, I just wanted to hear your dulcet tones! Babe, look, I need a favour...I know, I know, and I'll owe you one...Yep, can you take Zeppelin to her apartment in Notting Hill, please...She needs to grab some more stuff and bring it back to Jax's...I know, I know, I get you've been instructed not to let either of us go anywhere alone...I know, spare me the lecture, Jace...Ah awesome! Thank you, see you in five! Have I ever told you you're a prince among men? Aw, bless ya, see you soon! Byeeeee!"

She hangs up the phone with a beaming grin on her face, and I can't help but smile at her enthusiasm.

"I've got those boys wrapped around my little finger! Jace is coming to get you in five minutes. I have to be back at the shop for an afternoon appointment, but I can come back later if you're up to having company?"

I am grateful for her offer, as I begin to form a plan in my head of what I'm going to do once I get back to my apartment.

6

Zeppelin

The door slams shut behind me, enclosing me inside the place that once felt like home. Silence greets me as my eyes sweep across the room, and memories surge like a tidal wave. The day I moved in, the first night spent curled up on the recliner with a takeaway and cheap wine, and that impromptu flat-warming party with Rian. Just the two of us, dancing to eighties hits and laughing until our sides ached. He was my anchor in the chaos of the city, my only friend. My heart clenches, and I swallow back the lump that had formed in my throat.

The air was stale with nostalgia; my corner sofa still sat in its place, my faux-fur blanket draped over the seat, just as I had left it. The walls were still in their muted, neutral tones, but something felt...off somehow. A chill creeps along my spine as I turn toward the window overlooking Portobello Road Market. The blind clattering in the breeze, it was open. *Had it always been?* I didn't remember leaving it that way. *Maybe Pops had stopped by?* I pull out my phone, my thumb hovering over his name in my contacts, when a sound shatters the stillness, glass breaking, followed by a sharp, guttural yell. My body froze where I stood, the phone slipping from my hand and hitting the carpet with a dull thud. I couldn't move; I couldn't scream. My instincts had temporarily abandoned me, drowned beneath a flood of adrenaline and confusion.

Then, a figure lunged from the shadows. Clad in black from head to toe, face obscured by a mask with cut-out eye holes, he slammed into me, driving me to the floor. His weight crushed the breath from my lungs. His grip on my wrists was ironclad, his eyes dark and unreadable. I lay pinned, trembling, and for a second, my brain scrambled for reasons: Rian, the threats, and the unanswered calls. *Was this connected? Rian's death had left too many questions.* The room shrank around us, the silence deafening except for the thunder of my heartbeat.

I thrashed beneath the intruder, desperate to break free. My voice tore from my throat, raw and furious.

"GET THE FUCK OFF ME!"

The words echoed off the walls, and he flinched, just enough so I could twist, wriggle, and slip away from his grasp. I managed to scramble backward across the carpet; my eyes fixed firmly on the door. *Freedom. Safety.* He watched still as a statue, like a hunter waiting for the right moment to pounce. I crawled toward the phone, each inch a small victory, my limbs trembling under the weight of adrenaline. When I reached for it, he moved faster than I expected, his hand snatched my arm, yanking me back. The phone flew from my grasp and clattered away.

I lashed out, palm connecting with his masked cheek. He grunted and staggered, and for a heartbeat his hold loosened. I dove for the phone again, fingers closing around it, and managed to dial. The line rang once, twice, hope flaring, but in a split second, he was on me again, tackling me to the floor.

This time, he pinned me flat, his weight crushing the breath from my chest. Tears blurred my vision; the room narrowed to the press of his body and the frantic thud of my heart. I whispered, voice small and breaking,

"Please, don't hurt me."

The words felt useless in the face of his silence, but they were all I had.

His grip was unrelenting, and I let out a blood-curdling scream.

"NO! LET ME GO!"

I fought like hell, throwing my head forward, catching him with a sharp crack. He hissed in pain, loosening his hold. Dizzy and disoriented, I dove for the phone again. My vision blurred, but I managed to dial. It rang, once, twice, before he tackled me again.

I hit the floor hard; the breath knocked from my lungs. He pinned my arms above my head, his,

"Please."

I whispered, voice breaking.

"Don't hurt me...Please."

I plead again, as a tear rolls down my cheek and I succumb to the fact that no one is coming to my rescue.

7

Zeppelin

His movements are lightning fast, as he moves both of my wrists into one of his, and his other hand moves around my throat. He squeezes tightly, and I close my eyes, resigned to the fact that this is the moment that I die. It's been said that your life flashes before your eyes right before you die, but I see nothing, no fanfare, no blinding bright light, no figure welcoming me to the pearly gates. *Nothing.*

"Please."

I murmur weakly, my plea dying on my lips, as I feel the life draining from me. My mind gives up, as I unexpectedly hear the door swing open, ricocheting against the wall, and heavy footsteps across the carpet.

"GET THE FUCK OFF HER!"

My eyes snap open as I see Jace's large, muscular form barrelling towards me. The mystery figure moved quickly, lithely lifting himself and freeing me from his steel grip. He lunges for the door, knocking Jace out of the way, but not before Jace lands a meaty punch to the side of his head. He smashes his head on the door frame, but that doesn't hinder his escape, as I lie on the carpet staring up at the ceiling, feeling more than a little dazed.

"Zeppelin?"

Jace's Irish lilt filters through my foggy brain.

"Zeppelin, can you hear me, sweetheart?"

He asks again and mutters a curse low in his throat.

"Fuck!"

I let out a soft whimper as he kneels on the floor next to me.

"Sweetheart, where does it hurt?"

His voice soothing, as I succumb to the blackness.

***

"I want whoever is responsible for the security in that building here, right fucking now, or so help me fucking God!"

I hear Jax's low, threatening tone as my eyes flutter open, and I find myself in an unfamiliar environment. A feeling of dread settles in my stomach like a lead weight, my vision is blurred, and I struggle to focus on my surroundings as the excruciating pain explodes in my head.

"I'm not asking, I'm fucking telling you! No, no, no, you listen to me, and you listen fucking good! You're lucky it's me and not Sam! Great...good...ok...thanks."

I try again to focus, and that's when I see him, Jax, my handsome rock star. His familiar handsome face is marred with concern, sadness, and overriding anger. A frown line jumps between his eyebrows, and I start to wonder why he's here. *Isn't he supposed to be on the U.S. leg of Rancid Vengeance's World Tour?* He turns to me, and his features soften.

"Hey, beautiful."

He greets me with his familiar smile, as if his phone conversation never happened.

"Jax."

My voice doesn't sound like my own, as a dull throb settles at the base of my skull.

"It's going to be ok, *Jesus fucking Christ,* you had me worried there for a second. Please tell me why you thought it was a good idea to go back to your apartment, after I specifically told you it wasn't safe?"

He doesn't even try to keep the annoyance from his usually calm voice. I go to open and close my mouth because I've got nothing. *Why did I think it was a good idea to go back there*? Because the Nancy Drew part of my brain thought I could look for clues in Rian's murder. *What did you think was going to happen, Williams? That you were going to solve the crime? Have a word with yourself, for fucks sake.*

"I-I don't know."

I manage to croak out, he drags his hand through his long blonde hair, and closes his eyes briefly, then opens them to settle on mine. The anguish in his hazel eyes is evident, and my heart slams against my rib cage, knowing that I was the one who put that look in my handsome Jack's eyes.

"I'm sorry."

I let out a strangled sob, and he moves closer to the bed as I take in my surroundings. It's quite modern and spacious for a hospital room. There's a large navy suede chair in the corner, an array of abstract artwork adorns the walls, and it reminds me of a plush hotel room. On the wall is a plasma TV, and the décor is all pale pastels with clean lines, which are elegant and calming at the same time. The large square window has an open light-grey blind, and the floor matches the colour of the blind.

He drags the navy suede chair closer to the bed, the scrape along the linoleum floor causing the ache in my head to intensify. He takes my hand in his, and his calloused thumb brushes across my knuckles soothingly.

"You don't have to be sorry, it's a flying visit, but I flew back from America as soon as I heard. Jace called me, then I called my mum, she told me to get you brought to her private medical facility, so I got the wheels in motion and arranged for you to be transported here instead of a public hospital, where the press could get to you."

He explains, as I squeeze my eyes shut, the pain temporarily disarming me.

"Jax, my head hurts."

I let out a strangled sob as he plants a chaste kiss on the back of my hand.

"I know, I know it does, sweetheart. You have a concussion; you just need to rest for a few days and take it easy. Cole's back at the security cabin with Jace, going through the CCTV footage from your apartment, including the footage from the police. I'm not going to let anyone hurt you, Zeppelin, that's a fucking promise. Whoever's responsible for this, they're not going to get away with it, not on my watch."

Jax spits out angrily, and I struggle to comprehend the seriousness of the situation. Whoever is responsible for this could be linked to Rian's murder. What if their goal was to kill me, *too?* That thought alone terrified the shit out of me and sent a cold shiver through my entire body.

My thoughts are interrupted by a woman entering the room. She is a beautiful, slim waif, a few inches shorter than Jax, with her blonde hair piled up haphazardly on top of her head. She is wearing purple scrubs and white trainers; she has deep hazel eyes, almost an identical shade to Jax's.

"Hello, sweetheart, I'm Jamie-Leigh Chase, but you can call me Jay. I'm Jackson's mum."

She introduces herself brightly, her smile is infectious, and I can't help but smile right along with her.

"Zeppelin, pleasure to meet you, finally, Jay."

I say, unable to keep the nervous tone from my voice, as she checks my vitals.

"Well, I had the opportunity to meet the woman who captured the heart of my firstborn, and I took it! Not the circumstances I wanted to meet you, but he wasn't going to introduce us any other way! Little shit!"

She turns to Jax, chucking his cheek and narrowing her eyes playfully at him. Jax rolls his eyes and turns to me, his muscles bulging from beneath his heather grey t-shirt.

"Give it a rest, mum!"

He says with an impish grin as his phone starts ringing. He pulls it from his pocket and looks at the screen for a few seconds, looking between his mum and me.

"I have to get this; I'll leave you two to it for a minute."

He leaves the room, and I stare after him, curious to see who would be calling him.

"How are you feeling, darlin'?"

She asks to distract me, and I nod in response.

"Ok, I think, my head hurts, that's all."

She smiles sympathetically, brushing my arm softly.

"It will be a bit sore for a few days. You have a concussion. If you take it easy, rest, and take the pain medication I prescribe, you'll be back to normal in no time at all."

She explains in her soft demeanour as she sits down in the chair next to the bed.

"I like you; you seem tenacious just like the rest of the Rancid Vengeance women."

She busies herself with adjusting the saline drip next to the bed, as I regard her intently.

"I don't know whether to take that as a compliment."

I retort, and she chuckles softly.

"Definitely a compliment, darlin', the women of Rancid Vengeance complement the boys they're with. Peyton and Sam are a force to be reckoned with; she's the fierce mama bear to his warrior. Raleigh and Brody are both damaged human beings who fix and heal each other just by being together. You and Jax, I haven't quite worked out what you two are yet, but when he found out you'd been hurt, I hadn't seen him like that since..."

She doesn't have to say her name for me to know that she means Ruby, and I nod in understanding.

"It's been a rollercoaster, but those boys, every single one of them, deserves their happy ending, and I think you could be that for my Jackson, because God knows he bloody needs that."

She states with a long, drawn-out sigh, and even though I met her minutes ago, I feel at ease in her company.

"I get that he's got baggage but haven't we all. He doesn't bring women to meet us often, except for Ruby, so I know you must be special. Please don't break his heart, darlin', he's been through enough."

Her voice was almost a plea, and in that moment, I vow to be the woman who gives Jackson Chase the happy ending he deserves.

8

Jax

I turn to face the large garden, acres of green land for miles. I watch my daughter chase Jericho around the decking and down onto the grass. Her squeals of laughter fill my heart, and I exhale on a long breath. Her dark hair swishes around her pink cheeks, and I close my eyes, trying to commit every moment to memory. This was how I wanted to end my days, making precious memories with my daughter and the woman I love. I turn my eyes to Zeppelin, her bare legs stretched out on the sun lounger, her laptop resting on her thighs, lost in thought to whatever character was dominating her brilliant mind.

She's had a rough couple of months, and I felt awful for not being there for her when she needed me. Touring for six months a year was taking its toll on all of us. We were all missing out on watching our kids grow up and on spending time with the women we had committed our lives to. I had just returned from three months away from them, after a gruelling schedule of travelling from state to state in the U.S., and I was desperate to make up for lost time. We had just gotten our relationship on track when her best friend was murdered, and I had to go back out on the road. The overwhelming guilt that consumed me daily that I wasn't there in her time of need crippled me, and the thought of someone wanting to harm even a hair on her head made me feel physically violent.

The police and coroners still hadn't released Rian's body, so she could finally lay him to rest, and the murder investigation is still ongoing. They still hadn't found the mystery man Rian had taken back to his apartment; they still hadn't managed to trace the man who attacked Zeppelin and broke into her place. She had moved all her possessions from her apartment to my house, and she had officially moved in with me. We were rediscovering each other after a long time apart, and it felt like we were getting to know each other all over again. It was new, refreshing, and I relished exploring her body, as if for the first time. We were closer than we had ever been, and we were in the perfect honeymoon period; we couldn't get enough of one another. I watch her for a few minutes, unable to take my eyes off how beautiful she is, the sunlight reflecting off her blonde hair, making her look almost ethereal.

"I can feel your eyes on me, Chase."

She quips playfully, her eyebrow quirking, and I chuckle softly.

"I'd be disappointed if you couldn't, sweetheart."

I get up from my lounger and drop down on the chaise lounge, crawling between her legs, shifting her laptop onto the table beside us.

"I want to be buried inside you again. I can't get enough of you, Zeppelin."

I see her throat bob on a swallow, as she traps her full bottom lip between her teeth. I move closer to her, my thumb moving up to release her lip. I take a moment to look at her before crashing my lips urgently to hers. Her lips are so soft as I introduce my tongue, delicately caressing hers. She lets out a soft moan into my mouth as she wraps her arms around my neck, gently tugging on my hair.

"Mmm."

I hum against her lips, as I hear a loud sound.

"Ewwwww! Gross!"

Thea runs onto the deck and regards us intently, as we spring apart. I discreetly adjust my cock in my denim shorts, as I turn around to see my daughter covered in grass stains and her dark hair a tangled mess. She looks adorable, as Jericho stands to attention beside her, tongue flopped out and his tail wagging wildly. We both laugh at them, Marnie stepping out onto the deck, her long black maxi dress billowing in the early afternoon breeze. Her long dark hair loose around her shoulders, a soft smile on her face.

"Look at you two!"

She says, her voice melodic and filled with amusement.

"Let's get you cleaned up, ready for your Mad Hatter's Tea Party!"

Marnie states enthusiastically, as Thea bounces on the spot in excitement, clapping her hands. She bounds towards me and flings herself across my lap, planting a wet kiss on my cheek. I throw my arms around her and hold her close to me.

"Love you, daddy."

Thea whispers, and it never fails to melt my heart hearing her say those words to me. My heart almost feels too big for my chest, and it's the little things that make a huge impact. Watching her sleep, watching her play and interact with Jericho, seeing the way Freddie and Zachary take on the roles of her protectors whenever she's around them. The way Thea helps Raleigh look after the twins, she's so caring and so thoughtful, it makes me feel like I'm doing a good job at raising her right. My thoughts are interrupted by Thea wriggling in my arms. I kiss her again and whisper I love you to her, as she leaps off my lap. She makes her way towards Marnie, and she takes her hand, as she leads her into the house, closely followed by Jericho.

When the patio door slides shut, I resume my position between Zeppelin's legs.

"Now, where were we?"

I rasp in a voice that would rival Sam's, as I slide my hand beneath her shorts, shifting her knickers to the side.

"Jax, stop!"

She giggles, trying to bat my hands away.

"What if Thea and Marnie come back out? What if we get caught?"

She states nervously, and I quirk my eyebrow at her.

"Then I'd better be fucking quick!"

I say with a cocky wink, as I push my long finger deftly inside her, her head falling lax against the chaise. She lets out a long-satisfied moan of pleasure as I thoroughly finger fuck her.

"*Oh fuck, Jack!*"

She mewls, as her breaths change from slow and measured to sharp, laboured pants. My fingers continue their assault, moving deep within her slick channel.

"*Jesus*, I can feel you throbbing against my fingers. That's so fucking hot."

I croon, as I push two fingers deep inside her and she cries out.

"JACK!"

She moves her hands to cup her full breasts, and she couldn't look more beautiful if she tried. I twist my fingers expertly inside her, causing her to cry out, and I shush her gently, uber aware that someone could come out here any second.

"*Oh, fuck Jack,* that feels so good."

She moans out loud and bites down on her plump bottom lip. I move my fingers inside of her, moving in and out, increasing the momentum with each plunge of my fingers.

"*Fuck*, Zeppelin, you're so wet for me."

I growl as her breath becomes urgent, and she arches her back.

"That's it, come for me, sweetheart. Come hard all over my fingers, give it up for me."

I increase the pace, as she starts panting urgently. Her silver eyes lock with my hazel ones,

"Let go for me, Zeppelin, I want your orgasm."

That's all it takes for her orgasm to tear through her like a tsunami, like waves of absolute pleasure. She screams loudly as I squeeze every ounce of pleasure from her. As I watch her come down from her post-orgasmic haze, she looks so young and carefree. It makes my heart race as if I'm a teenager in love all over again. Our moment is short-lived as her phone starts ringing, a frown line jumps between her eyebrows, and she swipes the screen to answer.

"Hello? Yes...this is Zeppelin Williams."

She responds apprehensively, putting her hand to her mouth, her eyes glossy.

"Yes, erm...yes, thank you for letting me know."

She clears her throat on a swallow, as a tear rolls down her cheek.

"What's wrong, sweetheart?"

I ask, concern in my voice. But it's like she shuts down as she did all those weeks ago. *For fucks sake, back to square one.*

9

Zeppelin

It felt like the bottom had dropped out of my world again, listening to those words on the other end of the phone.

"We're releasing Mr. St. James' body so you can finally lay him to rest."

The blood pounded in my ears, my heart thudded in my chest, my hands began to shake, and my vision felt as if I was looking at the world through a fish-eye lens. I had to get away; I can't stay here any longer. I stand up on shaky legs, and I don't know if it was from the news I had just received or from the orgasm that Jax had just given me.

"Zeppelin?"

The concern in his voice made it harder to walk away, but I wanted to be alone. I needed to process what I had just been told.

"Sweetheart, talk to me."

I jam my feet into my white Birkenstocks, pick up my phone, and make my way inside, blindly grabbing a set of car keys from the rack hanging up in the kitchen.

"*For fucks sake*! Will you just stop for a second! Zeppelin!"

He curses, and I can feel his presence behind me, but I don't register his words. I just know I must get out of here, as I rush through the house and out of the front door. I point the key fob at the car parked in the circular, gravelled driveway, a black Ford Mustang. I open the door and climb into the driver's seat, closing it behind me, relishing the silence of the car's interior. I see Jax's lone figure in the rear-view mirror step out of the house onto the stone steps and rush towards me.

"ZEPPELIN!"

He roars as I press the stop-start button and take a long, slow, deep breath, as I drive towards the closed gate, a feeling of panic rushing through me. I manage to locate a black box on the dashboard, I push it, and the gates slide open as I approach. The group of at least ten photographers leaped to attention as the wheels screeched over the gravel. The click-click of their shutters sets my teeth on edge, and the blinding flashes temporarily disorient me, until I round the corner. They wouldn't follow me; I was out of sight for now, and that's all that mattered.

I clutch the steering wheel; my hands wrapped so tightly around it that my nails dig into my palms. I pull the car over to the side of the road, and I break down over the steering wheel. I cry harder than I've ever cried before, my chest growing tight, bile rising in my throat. Gasping for air between sobs, I clung to the steering wheel, cold and unyielding, the weight of my threatening to crush me where I sat. Tears blurred my vision, and my breath came in ragged sobs. The events of the past couple of months threatened to drown me: Rian's death, the mystery attacker, and the constant paranoia that there was someone out there who wanted to hurt me. The car was suddenly a cocoon of despair, and the pain, anger, and unbearable sorrow poured out in an unrelenting torrent. A dull, persistent ache settled deep in my bones, each breath a heavy reminder of what was gone. My tears were coming in never-ending floods, leaving behind an intense exhaustion I had never felt before. I was so tired of fighting, of losing everyone who ever meant anything to me. *My mum, my dad, Abel, Rian, where would it fucking end?*

My melancholic thoughts are interrupted by a car engine; a few seconds later, I hear a car door slam. I'm startled from my pity party for one by rapping on the window. I turn to see Jax, his hair mussed, and sunglasses pulled down to shield his eyes. His muscles bulge through the t-shirt he is wearing, the silver ring glints in the afternoon sunshine, and the full-sleeve tattoos on both arms stand in contrast to his golden tan from the three months spent in America. I swipe angrily at my tears and sniffle, cursing my emotions to hell and taking a few moments to compose myself before I press the button to wind the window down.

"Zeppelin."

The relief in his voice causes me to let out another strangled sob, and he climbs into the passenger seat of the car, shutting the door behind him. He envelopes me in his arms and pulls me against his warm chest, his unique scent offering me comfort. He cradles me close to him, stroking my hair softly, gently shushing me, and my tears make his t-shirt damp. He rests his chin on top of my head and wraps his arms tighter around me, as if he knows what I need.

"Shhh, I've got you, it's ok, I'm here, I've got you."

He croons, as he holds me for the longest time, until my wracking sobs have subsided. He breaks the silence between us, pulling away from our embrace, and I am instantly bereft at the loss of contact.

"Do you want to tell me what happened, sweetheart?"

He asks softly, and I shift my gaze, suddenly feeling embarrassed at my outburst, as I feel him move in his seat.

"Look at me."

He demands, his voice remaining calm, as I turn to meet his hazel eyes, marred with such concern it makes my heart break that little bit more. I fidget idly with my fingers, as I feel him reach across and take my hand in his. I draw comfort from his touch before I find the courage to speak.

"T-they released Rian's body."

My voice is shaky with unshed tears, and I will not let myself break down again. I hear him suck in a breath, and then he nods.

"I'm here for you, Zeppelin, you never have to go through any of this alone, I promise."

His voice is almost a whisper, and as he says those words, I have no doubt in my mind that he will stick to his promise.

IO

Jax

I set the treadmill in my home gym to a steep incline and begin pounding at a steady pace until I feel that delicious ache in my calf muscles. I need to get some of this pent-up frustration out of my system. I never realised being in a relationship would be such hard work. After Zeppelin's breakdown yesterday, I have been the attentive, supportive lover, but after being single for so long, she still finds it hard to rely on another person other than herself. We're both still adjusting to being in a long-term relationship, but she doesn't make it easy. I get more than most that she's grieving for her best friend, but she needs to open up to me more about how she's feeling and not just run away from me when all I want to do is be there for her. I let out a long-laboured breath as I turn on the TV, and the news channel piques my attention.

"Jackson Chase, also known as Flash to die-hard fans, has been spotted in a steamy clinch with a mystery blonde. Following the tragic death of his fiancée, Ruby Logan, at the wedding of Samson Newbolt and tattoo artist Peyton Harper in a Las Vegas chapel three years ago. Single dad

of one, Chase, has been linked to a string of beauties in typical rock star fashion, including fellow judge on UK's Finest Phoenix King, music mogul, and manager of rival band Devil's Henchmen."

I roll my eyes at the ridiculous, sensationalised bullshit, as a grainy picture of Zeppelin and me pops up on the screen. The photo was taken yesterday when I was comforting her, and I curse my fame to hell because that moment was private. I turn off the TV angrily, grab a towel, and wipe the sweat from my face, trying to clear my mind. Zeppelin's been through so much, we both have, and seeing that picture of us plastered all over the news feels like a gross invasion, a twisted exploitation of her vulnerability. I reach for my water bottle, taking a few deep gulps, hoping it'll help me calm down. I think about the past fifteen years, about the price of fame and the toll it's taken on all of us. I know this whole fame circus has always been part of the package, but days like this make me question if it's worth it. I power down the treadmill and step off onto the floor, reach for my phone, swipe up to my contacts, and call the person I need.

"So, I take it you've seen the news?"

Tate says in a way of a greeting with an amused tone, and I let out a drawn-out sigh.

"What exactly do we fucking pay you for, Tate? And Phoenix King, please, we all know that's a load of steaming horse shit!"

I can't keep the snippy tone from my voice as I start to pace the room, feeling myself getting agitated.

"Come on, Chase, it goes with the fucking territory, have you not learned anything from the last fifteen years?"

He chuckles, and I grit my teeth at his nonchalance, running my free hand through my hair.

"Don't come on, Chase me, Tate, don't treat me like a fucking child! I'm not Sam or Brody! *Jesus*!"

I raise my voice, feeling all rational thoughts disappear. *We're fucking human beings too!*

"Alright, alright, don't get your knickers in a twist!"

He states in his prominent London accent.

"Let me make a few calls, and I'll call you back."

I hear the phone click off, and it goes dead. *Fucking brilliant.*

***

I hurl the phone across the shelving unit and continue pacing the room, my agitation rising with each step.

"FUUUUUUCCCKKK!"

I roar as the familiar tension tightens my muscles, the feeling of helplessness in the face of this media circus gnawing at me. Tate's nonchalance is fucking infuriating, his casual dismissal of my concerns, as if this invasion of our privacy is something I should just accept. We've lived with it for almost fifteen years, but it's getting old and way past its expiration date. I crave the day when I can walk down the street without having a camera thrust in my face. I crave the day when I'm not hounded daily, constantly asked for photos, selfies, and autographs. My thoughts were interrupted by my phone ringing again.

"Alright, I've spoken to a few contacts."

Tate's voice was clipped and business-like. I hum my answer as he continues.

"We're working on damage control, but you need to keep a low profile for a bit, yeah? That means no PDAs or leaving the house without your security detail, is that clear?"

Tate instructs, and I roll my eyes. *No shit, Sherlock.*

"Well, that's easier said than done."

I mutter, glancing up at Zeppelin leaning casually into the doorjamb. I hold up my finger to gesture that I'll be a minute, and she nods curtly.

"Just make sure they leave Zeppelin out of this, or so help me God."

She cocks her perfectly arched eyebrow at the menacing tone to my voice and smirks, twirling her hair around her finger seductively.

"I'll do my utmost best, Jax. But you know how the vultures are, once they have their claws into a juicy story, they don't stop, it's relentless until you give them their pound of flesh."

He tries to placate me, but it's not working. I'm pissed off, fucking frustrated, and...oddly horny as I catch Zeppelin's lust-filled gaze. I clear my throat before continuing my conversation with Tate.

"Yeah, but that's what we fucking pay you for, Tate."

I can't keep the annoyance out of my voice, but it's short-lived as I spin around to Zeppelin stepping further into the room and stripping off her clothes down to her red lace underwear. I swallow hard at the sight of her pale skin, a stark contrast to the red material.

"Hang in there, mate."

Ignoring my previous statement, I hang up the phone without saying goodbye, my bad mood dissipating as she stands in front of me looking so beautiful, my cock stands to attention, instantly becoming hard. She moves closer until she's standing right in front of me, her eyes locking with mine, a knowing smile playing on her lips. She reaches out, her fingers grazing the edge of my t-shirt, damp from my workout, before slipping underneath to touch my skin. The warmth of her touch sends shivers down my spine, igniting a fire within me. I can feel my heartbeat quicken as she leans in, her breath hot against my neck, which makes my pulse race even faster. My hands move almost of their own accord, wrapping around her waist and pulling her closer.

The heat of her body pressed against mine, the scent of her perfume filling my senses and sending them into overdrive. I tilt my head down, capturing her lips with mine in a kiss that is both urgent and tender all at the same time. Her mouth opens to me as our tongues dance together, exploring, tasting, and needing more.

She moans softly into my mouth, and the sound sends a jolt of pure carnal lust through me. I deepen the kiss, my hands roaming over her back, feeling the gentle curve of her spine and over her marred skin. I deftly unclasp her bra expertly with one hand, freeing her pert breasts. She presses herself into me, as if she can't get close enough, her body moulded perfectly to mine.

Breaking the kiss, I look into her eyes, seeing the same burning desire reflected there. Without a word, she takes my hand and leads me across the room, the anticipation building with every step. She urges me to sit down on the padded leather cross trainer seat and turns to face me, her eyes never leaving mine as she straddles my lap. I take a moment to drink in the sight of her, every curve, every scar, every line of her body perfectly imperfect and inviting. My hands reach for her, eager to explore every inch of her, her breath hitching as I trace a path down her side, savouring the softness of her skin. I crush my lips to hers in a searing, white-hot kiss, my cock so hard it's verging on painful. Her fingers tangle in my hair, pulling slightly, a delicious contrast to the softness of her kiss. As I trail my lips down her neck, she tilts her head back, offering more of her skin to me. I take my time, kissing and nibbling my way down to her collarbone. She begins to move her hips, a slow, tantalising rhythm that drives me wild. My hands slide to her waist, guiding her movements, each grind bringing us closer to the edge. I can feel her dampness through the lace of her thong. I'm still fully clothed, but the anticipation is electric. Every touch, every kiss, every sound heightens the desire between us. Her breaths come out in ragged pants as she grinds harder on me.

"*Fuck,* Jack, I need you, I need you, please, oh God, please."

She begs, her voice needy and filled with desperation.

"Please, please, please."

She chants as I free my cock from the confines of my workout shorts. It stands at attention at full mast, and it's so hard I could hammer nails with it. I give her thong a sharp tug until it rips, the noise echoing through the silent room. I haphazardly discard it, and she lifts herself up, gripping my shoulders for balance, as she drops down onto my waiting erection. I enter her easily, *Jesus fucking Christ, she's so wet.* She moves against me, her eyes locked on mine, filled with a hunger that matches my own. I can see the flush spreading across her chest; her pupils dilated with desire. I slide one hand up to cup her breast, teasing her nipple with my calloused thumb, eliciting a gasp that sends a surge of arousal through me.

"*Fuck,* you're so beautiful right now."

I growl, unable to hold back any longer, I grip her hips firmly, lifting her slightly before bringing her down to meet me in a powerful motion. She cries out, a sound of pure pleasure, and I feel a surge of satisfaction knowing I'm the one making her feel this way. Our movements become more urgent, each thrust bringing us closer to that inevitable peak. She clings to me, her nails digging into my shoulders, her breath coming in short, desperate gasps. I bury my face in her neck, breathing in her scent, feeling the tension coil tighter within us both.

"Jack, Jack, Oh God! Fuckkkk, I'm so close! Oh, Jesus!"

She screams, her head tilted back, deep in the throes of passion.

"I've got you; I want you to come for me, Zeppelin."

I urge, as I increase the pace, her breasts bouncing with the punishing rhythm. I can feel her throbbing, and I know she's close. Finally, with one last, powerful thrust, we both come undone, the world shattering around us, waves of pleasure crashing over us. I shudder out my orgasm, spilling my hot seed inside her.

"JACK! OH GOD! JACK! I'M COMING! I'M COMING! FUCK! I'M COMING!"

She collapses against me, our bodies trembling and slick with sweat, our breaths mingling as we come down from the high together. She buries her damp face into my neck, as I wrap my arms around her, blanketing her in my scent.

"Well, that was unexpected!"

I say with an amused tone, and I feel her smile against me. We hold each other for long moments, the intensity of what we've shared leaving us both breathless and satisfied. She pulls back slightly, looking into my eyes with a soft smile, a mixture of contentment and lingering desire in her gaze. I brush a strand of blonde hair from her face, my heart still racing from our connection, and in that moment, I couldn't feel closer to her. Each time, felt like it was the first time all over again, and I don't think I could love her more.

II

Zeppelin

Those who died yesterday had plans for this morning, and those who died this morning had plans for tonight. I learned a long time ago not to take life for granted; everything can change in the blink of an eye. As I stand at the window overlooking Portobello Road Market in Notting Hill, where Rian and I used to reside. The sun is shining, blazing in the sky, and I start to think to myself that the sun shouldn't be shining on the day I lay my best friend to rest. The pain threatens to drown me where I stand, my stomach roils, and I feel like I'm going to throw up. It feels like my heart is breaking all over again, as I force my eyes shut to push back the image of his lifeless gaze.

I take a deep breath, attempting to steady my trembling, warring emotions, the weight of grief hanging heavy in the air. In the weeks that followed, the funeral preparations were a sombre reminder of the cruel reality that life continues, even in the wake of death. I force myself to turn away from the window, and a photo of Rian and me smiling vibrantly at a Gay Pride event, both with bright rainbows painted on our cheeks, catches my eye, and I can't help the tear that spills down my face. *Life is such a cruel bitch sometimes.* Rian didn't have any family; his parents disowned him when he came out as gay, and he had no other family to speak of. The gay community was his family, and they took him under their wing, accepting him as one of their own. He was well known in the community and advocated for them, even when society shunned them.

As we make our way to West London Crematorium in Kensal Green, I spot the eclectic array of people who loved Rian and find myself smiling softly at the colourful gathering. I squeeze Jax's hand as we approach, and he turns, kissing me on my forehead in a gesture of silent support.

"Who's this dish, peaches?"

A six-foot-two-inch drag queen called Gale Force flashes me a wide, toothy grin and a cheeky wink as she looks from me to Jax. Gale was one of Rian's close friends, and he always did her make-up and hair for events and shows. Gale is wearing a glittery blue dress and six-inch heels to match, her hair expertly twisted up into a stylish high, slicked-back ponytail. Her make-up was flawless and bright, matching the occasion.

"Peaches?"

Jax mouths, and I try to stifle my smirk, shaking my head in exasperation. *That's a story for another time.*

"Later."

I mouth in response, biting my lip as Gale leans in to give me a red lipsticked kiss on the cheek.

"It's so good to see you, Gale, it's been so long!"

I say genuinely, as I take a steady breath and head into the crematorium to say a final goodbye to Rian.

Rian's casket has a Pride flag draped over it, adorned with flowers, a stark contrast to the vibrant colours of life that once surrounded him. I approach, my heart heavy, and run my fingers gently over the smooth, glossy wood. The reality of his absence settles in, and the ache in my chest intensifies with each moment that passes. A single tear escapes my eye, tracing a lonely path down my cheek. *God, I miss you so much, Rian.*

I sit in the front row next to Jax and Gale, and as the powerful voice of Whitney Houston *I Have Nothing*, fills the small, intimate crematorium. The funeral service is a blur, a series of heartfelt eulogies and tearful goodbyes. I find solace in the shared grief of those around me, knowing that we are bound by our love for Rian. The ceremony concludes, and we gather for a final farewell as the strains of *I Am, What I Am by Gloria Gaynor* fill the room, the curtain closing around Rian's casket, symbolising the finality of this painful goodbye to a life taken far too soon.

After the final words are spoken, and the last strains of the music fade away, it's time to say my own private goodbye. I approach the closed curtain, the reality of the loss hits me all over again, and I struggle to find the words that can never truly capture the depth of my grief. I hang my head, and I make a silent promise to Rian that his memory will live on in the stories we share. Life, once taken for granted, now stands before me as a precious gift. I carry the weight of yesterday's plans, unfulfilled dreams, and the searing pain of loss. Yet, during the darkness, I find gratitude for having shared a chapter of my life with someone as extraordinary as Rian St James. I know that life will never be the same, but with each passing second, I vow to honour the memory of my best friend by holding onto the precious moments of the one we laid to rest today.

***

I step out of the dull crematorium and into the blazing sunshine, with Jax's arm slung around me protectively, his Ray-Ban aviators shielding his eyes, looking ever the rock star. I turn my head slightly to see Danny Debonair leaning against the side of the crematorium with his hands tucked into his pockets. Gale cupping his face in her hands, tears streaming down his cheeks. I can't help but take in their interaction, even though it feels like I'm intruding on a private moment; their shared grief is palpable. Danny squeezes his eyes shut, and her whispered words are too soft for me to hear, but I can see the way she's trying to soothe him, trying to hold him together when everything feels like it's falling apart. I can't tear my eyes away, as Jax squeezes my hand in a gesture of reassurance.

As we reach the car, I glance back one last time, catching a glimpse of Danny burying his face in Gale's shoulder, her arms wrapping around him like a lifeline. I swallow hard, the lump in my throat almost unbearable, as I observe them clinging to each other like a lifeline. Jax opens the car door for me, and I slide into the seat, the leather cool against my back. He follows, settling beside me in the driver's seat, his presence a silent source of comfort. As he starts the engine, the car's quiet hum feels like it grounds me somehow. As we pull away from the crematorium, my gaze lingers on Danny and Gale until they fade into the distance. I turn my head back to Jax, leaning my head back on the car's headrest. He reaches his hand over to me, resting it on mine, choosing to drive one-handed. His touch offers some well-needed comfort and reassurance. I exhale slowly, letting the tension of my body ease, as I relax back into my seat, my thoughts firmly on the events of the day so far, playing like a movie in my head. Saying a final goodbye to Rian was like allowing that chapter of my life to end and for a new one to begin. It was going to be a big adjustment, but I wasn't totally averse to it, and I planned to embrace it, no matter how hard it was going to be. I was fully aware that this chapter wasn't going to include Rian, and I had come to accept that.

***

"So, you never did tell me why Gale calls you Peaches!"

Jax says with an amused tone to his voice, as I throw my head back and laugh. I take a long gulp of my wine, allowing the warmth to settle in my stomach for a moment before continuing.

"Ah, I didn't, did I? Well..."

I set my glass down on the table, let my shoes fall to the floor, and tuck my legs under me. After the funeral, Jax had taken me to my favourite restaurant and treated me to some traditional Indian food. He was attentive, thoughtful, and I could tell he was trying to take my mind off today. We had some delicious food at Paradox and arrived back at Jax's. We were enjoying each other's company, chatting, reminiscing, and drinking wine outside in the beautiful, scenic garden, which seemed to go on for miles. Acres of lush green, open space. The evening was balmy for the time of year, and I wanted to enjoy the fresh air, the gentle breeze on my skin, reminding me that I was alive.

"Come on, Williams, don't hold out on me! Spill!"

Jax presses, as I take another sip of my wine, feeling my face flush.

"It's actually a pretty embarrassing story..."

I begin, and Jax reaches over to stroke my face.

"You're so cute when you blush, love."

He says with a soft chuckle as I continue my story.

"Rian and I lived in two separate apartments in Notting Hill, but we were in and out of each other's houses pretty much daily. I didn't keep the door locked; neither did he. We used to just walk in. So, one day, Rian comes into my apartment, and we're getting ready to go out for some drinks. I'm in the shower when he comes in. He makes himself at home, pours us a glass of wine each, but what he doesn't tell me is that his friend Gale is tagging along. She had just gone through a bad breakup and needed a blow-out."

I put my hand to my head, remembering what happened next.

"So, I get out of the shower, and I have a towel wrapped around me. I go from the living room and into my bedroom, not bothering to close the door. Rian was gay; there was nothing he hadn't already seen before, numerous times, and I was comfortable with that! But what I didn't pay attention to was when I got out of the shower, Gale was already in my apartment, and I dropped my towel in full view. Gale starts wolf-whistling, and I spin around, realising my error. She winks at me, and from then on, she's called me Peaches, because of my peachy arse!"

I cover my face in pure embarrassment as Jax almost chokes on his wine, and we both belly laugh at my recollection. We spend the rest of the evening laughing, telling each other stories of people we've lost. It was cathartic; we shed tears, we laughed, and at that moment, I was hopeful that we could remember all the people we had lost over the years.

12

Zeppelin

After a gruelling six-month tour, three months in the UK and three months in America, Rancid Vengeance have a well-earned month off, before they embark on writing and recording their sixteenth studio album. We have flown to the Maldives, a secluded oasis with its own stretch of beach. We are staying in a large eight-bedroom villa, which belongs to Jax. It has four fifty-five-inch smart TVs, all internet-ready, equipped with the latest streaming apps and state-of-the-art technology. It has a large open-plan dining area and living area leading out onto the beach, three outdoor showers, eight bathrooms, and a twenty-four-hour gym at the resort down the beach. All eight bedrooms have four-poster beds with glass floors, offering views of marine life in the tranquil turquoise waters of the Indian Ocean below. It was literal paradise.

Jax, me, Raleigh, Brody, the twins Bowie and Azalea, Sam, Peyton, Lucas, Nick, Freddie, Zachary, Cole, Amy, Addison, Dexter, Marnie, George, Danny, and the security team are staying in Jax's luxury villa. We flew out on the bands' private jet, Air Vengeance, and took a twenty-five-minute speedboat ride from the airport. The villa has its own housekeeper, cleaner, and chef to tend to our every need. Jax thoughtfully invited me and promised it would be an opportunity to get to know everyone and to relax after the last few months.

Jax, with his easy-going demeanour, made sure I was included, but I felt an immediate apprehension at being introduced to the diverse personalities within Rancid Vengeance's inner circle. Rancid Vengeance and their entourage were a melting pot of personalities. They were an eclectic mix of individuals, each with distinct quirks, making them all unique. They resembled a motley crew, brought together by their shared passion and love for music. The quiet ones observed the chaos around them with an air of mystery; the loud and obnoxious ones injected infectious energy into the group. There were those who weren't sure where or if they fitted in. I was one of them. I couldn't help feeling awkward. I lingered on the outskirts, grappling with the uncertainty of belonging in this family that had been through hell and back, but they had survived, together.

There was Gorgeous George, a big beast of a man, six feet seven inches tall, with long blonde hair that reminded me of a lion's mane, a gruff beard, and a laugh you could hear a mile away. He was one of the biggest personalities. Then there was Danny, who had a forlorn, faraway look in his eyes, and I get it, because I feel the same; our lives were empty without Rian. He was the opposite of George, but they complemented each other perfectly and bounced off each other with their laid-back banter to boot. It was easy to look at these as individuals, but they were a family, and I had learned fast that you didn't have to be blood to be family. I observed how they were around each other, and I found myself envious of their relationships. Sam and Peyton worshipped each other, his emerald eyes following her wherever she went. Brody and Raleigh had been through so much together, but seemed so in love; his silver eyes sparkled when she was within touching distance. I didn't know where Jax and I stood in that relationship, but I was looking forward to discovering who we could be together.

My short blonde hair is styled into damp, tousled waves, with my Michael Kors sunglasses perched atop my head. I am wearing a pink polka-dot bikini that complements my slender figure. I'm giggling along with Peyton and Raleigh, feeling carefree for the first time in a long time. The boys are gathered around sun loungers on the beach; they all look like they could model for GQ. I lick my lips at the sight of Jax's tanned washboard abs glistening in the fierce sun. Peyton and Raleigh gather round, Peyton cradling her baby bump. She's four months pregnant with a baby girl, and she is glowing in her red bikini and pink Ray Ban aviator sunglasses.

"I can see you drooling from here, girl, you got it bad!"

Raleigh laughs, and I find myself blushing at being caught ogling my man.

"What are you waiting for? Go get him, tiger!"

Peyton shoves me playfully, and I can't help the genuine laugh that bursts from me.

"How did you know you were in love with Sam and Brody?"

I ask thoughtfully, and Peyton sighs, unable to take her eyes off her husband. He's on the lounger next to Jax, and his huge body eclipses his; his thick biceps are twice the size of Jax and Brody put together.

"It was instant with Sam, I knew I was going to marry him from the first second I laid my eyes on him. It was...Wow, I can't describe it, fuck, it was like all the lights had finally come on, and I was seeing everything for the first time. I'd never felt like that in my whole life;

it was like I'd found the other half of me as soon as he walked in the shop."

Hearing her describe her love for Sam makes my heart melt; that's the kind of love I write about in my books. The type of love that spans across decades, an all-consuming kind of love. An idea for a new book is starting to form in my head; the familiar haphazard thoughts that somehow make sense to me have seldom made an appearance lately. I must go and grab my notebook to write it down.

"I'll be right back."

I mutter and rush across the sand, sliding the doors to the villa open. I walk into the bedroom and place my carry-on suitcase on the bed, unzipping it. I take out my notebook, as I feel a set of strong, tattooed, corded arms slide around my torso.

"There's my girl."

Jax buries his nose into my neck, and I lean back against him, loving the feel of his hard body pressed against me.

"God, you smell good."

He hums, tightening his grip around me. He smells of Diesel Only the Brave and faintly of beer, but that uniquely heady scent intoxicates me like nothing else. It's addictive and hard to put into words, but I was a mess of hormones. I felt like a teenager falling in love all over again.

"You loved me back to life, Zeppelin."

He breathes, his voice thick with emotion. As he says those words, I am a ball of sensation, a pent-up whirlwind of absolute want. I think I would weep if he didn't put his cock inside me right this second. I wanted him fiercely, possessively, and licks of desire unfurled deep within my stomach, and I was desperate for this man. He seems to read my mind and slides his hand into my bikini bottoms, finding my clit swollen and damp for him.

"*Fuck*, you're soaking wet for me, Zeppelin."

He presses his finger to my nub, and I throw my head back onto his shoulder, biting down on my lip and briefly closing my eyes.

"Jack, oh God, that feels so good."

I pant, my voice not sounding like my own. He shifts us forward until I'm facing the wall.

"Palm the wall."

I place my hands on the wall; my cheek pressed into the cool paintwork. I feel his cock thickening between us as he pushes my bikini bottoms down my thighs and taps my legs one at a time for me to step out of them.

"Lean forward."

He demands, and I do as I am bidden. I lean forward, bracing myself and squishing my boobs into the wall. He doesn't give me time to adjust to my new position, impaling me on his waiting stiffness. I cry out as he penetrates me deep, my bum pressed against him. He moves his hand around and circles my clit, my breath hitching, as he possesses me so completely. I push back against his urgent thrusts, moaning softly. I feel the familiar ripples of pleasure spiking between us like an electric current. He quickens his pace, as I moan out loud at the mix of sensations between us.

"OH FUCK! JAX! PLEASE MAKE ME COME!"

I scream, aware that someone could hear, but I'm so lost in the moment, I don't care who knows what we're doing. My pussy floods around his throbbing member, and my senses are in total overload, my mind short-circuiting, as the pleasure washes over me.

"JAX! FUCK! JAX! I'M COMING! OH, GOD!"

I feel his body tense as he grips my hips harshly, finding his own release.

"ZEPPELIN! FUUUCCKKK! I'M COMING! JESUS FUCKIN' CHRIST! ZEPPELIN!"

He growls out his release, as his hot seed spurts inside me, and I'm suddenly very aware that we didn't use a condom. He pulls out of me, and I shudder with tiny aftershocks, unable to move from my spot plastered to the wall. He helps me straighten, taking a few seconds for me to gather myself before tackling me to the wall and angling his face to mine until our lips lock. The contrast of my softness against the scruff of his beard feels amazing against my highly sensitised skin, and I can't help but want him again. I feel his smile against my mouth, his hot breath gusting out and tickling my cheek.

"Insatiable."

He whispers, and I laugh melodically at his ability to read me like a book.

"The boys and I have to help Brody with something, but make yourself at home, hang out with the girls, and I'll see you at dinner later?"

I nod as he kisses me chastely, and with those words, he's gone. I take a few quiet moments, as I watch him leave, to make myself presentable and pick up my notebook from the bed, holding it possessively to my chest.

"There you are! We've been looking all over for you!"

Peyton states, a sheer black cover-up over her bikini, her small but perfectly formed bump protruding in front of her, and her hair piled up into a loose ponytail, exposing the shaved sides of her head.

"Couldn't keep your hands off him, huh?"

She flashes me a wink and a wicked grin. I find myself blushing at her observation, clutching my notebook tighter to my chest. *If I were religious, I'd be clutching my pearls right about now.*

"Come on, don't be embarrassed! We need to teach you the ways of the Rancid Vengeance women! We take no prisoners!"

She says with a laugh, and I find myself laughing right along with her, instantly relaxing in her calming company. For the first time in a long time, I feel like I belong and, in that moment, I'm finally content with that.

13

Zeppelin

I spend the rest of the day scribbling ideas in my notebook and enjoying the sunshine, stretched out on a sun lounger on the beach outside the opulent villa. Surprised by Danny Debonair's unexpected presence, my pen hovers over the notebook, momentarily forgotten. The sound of the waves lapping against the shoreline provides an uneasy backdrop to the unspoken silence that lingers between us. His sad, desolate gaze doesn't waver, and for a moment, I catch a glimpse of vulnerability beneath the facade of the effortlessly cool demeanour he often wore like a shield. His dark hair is shorter than the last time I saw him, flat and damp from the sea, his long legs tucked underneath him in the lounger next to me. His jaw is tight as he idly plays with an invisible thread on his palm tree print board shorts. I regard him intently for a few moments, the prominent scars on his face a cruel reminder of the life he had before. His sheer presence creates a palpable tension in the air as I place my pen between the pages of my notebook, close it, and set it down on the cushioned lounger before I speak.

"It's not your fault, you know?"

I tell him sincerely, and he takes a long pull on his e-cigarette, blowing a cloud of sweet, tropical-smelling smoke into the air. The sun, still high in the sky, casts a warm glow on everything around us. Freddie, Zachary, Addison, and Thea are running around, squealing with delight across the sand, closely watched by Marnie and Amy. Despite the idyllic setting, there's a heaviness in the air, an unspoken understanding that both of us are here seeking refuge from the storms of our respective lives and to mourn the loss of Rian St-James.

"Whatever the reason for the break-up..."

I continue, as he looks up at me questioningly, a look of pure shock on his face.

"You mean you don't know why we broke up?"

He asks with an incredulous tone to his voice, and I cock my head to the side. The weight of unspoken words settles uneasily between us.

"He never mentioned the reason, I just thought he'd tell me in his own time when he was ready, so I didn't push. Rian could be incredibly proud and stubborn, never admitting his faults, never admitting when he was wrong, it used to drive me fucking insane!"

I say on a chuckle, and Danny's mouth quirks up into a half smile, his jaw relaxing somewhat.

"He met someone else online, I found out accidentally, stumbled upon their messages. It was like... walking in on a secret world I didn't know existed."

Danny blurts out, and my eyes widen like saucers at his admission. *What the fuck? What the hell were you thinking, Rian?*

"I thought he was the one, but obviously I was wrong again. I don't know how many frogs I'm going to have to kiss before I get the prince."

He states on a dramatic sigh, and my mouth is agape, as I'm still trying to process his bombshell. The sound of distant laughter from the villa seems to mock the solemn yet serious nature of our conversation.

"I...I had no idea. He was devastated when you broke up. I don't get it. Why the fuck would he do that?"

I say, the question is rhetorical and more to myself than him, but he shrugs at my statement.

"Why the fuck does anyone do anything? Besides, you knew him better than anyone. Why *would* he do that?"

I shake my head, my mouth opening and closing, unable to answer.

"If I meant so much to him, why the fuck would he mess around behind my back, Zeppelin? The guy on the CCTV footage, that's the guy he arranged to meet."

Danny divulges, and I narrow my eyes at Danny's unexpected revelation. It certainly has opened a Pandora's box of questions, and the path to answers appears more out of reach than ever.

"How do you know they'd arranged to meet?"

I question, as he smirks, feeling a mixture of frustration and sympathy. His pain is palpable, and I can't help but wonder if there's more to the story between Rian and him.

"Because Nancy Drew, I fucking followed him! I still had him under my tracker app on my phone."

He admits with more than a hint of prideful bitterness and shame to his voice. *So, Danny knows the man he arranged to meet? He could possibly lead us to the person who killed him.*

"Did you recognise the man he was meeting? This could be important, Danny."

I snap out impatiently, aware I'm being rude, but I can't seem to help myself. He hangs his head as I wait for him to continue.

"He caught on to the fact I was following him, we argued, it wasn't my finest moment."

He says on a sniff, with a nonchalant wave of his hand and a theatrical roll of his eyes.

“We said some awful things to each other, Zeppelin, things I'll never be able to take back, or apologise for.”

A lone tear slips down his cheek, and my heart hurts for the man in front of me. I reach over and brush his arm reassuringly. He gets to his feet and shakes his head, swiping angrily at the tears that have tracked their way down his face.

“I...I’m sorry, I can’t do this, I...I can’t.”

He rushes across the sand into the villa, sliding the door closed behind him. Gathering my thoughts, I reach for my notebook, flipping through its pages as if the answers might magically appear. The pieces of this puzzle seem scattered, and I’m left with a sense of urgency to uncover the truth of how my best friend was murdered.

***

The gentle breeze blows through the open windows of the lavish beach villa. The mirror reflects my contemplative expression as I continue to apply my makeup. Each stroke of the brush was a desperate attempt to silence the chaotic thoughts racing through my mind. I couldn’t seem to shake the feeling that something was off and that there was more to the story than meets the eye. As I finish applying my makeup, I take a deep breath, attempting to push aside the lingering questions. I step away from the dressing table, glancing at the elegant walk-in wardrobe where my chosen outfit hangs. I reach up, taking the simple yellow floral-patterned jumpsuit and step into it, pulling it up my body, settling the straps onto my red, lightly sunburned shoulders, cursing myself for being so careless in the fierce heat. I step into a pair of black diamante-encrusted sandals and give my hair one last fluff in the mirror, ready for what the night has to offer.

I leave the bedroom, and I step onto the wooden deck, the warm night air enveloping me. All I want is to see Jax. I want him to hold me, soothe me, and tell me that everything is going to be alright. My stomach roils with nerves and something else that I can't quite put my finger on, but I push that thought to the back of my mind as my feet sink into the sand. I hear loud chatter and laughter in the distance, plastering a smile on my face; I head in the general direction, the day's revelations temporarily forgotten.

Jax saunters towards me, his hand tucked casually into the pocket of his denim shorts. He is wearing a fitted black shirt, which showcases his muscular physique. He's cut off his long blonde hair since I last saw him; his beard is shorter, too, and resembles heavy stubble. He reminds me of a tattooed Thor, but the Ragnarök version of him. He catches my wistful gaze, and I instinctively look away, suddenly feeling shy. He cocks his eyebrow curiously as he reaches for my hand and I take it, as he strokes his thumb across my knuckles. I notice he isn't wearing his ring either, which surprises me, and I look at him questioningly, my mouth dropping open at the sight of him.

"You cut your hair?"

I manage, as he shrugs with a grin on his handsome face.

"Ah, it was time for a change, love."

He explains nonchalantly, my pussy instantly flooding with heat. I bite my lip as he pulls me into his warm chest. I wrap my arms around him, feeling that familiar comfort I had been craving all day.

"Come on, let's go inside, Brody is proposing to Raleigh, we're waiting to hear if she says yes!"

Jax states, on an excited chuckle, to his friend that was once so off the rails they thought he would be dead before he was thirty-five. I follow Jax into the villa where everyone is gathered, the floor-to-ceiling windows looking out across the beach where Brody and Raleigh stand in the distance. The stunning scenery seems to mirror the mixture of emotions within me. My thoughts drift to marriage. Jax and I have shared so much, but the idea of forever feels like a question I haven't dared to answer yet. As we wait for Raleigh's answer, I stand beside Jax, the future a quiet hum in the background, and for the first time in days, I let myself wonder what might come next.

14

Zeppelin

Laughter drifts across the beach, mingling with the rustle of palm trees and the soft lapping of the tide. The celebration is in full swing, Brody proposed, Raleigh said yes, and now the night glows with fairy lights and champagne toasts. They stand together beneath the stars, hands entwined, eyes locked in a way that makes the world around them disappear. Their joy is radiant, contagious, and yet something inside me stirs, something sharp and unexpected.

I smile, raise my glass, and sip champagne, but the bubbles bursting on my tongue do little to lift the heaviness in my chest. The music shifts, as P!nk's *Fuckin' Perfect* plays in the background, I observe Brody and Raleigh, surrounded by love, and a quiet ache blooms inside me. *Is it envy? Or something deeper, something I've never dared to name?*

I slip away from the crowd, my feet sinking into the cool sand as I walk toward the water's edge. I let my mind wander and start to think that I've never had a family like this, never belonged to something so whole, so safe and complete. My mother was a mystery, my father was a tragedy, and I've spent my whole life always on the outside, looking in.

"Penny for em'?"

Jax's voice cuts through the quiet, low and familiar. I turn to find him standing a few feet away, his silhouette framed by moonlight. His hair is shorter now, his beard trimmed, and for a moment, it's

like seeing him for the first time all over again. He steps closer, his eyes searching mine.

"You okay?"

He asks gently.

"I know today's been a lot, but they adore you. I bloody adore you!"

He admits shamelessly, and I try to smile, but something shifts inside me. A sudden, violent churn in my stomach, as I press a hand to my abdomen, the nausea rising fast and unforgiving. Without a word, I turn and stumble inside and collapse to my knees in front of the toilet, not registering the pain as the sickness comes in waves.

My body convulses, and I feel Jax's hand on my back, steady and warm. He doesn't speak at first, just stays with me, silently rubbing my back. When it finally passes, I flush the toilet and lean against the cool tiles, breathless and trembling. Jax hands me a glass of water, his expression etched with concern. I rinse my mouth, the acrid taste lingering, and I catch my reflection in the mirror, pale, shaken, and stomach still roiling.

"What was that about?"

He asks softly.

"I don't know."

I whisper as I wipe my mouth with the back of my hand.

"Maybe the heat, something I've eaten didn't agree with me, or maybe everything just caught up with me."

He nods, brushing a strand of hair from my face.

"We don't have to go back out until you're ready."

I lean against the counter, the weight of the moment settling over me. A thought flickers, quiet, persistent, as a chill worked its way down my spine. *Could it be more than exhaustion? More than emotion? Could it be...pregnancy?*

The word hangs in the air, unspoken but loud. I close my eyes, letting the possibility wash over me.

It's terrifying, it's thrilling, and it's everything I didn't expect all at once. Jax's presence feels different now, and if this is real, everything changes. I open my eyes and meet his gaze; he's observing me closely, an obvious question hovering behind his silence. But neither of us speaks it aloud, not yet.

Saying it would make it real, and I'm not ready for real, at least not tonight. I offer him a smile, soft, uncertain, and he takes my hand. Together, we step back into the night, and the celebration continues, unaware of the quiet shift that's taken place. As the music swells and the stars shimmer above, I carry the weight of the unknown with a strange, fragile hope. *Whatever comes next, we'll face it together, one heartbeat at a time.*

15

Zeppelin

Today is Brody and Raleigh's wedding day. After a week of non-stop preparations and meticulous short-notice wedding planning, they gathered a small group of close friends and family and flew them first class to the Maldives. I had been welcomed wholeheartedly with open arms into the madness of the Rancid Vengeance family. The sun was blazing down; there was a white canopy with pink hibiscus flowers hanging from it, and at the ends of each aisle sat pink fairy lights. Spread down the centre aisle were pink rose petals, and on either side of the aisle sat white chairs set up on the sand. It was truly magical, and I could not be happier to witness this amazing couple become husband and wife.

Amidst the celebration, the memory of that unexpected episode on the first day lingers, casting a shadow over what should be a happy occasion. Despite the undeniable happiness around me, the unspoken question nags at my thoughts. *Could there be more to that incident than just a random bout of nausea?* I discreetly glance at Jax, my handsome man, partner, soul mate, and confidant. We exchange subtle looks, a silent acknowledgement of our situation. Ever since that day, he has become more attentive, more aware of my feelings, and we have spent almost every day together, starting and ending our day making long, slow, sensual love beneath the sheets. Holding hands, taking long strolls along the beach, and having long, meaningful discussions about life, love, and everything in between. We have been swimming in the sea, enjoying the company and the sunshine. I had never been this relaxed, and I hadn't had another chance to speak to Danny since our previous conversation, but I was determined to pursue it once we were home. I still wanted justice for Rian.

Jax, who is standing to the left of Marlowe Newbolt, Sam Newbolt's father and one-third of iconic rock band The Lightning Bolts, agreed to marry Brody and Raleigh after he was ordained online to officiate Sam and Peyton's wedding. He is wearing a clerical collar, a short-sleeved black shirt, and sunglasses. He looks ever the rock star, as Jax starts to play a rock version of the wedding march on his electric guitar. I can't help the smile that spreads across my face. I'm so proud of him, and I couldn't be more honoured to witness this day alongside him.

"Friends, family, and everyone in between, we are gathered here today to celebrate the marriage of Brody and Raleigh. This is my second Rancid Vengeance wedding!"

Marlowe pulls a face, and everyone starts to laugh at his joke, as he pushes his sunglasses further up the bridge of his nose. Brody whispers softly in Raleigh's ear so only she can hear, his hands clasped with hers. With the wedding celebration for Brody and Raleigh in full swing, the air was alive with the soft music of laughter, unforgettable memories for the newlyweds and those present for their special day. The magic of the occasion washed over me, and I revelled in the pure happiness that enveloped everyone.

"So, are we going to talk about what happened on our first day here?"

Jax asks out of nowhere, and I take a long gulp of champagne before turning to face him. His expression sombre, a mixture of concern and quiet annoyance.

"Are you pregnant?"

He leans into a whisper so only I can hear him, as I place my glass slowly down on the table. To an observer, it looks like he's whispering sweet nothings in my ear. *Fuck my life.*

"I thought you were on birth control?"

His statement is more of an accusation than a question. I had once contemplated having kids with Abel, but neither of us was equipped emotionally to handle raising a child. We were young, and I would never have been so careless as to bring a child into the mix back then. Since meeting Thea, I've had hope about what it would be like to be someone's mum.

"I...I..."

I manage to stutter out, but our conversation is interrupted by all the boys shouting in unison.

"SHOTS!"

As they drag Brody off to the bar, Jax follows closely behind them. I swallow back the lump that has formed in my throat, and I feel the familiar sting of tears burning behind my eyes. *Come on, Williams, pull yourself together! You will not cry in front of all these people!* I get up from my seat and head down towards the beach, the quiet lapping of the waves a welcome change to the noise in my head. I drop heavily down onto the sand, and an overwhelming sense of guilt washes over me; he doesn't deserve this. He's been through enough in his life already; he lost the woman he was going to marry, and his daughter is growing up without a mother. *How could you do this to him, you selfish bitch!*

"Hey, whatcha' doing down here all by yourself?"

The familiar American drawl of Lucas cuts through my thoughts. I turn to him, a playful smirk tugging at the corner of his lips. I force a small smile, attempting to mask the storm of emotions swirling within me.

"Just needed a breather, some quiet time, ya know. It's all a little overwhelming."

I reply, my gaze fixed on the distant horizon where the ocean meets the sky. Lucas settles on the sand beside me, his presence a comforting anchor amid my internal turmoil. The rhythmic sound of the waves seems to synchronise with the ebb and flow of my conflicted thoughts.

"You sure about that?"

He asks, a knowing look in his eyes. Lucas has always had a knack for sensing when something's amiss. From what Jax has told me, Lucas is very mysterious and guarded about his past, even to those close to him. He had a rough childhood and was raised by Kyle Landon, the movie director, and his wife, Ava. He's very observant, and he has a unique way of reading people.

"Those pretty eyes don't look so convincing."

He states matter-of-factly with a wry tone to his voice.

"Shouldn't you be with the boys? It is a celebration after all?"

I counter, and he cocks his eyebrow.

"Well, shouldn't you be with Jax? He was looking for you."

I let out an audible sigh, the guilt weighing heavily on my conscience. Lucas's perceptive gaze lingers on me, his expression thoughtful.

"You can't distract me that easily."

He says with a playful glint in his eyes. I take a moment before responding, deciding to be honest.

"It's just...complicated. Jax and I...we're in a strange place right now."

The truth lingers on the tip of my tongue, but Lucas, however, has a way of unravelling the unspoken.

"I guess you can run from it, but it catches up to you eventually."

He states with a half shrug, and I nod, acknowledging the wisdom in his words. The mention of Jax stirs a mix of emotions, longing, regret, and the weight of his statement lingering between us.

"I know he loves the shit out of you, I know that much, any fool with a pair of eyes can fucking see that."

Lucas continues, his tone gentle, and I find myself smiling at his blunt reply.

"Maybe it's time to face whatever's keeping you two apart."

I regard him with wary eyes, thinking back to something Jax said all those months ago.

"Like whatever's keeping you and Nick Slade apart?"

I regret the words as soon as they leave my mouth, and Lucas looks like I've just slapped him in the face.

"Jax has a really big fuckin' mouth."

He spits as I place my hand on top of his, and he flinches away from me. My heart slams against my rib cage at his reaction. *What happened to this man to make him react that way? Who did this to him?*

"I'm sorry, I don't know very much, and I don't know any of you very well, but Jax cares about you more than you'll ever know, all of those boys do."

I tell him. He seems to relax a little and takes my hand in his as he turns back towards the villa. His eyes landed on Nick Slade. Nick is classically handsome, but not in the traditional sense. He is six feet tall, extremely muscular, has lean, narrow hips, and has dark brown, almost black eyes. His dark brown hair is neatly styled into a soft quiff. He has a tattoo of a set of dice, playing cards, a lucky '8' ball, and the words '*You make your own luck*' extending up his throat and neck. He is wearing denim shorts and a white shirt open at the collar, with one hand tucked casually into his pocket and the other holding a bottle of beer. He half turns, and his eyes lock with Lucas, and Lucas quickly looks away, turning back to me.

"Nick and I...*Jesus Christ*, it's fucking complicated at best, ok? I'm not gay, it's...it's just...him, *just him*."

He breathes and squeezes his eyes shut briefly before continuing.

"God...he's...he's all I've ever wanted for fifteen fucking years! I slept with Noa Vega to get over him and now...now...it's all fucked to hell!"

He raises his voice, dropping his head into his hands. I sit beside Lucas, the weight of his confession hanging in the air. I give his hand a reassuring squeeze as I turn slightly to face him. The early evening breeze was blowing a strand of hair in his face.

"I'm sorry, Lucas. I didn't mean to pry."

I say softly, realising the depth of his feelings for Nick and the open wounds he is nursing. He takes a shaky breath, looking at me with a mix of gratitude and pain.

"No, it's...I...I needed someone to know. It's eating me alive, Zeppelin."

It's a moment of shared vulnerability. My heart hurts for him and the burden he is carrying on his own. My own issues fade into insignificance in comparison.

"I can't pretend to understand the depth of your feelings, but I see the way he looks at you. It's like he sees no one else..."

I begin, choosing my words carefully, as I glance to where Nick is standing, his attention firmly fixed on us.

"But it sounds like Nick means more to you than you're letting on."

Lucas nods, his gaze distant.

"More than I can ever admit to myself, let alone anyone else."

Lucas looks up at the stars, as if seeking guidance from above.

"I don't even know where to fucking start with that."

He says with a bitter laugh.

"Start by being honest with yourself and with Nick. The rest will figure itself out, and if it's meant to be, it's meant to be."

I suggest, and he takes a deep breath, his grip on my hand tightening.

"I don't want to lose him, but I don't want to lose myself either."

The journey ahead may be uncertain, but in the honesty of the moment, a glimmer of hope emerges for Jax and me and for Lucas and Nick.

16

Jax

This place is idyllic, my own private paradise. There's something about the sound of the sea that has always soothed me. The calming lap of the crystal-clear water and the quiet that follows are so peaceful; they clear my head, stop the noise, and I can finally breathe again. Watching another one of my best friends marry the love of his life is a joyous and momentous occasion. *It should have been Ruby and me.* That thought has weighed on me all day; it has tainted what should be a happy occasion, and it feels like it's fucking crushing me. I'm starting a new chapter; I can't help but think back to the old one and crave so desperately the life I had before.

As the sun sinks below the horizon, casting hues of orange and pink across the sky, I find myself standing on the edge of the tranquil beach, a bottle of beer in hand, grappling with thoughts of the past and the promise of a new beginning. The laughter and cheers from the celebration going on behind me only intensify the ache in my chest. The conflicting emotions barrelling through my exhausted body made me question everything about mine and Zeppelin's relationship. *Was she really the woman I wanted to spend the rest of my life with? Was she really the one? Was I kidding myself that the feelings I had for her were one hundred percent real? Was she nothing but a rebound?*

I hadn't thought about the concept of having more kids with someone who wasn't Ruby. *Was I ready to be a dad again?* The unanswered questions that plagued my mind were unrelenting. Zeppelin, a chapter of my life that had seemed so promising, now stood under the crushing weight of my still broken heart. The dreams of building a family, a future with her, brought with them a pang of guilt, as if I were betraying another life, the one I had envisioned so clearly with Ruby. It made me feel unknown, unfathomable emotions that I hadn't quite gotten to grips with yet. Doubt filled my mind as I questioned whether my feelings for her were genuine or a lame attempt to fill the void left by a past love. The love I had for Ruby was a cherished chapter, but it was a chapter that had long since closed. Zeppelin, with her own uniqueness, offered an opportunity for a new story, one that could be just as vibrant and meaningful if I only gave it the chance it deserved.

As I turn back towards the celebrations, my eyes seek out Zeppelin's. Her eyes sparkling with joy, as she danced under the moonlit sky. In that moment, I realised that doubt was natural and normal, but it didn't have to be the deciding factor. The love I had for Ruby, though irreplaceable, had become a part of my history. Zeppelin, with her own quirks and unique personality, represented a chance for a different kind of love. Her silver eyes glittered as her body moved fluidly, her arms raised in the air, letting the music wash over her as Morgan Wallen and Post Malone's "I Had Some Help" blares through the speakers. I made my way towards her as I watched her gracefully move to the rhythm of the music. The weight of doubt that had lingered in my heart began to lift, replaced by the stark realisation that love, in all its forms, was a journey of self-discovery. Ruby had been an integral part of shaping my experiences and memories. Like Zeppelin's books, we were responsible for creating our own happy endings, and I had no doubt in my mind that this was meant to be mine.

The moonlight cast a gentle glow on her face, accentuating the contours of her features. Her laughter mingling with the music drew me towards her magnetic energy, and as our eyes met, I saw not only a reflection of her happiness but also a potential for shared moments that could redefine the meaning of love in my life. The music enveloped us, as Zeppelin's hand found mine, and together we moved through the night, leaving behind the shadows of doubt and stepping into the uncharted territory of a new beginning. The celebrations continued, and in Zeppelin's arms, I found solace in the knowledge that love could conquer all and lead us to unexpected and beautiful destinations.

17

Zeppelin

Life in the UK had resumed its familiar rhythm. The return home after two weeks in paradise marked a continuation of our love story, one that had deepened amid the sunsets and gentle waves of our tropical escape. The shared experiences had woven an unbreakable bond between us.

I sat on the toilet after peeing on the stick and waiting with bated breath for the results to develop. Jax stood beside me, leaning against the sink, his hand clutched in mine. The turmoil apparent in his hazel eyes, my stomach roiled with nerves, and I couldn't bring myself to look. I held the stick with trembling hands, terrified of the impending result. *Did I want to embark on the journey of parenthood? Was I ready and equipped for it? Was our relationship stable enough to withstand the prospect of bringing a new life into the mix?* My mind was swimming with unspoken thoughts, thoughts I was scared to say out loud. A few minutes pass, and I glance down at the result, which reads *'Not Pregnant.'* A sigh of relief accompanied the negative result of the pregnancy test, a mutual acknowledgement that neither of us was ready to become parents, at least not yet. We didn't acknowledge the news, but an unspoken understanding passed between us as he wrapped his arms around me and enveloped me in his tight embrace. *We had a lucky escape this time.*

Jax had gone back into the studio with Rancid Vengeance to start writing and recording their sixteenth studio album. It was a whole new creative chapter for him, and it was showing in the music they were creating together. His dedication to the craft mirrored our commitment to each other, a shared understanding that allowed us to pursue our individual dreams while supporting one another. The music became a backdrop to our shared journey, a soundtrack that captured the essence of our love story. As the days turned into weeks, we found solace in the simple pleasures, the comfort of each other's presence, the laughter in our shared moments, and the anticipation of the adventures that lay ahead.

Since our return, I had made a solid start on book number ten, which was a romance with a murder mystery twist. For the first time in years, I was excited to see where the story went. I had a passion for it again, and it was refreshing. I looked forward to the time that I sat down at my laptop and got lost in the fictional world of Roxie and Sully. I had found my love for writing again, and even though I was heading in a completely different direction from my usual conventional romance stories, I had learned to just go with it.

"Hey girl, just doing my monthly check-in! How's it going?"

My publisher, Sara Stapleton-Smythe, from Raven Rebellion Publishing, with her ash-blonde hair cut into a long bob, framing her golden tanned face after spending far too much time on the sunbeds. Her black-rimmed glasses rested on the bridge of her nose, her bee-stung lips over-inflated from her monthly filler appointments. She wore a bright pink kimono over a black bikini, with a blue, cloudless sky and a blazing sun as the backdrop for our monthly Teams call to catch up on my next book. I had sent her over some pages, and even though she was on holiday in Santorini with her husband, Thom, she had bought our call forward.

"I must say, you are looking fabulous, babes!"

She gushes, and I smile genuinely at the camera as I take off my glasses, placing them down on my desk next to me.

"That's what two weeks in paradise will do for you!"

I say with a grin, my smile genuine.

"It looks good on you! You and the rock star! You're hot property! I'm so happy for you!"

She states in her over-the-top fashion, and I can't stop smiling. I had returned home relaxed, refreshed, and ready to take on the world. I was determined to move on from the last few months, and I was finally content with the hand life had dealt me. I was in a meaningful relationship and writing again.

"So...onto the new book."

Interrupting my thoughts, she changes the subject, her face turning serious, and I'm nervous at her sudden switch.

"It's not your usual...style."

She says, tapping her nail against her front tooth, and I'm silent for a moment, eagerly anticipating her next words.

"And while that's not necessarily a bad thing...per se...but with your current fan base...I don't think it's what they want. They want your typical schmaltzy, spicy romance that you're known for."

My mouth drops open at her blunt but honest response.

"Sara, with all due respect, for the first time in a long time, I'm in love with writing again! I really think this story is special, and I truly believe in it! I love my fans, I do, but would you be content with just churning out romance after romance? It's becoming boring! They meet, drama ensues, they inevitably fall in love, the end! Same old, same old, same shit, different characters! Come on! I don't want to be pigeon-holed; I don't want to be known just for that!"

I explain, frustration evident in my voice, and she sniffs.

"Your reader base is bored housewives with nothing better to do than fantasise about fictional men in their beds doing the wicked things that their husbands don't do! They want the happy ever after, they want a bit of hot and heavy erotica that they can use with B.O.B late at night when the kids are in bed! I'm sorry, but I don't think this will work. It's probably not what you want to hear, but bottom line, it's the way of the book world, babes."

I clench my jaw tight at the way she says *'babes'* in that nasal tone, condescending and patronising way of hers.

"You're either going to have to change the story, or we're going to have to re-negotiate your contract."

There is a threatening undertone to her voice, and I nod curtly. For the first time in a long time, instead of shying away from confrontation, I square my shoulders and steel myself to reply.

"Then I'm sorry, Sara, but we'll have to re-negotiate. I'll be in touch."

Her eyes widen as she goes to speak again, and I click leave, reeling from the conversation. I lean back in my chair, taking a few moments to process the last twenty minutes. My thoughts are interrupted by a tap on the door. I swivel my chair around as Jax comes into view. I still can't get over his transformation since our break in the Maldives. His short blonde hair mussed from running his fingers through it, his faded, ripped blue jeans hanging off his lean hips, the white t-shirt he is wearing clinging to his biceps in that delicious way, and I can't take my eyes off him. He really is perfection. I have to stop myself from eye-fucking him, as Jax smirks at me, sensing the tension in the air.

"Everything okay, sweetheart?"

He asks, leaning against the door frame, his t-shirt riding up to reveal his golden tanned abs. I let out an audible sigh, trying to shake off the frustration from the call.

"Not really."

I admit, scrubbing my hands down my face, feeling absolute despair and annoyance.

"Sara thinks my new book is...too different and not what the readers want."

His hazel eyes narrow slightly, a protective glint in them.

"And what do you want?"

He cocks his head to the side, and I pause, considering his question. No one has ever asked me that before, and it's refreshing, as I consider his question. *What do I want?*

"I want to write something that excites me, something that makes me fall in love with writing again. I don't want to be confined to a single genre just because it sells."

Jax steps closer, his long fingers gently tracing the edge of my desk.

"Then don't let her push you around. You're a fucking great writer, Zeppelin, and you should do what makes you happy. If this book makes you happy, then go with it. I'll support you whatever you decide."

A smile tugs at the corner of my lips, grateful for his support.

"Thank you, babe. I really needed to hear that, more than you'll ever know."

He grins, leaning down to plant a soft kiss on my forehead.

"Anytime, love. Now, tell me more about this not-so-typical book of yours. I'm curious."

As I begin to share the details of my unconventional story, I see the spark of interest in Jax's eyes. He listens intently, offering suggestions and encouragement. It's a stark contrast to the discouragement I faced moments ago. In that instant, I realise that Jax is not just my rock star boyfriend; he's also my muse, my confidant, and my biggest supporter. With his encouragement, I feel a renewed sense of determination, and whether it's love or writing, sometimes you have to fight for what sets your soul on fire.

18

Jax

Past

A figure dressed from head to toe in leather, wearing a motorcycle helmet, emerges from the chapel entrance. The figure is holding a box, and before anyone gets a chance to register what is going on, the figure pulls out a gun and opens fire, spraying the room in a never-ending torrent of bullets.

As the bullets fly, I hear Sam roar Peyton's name. He hits the floor first, and I can't contain my disbelief. I'm frozen to the spot as Peyton lets out a blood-chilling scream. My first instinct is to protect Ruby and our unborn child. No hesitation, no regard for my own safety and well-being, it's all about her and our baby. I grab her trembling hand in mine, her engagement ring glistening in the sunlight blazing through the small window above us. I swing her around, a bullet narrowly grazing her hair, as she starts to sob.

"Jack."

Her melodic voice trembles, pulling her close to me. I shake my head, cupping her face in my hands.

"No, no, no, look at me, shhh, shhh, it's alright, buttercup. Just focus on me, don't take your eyes off me, everything is going to be ok."

I flash her a smile, even though, inside, I'm fucking terrified.

The next thing I heard was continuous loud, almost deafening popping noises from behind me. At first, I didn't even realise I had been hit. I don't know if it was because of the adrenaline and my fight-or-flight instinct, but I didn't feel a thing on impact. It was only after I felt the warm trickle of blood and the crimson smear across my hand as I touched it, the blood soaking through the shoulder of my shirt. A few moments passed, and the adrenaline finally wore off; it became the greatest pain I had ever felt in my entire fucking life. The only way I can describe how it feels is like your body is being scorched from the inside out. After what feels like an hour of standing still, when it's only seconds, I look down, fixating on the wound. So much fucking blood. I manage to take a few steps back, and I collapse to the floor.

Jax

Present

I'm startled awake and sit bolt upright in bed, my breath coming in sharp gasps, my heartbeat thundering in my bare chest. I'm covered in a thin sheen of sweat, and it takes a few minutes for me to realise it was a nightmare. I look around the dark room, like a deer caught in headlights, the familiarity of my bedroom and Zeppelin sleeping soundly next to me calms me somewhat. *Fuck me, I haven't had that nightmare in ages.* I run my hand through my short hair as I swing my long legs out of bed, careful not to wake her. I pad across the carpeted floor and head downstairs. Thea is on a sleepover with Addison, which I am thankful for. I make my way into the open-plan kitchen, finding a pile of neatly folded washing on the countertop. I pull on a pair of freshly laundered black jogging bottoms, a soft heather grey t-shirt, and a black Rancid Vengeance hoodie. I jam my feet into my trainers, my footsteps soft as I head out to the front door. I put my Beats earbuds in and quietly unlock the front door. I get to the bottom of the stone steps, my footsteps crunching on the gravel, and I begin with a gentle jog around the perimeter of all five looming mansions that make up Vengeance Estates. All were modern concrete buildings with tall glass windows that offered panoramic views across acres of lush greenery and woodland that seemed to stretch for miles.

I breathe in the cool, crisp air, enjoying the peace running brings me. Taking in the inky blackness of the night, as the pounding beat of my music drives me on, as Apocalyptica sing about not being strong enough, and soon, I hit my stride. I am pounding the dirt trail that leads into the dense woodland at a punishing pace. My mind clears with each mile I run, my calf muscles are deliciously sore, and I look up to see Sam jogging towards me. He approaches, his breath visible in the cool night air. He nods in acknowledgement and falls into step beside me. The dense woodland around us seems to enclose us, as we resume our run. The path ahead is dimly lit, and the sounds of our footsteps echo through the quiet woods. The music in my ears continues to drive me forward, the beat matching my strides. The cool breeze rustles the leaves overhead as we run side by side. Sam and I exchange knowing glances. There's an unspoken understanding between us, a shared appreciation for the escape that running provides. With each step, the tension seems to dissipate, and the world fades away. I pull out one of my earbuds, turning briefly to Sam.

"Don't you ever fucking sleep?"

I say wryly, and he cocks his pierced eyebrow.

"Could ask you the same question, brother."

He rasps with a smirk, and I chuckle softly.

"Fair point."

I say with a shrug as the trail takes a turn, and we push ourselves, the endorphins pumping, all traces of my nightmare long gone. I stop briefly to catch my breath, bouncing from one foot to the other. Sam comes to a halt, too, and it looks like he hasn't even broken a sweat. *Fucking show off, he works out like a machine.* We all stopped working out with him because none of us could keep up.

"Wanna' talk about it?"

He asks, as I glance at him, appreciating the concern in his eyes. The moonlight casts a soft glow on his features, emphasising the subtle lines of fatigue and determination etched on his face. I take a deep breath, feeling the cool night air fill my lungs.

"I had another nightmare; it hasn't happened in a long fucking time. It was one of those that stays with you for a bit, I can't seem to shake it off, ya know?"

I shrug, attempting to downplay the lingering unease.

"I was back in that chapel again..."

I shake my head, attempting to push it to the back of my mind, and Sam nods as if he just gets it.

"When I imagined Ruby walking down the aisle, I never in a million years thought it would be in a casket."

I swallow past the lump in my throat and run my hand through my short hair. Sam's expression shifts, his eyes reflecting a mixture of empathy and understanding. He places a comforting hand on my shoulder, a silent gesture of support.

"I get it, I really do. Those nightmares haunt me on a nightly basis; that, twinned with my insomnia, is not a great combination."

Sam says, his voice low and somewhat soothing.

"The chapel, the memories, it's all too...vivid. I have no idea what brought it on; it hasn't happened in a while. I can't believe it's been three fucking years."

I admit.

"Maybe Zeppelin and I are too happy? I can't help waiting for the other shoe to drop, I mean...we had a pregnancy scare."

He quirks his eyebrow.

"How come you never mentioned any of this before, man?"

He asks, and I shrug.

"You've got your own shit to deal with; you don't need to listen to my fucking problems."

I laugh bitterly, and he shakes his head, his expression hard.

"Don't ever say that I'm never too busy with my own shit to listen, dude. Trust me, it would be a welcome change for me to listen to something other than the shit in my own head."

His voice was tinged with sadness, and I suddenly felt bad for my flippant statement.

"It's just... Zeppelin and I have been through a lot, you know? The ups, the downs. Every time things seem a little too perfect. I can't help but worry that it's all too good to be true."

He studies me with a thoughtful expression.

"Life has a way of throwing curveballs when you least expect it. But that doesn't mean you can't enjoy the good times, man. You're well overdue for some happiness."

I nod, appreciating the wisdom in his words.

"You're right...I know you're right, I mean, the pregnancy thing...it was a false alarm, it was a rollercoaster of emotions, though. Made us reevaluate a lot of things, I'm not gonna lie, it shook me, man. It made me question everything, but we're stronger for it, I think. I've got this nagging, irrational fear that the universe is keeping score, and at some point, it's gonna' cash in."

I let out a sigh as he places a hand on my shoulder, offering a reassuring squeeze.

"Listen, life is unpredictable at best, and we can't control everything that happens. But what we can control is how we handle it. You've got a good thing going with Zeppelin. Don't let fear ruin what you've built, and if you're going through shit, you don't have to face it alone. We might not be blood, but family is here for each other, through the good and the bad times."

I appreciate his words, and for a moment, the weight on my shoulders feels a little lighter. I offer a small smile, grateful for his friendship.

"Thanks, man. I needed to hear that."

With those words, we continue our run, and my nightmare fades away with the rising of the early morning sun.

19

Zeppelin

Expecting to find the warmth of Jax's body next to me, I sleepily reach over, and I'm met with cold sheets and an empty bed. I rub the sleep from my eyes and notice it's still dark outside. Judging by the coolness of the sheets, he's been gone for a while. I look at the digital clock next to the bed, and the glowing blue LED numbers tell me it's 5:02 am. I swing my legs out of bed, my feet hitting the soft carpeted floor in Jax's bedroom and sinking into it. I make my way over to the chest of drawers, pull open the top drawer, and take out one of Jax's black t-shirts from his vast collection. I pull it over my head, relishing the softness of the material against my naked skin. I inhale deeply, it smells of him, the unique, masculine smell of Diesel Only the Brave and pure Jackson Chase. I pad quietly across the room and head down the stairs. The t-shirt hangs loosely on my frame as I navigate my way to the kitchen, where a soft glow emanates from the large American fridge. I open it and grab a bottle of water, taking a long, soothing sip, as I hear the soft tip-taps of Jericho's paws across the marbled floor. I stroke his ears and pat his head, as his tail starts wagging wildly. I chuckle softly to myself and dramatically roll my eyes at his excitement to see me.

"*Fucking traitor*, you only want me because Thea isn't here!"

I grumble playfully, and his tongue flops out of his mouth as I take another sip of water. The cold liquid does little to ease the ache of Jax's absence. *Where could he be at this hour?* I fell asleep in his arms after a marathon lovemaking session. I glance at my phone on the kitchen counter, the screen background a picture of Jax and me laughing, lying in bed one morning. I smile at the memory, but there are no messages or missed calls. I'm wide awake now, leaning against the kitchen counter. I let my mind wander, replaying the warmth of Jax's embrace and the scent of his t-shirt that now envelopes me. I enjoy the quiet moment and anticipate his return, the clock on the wall ticking away the minutes, but time seems to slow down.

I contemplate the times we've shared, the laughter and the quiet, contemplative moments. I can't help but feel grateful that we found each other in that chat room on that fateful day. As the sky outside gradually lightens with the approaching dawn, a faint sound catches my attention, and with curiosity guiding me, I follow the soft melody. I find myself at the door of Jax's music studio. I don't bother knocking and push the door open gently. The room is bathed in a soft, ambient light and surrounded by instruments, bathed in the harsh glow of monitors, which is Jax. His fingers dance gracefully over the piano keys, creating a hauntingly beautiful tune that fills the room. I lean against the doorway, captivated by the sight of him lost in the music. The love and passion he pours into his art are palpable. As the last notes linger in the air, he hums quietly to himself as he scribbles something in his dog-eared notebook and turns to me. A mixture of surprise and warmth in his hazel eyes, a faint smile quirking at the corners of his lips.

"I couldn't sleep."

His voice was a gentle murmur, exhaustion evident in his deep timbre.

"I went for a run, and I bumped into Sam, then came here to write. I didn't want to wake you."

He explains, as I step further into the room, drawn to him like a magnet, and I reach out to intertwine my fingers with his.

"I woke up, and you were gone."

I idly play with a loose thread on his t-shirt, biting down savagely on my bottom lip.

"I'm sorry, love."

He says, his thumb reaching over to free my lip from my teeth.

"I didn't mean to worry you. I had a nightmare, that's all. I just lost track of time."

He admits, and I offer him a concerned look, as he shakes his head in warning. I don't push him to tell me, I just nod in understanding, his hazel eyes holding a mixture of vulnerability and gratitude.

"I'm just glad you're ok."

I offer softly, leaning in to place a gentle kiss on his stubbled cheek, and he pulls me into a warm embrace, his arms enveloping me in a comforting hold. I nestle my head against his shoulder, feeling the gentle rise and fall as he takes a deep breath. He reaches around me, and with a few clicks, he shuts down his computer. He gets to his feet and pulls me up with him. I take him in: he is wearing a pair of loose-fitting grey shorts that hang off his lean hips, his tattooed chest bare, and his damp hair from a recent shower looks perfectly mussed. His hazel eyes were heavy and weary.

"Let's go back to bed, sweetheart."

Jax's voice is a soothing whisper, and I willingly follow him, hand in hand, back up the stairs. The soft glow of the sunrise spills into the room as we enter, casting a serene atmosphere that contrasts with the earlier emptiness. He presses a button on the bedside table to activate the blackout blinds. As we settle back into the bed, Jax tucks the covers around us. I snuggle close, finding refuge in his bare chest, and I can't get close enough to him, wrapping myself around him like a vine. Within minutes, his breathing evens out, and I take a few moments to watch him sleep. He looks so peaceful, and I can't help wondering what his nightmare was about, but I decide to push that thought to the back of my mind, as I drift off to sleep in the arms of the man I love.

***

I wake with a start to the sound of raised voices downstairs, and I take a few moments to rub the sleep from my eyes.

"WHAT THE FUCK, COLE?"

I hear Jax bellow, and I've never heard him sound so angry. I swing my legs out of bed, dress quickly, and rush down the stairs barefoot.

"Jax?"

I say softly, as he turns to look up at me. Cole has what looks like a bunch of letters tied together with brown twine in his hand. My stomach drops at the sight, and my eyes widen, as I shake my head vehemently.

"No! No! No!"

My legs buckle beneath me, and I drop down onto the step, my stomach roiling violently. Jax runs up to meet me and gets down on his haunches in front of me, cupping my chin in his hand.

"It's gonna' be ok, sweetheart."

A lone tear tracks its way down my cheek as I look over his shoulder at Cole, who is leaning heavily on his cane. He has the letters in his other hand, and I shake my head.

"How? Whoever was sending those letters before, they've found me! You're not safe, Jax, I couldn't bear it if anyone hurt you because of me!"

My voice is thick with panicked emotion, and I can't comprehend the events of the past few minutes. Jax's concerned eyes search mine, brushing the tear away from my cheek with the pad of his calloused thumb.

"Cole, what the fuck is going on?"

Jax's voice was unwavering, and Cole's steely gaze shifted between Jax and me.

"These letters showed up at the security cabin this morning, addressed to Zeppelin. They're filled with threats just like the ones before, but whoever is behind this sounds fucking unhinged. We can't be sure what we're dealing with. I had a feeling they'd find her eventually, but I thought I could handle this quietly and discreetly."

Cole squeezes the back of his neck and lets out a long, laboured breath. Jax's expression darkens, but he turns back to me, steely determination in his eyes.

"Listen, sweetheart, no one is going to hurt you, I fucking promise you that."

He says, his jaw tight. I wipe away another stray tear and nod, trying to regain my composure.

"But they know where we live. What if they come after you or..."

I slap my hand over my mouth to stifle the sob. I can feel a panic attack threatening, as my breath comes in short, shallow bursts. Jax's thumb gently brushes my cheek, his touch grounding me, as I feel my breathing return to normal almost instantly.

"Whatever it takes. Cole, we need a plan. Now."

Cole nods, a mix of guilt and determination on his face.

"I've got some connections, old Bill, ex-military, we can figure this out, but I'm going to need some time."

As Jax helps me to my feet, I shoot a worried glance at the letters still in Cole's hand.

"What's in those letters, Cole? Are they like the ones from before?"

I ask, suddenly terrified of the answer. Cole hesitates for a moment before replying, as he nods and puffs out his cheeks.

"Someone who knows about your past, they know everything about Rian, Abel, Jax."

My heart sinks, and I feel an unwelcome chill run down my spine. The shadows of my past seem to be catching up to me, threatening the fragile peace I've found with Jax. Jax takes my hand, squeezing it reassuringly.

"We face this head-on, together. No one messes with our family; we've lost enough fucking people. This ends now."

He grits out, his index finger pointed harshly in Cole's direction. Whatever challenges lie ahead, we're ready to confront them, ready to protect the love we've built, against the shadows that seek to tear us apart.

20

Jax

"I can't hear what's going on."

I pull my headphones off, as I wave my hand through the glass at M.J, his dark sunglasses shielding his eyes. His hand was tucked into the pocket of his dark skinny jeans, his elaborate yet gaudy silver belt buckle glinting in the studio lights. He leans into the producer of our new album, the legendary rock producer Xander 'X' Rogers, his red Chicago Bulls baseball cap worn backwards, his long, dark beard braided at the end. He reminds me of Slash, but without the top hat. His jaw was going ten to the dozen, chewing furiously on some gum. We've wanted to work with Xander for years. He's the most sought-after producer in the industry, and he jumped at the opportunity when M.J approached him to work on our new album, *Rancid Vengeance - XV (The Next Chapter)*. We're going for a brand-new experimental sound on this album, and it sounds very different from all of our other albums. It was refreshing to write, and it reignited my passion for music. I press the intercom button, allowing my voice to carry through from the recording booth into the main studio.

"I can't hear anything."

I repeat, as the guitar riff and pounding drum beat suddenly come to a halt. Xander cocks his eyebrow, the gum still working overtime. M.J adjusts his sunglasses, his expression unreadable. I exchange a quick glance with Sam, Brody, and Lucas, who are sitting on the studio sofa. They're just as nervous about this album as I am. Sam leans forward, twisting his wedding ring around his finger. Brody looks bored, and Lucas is looking at his phone with an impassive expression on his face.

"What's going on, man?"

Xander asks, his voice gruff, as I lean closer to the microphone.

"I can't hear anything, something's wrong with the fucking audio in here!"

Frustration is evident in my tone, and M.J smirks, tapping his foot impatiently.

"Come on, Jack, we don't have all day. Xander's time is extremely valuable."

M.J says in his familiar American drawl, as I pull my headphones off and Xander holds his hand up.

"Give me a minute, dude, I'll check the levels, and we'll figure this shit out, yeah?"

He offers me a reassuring wink, and after a few tense minutes, the sound engineer signals that the issue is resolved. The music kicks back in, and I can finally hear the powerful backing track pounding through the speakers. I slide my headphones back into place as the music envelopes the studio once more. I feel the familiar rush of adrenaline, and I lock eyes with M.J, his smirk fading as the music resumes its thunderous course. He nods his head to the beat of the music, the frustration from earlier replaced by a renewed sense of determination. Xander gives a subtle nod, signalling that everything is back on track.

"Let's pick up where we left off, yeah?"

Xander announces, and I adjust the strap of my guitar, as the other boys enter the recording booth. Lucas takes his place behind the drum kit, Brody picks up his guitar, and Sam resumes his place next to me, his cool demeanour from a moment ago turning into a full-on swagger, as he steps up to the microphone, a beaming grin on his face. The familiar melody takes over, and we launch into the next part of the song, the booth coming alive with the sound of old and new Rancid Vengeance music. Xander, with his gruff exterior, nods approvingly as he works the mixing desk with expert precision and fine-tunes the levels to perfection. Brody's fingers dance skilfully across the guitar strings, adding depth to the sound. The energy in the studio is palpable, and Sam's vocals blend with mine and Brody's impressive guitar riffs. A thrill weaves its way through my consciousness, and a smile spreads across my face, the nerves from moments ago dissipating with each note we play.

I feel my phone vibrating in my pocket, but I ignore it, temporarily engrossed in the music we are making. The vibrating stops, only to start again seconds later, the persistent buzzing becoming increasingly distracting. Sam flashes me a concerned look, and I shake my head, continuing to play until the song fades out. I pull my headphones off and take my phone out of my pocket. The screen lights up with multiple missed calls and messages. Concern furrows my brow as I notice they are all from Zeppelin. *Fuck.*

A sense of dread washes over me as I scroll through Zeppelin's missed calls and frantic messages. With each passing moment, the weight of the situation intensifies. Sam and Brody exchange worried glances, sensing that something is off.

"What's going on, man? Is everything ok?"

Sam asks in his familiar rasp, as he looks from me to Brody and back again. I run my fingers through my short hair.

"I don't fucking know!"

My voice strained, and without further explanation, I dial Zeppelin's number, the tension in the room escalating with each ringing tone. Finally, she answers, her voice urgent and panic-stricken.

"Jack! Jack!"

Fear settles in my gut, and my heartbeat quickens at the terror in her voice. A blood-curdling scream echoes through the phone as I hold it in a death grip to my ear, and my jaw clenches tight.

"JACK! JACK!"

She repeats, a loud commotion in the background and the distinct sound of traffic.

"Zeppelin, baby, I need you to talk to me. Where are you? Are you ok? What's going on?"

I manage to choke out in garbled gibberish, the blood freezing in my veins as I hear the pure terror in her voice.

"Please, please, Jack, don't let him hurt me! I'm coming to you!"

Then the phone goes dead, and I can't make my feet work. My phone slips out of my hand and thuds on the floor, leaving me with the haunting echo of Zeppelin's desperate plea. Sam, Brody, and Lucas exchange anxious glances, realising the severity of the situation. I take a moment to gather my thoughts, trying to shake off the paralysis that has me frozen to the spot.

Unexpectedly, my synapses fire, my brain sending a message to my legs to move. I rush out, the door ricocheting off the wall with a loud bang, as the urgency of my footsteps matches the pounding in my chest. I run down the stairs two at a time, followed closely by Sam, Brody, and Lucas. The sound of M.J shouting '*where the fuck do you think you're going*' echoes down the stairwell. By the time I get to the bottom, I haven't even broken a sweat, the adrenaline and pure need to get to Zeppelin driving me on. I push open the fire door out onto the busy London Street. I look from left to right, scanning my surroundings, as I see her running barefoot in the distance, her dishevelled appearance a stark contrast compared to the suited business types going about their daily lives.

"Jesus Christ!"

Sam mutters as I spin on my heel and run towards her.

"Zeppelin!"

I yell, the fear in her silver eyes causes every hair on the back of my neck to stand on end, and my heart to slam violently against my rib cage. As I sprint towards Zeppelin, weaving through the bustling crowd of city dwellers, the chaos of traffic and city life fades to a distant hum as my focus narrows on her. She looks terrified, her wild, blonde hair a mess of loose curls. My need to reach her grows more desperate with each passing second.

"ZEPPELIN!"

I call out again, as she stumbles, glancing over her shoulder, and our eyes lock for a moment. In that instant, I see a mixture of desperation, fear, and a plea for help in her watery gaze. I have to get to her, as I try to close the distance between us. Unexpectedly, horror washes over me as I watch Zeppelin being flung into the air, her body twisting unnaturally before landing with a sickening thud on the unforgiving pavement. Time seems to freeze as the horrifying scene unfolds before my eyes. The screech of tyres and the blare of car horns ring in my ears. Panic surges through me, and my legs carry me towards Zeppelin's crumpled form on the cold asphalt.

"ZEPPELIN!"

I scream, a gut-wrenching mix of fear and disbelief gripping me, as concerned onlookers gasp and recoil at her motionless, bloody form.

Kneeling beside her, her blonde curls spill over her face, blood staining her dishevelled hair. My hands tremble as I reach for her. I check for a pulse, desperate to find any signs of life. Her pulse is weak, but she's breathing. She groans softly, and the feeling of relief washes over me as I let out the breath I didn't know I was holding.

"Someone call a fucking ambulance!"

I roar, my voice cracking with desperation and not sounding like my own. Sam, stunned by the sudden turn of events, fumbles for his phone, frantically dialling for help. Zeppelin's silver eyes, now glazed with pain, meet mine, and I feel a lump forming in my throat. *Please God, no, not again, please don't take her away from me.*

"Hold on, baby, please, oh God, please Zeppelin, hold on."

Time seems to stretch into agonising eternity, as I cling to Zeppelin, my hands stained with her blood. Sam's voice on the phone with emergency services is drowned out by the nightmare unfolding before me.

"Stay with me, Zeppelin. Stay with me, sweetheart."

I whisper, my voice choked with emotion. The lump in my throat grows larger, threatening to suffocate me. Her eyes reflect a painful vulnerability that pierces through my soul. I cradle her in my lap, tears blurring my vision as I murmur desperate pleas.

"Hold on, Zeppelin. You can't leave me, not like this. Stay with me, please."

The weight of her frail body in my arms is a stark reminder of the fragility of life, as her eyes flutter closed, and she succumbs to the darkness.

21

Zeppelin

After a restless night's sleep, plagued with nightmares, haunting thoughts of poison pen letters, severed heads, and terror-filled eyes. I wake to a text from Sara, my publisher, asking me to come to her London office for a meeting to renegotiate my contract and discuss my books moving forward. Jax has a full day in the studio today recording Rancid Vengeance's new album. After the pile of letters appeared yesterday, he was reluctant to leave, but I insisted I would be fine. He was gone before I woke up, and I rolled over to a note placed on his pillow.

Love you, sweetheart.

Stay safe.

Your J xx

I smile at his neat, elaborate penmanship as I hold the note close to my heart and place it down on top of my notebook on the bedside table. I swing my legs out of bed and onto the soft pile of the carpet. After a quick shower and a cup of strong coffee to shake off the remnants of sleep, I dress quickly, opting for smart black shorts, black heels, and a sleeveless dark denim shirt, tied at my midriff, and my hair styled into loose, tousled waves. I grab my notebook and Jax's note, tucking them both into my slouchy tan suede bag. As I head out the door, I can't shake the feeling of unease that clings to me. I crunch unsteadily across the gravelled driveway, regretting my decision to wear heels. I climb into Jax's black Audi R8, the sleek black leather bucket seats hugging every inch of my body, and I take a few minutes to connect my phone to the car's Bluetooth. Soon, the quiet interior is filled with the sound of *"Honey I'm Good" by Andy Grammer as I slide the car into drive, its* powerful engine roaring to life. I set about my journey to my publishers' office in Central London, leaving the looming gates of Vengeance Manor in the rearview mirror.

The sleek black Audi R8 glides smoothly along the road, its powerful engine purring beneath me. My country music playlist continues with *"Arlington" by Trace Adkins, my fingers tapping lightly on the steering wheel to the poignant lyrics* as the countryside zips past me in a blur of greenery. As I navigate the winding roads, I find solace in the beauty of the countryside, a reminder of the simple joys that life has to offer. With each passing mile, I feel a sense of clarity and purpose settling over me, guiding me ever closer to my destination. I hit heavy traffic as I drive closer to the city. I flick a glance in the interior mirror, noticing a distinctive white Mercedes following close behind. I signal to move into the right lane, and I see the Mercedes make the exact same move. *Are they following me? Why would they be following? Fuck my life.* I push my foot down on the accelerator, and the car speeds up too, like an angry kitten, throwing me back in my seat. My heartbeat quickens as I try desperately to figure out who the fuck is in the driver's seat, but I'm too focused on the road ahead. I grip the steering wheel so tight, my knuckles turn white. My mind is racing with a whirlwind of questions as the white Mercedes continues to trail behind me, mimicking my every move. *What do they want? Is this something to do with Rian's death and the poison pen letters?* Panic begins to claw its way up my throat, threatening to overwhelm me. I try to steal another glance at the driver in the rearview mirror, but all I can see is the blur of their silhouette, obscured by the tinted windows. The cityscape flashes by in a dizzying array, my thoughts racing as I try to formulate a plan, but fear clouds my mind, leaving me in a state of panic and pure helplessness.

As the adrenaline courses through my veins, I make split-second decisions, darting down random side streets in a desperate attempt to lose Mr. Mercedes. But no matter how hard I try, they remain hot on my tail, as I feel tears burning behind my eyes.

"Call Jax."

I say to the screen, and the car's interior is filled with the dial tone of my phone as it continues to ring.

"FUCCCKKK! COME ON! COME ON!"

I shout as his voice comes through the speakers.

"Hey, it's Jax, you know what to do, leave me a message at the beep!"

A loud beep makes me jump, as I swallow past the lump in my throat. It takes a few seconds for me to compose myself before I speak.

"Hey, it's me, please, pick up, I need you, Jax. Call me back, please."

I end the call, as I swing right into a side street and realise it's a dead end. *Fuck my life.* I push heavily on the brake and skid to a stop, noticing the white Mercedes sailing past the street. *Thank God.* I breathe a sigh of relief as I grab my bag and open the door, getting out of the car and leaning on the bonnet of the car with shaky legs. I pull my phone out of my bag and dial Jax again, it rings out as I feel a hot tear slip down my cheek. *This can't be happening.* The adrenaline that had fuelled my frantic escape now leaves me feeling drained and vulnerable. With each unanswered ring, my desperation grows, a knot tightening in my stomach with every passing second.

As I brace myself against the bonnet of the car, my hands trembling and tears threatening to spill from my eyes, a sense of helplessness washes over me. An uncomfortable knot tightens my stomach, as the reality of the situation sinks in, I realise that I am alone, stranded in a dead-end street with no one to turn to for help. The weight of fear presses down on me, threatening to crush me. I wipe away another tear that trails down my cheek, drawing in a shaky breath, as I try to steady my racing heart. *Come on, Zeppelin, fucking think!* Drawing in a deep, steadying breath, I force myself to think clearly, to assess the situation and find a way out of this nightmare. My eyes scan the deserted street, searching for any sign of hope, any opportunity to escape this nightmare I have unknowingly found myself in. I swipe the screen of my phone and dial the one person who knows where I can find Jax. *If I can get to him, everything will be ok, he'll know what to do.*

"Hey girl, what's up?"

Peyton's melodic voice fills my ears, and I breathe a sigh of relief at hearing a familiar voice.

"Hey, hon, sorry to call you like this."

I try to keep the fear out of my voice.

"It's ok, is everything alright, babe?"

She asks, concern in her voice.

"Yeah, yeah, everything's fine, babe. I'm in Central London for a meeting with my publisher, and I wanted to surprise Jax with lunch. Can you text me the address of the studio, please?"

I ask apprehensively, as she chuckles softly.

"Aw, that's sweet, yeah course, I'll text it to you now, babe, are you sure everything's ok?"

She asks again, giving me every opportunity to confess what's going on, but I choose not to.

"Everything's fine! Honestly!"

I say brightly, trying to sound convincing.

"If you're sure? I'll text you the address now, call me if you need me, yeah?"

"I will do, and thanks, Peyton."

We say our goodbyes, and I hang up the phone. Almost instantly, she texts me the address. I type it into my phone's navigation app, and it says it's 20 minutes on foot. I can't risk driving there in case I'm followed again, I can't put Jax in danger...*I won't put Jax in danger.* I push away from the bonnet of the car and sprint towards the alleyway, the click-click of my heels against the pavement echoing loudly in the stillness. Adrenaline fuels my movements as I dart between the looming buildings, my heart racing with every step. I curse my decision to wear heels, as I slip them off, opting to go barefoot. As I reach the entrance to the alley, I hesitate for just a moment, my pulse thundering in my ears. The navigation app tells me to turn right and then continue straight on. I follow the instructions, my fingers trembling, as I dial Jax's number once more, praying for him to answer. But as the call goes unanswered again, a wave of frustration washes over me, and I start to lose all hope. With each step I take, the urgency of the situation propels me forward, my bare feet slapping ungracefully against the pavement, as I dodge suited business types who flash me looks of annoyance. I spot the white Mercedes, crawling at a snail's pace, in the busy London traffic. My stomach roils, and I gasp in sheer terror as my phone starts ringing, and I can't answer it quickly enough. I try to blend in with the flow of the crowd so the driver of the Mercedes can't catch sight of me, and I can buy myself some more time.

"Jack! Jack!"

I answer, with more than a hint of desperation in my voice.

"Zeppelin, baby, talk to me. Where are you? Are you ok? What's going on?"

"Please, please, Jack, don't let him hurt me! I'm coming to you!"

I hang up the phone, as my pace quickens. I'm breathless, and I can feel beads of sweat pooling at the base of my spine. I have never been more scared in all my life, and all I want to do is curl up in Jax's lap while he holds me and tells me that everything is going to be alright. I continue to follow the navigation app, and it tells me I am five minutes away from him. I start to sprint towards my destination, as I see a fire door spring open ahead, and he steps out, as if he's my guardian angel. He's followed by Sam, Brody, and Lucas. His eyes find mine through the crowd, as I hear him call out my name.

"ZEPPELIN!"

He starts towards me, the world around me blurring. I stumble, and as I look up, I see familiar hazel eyes. I couldn't be more desperate to get to him. I step out into traffic, and it all happens so fast, it's as if I'm looking from the outside in. My body contorts and is flung up into the air. I watch in horror as the world spins around me, a cacophony of noise and motion. As the ground rushes up to meet me, a sense of calm washes over me, and time seems to stand still. I hit the ground with a bone-jarring impact, and the cold pavement pressed against my battered and broken body, a searing pain radiating from every inch. I'm vaguely aware of being cradled in familiar arms, the sound suddenly muffled, my last thought before I succumb to the darkness.

"I'll see you soon, Rian."

22

Jax

I was glad I couldn't hear my thoughts over the dull, but incessant, low humming beep of the machines. The sound set my teeth on edge and stirred up images I would rather forget. I gnaw viciously on my thumbnail, and my leg bounces restlessly. I was a mess of raw emotion, hanging on by a fucking thread. I hadn't slept for four days straight, and my mind filled with unwelcome thoughts, as she lay there looking tiny, pale, and so fucking fragile against the stark, sterile white sheets. There are wires coming from all directions, and I swallow hard, pushing back the surge of regret that threatens to overwhelm me. *If only I had gotten to her in time.* I clench my jaw, trying to drown out the cacophony of thoughts racing through my mind. With trembling hands, I reach out to her, grasping her hand in mine and pressing a kiss to the back of her hand. I take a few moments to feel the warmth of her hand in mine, reminding me that she was still living, still breathing, and I took comfort in that thought as the door swung open.

I look up to see Lucas casually standing in the doorway with two cups of coffee in his hands. He steps further into the room and hands me a cup wordlessly while taking a sip of his own, nodding my thanks as I take it from him. The warmth seeping into my hands provided a brief respite from the cold grip of fear that crept its way through every inch of my body. Taking a sip, the bitter taste of the strong, steaming black liquid offered me the caffeine buzz I so desperately craved.

"Dude, go home."

Lucas states matter-of-factly, his tone placating.

"You look like shit, you've been here for four days straight, man. Go home, get some rest. I'll call if there's any change."

I quirk my eyebrow and smirk, as I swallow the hot liquid.

"*Wow*, you don't fuck about, do you, mate?"

I quip, and he chuckles softly.

"Nope, it's all part of the charm! Seriously, though, Kai and Trey are taking it in shifts, Jace is on call as a back-up, besides, I think Thea's missing her daddy."

Lucas says with a shrug, and my heart slams against my rib cage when I think of Thea, listening to the sound of her hiccupping sobs when I explained to her in the dimly lit room that Zeppelin had been hurt. The image of her tear-streaked face, her small hands clutching onto Jericho's soft fur, and he whined as if he was crying too, haunts me. She's too young to understand why this was happening, and she's too innocent to understand that there are people out there who want to hurt other people just for the sake of it. I wanted to grab the person who did this to her and nail him to the fucking wall. I wanted to look him in the eye while I watched him bleed for his fucking sins. But I could never act on those impulses, not with Thea depending on me to be her rock in this fucking shit storm. As much as I wanted to unleash my rage on whoever had harmed Zeppelin, I knew that my priority was to comfort my daughter and make sure that she was safe.

Taking a deep breath, I force myself to push aside the thoughts of vengeance and take another sip of my coffee. Lucas regards me intently, anticipating my answer.

"You're right, man, my priority is Thea and making sure she's safe, I can't let my emotions cloud my judgement. We need to double security, I can't, and I won't fucking lose anyone else, Luke."

I say with a steely resolve, and he nods curtly, a look of quiet understanding passing between us.

"I'll touch base with Cole, and I'll call if there's any change, go be with Thea, get some rest."

He squeezes my shoulder in a gesture of reassurance, as I place my now-empty coffee cup in the bin next to the hospital bed and lean down to place a chaste kiss on the corner of Zeppelin's mouth.

"I'll be back soon, love. I love you."

I whisper as I turn to leave the room, closing it with a quiet click behind me. As soon as I leave the room, I lean against the door, feeling an overwhelming sense of guilt for leaving, but I know it's what I need. I'll be no good to her exhausted, so I start to walk down the corridor, Jace falling silently in step a few paces behind me. We go down in the lift, and as I step out, I hear them, the loud hum of reporters and photographers at the entrance of the hospital. Jace touches his ear as he moves in front of me.

"On the move, boss. Yep, on it, it's just Jax."

He says in his familiar Irish lilt, and I pull my Raybans down to shield my eyes. As soon as we step outside, I am momentarily blinded by the wild flashing of flashbulbs and loud catcalling.

"Jax! Jax! Is it true that someone tried to murder Zeppelin? Is it linked to Rian St James' murder?"

My blood runs cold at the question, but I don't get time to dwell, as Jace encourages the crowd to move back, opening the passenger door and ushering me into a black Range Rover with tinted windows idling at the kerb. I climb in, and he slams the door shut behind me. I settle into the soft, cream leather seat and pull my sunglasses off, allowing myself a second to breathe before I contemplate the vile question.

"Is it true that someone tried to murder Zeppelin? Is it linked to Rian St James' murder?"

As we pull smoothly away and into the traffic, I pull up the privacy glass and let out the emotions I have been holding back. I sob, tears streaming down my cheeks. The question had been thrown at me like a dagger, and the chilling thought sent shivers down my spine, igniting an inferno of anger, rage, and deep-seated fear within me. The sound of the radio interrupted my wayward thoughts.

"Rock band Rancid Vengeance seems to be the unluckiest band in history, as it has been reported that Jackson Chase's lover, author and New York Times bestseller Zeppelin Williams, has been involved in a dramatic hit and run on a busy London Road. Chase, also known as 'Flash', to die-hard Rancid Vengeance fans, was photographed leaving the Queen Elizabeth Hospital earlier today. Williams, thirty, has been spotted on a string of romantic dates with Jackson over a three-month period and is said to be 'head over heels in love.' After losing his fiancée, Ruby Logan, three years ago at the ill-fated Las Vegas wedding of bandmate Samson 'Bolt' Newbolt and celebrity tattoo artist turned entrepreneur, Peyton Harper. The extent of Zeppelin's injuries is yet to be confirmed. For Rancid Vengeance, a band already marred by tragedy and misfortune, this latest incident feels like yet another cruel twist of fate. It begs the question, what led to this tragic event? And what does it mean for the future of Rancid Vengeance, a band already teetering on the edge of collapse? A spokesperson for the band has been contacted for further comment, and we will keep you updated as this story unfolds."

The unforgiving world of rock n' roll, where triumph and tragedy go hand in hand, is fraught with danger lurking in the shadows, and the recent events surrounding Rian's murder have shattered the illusion of safety that once enveloped us. We were untouchable, but after Peyton's kidnapping, Ruby's death, Raleigh's crazy ex, and Brody embroiled in an attempted murder charge, we really were the unluckiest band in the history of the world. I couldn't help but think that we were truly fucking cursed, misfortune seemed to follow us around like a looming spectre, and it was an endless cycle of despair. As we left the city behind, the concrete jungle gave way to lush, rolling green hills. All I wanted to do was lock myself in my house and hope this all goes away.

23

Jax

I never realised how much I enjoyed being a girl dad. The rough early months with a chunky baby that soon turned into a toothless and active toddler. She was replaced by a jabbering little girl who looks at her daddy with a love I never knew or could ever imagine. I lived for the nights when she slept and snuggled with me, safe in my arms. Yet I couldn't get a wink of sleep because I was terrified, she was going to be taken away from me, just like her mum. I've loved my journey as a dad. I've grown so much as a person, even when I thought I wasn't good enough or strong enough to carry on. That's why I was grateful that my mum and dad were looking after Thea and Jericho; I didn't want her to see me like this. *This out-of-control fucking mess.*

The fear of history repeating itself scared me; my past, present, and uncertain future were colliding spectacularly, and there was nothing I could do to fucking stop it. I felt refreshed after a full twelve hours of sleep, but my mind was still restless and drowning with memories I thought I had long since buried.

It was the middle of the day, and I was in my bathrobe, slumped in my buttery leather chair in my home studio. *Proper rock n' roll.* My arm hung limply at my side, clutching a bottle of whiskey, alone with nothing but my thoughts. I lifted the bottle to my mouth and gulped it down as if it were an oasis in the middle of a dry desert. *Oh well, it's five o'clock somewhere.* Or at least that's what I had convinced myself. My stomach churns from lack of food, and I can't remember the last time I ate a full meal. My mind starts to race with thoughts of the events from the last few days. But I don't want to think, I just want to forget. I want to erase the image of the woman I love being flung up in the air and hitting the ground. I wanted to erase the look of sheer terror in her eyes as she desperately tried to get to me. The sheer terror in her eyes was etched into my memory, fuelling my need to take another long pull from the bottle. The whiskey burned my throat and created a comforting warmth in my stomach, momentarily numbing the pain. However, it did nothing to quiet the inner storm raging inside me.

With a shaky hand, I set the bottle of whiskey aside and force myself to stand up from the chair. I glance around the room. My home studio, once a place of solace, my sanctuary, now felt...suffocating. I had to get out of here; I had no sense of time or how long I had been here. I just know I need to get out of here; I need some air. My legs wobble like a toddler just finding his feet, and I blindly reach out for something to steady myself. My breath starts to come out in short, sharp pants, and my chest tightens. *Shit, this hasn't happened in a long fucking time.* I run my hand through my hair and make it to the door, placing my hand on the handle. I press my forehead to the cool, unforgiving wood. *Come on, Chase, deep breaths.* I inhaled through my nose and exhaled through my mouth as I took a minute to compose myself.

I swung the door open and stepped out into the hallway, my steps unstable and tentative. The house was quiet, eerily so, the kind of silence that makes you feel you're the only person left in the world. I started down the hallway, my bare feet sinking into the plush carpet with every step and the faint scent of whiskey lingering in the air behind me. I tried to remember the last time I'd walked these halls without feeling like a stranger in my own home. When Thea's laughter echoed through the walls, Jericho's comforting tippy taps of his paws on the floor, and the sound of Zeppelin's quiet humming of some random tune. When the house was alive with the sounds of family, the people I loved, not haunted by the ghost of who I used to be. The rock star who had the company of a female for twenty-four hours, not a moment longer. After Ruby, I was infamous for fleeting romances, each encounter brief. I was known for living in the moment, never allowing anyone to get close enough for happy ever after. The sex was always overshadowed by an impending sense of goodbye. Whether it was champagne-fuelled evenings in penthouse suites or impromptu drives through the city that seemed to exist outside of reality, these women became part of my lavish lifestyle for a day, then slipped away as quickly as they arrived.

I stopped at the threshold of Thea's room, the door ajar, and peeked inside. Her room was a chaotic blend of pinks, purples, and glitter, stuffed animals scattered everywhere, her favourite blanket half hanging off the bed, half-chewed dog toys haphazardly on the floor. I could almost see her there, curled up with her thumb in her mouth, the way she did when she was deep in sleep, Jericho on the floor next to her bed, but she wasn't there. Instead, there was just an empty room, and the aching void in my chest that came with it.

I tore myself away and continued down the hallway, my breath shallow and fast. The need to get out, to escape. I stumbled carefully down the stairs and into the kitchen. My stomach growled again, louder this time, but the thought of eating made me want to vomit. My hands were trembling, but I managed to clumsily grab my keys off the counter, the cold metal grounding me for a moment. I needed to get out of here, *but where would I go?* The hospital wouldn't let me in drunk, plus that would give the press a fucking field day, and I couldn't risk that. I could barely trust myself to stay upright right now, let alone navigate the world outside. I thought about calling my parents, asking them to bring Thea home, to surround myself with the only people who still saw something good in me, something worth saving, but I couldn't. *Not like this.* Not when I was one breath away from falling apart completely. They deserved better, and right now, they were better off not seeing me at all. I deserved to continue my pity party, all alone. That way, I couldn't hurt anyone or say something I'd regret in the morning.

I took another deep breath, forcing air into my lungs, and made my way to the front door. The handle was cold under my palm, and for a moment, I hesitated. Leaving felt like admitting defeat, like acknowledging that the walls were closing in on me, that I wasn't strong enough to hold them back. But staying wasn't an option either. Not when every corner of this house reminded me of what I'd lost, and what I was continuing to lose. *Ruby, Zeppelin, my fucking sanity.* My mind was awash with dark thoughts that I couldn't seem to shake. *Who would want to hurt Zeppelin? Was this my punishment? Was this all my fault for putting her directly in the firing line?* I knew what we were getting into at the beginning. Why couldn't I just have carried on pretending to be Jack Logan? *Because she would have found out eventually, dickhead.* I shook away the wayward thoughts as the door creaked open. The bright afternoon sun hit me full force, and I squinted against the light, my eyes adjusting slowly. The air was cool, a welcome contrast to the stifling heat inside, and I stepped out onto the gravelled driveway, feeling the rough, uneven stones beneath my feet. For a moment, I just stood there, breathing in the fresh air, trying to calm the storm inside me. I briefly closed my eyes and took in another gulp of air, my heart heavy with unsaid things. The memories are still very much at the forefront of my temporal lobe. The guilt, the fear, the overwhelming sense of loss, the underlying sense that none of us were safe.

I needed to run, to move, to do something, anything that would drown out the noise in my head. My feet shifted on autopilot, one foot in front of the other, but my mind was stuck in a loop of memories, frozen in the past. Thea's laughter, her tiny hand in mine, the way she looked at me like I was her whole world. The chapel in Vegas, the screams, the blood, the moment everything changed, and my perfect world ended. Ruby's face morphed into Zeppelins. As I cradled her in my lap, I heard my desperate screams, the light fading from her eyes, and the unforgiving coldness of the asphalt beneath me. I didn't realise I was crying until I felt the dampness on my cheeks. I swiped at them angrily, frustrated at my weakness. But no matter how hard I tried, the tears kept coming; the pain was too much to contain. I wanted to scream, to break something, to rage at how unfair all of this was, but all I could do was hope that somehow the pain would stop.

Deep down, I knew it wouldn't. The pain was a part of me now, just like the memories, just like the fear, the sadness, and the anger. It was the price I paid for loving so freely, so deeply, and for letting people too easily into my heart. I always knew that love would tear me apart, just like that Joy Division song, and as much as I wanted to escape it, I knew I couldn't. All I could do was keep moving forward, taking one step at a time, until the day I found a way to live with it, or until the day I finally allowed it to consume me.

***

I felt sick, my stomach roiling from lack of food, and my head pounded from all the whiskey I had drunk. My throat was dry, the edges of my vision blurred into a hazy fog, as I turned and headed back up the stone steps to my house, which felt like a prison right now. I struggled to get the key into the lock and closed one eye to focus. My hand trembled, and the key scraped uselessly against the metal before finally slipping into place. I turned it, and I stumbled across the threshold, my legs feeling like jelly. I stood there for a moment, swaying slightly, my hand still clutching the door handle, as if it were the only thing keeping me upright. The overwhelming sense of dread gnawed at my insides, and the silence that greeted me pressed down on me with an almost crushing, suffocating weight.

I finally forced myself to let go of the door handle and stumbled forward, my footsteps echoing in the emptiness. The house suddenly seemed unfamiliar, and everything seemed like a harsh reminder of how hollow this place had become. It was supposed to be my sanctuary, a place of comfort, safety, and warmth, but now it was just a cold, empty shell that mirrored the hollow ache in my chest. I made my way across the floor and into the living room, collapsing onto the large corner sofa with a heavy sigh. My eyes scanned the room, photos of happier times, awards that were a reminder of our achievements, but it all seemed to fade into insignificance as my head throbbed relentlessly, each pulse sending sharp stabs of pain behind my eyes. *Fuck my life.* I leaned back, closing my eyes against the spinning room, but even then, the darkness offered no relief. It only amplified the thoughts I had been trying so hard to drown in alcohol, the regrets, the mistakes, the endless loop of what-ifs that played out in my mind. I was too exhausted to do anything, so I sat there, letting the minutes stretch into hours, staring blankly at the ceiling as the nausea in my stomach slowly gave way to an empty, gnawing hunger. I knew I should eat something, anything, but the thought of food made my stomach twist uncomfortably.

I'm not sure how much time passes, but I'm about to drift off as I hear unrelenting footsteps, heavy and almost too loud, across the floor. *Why the fuck is that so loud?* My heart jumps in my chest, my eyes fly open, and I bolt upright, the haze of alcohol and fatigue clearing just enough for the anxiety to take over. I scan the room carefully and cautiously, as my eyes land on Lucas.

"You scared the shit out of me, you fucker!"

I yell almost incoherently, the noise causing the throb in my head to return. He chuckles softly as I look up at his amused face. His beanie covered his head, his jeans were loose and baggy, and the belt did little to hold them up.

"Are you drunk?"

He says with a laugh, and I frown in his general direction, suddenly finding myself unable to focus on my surroundings. I pause for a moment, as I blink, attempting to steady myself, but the spinning sensation only worsens. Lucas is still standing there, grinning like an idiot, but his voice seems to come from far away, muffled and distorted. *Fuck, how much did I drink again?*

"Are you drunk?"

He repeats, this time with more amusement, and I can see the way his eyes dance with mischief.

"I might be. Why is it any of your fucking business?"

I mumble grumpily, as he quirks his eyebrow.

"I'll let you have that one because you're quite clearly upset."

He states softly as I lean back against the sofa cushion, my head throbbing with each beat of my heart. The anger I felt a moment ago fades, replaced by a wave of exhaustion.

"Why the fuck are you even here? Are you trying to give me a heart attack?"

He shrugs as he plops down on the couch beside me, his weight causing the cushions to dip.

"Well, someone had to come and check on you. I guess it was me who drew the fuckin' short straw."

He says wryly as I narrow my eyes at him.

"Arsehole."

I mutter, but there's no real heat behind the words. I rub my temples, trying to ease the pounding in my skull, but it's no use. The alcohol has done its damage, and now I'm stuck in that uncomfortable space between drunk and hungover, where everything feels too loud and too bright. Lucas leans back, stretching his legs out in front of him. I catch a glimpse of the frayed hems of his jeans and his chunky motorcycle boots. The silence stretched between us for a few moments.

"Everything feels like it's been spiralling out of control, Luke. I've been doing my best to just keep my head above water. But I'm tired, so damn tired of it all. This whole fucking mess with Zeppelin..."

I admit, as I scrub my hand down my face, all I want to do is sleep.

"It's just...too much. I don't know how much more I can take. First, the attack at her apartment, the poison pen letters, and now this. I'm at breaking point, Luke."

I confess, my voice is barely a whisper. My hand trembles slightly as I lower it from my face, the exhaustion etched deep into my bones. Lucas is silent for a moment, his eyes searching mine with a mixture of concern and understanding. He's always been the steady, reliable one in the band, the anchor holding us all together when everything is in chaos and goes to shit. He takes a breath, about to speak, when my phone rings. I glance at the screen, and it's a number I don't recognise. I swipe the screen to answer and put it up to my ear apprehensively.

"Hello?"

My voice doesn't sound like my own, and suddenly, I've never felt more sober.

"Jax, son, it's Jimmy, Zeppelin's granddad. She's awake, and she's asking for you."

Jimmy's concerned voice echoes in my ear, and I let out the breath I didn't realise I was holding.

"Ok, thanks for letting me know, Jimmy, erm...yeah, I'll be right there as soon as I can."

I hang up without saying goodbye and turn to Lucas.

"She's awake."

I can't keep the joy out of my voice as Lucas' eyes widen in surprise, and for a moment, neither of us moves. The weight of the words hangs in the air between us.

"I have to go to her."

I say quickly, and he nods.

"Then let's fucking go."

We both stand up and head out the door. My mind is a whirlwind of thoughts and emotions. The last time I saw Zeppelin, she was so still, so pale, it felt like she was slipping away, and I thought I'd never see her again. Now, the thought of her being awake, of her asking for me, feels surreal.

The drive to the hospital is a blur, and before I know it, I'm standing outside her room, my heart pounding in my chest. I take a deep breath, trying to steady myself, but it's no use. The anticipation was almost too much for my mind to focus on. Pushing the door open, I step inside. Zeppelin is lying in the bed, her silver eyes open and focused on the ceiling. When she hears me enter, her gaze shifts to mine, and for a moment, neither of us says anything. The silence is thick with unspoken words, relief, and something else I couldn't quite put my finger on.

"Jax."

She finally whispers, her voice raspy but unmistakably hers. The sound of it almost brings me to my knees. I shift farther into the room to remind myself that this is real, not just a dream. I pull up the chair beside the bed and drop down onto it, taking her hand in mine. It's warm and so distinctly Zeppelin that I can't help but give her hand a squeeze. She flashes me a small smile, and as we sit there, the world outside the room fades away. There's just the two of us, and for the first time in what feels like forever, I believe that maybe, just maybe, everything will be okay.

24

Zeppelin

It's too bright, I'm struggling to focus on my surroundings. The light floods my vision, overwhelming all my senses. It's hard to distinguish shapes and colours. My eyes squint involuntarily, seeking refuge from the blinding glare. I take a deep breath, trying to steady myself, but it's relentless, casting everything in a harsh, unforgiving, stark white. I can feel my heartbeat quickening, a sense of disorientation creeping in. I force my eyes open again, slowly, painfully, and the shapes around me start to come into focus. The harsh white softens, giving way to muted outlines and blurry figures. I can just make out a face, a concerned face, leaning over me.

"Zeppelin, sweetheart, it's me. Can you hear me?"

The familiar voice asks again, clearer this time. It's my granddad, Jimmy. *My Pops.* I realise, with a jolt, that his worried eyes are the first things I see clearly as the light begins to recede.

"Pops..."

I manage to croak out, my throat dry and my voice weak. The sensation of his rough, warm, calloused hand on mine is an anchor, pulling me back from the edge.

"You're alright, my girl. You're safe. You gave us all a bloody fright!"

His voice shaky, trying and failing to chastise me, as he grounds me in the here and now. The light is still too bright, but it's no longer all-consuming. The room comes into focus: the sterile hospital walls, the beeping of machines, the soft hum of voices in the background. *I'm here, I'm going to be ok.*

As my vision clears, I realise I'm lying in a hospital bed, the room now fully taking shape around me. I turn my head slowly to see a man in a white coat, tall, middle-aged, and balding. His face is kind.

"Ah, it's good to have you back with us, Zeppelin. I'm Doctor Cooper."

The corners of his eyes crinkle as he holds a clipboard and pen in front of him, pushing his glasses further up the bridge of his nose. He glances down for a moment before he speaks again.

"You were very lucky, Miss Williams. You suffered some minor cuts and bruises, two broken ribs, and a mild concussion, which seems to have healed nicely since you were in a coma."

My mouth opens and closes, struggling to come to grips with what happened. I shudder at the thought; it could have been so much worse. I'm so fortunate that I didn't get killed. My mind can't seem to grab on to any memory. It's all such a blur. I don't have time to dwell on forgotten memories. As I look up, I'm greeted by familiar, concerned hazel eyes. *My Jax, handsome Jack.* His eyes lock with mine, silver on hazel, and I can't look away from him. He looks slightly dishevelled and a little less put together than usual, but he is a sight to behold. His short blonde hair, his neatly trimmed beard, the heather grey t-shirt that clings to his muscles, his tattoos peeking out from beneath his sleeves, and the way his jeans sit just so on his lean hips. I take all six feet of him in, and I let out the breath I didn't realise I was holding.

"Jax."

He pulls up the chair beside the bed and drops down heavily onto it, taking my hand in his.

"It's ok, you're safe now, I'm here, shhh."

He hushes me as a tear slips down my cheek and presses a soft kiss to the back of my hand. I shake my head slowly.

"I-I don't remember..."

My voice is barely a hoarse whisper as he lifts my hand up to his face. His jaw tightens, his eyes narrowing slightly, as he stares at the blank space behind me, as if searching for the right words.

"I know."

Jax whispers, his voice laced with both frustration and sadness.

"You don't have to remember right now, it doesn't matter."

His grip on my hand tightens, just enough for me to feel his silent desperation.

"What matters is that you're here, you're alive, that's all that counts. You scared the shit out of me, Zeppelin."

I can hear the struggle in his voice, see the way his free hand curls into a fist in his lap, the tension in his shoulders that tells me he's fighting his own demons just as much as I am. I wish I could comfort him, tell him that it's all okay, but how can I, when I can't even remember what happened to me right now?

"I wish I could remember."

I murmur, my voice shaky. Another tear escapes, tracing a path down my cheek, but this time I don't bother to wipe it away.

"I feel like... like I'm missing a part of myself, I don't feel...whole."

Jax's gaze drops back to mine, his hazel eyes softening as he cups my cheek with his large, calloused hand. His thumb brushes away the tear, and for a moment, the room feels smaller, quieter, just the two of us and nothing else. His touch is gentle, grounding me in a reality I can't fully grasp.

"You don't need to remember right now."

He repeats, his voice firmer and more resolute this time.

"When you're ready, it'll come, and when it does, I'll be right here. I'm not going anywhere, not now, not ever."

I nod, but the weight in my chest remains. There's a void in my mind, a dark space that I can't reach, and it fucking scares the shit out of me.

***

"Hold on, baby, please, oh God, please Zeppelin, hold on."

Jax's desperate voice breaks through my unconscious state. I am vaguely aware of the dull cacophony of a random Monday in London. The hum of the traffic, the sound of car horns blasting, and the sound of a mildly panicked voice in the distance. *Where am I? What the hell happened? Fuck, that hurts.* I can smell a strong, warm, metallic smell lingering in the air that makes me feel nauseous.

"Stay with me, Zeppelin. Stay with me, sweetheart."

Jax's voice feels so far away now. I can't focus on his voice, only the bright light that is tempting me to walk towards it. My body feels heavy, like I'm sinking into the hard, cold ground beneath me, but that light... It's pulling me. It's so warm, so inviting. The pain starts to fade as the light brightens, and for a second, I consider letting go, letting it wrap me in its warmth and safety.

But Jax's voice...his voice cuts through, tethering me to this world. There's fear in it, raw, pleading fear that twists something deep inside me. I try to focus, try to hold on to the sound of his voice, but everything is slipping away so fast.

I blink, and for a moment, I see his face above me, pale and desperate, his hands covered in something dark. *My blood*. That metallic scent hits me again, the nausea swells, causing my stomach to twist and roil violently.

"Hold on, Zeppelin. You can't leave me, not like this. Stay with me, please."

I want to respond, to tell him I'm trying, but the words won't come. They're trapped somewhere in my throat. The light pulses again, closer, and for a second, the pain vanishes entirely.

But then I remember Jax. His laugh, his touch, the way he always looked at me like I was his whole world. *I can't just leave him. Not now, not ever. He's lost too much already.*

I fight to stay, gripping onto that thought. But the light is so strong, and the darkness is creeping in at the edges of my vision.

"Zeppelin, please."

His voice cracks, and I hear him choke on a sob. That's when everything goes dark.

***

"I thought I'd lost you, Zeppelin. I can't bear the thought of losing anyone else. I won't survive it, not this time. You have the ability to wreck me like no one else."

His breath hitches as the weight of his words hangs in the air, heavy and raw with intense emotion. My chest tightens as I watch him, his eyes glossy and filled with a vulnerability I've rarely seen in him since we've been together. Jax doesn't show weakness. He's always been the strong one, the protector, the fierce Papa Bear, the one who holds it all together. But right now, sitting at the edge of my hospital bed, he looks broken, as if this fucked up mess has finally brought him to his knees. His hands are trembling, and his eyes have lost their familiar sparkle. He reaches for my hand, hesitant, as though he's afraid I might slip away again. The memory of the accident is still fuzzy, flashes of light, pain, his voice calling out to me. But the fear in his eyes now is more real than anything. I can't stand listening to the man I love laying himself bare like this. He doesn't deserve any of this. He's been through enough, he's lost too many people, he deserves to be happy, to be loved by someone whole, someone a little less broken by life.

I know what I must do; I have to let him go. As much as it will break my heart, I have to set him free. I swallow hard past the tennis ball-sized lump in my throat, as the thought truly sinks in. I must let him go; it's the only way to save him from the inevitable pain I continue to cause him daily. The last thing I want is to drag him down with me. When I look at him, I see his hand trembling as he holds mine, his eyes fixed on me like I'm the only thing keeping him tethered to this world, and my resolve starts to crumble. *He doesn't deserve this, but he's here, and he's fighting for me. For us.*

I feel the weight of my decision, like a rock lodged deep in my chest, suffocating me, crushing me from the inside out. I need to say it, to push him away before it's too late, before he gets hurt even more. But the words get stuck in my throat as Jax's eyes meet mine, searching, pleading.

"I can't do this to you."

I manage to choke out, my voice barely above a whisper.

"You deserve better, Jax. You deserve someone who isn't...broken."

His brow furrows, and the hurt that flashes across his face makes my heart ache even more. He shakes his head, squeezing my hand tighter as if he's trying to ground me and bring me back to the present.

"No, don't fucking do this, Zeppelin. I won't let you do this to us!"

I close my eyes, trying to gather the strength to say what I need to.

"I can't keep hurting you, Jax, don't you see? You've lost so much already. I...I don't want to be another person you have to lose."

I explain with more confidence than I feel, as his grip tightens even more, almost desperate now, and when I open my eyes again, there's fire in his gaze.

"You think I want to carry on without you? Live my life without you? You're the reason I'm still fucking breathing, Zeppelin!"

His voice is raw, low, filled with a kind of pain, and it hits me harder than I expected. He rubs at his chest as if to soothe a physical ache, and my heart slams against my rib cage. *You really can't help yourself, can you, Williams?*

"You don't get to make that fucking decision for me, Zeppelin! You don't get to decide, watching that car hit you, watching your body being flung up into the air, and landing on the ground. It fucking broke me! It broke something inside me, it reminded me that life is so precious, it can be taken away in the blink of an eye, and I'm not about to give up on you, on us, on the family we're trying to build here! You're my home, you're...you're fucking everything! You're the moon, you're the stars, you're the sun, fuck, you're the whole God damn universe!"

His voice cracks on the last few words, and I squeeze my eyes shut briefly.

"Look at me, Zeppelin, if you're going to break my heart anyway, you may as well look me in the fucking eye while you're doing it!"

The tone of his voice was bitter, as if he already knew I'd made my decision. I open my eyes, and when they meet his, I see the hurt, the kind of hurt that runs deep, the kind you can't just talk your way out of or walk away from. His chest rises and falls, his breathing ragged, as if each second waiting for my response is another knife twisting in his heart. His jaw clenches, his hands balling into fists at his sides, but he doesn't say a word. He's waiting, waiting for me to tear everything down. I steel my resolve and take a breath.

"I'll never be Ruby fucking Logan! I'll always be a poor substitute! I don't want to be a mother to someone else's kid! I deserve to be someone's first choice, Jax."

I spit out, as he throws his head back and laughs bitterly.

"Wow! So that's what you're going with? It sounds like you've already made your mind up."

He runs his hand through his short hair, and I bite my lip, fighting back the surge of frustration and guilt that rises in my chest.

"Don't you fucking dare twist my words, Jax. This isn't about her; this is about me. About what I want, what I need! What you can't give me! I've tried so fucking hard, but it's not enough, it'll never be enough! I'll never be enough, and that's the fucking truth!"

He steps forward, eyes flashing with anger, his voice low but sharp.

"And what you want is to run? To throw away all that we've worked so hard to build because you're scared? That's a poor excuse even for you, Zeppelin. Just because you don't think you can live up to some *imaginary* standard you've created in your head?"

He states with an incredulous tone to his voice, and I shake my head, wrapping my arms protectively around myself.

"It's not imaginary, Jax. She's everywhere, she's in my home! Her memory, her influence, the way people look at me like I'm just here to fill the space she left behind...I'm not her, I'll never be her! And it's like...like I'll never measure up."

A tear slips down my cheek, and I hate my stupid emotions for betraying me right now.

"You think I *want* you to be her? What the fuck!"

He snaps, his voice incredulous and rising with each word.

"I don't want another Ruby! I don't need another Ruby! I need *you,* damn it. But if you're gonna' stand here and tell me that you're nothing more than a placeholder, then you don't fucking get it at all."

His words hit me hard, like a punch to the gut, but I force myself to meet his gaze, even though my heart is breaking.

"I deserve to be someone's first choice, Jax."

I repeat, my voice shaking.

"You know what, Zeppelin, you're right, you're right."

He gets up and starts pacing the room.

"You and me, I'm done, we're done."

His voice is filled with defeat, and the silence that follows is suffocating, and I feel like the ground is crumbling beneath me. I force myself to meet his gaze, even though it feels like it's tearing me apart from the inside out.

"I'm sorry, Jack."

I choke out, my voice breaking.

"I'm so, so fucking sorry."

With those words, he turns and walks away, leaving me alone, a sobbing wreck in my hospital bed, mourning the loss of my Jax.

25

Jax

Listening to her throw her hateful, vitriolic words at me like daggers was a slow, excruciating torture. Each word sliced through me, sharp, measured, and deliberate, aiming for the most vulnerable parts of my heart and already fragile soul. It felt like I was standing in the eye of a storm, helpless, as her fury raged around me, tearing down everything I thought we were. Her voice, once familiar and warm, was now cold, venomous, and unrecognisable.

I wanted to defend myself, to throw something back at her, but the weight of her accusations pinned me down, paralysing me. Every bitter syllable she spat at me felt like a confirmation of the darkest fears I had hidden inside. Maybe I deserved this, maybe I wasn't enough, maybe I made her feel like she wasn't enough. *Did she really mean those hurtful words, or was it all an act to throw me off the bigger picture?* I didn't stick around to find out; I wanted to be as far away from her as possible so I could lick my wounds and adjust to life without her in it.

After I left the hospital, I spent long days rehearsing with the boys, not really taking time to dwell on the fact that my heart was breaking.

Tonight, we were performing an intimate gig at the O2 Academy in Brixton, for 2,500 people, previewing some tracks from our new album. We are waiting in the dimly lit corridor, about to go on stage. Donovan and Caleb are setting up our wireless headsets as I swing my guitar around to the front of my body, so it hangs loosely off my shoulders. Lucas expertly spins his drumsticks, throwing them elaborately up in the air and catching them like a pro. Brody is leaning casually against the wall, his hand gripping the fretboard, and Donovan moves across to Sam, handing him a microphone, as he clips the mic pack to the back of his leather trousers.

"Are we fucking ready, boys?" Brody shouts.

"Let's rock."

***

The crowd roared as the lights dimmed, and we ascended the stage. I opened with my signature elaborate guitar riff, as Lucas' drums thundered in perfect unison and Brody joined with an equally elaborate guitar riff to match mine. I could feel the waves of energy palpable through the crowd, and I couldn't help the grin that spread across my face. This was what I fucking lived for. Sam struts towards the microphone, a smirk on his face as he takes in the audience before us, swaying and bouncing to the beat. He begins to sing the opening lyrics of our new single 'Devil May Care.' The lights were flashing and pulsing in time with the music. The air was charged with excitement, and Sam sang with such passion that a woman in the front row sobbed. We all moved across the stage in perfect sync because, when we performed, our private lives didn't exist; it was just us and the music. As the first song draws to a close, Sam moves fluidly towards the front of the stage, addressing the crowd directly.

"London! You guys are fucking amazing! You're all looking beautiful out there tonight!"

His voice was husky with pure emotion.

"Let's keep this party going, shall we? This next song is what put Rancid Vengeance on the radar, and I want you to all sing your motherfucking hearts out! Yeaaahhh!"

He growls, and I flash him a beaming grin.

"Let me hear Corrupted, Flash, you know what I need, brother, give me that riff!"

I strum out the opening chords, and he rests his foot on the amp at the edge of the stage, leaning towards the crowd, and he has them eating out of the palm of his hand, hanging on to his every word. They have their hands in the air singing the lyrics back to us, Sam's face contorted in ecstasy as he pours his soul into every note. I notice that Peyton isn't in her usual spot, which I find very odd; she's in the front row, middle seat at every show. She never misses, ever. Sam glances across at me, and I flash him a questioning look, gesturing with my eyes to where Peyton should be, and he gives me a warning look in return. It appears it's not just me who's having relationship issues.

The first half of the show goes by in a blur of screaming, adoring fans, and by the time we hand off our instruments to Donovan and Caleb at the interval, I'm wired and running completely off adrenaline. I catch up to Sam as we both head into the empty dressing room. He grabs a towel from the back of his chair and wipes the sweat from his damp face.

"Hey, where's Peyton?"

I ask, curiosity getting the better of me. He holds the towel in front of his face as he stands stock still in front of the mirror. His black eyeliner smudged, making him look like he has panda eyes. With a final, vigorous rub, he clears the black residue from his eyes. He blinks a few times and takes a gulp of clear liquid from a bottle on the dressing table. I'm not sure if it's water or vodka.

"Don't."

He rasps, his tone low, as he discards the towel and folds his arms across his broad chest, his muscles bulging, veins protruding through his tanned skin. I look up at him, and I narrow my eyes on him.

"Have you got something you want to get off your chest, mate? I'm right fuckin' here."

I ask cautiously, and I don't know why I'm pushing because I know he'll share when he's ready, but I guess I'm a glutton for punishment. He unfolds his arms and scrubs his hands down his face, but he remains silent. His hesitation confirms my suspicion, and he's looking everywhere but at me. He sniffs, shifting his gaze and scuffing his boot on the floor. He's using again, the tell-tale signs are there, his face is pale, he's sweating profusely, and he's unusually twitchy.

"*For fuck's sake*, Sam."

I growl as he puffs out his cheeks.

"I didn't ask for a fucking lecture, Jax. Just drop it, yeah?"

A bored, uninterested tone to his gruff voice.

"She's gone to her parents' house in Brighton with the boys."

He volunteers to fill the awkward silence, and I cock my head to the side. At least he's communicating, which is always a good start. He's been in the midst of an episode for months and it hasn't come to a head yet.

"She said she needed space, so I gave it to her."

He states with a shrug, swiping the back of his hand across his nose. As he pulls his hand away, I notice his nose is bleeding.

"Ah, fuck."

He stumbles to the side, and I steady him before he falls to the ground, guiding him to the chair in front of him. He drops down heavily onto it, his nose dripping with blood. I get down on my haunches in front of him and grab a tissue from a box on the nearby table. I press it gently to his nose, as he tilts his head forward slightly. He grunts in response, one hand coming up to hold the tissue in place, as his green, bloodshot eyes drop to the floor. The silence is thick between us, heavy with things left unsaid. His breath comes out ragged, more from exhaustion than pain. I can feel the weight of his struggle; it's like watching a dam about to burst, but he's too fucking stubborn to let it.

"You can't keep doing this to yourself, man."

I say quietly, and I know he doesn't want another lecture, but I can't seem to help myself; he needs to fucking hear it. However painful it may be for him.

"Running yourself into the ground, shutting everyone out...self -medicating...it's not going to make it any better. Even you know that you're not stupid, Sam."

He doesn't respond right away; he just sits there, broad shoulders slumped, staring at the floor like it holds all the answers he's been searching for. Eventually, he sighs, a long, defeated sound, as he moves the tissue away from his nose, the dark crimson a stark contrast to the white tissue, stirring up memories we'd both rather forget. But I push that thought aside and focus on the here and now.

"What's the fucking point?"

His voice is quieter now; the usual Sam Newbolt bravado vanished.

"She's not coming back."

He says, his tone final, as I get to my feet, crossing my arms and leaning against the table.

"You don't know that."

His head tilts slightly, a bitter laugh escaping his lips.

"She's better off without me. The boys...they're better off, too. I'm just a fuckin' mess. I haven't got enough fingers and toes to count how many times I've fucked up. She doesn't need me; they don't need me. I'm a fuck up, just like Brody, but he had the sense to realise it sooner rather than later."

This isn't just the episode talking; it's something deeper, darker, and it's been eating away at him for months.

"I'm fucking exhausted, Jax."

There's fear in his eyes now, barely masked by the rough exterior he's so good at putting up. He's fighting to keep it all together, the weight of everything crashing down on him, but he's balancing on the precipice. His jaw clenched tight, like he's trying to hold back the flood of emotions that threaten to spill over.

"I don't have anything left to give, Jax. I'm fucking done."

He mutters, his voice hollow.

"I'm running on fucking empty."

I'm about to speak when we're interrupted by a voice on the P.A system.

"Five minutes to show time, five minutes to show time."

It's as if a switch has been flipped. He tosses the tissue into the bin beside the dressing table and gets to his feet as if these past thirty minutes haven't happened. He slaps me on the shoulder and plasters an almost convincing smile on his face.

"Let's fucking do this!"

As he breezes past me, I'm left wondering what the fuck just happened.

26

Zeppelin

"*Samson 'Bolt' Newbolt is the brooding, yet charismatic lead singer and frontman of Rancid Vengeance. His raw energy, effortless showmanship, and catchy melodies have made him a true rock icon. With hits like 'Corrupted' and 'Angel's Kiss,' he has captured the heart of millions along with his bandmates Jackson 'Flash' Chase, Brody 'Snake' Hart, and Lucas 'Axeman' Landon. The quartet has dominated the rock charts for almost two decades, with no signs of stopping anytime soon. The band is busy in the studio recording their new album, for a yet to be decided Autumn release date, after a preview gig last night at the O2 Academy in Brixton...*"

I had mastered the fine art of grey rocking. I hadn't thought about him or seen anything to remind me of him for weeks. Pops had collected my things from Jax's mansion in Chislehurst, Kent, and I had moved back into my apartment in Notting Hill. I had dyed my hair dark brown and cut and styled it into a cute side-swept pixie, with the sides shaved. I wore quirky bandanas and spiked it if the mood took me. I had lost weight in my time back here, spending my days in the gym or walking Jericho for miles. I had gotten a nose piercing, wore my thick black-rimmed glasses more often, and my smile was becoming more genuine as the days went on. It was as if Jax never existed. I didn't want to be reminded of the look in his eyes as I broke his heart. I didn't want to be reminded of the things that I'd lost along the way. I hated myself for putting that look in his eyes, but it was necessary; I couldn't bear the thought of someone wanting to hurt even a hair on his head. It had to be this way; I had to protect him and Thea at all costs. They'd lost enough people in their lives, and this was the sacrifice that I had to make, no matter how painful it was.

So far, I had managed to avoid all things Jackson Chase, but now, he seemed to be everywhere I turned. It was like he was taunting me as I pointed the remote at the TV and flicked through the channels.

Now, a band that has been regulars on the rock-metal scene for almost two decades. With countless awards, number one albums, and a coveted spot on the rock music hall of fame, please give a warm welcome to Rancid Vengeance!

The applause is deafening, and as I look up, I'm met with warm hazel eyes. Hazel eyes that studied and roamed every inch of my body with care and precision, a blonde beard that had scraped my inner thighs often, and the mischievous smile that melted me every time he flashed it in my direction. My heart slams violently against my rib cage, and I rub my chest to quell the ache I can feel building there. Jericho whines as he sits at my feet, resting his head on his paws. I reach down and stroke the top of his head, occasionally scratching his ears, not only to offer him comfort, but for me too.

I flick the channel on the TV, not wanting to torture myself for any longer than necessary.

"The Red Quill Killer Strikes Again. London is a city on edge after another apparent brutal murder, linked to the so-called Red Quill

Killer, police confirmed tonight. The latest victim, an aspiring novelist in their late twenties, was discovered in their home early this morning; investigators say evidence at the scene matches previous attacks that targeted writers and writing students. Police were called to a residential address at approximately 3:20 a.m. after a friend conducted a welfare check. Officers found the victim unresponsive; detectives describe the scene as grisly and consistent with the earlier cases. Authorities have not released the victim's name pending family notification, and they stressed there is no public information yet to indicate a motive beyond the pattern of victims' occupations and creative pursuits."

I shudder as I point the remote at the TV and turn it off. My mind started to wander to the fact that I had walked away from my happy ever after, so I was throwing myself into writing happy ever afters, even if I couldn't have one of my own. I had immersed myself in my book world and was more present on social media. I had a guest spot on a writer's podcast, was almost finished with book ten, and, once the book was released, embarked on a book tour to celebrate my tenth release. I found myself looking forward to the future, even if it didn't include Jax. I'd break my own heart, just to protect his, and that's the way it had to be. I had learned to accept the pain and heartbreak that came with making that choice. *The right choice.* It wasn't easy, and there had been days when I stared at his name on my screen and hovered over his number on my phone, where I wanted to go to him, crawl into his bed, and demand he make love to me, but I knew I had to resist those deep-seated, carnal urges.

Writing gave me a way to channel my sorrow into something beautiful, bittersweet. Each chapter I wrote was a step toward healing, a way to reclaim my story and, in some way, take back what I had lost. I made myself what seemed like my twelfth cup of coffee today; I was on a roll. I could feel a headache building behind my eyes as I pushed my glasses further up the bridge of my nose, as Jericho's tail wagged wildly, and his tongue flopped out to the side. I ran my fingers through his soft fur as my country playlist was blasting loud and proud. Luke Combs sang his version of '*Fast Car*' as I typed the final words of my tenth novel. I felt a bittersweet satisfaction in seeing the words *'The End'* on my screen. The story I had carefully constructed was filled with love, hope, and the promise of forever, the kind I once believed in for myself. I was fucking proud of what I had accomplished in the years since I had embarked on my writing journey. Ten books, ten worlds where love triumphed, and ten extremely hot fictional book boyfriends. But from now on, there would always be one name missing from the dedication pages, *Jackson Chase.*

***

I had submitted my tenth novel to my publisher a month ago, and the book tour was looming ever closer. Meeting my readers, signing copies, seeing my name in big, bold letters, and hearing how my stories had touched lives would bring me immense joy and a sense of great achievement. But there would also be the inevitable silence at the end of each day, where I'd return to another hotel room without *him.* Still, I promised myself one thing: I wouldn't look back. I wouldn't give in to the wild temptation and reckless abandon by going to him. I would celebrate this milestone and embrace the future that lay ahead of me. Despite my heart being fractured beyond repair, it wasn't broken. *Not really.* I was still standing, still writing, still dreaming, and perhaps, in time, I'd find my own happy ending again, even if it wasn't the one I had imagined with Jackson Chase. My heart ached in a way I couldn't seem to suppress, and there would always be a part of me that would wonder '*what if?*' But life didn't work in '*what ifs,*' at least that's what Peyton told me all those months ago. It worked in the cold, harsh reality of the choices I made and the paths I followed. As much as I wanted to rewrite my story, I had to accept that some endings weren't meant to be changed.

27

Zeppelin

After the release of my tenth book, I embarked on a country-wide book tour. I was currently in the heart of London at a well-known bookshop. It was so surreal to see my face on the display posters, my name emblazoned in the window, and the stacks of books neatly arranged on tables. Just a few years ago, I had been on the other side, an eager reader, roaming the shelves for stories that would pull me into new worlds, and now, my worlds had become the ones others sought.

I stood near the large windows, watching as people trickled in. I noticed most were women, some clutching my book tightly, and others flipping through its pages, as if unsure whether to commit to the purchase. Every smile, every curious glance felt like validation, not just of the hard work I had put into writing, but of the journey itself, the late nights, the self-doubt, and the rewrites that never seemed to end. I had been preparing for this day for weeks, and now it was finally here; I was second-guessing my decision. It was as if all those four and five-star reviews meant nothing, and I was a fraud. I was just some girl who wrote a few books and got lucky. My hands were clammy as I squirmed in my seat and took a few deep breaths, ready to greet my fans with a smile. My stomach roiled as I saw the queue of people approaching, and I swallowed hard to suppress the nausea I felt in the pit of my stomach. *Come on, Williams, you can do this! You got this! This is your moment. You deserve this! Pull up your big girl pants and stop being a twat!* I mentally gave myself a pep talk as I looked up to see the bookstore staff bustling around, and I couldn't help but think back to my first signing event, when only a handful of people had shown up. Now, this London shop was buzzing with excitement, and I was still trying to wrap my head around the fact that they were here for me.

A stack of freshly printed books was beside me, and my favourite pen engraved with my name was poised in my hand. The first reader stepped forward; she was around five feet two inches tall, with long, black hair that trailed down her shoulders. She was wearing dark jeans, black Converse, and a white t-shirt that read 'All my boyfriends are fictional,' and she looked to be in her late twenties. She approached me with a nervous smile that mirrored the way I felt inside.

"I've been following your work since your first book."

She said, awe in her small voice, as she clutched her copy to her chest as if it were something precious.

"I can't believe I'm meeting you! Oh my God!"

The sincerity in her voice struck me, and suddenly, the nerves melted away. This wasn't about proving myself anymore. It was about connection, about the fact that my words had reached someone in a way that truly mattered.

"Thank you."

My voice was softer than I expected, as she placed the book down on the table in front of me.

"I can't believe it either, to be honest."

I gave her a genuine smile as I flipped open the first page and signed her book. I scribbled my name and a small note of gratitude; she politely asked for a selfie, and I obliged as she held the camera in front of us. We both posed, and she nodded her thanks as she scurried away. The next person in line stepped forward. A calm settled over me, replacing my earlier anxiety. These weren't just readers, they were people who had, in some small way, been on this journey with me over the years and encouraged me to keep going when I lost all sense of belief in myself and my words. They were with me through the crippling writer's block until I found out that my book was a New York Times bestseller.

A few hours had passed, and I was making small talk with the large queue of fans, signing copies of my books as if it were the most natural thing in the world. I couldn't stop smiling. I was having a blast as I listened to their stories, anecdotes, and their requests for what I should write next. My hand was starting to cramp as I signed the next book and passed it across the table with a smile that seemed to come more easily with time. The next person approached, and I don't look up, as the book lands on the table in front of me.

"Hey!"

I say brightly, and I regret my decision to look up as I'm greeted with the familiar brown eyes of Jackson Chase. He has a navy baseball cap pulled low down, trying to stay under the radar, but I would recognise that face anywhere. The time that had passed hadn't erased the sharp line of his jaw or the intensity of his dark gaze. I swallow hard as I shakily open the book, my pen poised over the page.

"Hey, yourself."

His voice is gruff as his eyes lock with mine, carrying the weight of the history we share. His eyes lock with mine, silver on brown, and for a moment, the world around us blurred and seemed to stand still. I could hear the idle chatter and the hum of hushed conversations.

"Is that Jax Chase from Rancid Vengeance?"

The words hung in the air, sending a ripple of excitement through the small crowd. I caught a few more murmurs from nearby fans and readers, their curious glances darting towards him, recognising the rock star who had once been my whole world. A wave of disbelief crashes over me, and I shake my head, exasperated. *Of course, someone would fucking recognise him. He's Jax 'Flash' Chase from Rancid Vengeance, from one of the biggest rock bands in the world.* Even with his baseball cap pulled down low in a place like this. Fame never really lets people hide for long, no matter how hard they might try to stay incognito. *What the fuck was he thinking, turning up here?*

Jax stiffens slightly, his gaze still tethered to mine, as if waiting for me to react. I open and close my mouth, about to speak, but somehow unable to find the words that were stuck in my throat. Last time I saw him, I told him in no uncertain terms that I didn't want to be with him, but here he was standing in front of me. I didn't have time to process the way his presence seemed to suck all the oxygen out of the room. All six feet of him, his shoulders seemed somehow broader, his hips leaner and his biceps thicker. I couldn't help but lick my lips at the sight of him, as he flashed me his familiar smirk. The line of readers stretched behind him, each one here for me. Yet somehow, Jax's unexpected appearance had thrown everything off balance. *Talk about stealing my limelight, this was my time to shine, not his! He gets to perform nightly!* A small group of fans near the back of the queue was already looking his way, pulling out their phones, eyes wide with recognition, and bouncing up and down with excitement. I wanted to take back control of the moment, but the tension between us lingered, unspoken and heavy, as if we both knew this wasn't over.

My phone buzzed an alert, as I turned it over on the table and glanced at the headline flashing up '*Jax Chase spotted at a London bookstore signing.' Fuck my life.* It hadn't even been ten minutes, and already the vultures were circling. I wondered how long it would take for word to get around that he was here, but deep down, I already knew the answer. *Absolutely no time at all*. Before I could even fully take in what was happening, I heard the high-pitched squeal from across the shop.

"JAX CHASE! FLASH! OH MY GOD! OH MY GOD!"

Heads whipped around, searching for the source of the chaos. The excited shriek seemed to electrify the air. Several people jumped up, phones in hand, snapping photos and rushing towards the door. I could see Jax from the corner of my eye, his broad frame tightening as the crowd surged toward him and seemed to circle around him. He tried to pull his cap lower, ducking his head as he tried to go towards the exit, but it was too late. The whispers had turned into a full-blown frenzy, cameras flashed, and voices called his name.

"Fuck!"

He curses low in his throat, and I see him pull his phone out of his pocket. The crowd surging around him left his expression a mixture of frustration and panic. I wanted to help; I wanted to get him out of this situation, but I was frozen to the spot, helpless to watch from the sidelines. He swipes the screen and puts the phone up to his ear; I don't hear what he says as the crowd is gathered around him now, closing him in, the wild flashing of cameras almost blinding. I clenched my fists, frustration coursing inside me. Part of me hated him for showing up like this, for bringing this chaos into what should have been my moment. But another part of me ached for him, yearned for him. I wanted him to sweep me off my feet like one of my book characters and kiss me like it was the first time. But I knew now wasn't the time for romantic bullshit. I watched as his face tensed as he spoke into the phone, probably calling his security detail for backup, for an escape route out of this fucking gigantic mess. He had taken off his baseball cap, which was rendered useless. Everyone knew it was him, and no amount of disguise could mask the fact that he was rock royalty. I could see the sweat beading on his forehead, the muscles in his jaw tightening with each passing second. He was used to the spotlight, but this was different somehow. This wasn't a concert stage with screaming fans that he could control. This was raw, uncontrolled, a mob that had come out of nowhere.

One of the store managers rushes over to me, his face pale with concern.

"I'm so sorry about this."

He stammered, as if apologising for the chaos would make it all disappear. I forced a tight smile, shook my head, and dismissed him with a nonchalant wave of my hand, but my focus remained firmly on Jax. Suddenly, I saw movement in the crowd, a group of three familiar security guards pushing their way through, parting the sea of people like Moses parting the Red Sea. I recognised them from my time as part of the madness of the world of Rancid Vengeance: Kai, Trey, and Jace. They reached Jax and began ushering him toward the back exit, creating a human shield between him and the screaming fans and the relentless cameras. He glances back at me for a split second, and in that moment, our eyes meet again.

There was something in that look, an apology, regret maybe, or a goodbye, I wasn't sure. All I knew was that in the chaos, we still somehow maintained a connection, even if neither of us knew what to do with it anymore.

28

Jax

"What the fuck were you thinking, Jax?"

M.J, our manager, yells at me in his familiar American drawl, and I suddenly feel like I'm six years old again, getting chastised by my parents.

"I clearly wasn't fucking thinking, was I?"

I say with a wry tone to my voice, and M.J looks as if he's about to blow a gasket. His usually cool demeanour seems to have abandoned him.

"How can you sit there and be so nonchalant about this? It could have ended badly! Anything could have happened! All of you boys make my fucking balls itch, ya know that. *Jesus fuckin' Christ!*"

He shouts, running his fingers through his salt and pepper hair.

"I...I had to go to her. She wouldn't have agreed to see me otherwise. I fucking miss her, M.J, I love her so much. I had to make her see that! But I've gone and fucked it all to hell!"

I get up from the chair and start pacing the room like a madman, my heartbeat thundering in my chest. I feel like every ounce of control

I had up until now has been completely abandoned by me. I'm a man teetering on the edge of insanity, and the worst part it was all because of a fucking woman!

"FUUCCCKKKK!"

I curse, filling the room with the sound of my rage. When she left me all those weeks ago, I thought I would be able to handle it, that the time and distance would somehow numb the pain, but every day without her felt like I was dying, slowly bleeding out until there was nothing left, and there was nothing I could do to stop it. I tried to bury myself in distractions, in the band, in spending time with Thea, in touring, in the endless cacophony. But nothing seemed to work. Nothing filled that hollow void she had left behind. Seeing her again today and hearing her voice brought everything flooding back to the surface. The way her eyes had widened when she saw me, the shock, the hurt, the love, the sheer lust as her eyes smoked out when they locked with mine. I thought maybe I could get through to her, that I could fix what she broke. I kicked at the chair, sending it skidding a few inches across the floor. The sharp scrape of wood against tile echoed in the room, setting my teeth on edge. I knew M.J was watching me, waiting for me to calm down, but I couldn't. I couldn't calm down. *I couldn't fucking breathe, not without her.*

"What the fuck was I thinking?"

I muttered, dragging my hands down my face, my voice hoarse.

"Showing up like that... at her signing. I'm a fucking idiot. I thought...God, I don't even know what I was thinking. That she'd see me, we'd go back to her hotel room and make love like we used to, and suddenly everything would be okay? Like all those weeks apart meant nothing?"

I trail off, unable to finish the thought, because I knew how it ended: she was gone, and I'd fucked it up again. M.J rounded the table, his arms crossed, watching me carefully.

"You've gotta' stop torturing yourself like this, Jax. You're spiralling. If she wanted to talk, she would have."

I laugh, but it was hollow and bitter.

"Yeah? Well, maybe she would have, if I hadn't been such a fucking coward. Maybe if I'd fought for her and not let her go so easily, we could have worked it out!"

The words tore out of me raw and desperate, as I shook my head, the reality of it sinking in. I let fear get in the way of everything good between us. I let the fear of losing Ruby push her away, each time pushing her further away from me. Now I was standing here, alone, teetering on the edge of losing my Goddamn fucking mind.

My chest tightened, the familiar weight of regret settling in like a vice grip. I had one shot today to fix things, and I blew it. I had never felt more powerless in my life, and it was killing me. Regret settled deep in the pit of my stomach at how I had stood right in front of her, ready to tell her everything, but instead, I allowed the chaos to swallow me whole. I let out a sharp breath, my hands trembling as they dropped to my sides. I had never felt more powerless in my life. This wasn't like anything else I had ever faced in my life; it wasn't a bad review or a tough crowd. This was Zeppelin. This was the woman who made everything in my life make sense. She made me believe in something more than the empty, unfulfilled life I had been living, and I let her slip right through my fingers.

"She made her choice; you can't force her to change her mind, Jax."

M.J's voice broke through the silence, soft but firm, like he was trying to talk me down from the ledge I was standing on. But his words hit like a punch to the gut, the final nail in the coffin of everything I had tried to hold on to. I shake my head and continue to pace the floor, unable to unhear his harsh words.

"I...I can't fucking do this anymore, M.J, I can't..."

My voice was cracking under the weight of everything I had been holding in for weeks. Tears burned behind my eyes, and no matter how hard I tried to keep it together, I could feel myself unravelling. The sob that had been threatening to choke me finally broke free, shaking my entire body as it escaped. I sank to the floor in a heap, as I buried my face in my hands, the sobs coming harder now, raw and unfiltered. I hated how weak and vulnerable I was in this moment, how the pain I had tried so desperately to shove down kept flooding its way back to the surface. I couldn't hold it back anymore. I couldn't pretend that I wasn't broken inside. I had the sudden urge to run. I couldn't be here a moment longer. I had to go home; I had to be away from here. I wanted to hide away and pretend today hadn't happened, that my selfish actions didn't fuck it all up. I get up from the floor, feeling exhausted, and I turn and run out of the room as fast as my fucking legs will carry me.

***

I stare up at the ceiling, unable to switch my brain off. It offers me a selection of everything bad that's ever happened in all my thirty-four years on a loop. From losing Ruby, from all the bad decisions I made at the beginning of our relationship, to Thea, to the band, to Zeppelin. *What had I done so wrong? I didn't deserve this, did I? Was I really that bad of a person for her to just leave like that?* I let out a laboured breath and swing my legs out of bed; it would do no good to just lie here and torture myself. I pull on a plain black V-neck t-shirt and grey jogging bottoms. I had to do something to take my mind off this shit, I had to run, or go into my studio, something to take away this numb feeling inside. As I head down the stairs, I hear a knock at the door. I make it to the bottom and across the marbled floor to the door. I open it apprehensively, my eyes wide as I'm greeted by the familiar silver gaze of Zeppelin.

29

Zeppelin

After the book signing, I went back to my hotel room, and I couldn't get Jax out of my head. He was everywhere, his voice, his sheer presence, the familiar heated gaze in his deep brown eyes, and the wicked smirk he flashed me as my traitorous body gave me away. *How could he still affect me like this, after everything we had been through?* I had convinced myself I was over him, that I had moved on, but seeing him today had shattered that illusion. With a sigh, I turned on the taps to the large claw-footed bathtub in the corner of the room, and the hot water poured in, filling the air with a perfumed steam. I undressed slowly, trying to let go of the knots in my muscles. But even as I slipped into the warmth, sinking down until the water covered me completely, I couldn't shake the feeling that we really did have unfinished business.

The bath was supposed to relax me, but instead, my mind drifted back to every moment with him, the laughter, the fights, the passion. The way he used to make me feel like I was the only woman in the world when he looked at me, and then the inevitable heartbreak. I thought time and distance would have dulled that pain, but it seemed like the wounds had never fully healed. I leaned my head back against the cool porcelain of the bathtub, staring at the ceiling as the memories washed over me like the water lapping at my skin. I slipped my hand beneath the water; I pressed one finger into my slit and gently rubbed and teased my wet folds. I bite my lip as I cup my breast with my free hand, pinching my nipples between my thumbs and forefingers and tweaking them, causing me to gasp aloud at the pleasure-pain. I grow desperate to feel Jax's cock inside me, as my breath comes in short, sharp bursts. I continue to rub my pussy in deliberate circles, as the water splashes and laps around me. The ache between my thighs is unbearable as I think back to the last time I felt his cock inside me. I push a finger inside myself and moan aloud as I begin to quicken my pace, moaning softly as I feel my heartbeat quickening in my chest.

"Fuuuuccckkk!"

I hum with pleasure, almost frantic for the orgasm I can feel building deep within me. I introduce a second finger and a third, as I gasp at the feeling of delicious fullness. I squeeze my eyes shut as I continue my assault on my swollen nub, and I can almost hear him whispering in my ear.

"I want you to come for me, sweetheart."

My eyes fly open as my orgasm detonates through my whole body. My breath comes in ragged pants, and I'm boneless as I relax back against the cool porcelain. A stark contrast to the heat surging through me, and in that moment, I make the boldest decision I've ever made in my whole life. I know what I have to do: I have to go to him. I want him too much; I want him with everything in me. I rise from the bath, water dripping from my pink, still sensitive skin, a reminder of the ache burning deep inside me. Wrapping a towel around my body, I pause, just for a second, questioning my decision. But the thought of him, his touch, his presence is too fucking powerful for me to ignore. I dry myself quickly, carefully choosing my outfit and opting for a denim dress. I lay it on the bed, and I decide to go without underwear. I feel wanton and reckless. As I apply my make-up in the mirror, I don't recognise this version of myself, but I oddly like it. My reflection stares back at me, silver eyes glittering with a new kind of hunger. There's a wildness in my gaze, a recklessness that sends a thrill through me. I feel untamed, like I'm shedding every layer of control I've ever clung to. The denim clings to my curves as I slip into the dress, the absence of underwear making me hyper aware of every movement, every breath. It's electrifying, knowing I'm going to him bare, exposed, daring. I smooth my trembling hands over the fabric, taking one last look in the mirror before grabbing my keys. My pulse quickening, there's no turning back now. This is all I've wanted for the past few months; this is who I am tonight. I leave my hotel room, I go down in the lift, my stomach a riot of emotions and nerves. As I step out of the building, the cool night air hits my skin, but nothing can extinguish the fire building inside me.

***

I make the long journey to Chislehurst in Kent, and with each mile travelled, I second-guess and regret my decision to come here. *What if he turns me away? What if he doesn't want to see me?* I'm a ball of nervous energy as the taxi crunches up the gravelled driveway and up to the security gate. He buzzes us in, as Jace leans his head down, to see who is in the car, recognising me instantly. He greets me with a nod and a warm smile as we drive through the gates and pull up in the circular driveway. I smooth out my dress as I get out of the taxi and make my way up the stone steps. My heartbeat is thundering in my chest as I knock on the door. I wait patiently for him to answer the door, almost bottling it and turning around to leave.

He swings the door open, and there he is, all six feet of him. His eyes are dark and intense as they lock onto mine. For a split second, I forget how to breathe. The air between us is charged with all the things we left unsaid. His heated gaze travels slowly down my body, lingering on the hem of my denim dress, and I swear I can see the flicker of realisation in his eyes. *He knows. He knows what I'm here for. Of course, he knows, you stupid cow!*

For a moment, neither of us moves, and my heart is pounding so hard I'm afraid he can hear it. I open my mouth to speak, but the words get trapped in my throat, and before I can find them, he steps forward, his hand brushing lightly against my arm. He sends a jolt of electricity through me as he did all those months ago. The tension between us is thick and charged with the promise of all the wicked things I know he wants to do to me. I can feel the heat rolling off him as I take a deep breath, steadying myself. Without a word, I step forward, closing the distance between us, my fingers brushing against his hard, warm chest. He doesn't move, he just stands there watching me, waiting. *Fuck my life, is it possible that he looks hotter than he was when I saw him earlier?* His biceps are thicker, his shoulders are broad, and his thighs are taut and powerful. His tattoos stand out against the light bronze of his tanned skin. His beard is neatly trimmed; his short blonde hair is perfectly mussed as if he has been running his fingers through it. We stand there both mute, just staring at each other. He tilts his head to the side and crushes his lips against mine. The unexpected feel of his lips against mine causes a rush of heat to flood between my legs. The cool night air was causing me to shiver. He pulls away briefly, resting his forehead on mine and cupping my face in his large, tattooed hands.

"Fuck!"

He curses, squeezing his eyes shut briefly, as if he is having an inner battle with himself. He hauls me inside, kicking the door shut with his bare foot, and I tackle him against the wall. I feel his solid erection pressing into my lower abdomen, my pussy throbbing, and I rub my thighs together to satiate the ache I feel building there. I can feel his tumultuous need for me emanating from him in tsunami-like waves because it matches my own. He moves closer and presses his lips to mine. I moan softly into his mouth, as his tongue seductively dances with mine, frantic and urgent. I feel his hand snake down my ribs, and I silently plead with him to take me right there against the wall. He pulls away from our kiss, and I'm bereft at the loss of contact, as he chuckles against my mouth. He shakes his head slowly.

"Not yet, not here."

He whispers, his voice rough. I can feel the slick heat pooling between my legs, as a fierce, burning ache begins to blossom within me, and I need him to take it away. He pulls me closer to him until I can feel his erection solid between us.

"I need you, Jax. *Oh fuck,* I need you."

My voice doesn't sound like my own; it's breathy, desperate, and needy as I beg him with my eyes to worship me like only he knows how. In that moment, everything else fades; there's only him, only us, and the desire that's been simmering between us for far too long.

30

Jax

As we make it to my bedroom, it's a race to see who can get undressed the fastest, and I growl as I see that she's not wearing any underwear. I swallow hard at the sight of her, naked and perfect, sprawled out on my bed. She's dyed her hair since I last saw her at the hospital. I was shocked at just how different she looked when I turned up at her book signing earlier on today. She seems more confident, her smile is no longer forced, it's genuine, and it is a sight to behold. We're both naked in record time, as I crawl up the bed like a lion ready to claim its prey. Her silver eyes disarmed me and rendered me speechless, as I settled myself between her thighs.

"You weren't wearing any underwear, you little minx."

I taunt, as I blow a gust of air onto her pussy, glistening with her juices. She shivers at the sensation and writhes beneath me.

"Mmmm!"

She hums, and I shake my head, exasperated.

"You weren't wearing any underwear."

I repeat, as her gaze shifts to mine, as she traps her lip between her teeth.

"Well, I had to get your attention somehow."

She states sassily, and I chuckle softly.

"Sweetheart, you have my undivided attention every time you walk into a room. You had me wrapped around your fucking finger from the very first day we met."

I compliment, as her silver eyes hold me hostage, and I can't look away. I sweep my finger through her slickness, and she moans aloud. I slowly suck her juices from my finger, as she grasps her full breasts in both hands, playing with her erect nipples.

"Spread your legs, it's been far too long since I've made you come."

I demand, and she does as she's bidden, spreading her legs wider. I push my long, deft finger inside her, moving in and out, increasing the momentum with each plunge of my finger.

"*Fucking hell,* you're soaking wet. Is that all for me?"

I ask, my voice low and seductive.

"Oh, God! Jax! Yes, yes, yes, it's all for you, only you!"

She pants, and I introduce a second finger, as her breaths become urgent. She arches her back, her slender frame slight and sexy as hell.

"It fucking better be."

I say with a hint of warning to my voice, suddenly feeling a wave of jealousy that another man might have had her while we weren't together. But I push that wayward thought to the back of my mind. *Where the fuck did that come from, Chase?*

"*Fuck*! That feels so good, Jax!"

She screams out.

"Jax! Jax! Jax!"

My name is a plea on her lips.

"That's it, I want you to come for me, sweetheart. I want your orgasm."

She starts to grip and bunch the sheets in desperation, as I expertly twist my fingers inside her, and that's all it takes for her orgasm to tear through her like a raging inferno. She screams loudly as I squeeze every last drop of pleasure from her. As she comes down from her release, she flashes me a lazy grin, and I swear to God, she has my balls in the palm of her fucking hand.

"I want you to fuck me, Jax."

Her voice is confident, and I cock my eyebrow at her with a smirk.

"Is that so? Demanding, aren't we this evening? Where's this new Zeppelin come from?"

She narrows her eyes at me defiantly, and her personality is shining so bright, it's almost blinding. This is the Zeppelin I met online all those months ago.

"Are you denying me, Chase?"

Her voice is seductive, as I kneel between her thighs, fisting my cock a few times before I find her slick entrance and shove forward to enter her still slick channel.

"JESUS FUCKING CHRIST! JAX! OH, GOD!"

She cries out as I bury my cock deeper inside her. My eyes find hers as I look at her beneath me. She looks so fucking beautiful. She's cut her hair off and dyed it brown; it's short, but it suits her. Her silver eyes were dancing with lust. I still for a moment, taking her in, and I can't believe that she's here after I got unceremoniously mobbed at her book signing this afternoon. Not my finest hour, but I had to see her. I'd been seeing her pop up on my news feed; everywhere I turned, it was like she was taunting me, reminding me of what I'd lost. I couldn't let her go a second time without making her see that we were inevitable, that we were in it for the long haul, for keeps. She shifts up, snapping me from my reverie as I build up a punishing pace.

"Oh shit, Jax!"

My thrusts become urgent as I move in and out at a frantic pace, each measured plunge a reminder of what we had both been missing over these past few months. She moans softly, and I feel the flutters of her orgasm, her inner muscles rippling around my stiffness.

"*Fuck*, you're close. Come for me, Zeppelin."

She lets out an ear-piercing scream as she explodes around my throbbing cock.

"OH, GOD! JAX! JAX! I'M COMING! OH FUCK! JAX! I'M COMING!"

I throw my head back, finding my release and yelling her name in garbled ecstasy. We still for a few moments, before I pull out of her and crawl up the bed to lie down next to her. She snuggles into me, resting her cheek on my pec. I wrap my arm around her, both silent for long minutes, relishing in post-orgasmic cuddling, and for the first time in months, I'm content to just lie here with her in my arms, back where we both belong.

31

Zeppelin

There were a million things I wanted to say to him as I lay naked in his arms. Every thought went unspoken, and every word I opened my mouth to say was stuck somewhere in my throat, trapped and unable to speak the words I knew I needed to say out loud for them to become real. The rise and fall of his chest and the sound of his heartbeat against my cheek, as I lay on his warm chest, lulled me into a quiet sense of calm. But I knew it was going to be short-lived; it was a mess of confessions, dark truths, and everything I couldn't put into words. I wished I could stay like this forever, safe and wrapped in the warmth of his embrace. My fingers traced idle shapes across his chest as I felt him shift beneath me. He pressed a soft kiss to my forehead, pulling me closer into him, as if sensing a storm brewing in the silence. I wanted to apologise, I wanted to tell him I loved him, I wanted to tell him there was a future for us, I wanted to promise him forever, but I couldn't find the right words. For now, I would let the silence linger, allowing myself to savour the safety of being wrapped in his strong, muscular, tattooed arms, at least until the sun came up.

***

I slept soundly in Jax's bed, and he's wrapped around me like a spider, all arms and legs entwined with mine. I try desperately to shift without waking him, but his arm tightens around my waist, his warm breath stirring against my neck.

"Are you really trying to leave without saying goodbye?"

He murmurs, his voice thick with sleep. His hand slides down to my hip, pulling me closer, until there's barely any space left between us. His grip pulls me closer, anchoring me in place, his warmth radiating through me. I feel his lips brush my shoulder, a lazy, half-conscious gesture that sends shivers down my spine. He shifts, propping himself up on one elbow, and he looks down at me, his eyes still heavy with sleep but softened by something that feels a lot like...love. His fingers trace gentle patterns along my side, a small, unspoken plea for me to stay.

"What's it going to take for you to realise that this is it, Zeppelin? And don't you dare give me that bollocks that you're trying to protect me because I'm in one of the biggest rock bands in the world, security is of the utmost importance to us, for fucks sake!"

I stare at him incredulously. His words hang in the air, raw and vulnerable, and for a moment, I'm too stunned to respond. No one's ever spoken to me like this, with that mixture of frustration and conviction, like he's silently begging me to understand just how serious he is.

"Jax."

I say, swallowing hard, my voice barely a whisper.

"It's not that simple. The person who ran me over, it's got something to do with Rian's murder, I know it has!"

I admit, aware that I sound ridiculous and slightly unhinged.

"Come on, Zeppelin, for fucks sake!"

He challenges, laughing bitterly, and his hand pauses on my side.

"You're not Nancy fucking Drew! Be realistic! I get that you're still grieving, but come on! There's no mystery to be solved here; he was murdered, end of! Leave it to the police."

My heart slams against my rib cage at his harsh words. *Is he really mocking me right now?* He doesn't give me a chance to protest, as he continues.

"You keep saying you're protecting me, but I'm right fucking here! I've always been here! I know what I want, and I want you. How many fucking times can I say it? What's the point of all of this if you're just going to keep running away from me? You stayed away for months, without a fucking word! How do you think that made me feel? I had to explain to my daughter that you'd gone, and you wouldn't be coming back! *Jesus fucking Christ,* Zeppelin! We're both adults, it doesn't have to be like this!"

He sits up, swinging his long legs out of bed and resting his elbows on his knees. His words cut deep, each one feeling like a fucking punch to the gut. I try to put up the walls that have protected me for the past few months, but the anger and hurt in his voice break through.

"I stayed away because I was trying to protect you, and I was a fucking mess after Rian died, Jax!"

I snap, my voice cracking under the weight of the past few months.

"Because losing someone changes you in ways that you can never come back from! I didn't want to drag you or your daughter into this fucking chaos! I thought I was doing the right thing."

Exasperation evident in my voice, and I instantly regret the words as soon as they are out of my mouth. *Really? You had to go there, didn't you? Fuck my life!* He shakes his head, the incredulity clear in his eyes, and I bite my lip to quell the tears I can feel burning behind my eyes.

"The right thing? For who? For you? Because I'll tell you right fucking now, it sure as hell wasn't the right thing for me, or for her. She adored you, Zeppelin! You left without so much as a goodbye, and you think I don't get it? I've lost people, too! Vegas fucking changed everything for us! I lost everything that day, so don't you dare fucking stand there and say I don't understand because frankly, it's insulting!"

I feel the guilt overwhelming me, thick and heavy, making it hard to breathe, as a tear slips down my cheek.

"I got fucking shot, Zeppelin!"

He yells as he jabs his finger into the angry purple jagged circular scar on his shoulder, reminding me of my own scars on my back, and I'm instantly transported back to a time I'd rather forget.

Past

Zeppelin

I lightly trace the bandages on my back, careful not to apply any unnecessary pressure. My hands are trembling as I think of the months of pain and skin grafts I've suffered through. My nana and Pops keep saying I'm brave, but I don't feel very brave. I just feel weak and pathetic. I can barely get through a day without sobbing my heart out, in pain, and at the memory of the carnage of that day. Losing Abel, waking up in a cold sweat, and the acrid smell of burning flesh permeating my nostrils. I thought back to the months that the mere twitch of my back muscles would cause daggers of pure agony to shoot through every part of me and how far I've come. I'm grateful to whoever for sparing me that day, but I can't help thinking of the lives that were lost.

I sigh, my hands falling limply to my sides as I shift my gaze to the nurse, Lauren, who is patiently waiting by my side. I nod my head slowly as she approaches me and cautiously peels away the dressing covering my back, flinching each time I wince. Time seems to slow, and my breath lodges in my chest, my body instinctively freezes, and I can't help but wonder if I'll ever escape the shadow of that day. My scars a daily reminder of the life I had before, the life I had built with Abel before it had all come crashing down around us. Lauren's touch is gentle, her fingers nimble as she works with practised care, but even her kindness can't soften the impact of each reveal. The cool air hits my raw skin, and I bite down savagely on my bottom lip, tears filling my eyes. Lauren speaks softly, a calming murmur as she peels away the last part of the dressing and disposes of it in the bin next to the sink. She takes off her gloves, placing them in the bin, washes her hands, and puts on a fresh pair. I regard her intently. She's unusually quiet today; she's usually bubbly and extremely chatty, but I can sense she's reading my mood. She busies herself with taking out a fresh dressing, and she goes to unpeel it, but I stop her.

"I want to see."

She pauses for a moment, her eyes widening as she searches my face to see if I really mean it. There's a flicker of hesitation, but she nods slowly, understanding the weight of what I'm asking. She reaches up to the small cabinet above the sink and hands me a small mirror, glancing away to give me a moment alone.

With trembling hands, I bring the mirror up, angling it to catch my reflection. My breath catches at the sight of my back, a landscape of raw, pink scars stretching across my skin, jagged lines where smoothness once was. Some scars are thick and raised, others thinner and more faded, but each one is a reminder of that day, of the fire that took so much and left its mark on every inch of me.

A wave of nausea rises as I stare, my chest tightening at the sight of the person looking back at me. I feel like a stranger in my own skin, someone transformed, reshaped by pain and survival. I trace one of the larger scars in the mirror, feeling the familiar, uneven texture beneath my fingers, my own touch tentative, almost fearful. I can't help the sob that escapes and the tears that track their way down my cheeks. Lauren's hand rests on my shoulder again, her fingers warm and reassuring.

"You're still you."

She says softly, cocking her head to the side, as if sensing the turmoil inside me.

"Your scars are just part of your story, but they don't define you."

Her words linger, weaving themselves into the silence between us. I close my eyes, breathing in the quiet comfort she offers. Maybe I don't recognise the person I see in the mirror yet, but for the first time, I feel a hint of acceptance. The scars will always be there, but maybe one day, they'll just be another part of me.

Present

Zeppelin

I'm snapped back to the present as I feel the bed dip beside me, panic rising as Jax gets to his feet and pads across the floor.

"W-where are you going?"

Hesitation in my voice because I feel like I don't have the right to ask. Jax pauses mid-step, glancing back at me, his dark eyes softening, his tattoos taking on a life of their own in the moonlight peeking through the window. He shakes his head and runs his hand through his hair.

"I-I can't do this, I can't do it anymore, Zeppelin, I'm sorry, I'm fucking exhausted, and I'm done...I thought turning up to your signing today would change things between us, make you realise how good we are together, how right we are for each other."

I stare at him, disbelief in my wide eyes.

"How can you say that? I was shocked that you'd just shown up like that, out of the blue, without a fucking word! How did you expect me to react? For me to fall at your feet and beg you to whisk me away? This isn't one of my romance novels, Jax!"

He throws his head back and growls at the ceiling.

"I can't keep holding on if I'm the only one fighting for us."

The words hang in the air, sharp and unyielding. I feel my heart slam against my rib cage, the sting of his words cutting deeper than I expected. For a moment, all I can do is stare at him, taking in the tired lines on his face, the way his shoulders slump, and suddenly, I feel the urge to scream, to make him understand that I'm just as lost, just as scared, and just as desperate to be loved as he is.

"Fighting for us?"

I spit back, feeling anger surge to the surface, and I can't keep the vitriol from spilling from my lips.

"Jax, I don't even know who I fucking am anymore! I can't just pretend everything's ok, like I haven't been through hell and back. Losing Rian, the yacht accident, I can barely get through a day without wondering if I'll ever feel whole again. You...you just show up with your tattoos and your fucking charm and expect me to snap out of it?"

He takes a step back, hurt flashing across his face, and guilt twists in my stomach. I hadn't meant to be cruel, but it feels like he's pushing me, expecting something from me that I'm not sure I can give him right now. The silence stretches between us as he starts to pull on his discarded grey jogging bottoms, which hang loosely off his hips.

"Am I enough for you? Am I really what you want?"

He asks, unease in his voice, and the question blindsides me. I don't know what he's expecting from me at this moment. But whatever it is, I know I can't give him the answer he wants, so I shake my head slowly.

"Then there's nothing left for us to say to each other."

I watch as he grabs his shirt from the floor, slipping it over his head. His jaw is tight, his eyes dim, and I know he's closing off the part of himself he once offered to me so freely. I want to reach out, to pull him back and tell him that I just need more time, that I'm trying to find my way through the pain and grief that has consumed me for so many years. But as I open my mouth, no words come. I realise that he's been waiting for so long, and now he's finally letting go of me and of us.

32

Jax

I wanted her in the worst way and in the best way, all at the same time. I wanted to hold her close, to feel her warm softness pressed against me. I wanted to unravel her completely, to peel back every guarded layer and know her in ways no one else ever could or ever would. She was a mystery I feared and craved all at the same time, a storm I wanted to shelter against and lose myself in. I wanted to be her calm and her chaos; to offer her everything I had and take everything she was willing to give. Maybe it was selfish, but I didn't care. I wanted her, entirely and unapologetically, knowing that she could shatter me or make me whole in ways I never thought possible. I couldn't stand to watch her leave, but I couldn't let her stay either, not when it seemed we were both at an impasse in our relationship.

I found myself feeling envious of Sam and Peyton and Brody and Raleigh. Their relationships seemed so easy, so effortless, a kind of harmony that I had always told myself didn't exist outside of fairy tales. They made it look real, like love could be simple, like you could just fall into someone without constantly bracing for impact. *Why did it have to be so complicated for us?* She was the total opposite of Ruby, yet drama seemed to follow her wherever she went. Ruby had been a calming presence, predictable, a shelter from the chaos that seemed to follow us around. She grounded me somehow, and I missed her with an intense longing. But with Zeppelin, it was fire, unpredictability, and a constant need to keep my guard up, even as I let her in and let her know the real me. As I stood at the floor-to-ceiling windows watching her get into an Uber, she glanced up, holding my stare for what felt like minutes, when in reality it was only seconds. She defeated look in her red-rimmed eyes mirrored exactly how I was feeling at that moment. I felt as if I was closing the book on that chapter of my life, and I'd never felt more uncertain about anything.

***

I was a firm believer that when you're happy, you enjoy the music. But when you're sad, you understand and identify with the lyrics. As I stood in the recording booth listening to Sam's familiar gravelly rasp sing one of our new songs on our new album, I couldn't help but quietly observe him. He was struggling today; his voice wavered on certain lines, as if the lyrics held him prisoner, even as he tried to deliver them flawlessly. I could see it in his posture, his broad shoulders hunched forward, fists clenching and unclenching at his sides, the slight tension in his jaw.

He had closed his eyes for parts of the chorus, as if shutting out the room might somehow ease whatever was twisting inside him. Each line felt like a battle for him, his voice cracking in places it usually held strong, his breaths shallow and uneven. Unexpectedly, the music stops, and X waves his arms through the window.

"Something you want to share, dude?"

He leans into the microphone, the booth suddenly filled with his voice, rich and steady. Sam takes off his headphones, his lips forming a straight line, and he shakes his head.

"Na, man, all good."

He states, as I look from Brody to Lucas, and we all settle our gazes on Sam.

"Do you want to say that again, but without the bullshit?"

Brody says with a quirk of his eyebrow, and Sam's biceps flex as if he's ready to strike.

"Look, I don't know what it is you want me to say, but I'm fine. Everything's fine."

He rasps, and Brody laughs sarcastically. He crosses his arms across his chest, leaning casually against the console, eyes fixed on Sam with that knowing look he's perfected over the years.

"Right."

Brody says, drawing out the word.

"Because 'fine' explains why you've sung that same verse five times, like you're on the verge of either bursting into tears or punching the shit out of something."

Sam clenches his jaw, his hands flexing into tight fists, the knuckles turning white. He shifts his weight, clearly trying to keep his cool, but it's there, the storm brewing in his eyes. We've all seen it before, right before he has one of his all too frequent episodes.

"If you're struggling, mate, we get it, but don't fucking stand there and lie about it."

Sam looks at each of us, his expression hard, like he's weighing up whether to drop his guard or just keep his mouth shut. There's a flicker of something vulnerable in his gaze, but he shoves it down, swallowing hard.

"Appreciate it."

He states, almost robotically, as if he's rehearsed it in his head.

"Now, can we go again?"

His voice is dismissive, as I turn to the window to X, who nods curtly and starts the music again.

The rest of the day goes by in the blink of an eye, and it's been productive. We've almost finished recording the new album, and we couldn't be prouder of the music we've been making lately. It's fresh, and it's made us all fall in love with the music again. I haven't thought of Zeppelin once, and all I want to do is go home to Thea. As I step out of the studio, the cool evening air fills my lungs, the streetlights flickering and casting a soft glow down the still busy London Street. The drive home is a blur, and I'm filled with such relief as I pull up in my driveway. The first thing I see is Thea in her pink-and-white striped pyjamas, her penguin hanging limply at her side. Her big expressive brown eyes light up as they land on me, and she runs towards me. I catch her in my arms and swing her up, pressing kisses all over her face.

"Daddy's missed you, Princess!"

I say enthusiastically, and she giggles.

"Missed you too daddy, me and Marnie have got a surpwise' for you!"

She bounces excitedly as I look over her shoulder at Marnie, who shrugs with a huge grin on her face.

"It wasn't my idea, but she insisted! We've ordered pizza, your favourite, and now my work here is done!"

She says with a laugh, and I cock my eyebrow, more than curious as to what surprise awaits me as I step into the marble-floored foyer. I close the door behind us, and Thea wriggles for me to put her down. She takes off at speed, and I follow her. What greets me is a blanket fort with fairy lights hanging down and a duvet, two pillows, and a pizza box all laid out inside.

"I love it, baby girl!"

She grabs my hand, and I settle down in the blanket fort with her. We spend the evening watching her favourite Disney films, eating pepperoni pizza, and doing the daddy-daughter thing. Thea has fallen asleep. I carefully manoeuvre my way out of the blanket fort, and that's when I hear a blood-curdling scream. My feet are moving before I can stop myself, and I'm heading towards the door. I swing the door open and step out onto the driveway. I can see Sam's front door wide open, the light spilling out across the gravelled driveway. I sprint across the gravel and hover on the threshold for a minute.

"Sam? Sam?"

I call out, and the sight that greets me makes my stomach roil. He's covered in blood, and he's sobbing uncontrollably.

"Sam! Sam! What the fuck happened? Sam! Talk to me, man!"

I grab both of his arms and shake him gently, desperately trying to get him to tell me what's happened. He swallows hard, tears streaming down his cheeks.

"I-I-It's all my fucking fault, Jax."

He chokes out, his voice unsteady and his head shaking from side to side, as if in disbelief.

"You're not making any sense. Where's Peyton?"

He drops to his knees and the sound that comes out of his mouth doesn't sound human; it sounds like a wailing sob, and he rakes his hands through his dark hair.

"Sam? I need you to tell me what's happened. I can't help if you don't tell me. *For fuck's sake! Get your shit together!*"

I say firmly, my tone impatient. He doesn't speak; he just gestures to the door with his eyes. I head across the foyer and into the large open-plan kitchen. The sight in front of me stops me in my tracks as my eyes land on Peyton. She is unconscious on the floor, covered in blood. *What the actual fuck.*

33

Zeppelin

I had spent the last seven days travelling, doing book signings, and meeting my fans. I've had the best time interacting with them, hearing their stories, and I left the last book signing feeling completely humbled and in awe of every single one of them. Their stories inspired me to write, and on the train home, I lost count of how many pages I scribbled down, losing myself in new worlds. It had been an experience I would never forget, but I was glad to step back into my apartment in Notting Hill. Jericho greeted me with a wagging tail, a welcoming lick, and a single bark, letting me know he was happy I was home. I hadn't had time to think of Jax and the state of our relationship, but I knew I had to acknowledge it at some point. I went through the pile of post on the kitchen worktop that my Pops must have left for me, and my stomach dropped when I saw the familiar scrawl. *I knew it was too good to be true.* I turned the poison pen letter over in my hand as if it was going to jump up and bite me. I opened it carefully and unfolded it, the rustle of the paper echoing through my apartment as if it were taunting me somehow.

Guess who?

Thought you had escaped me, didn't you?

But you can't hide from the truth, no matter how fast you run.

And soon, everyone else will know it too.

I see you; I always have.

We're just getting started, sweetheart.

The rest of the letter was a muddled mess of veiled threats and cryptic references to things only someone disturbingly close to my life would know. Memories, fragments of conversations, and haunting phrases I had written in each of my novels, all of it twisted and used against me. This person was willing to expose themselves to let me know that they knew me, and that shocking realisation sent a chill down my spine. My heartbeat started to quicken, and cold sweat prickled at the back of my neck. Jericho, sensing my tension, let out a low, almost questioning whine and nudged my leg with his nose. I took a shaky breath and reached down to scratch behind his ears, and I'm not sure whether it was to comfort him or myself.

The crippling fear replaced the adrenaline from the week of travel and meeting so many inspiring people. My first instinct was to tear the letter up and not give them the satisfaction of knowing they're getting to me, but I didn't. I steadied my breath, set the letter back on the counter, and closed my eyes briefly, willing my hands to stop trembling. My mind is racing at a hundred miles an hour. There were so many things I wanted to do in that moment, but I didn't. Something kept me frozen to the spot, and I no longer felt safe in my own home. I was beginning to regret the decision to return here. I thought about calling Jax, despite everything being complicated between us right now; he would understand, maybe better than anyone. But I couldn't bear the thought of explaining why I was unravelling right here in my own kitchen, rattled by words on a page.

Instead, I turned away from the letter, leaving it on the counter, like an unwelcome guest. I walked into the living room, Jericho padding softly behind me, and collapsed onto the sofa, my body heavy with fatigue. Maybe tomorrow I'd deal with it, but for tonight I decided to let it go, let myself get some sleep, and hope that in the morning things might feel a little better.

***

I wake with a start to Jericho barking wildly. I rub the remnants of sleep from my eyes and swing my legs out of bed.

"Hey, calm down, buddy."

I say softly, trying to placate him.

"What's got you so rattled, eh?"

I ask, more to myself than to Jericho, and I always find myself talking to him as if he's somehow going to answer me back. I pad out into my apartment, barefoot, the cool floor sending a shiver up my spine. Jericho's nails click frantically against the hardwood as he paces near the front door, his ears pricked and body taut like a coiled spring.

I glance at the clock 5:21 am, the silence outside is thick, broken only by the occasional hum of a distant car. I move toward the window, pulling the blind aside just enough to peer out. The street is empty, bathed in the pale orange glow of the streetlamp. Nothing unusual, no movement, no sound.

Jericho lets out a low growl; his gaze is fixed on the door now. I feel unease crawl up my neck.

"All right, all right, Jericho, it's alright, buddy."

I whisper, reaching behind the coat rack for the baseball bat I'd started keeping there. I didn't expect to use it, but the weight of it in my hands seemed to ground me somehow.

I moved slowly to the door, heartbeat thundering in my chest. Jericho pressed himself close to my leg, his growl deepening. I held my breath and looked through the peephole. Nothing. I breathed a sigh of relief. But just as I started to turn away, I saw a flicker of movement. A shadow, too quick for me to register. I froze on the spot, as Jericho barked again, loud and sharp, almost as if he sensed a looming threat. I stepped back, gripping the bat tighter, my breath coming in short, shallow bursts. Whoever it was, they were close, too fucking close for my liking. I didn't open the door, I didn't speak, I just stood there, listening to the silence stretch around me. Unexpectedly, a slip of paper slid under the door; it curled at the edges. I stared at it, my pulse roaring in my ears. Jericho whimpered, his body rigid. I didn't pick it up, I couldn't. The message was clear; they knew where I lived. They had been close enough to touch the door, close enough to hear Jericho bark, close enough to know I was awake. I backed away slowly, the bat still clenched in my hand, and reached for my phone with trembling fingers. Maybe it was time to call Jax, or maybe it was already too late.

34

Jax

My stomach twists violently at the sight of Peyton lying unconscious on the cold, tiled floor. Her skin is almost as pale as the tiles beneath her, blood pooling around her, soaking into the soft fabric of her pale denim dress. I can't tell if she's breathing. I drop to my knees beside her, hands trembling as I reach for her pulse, and for a terrifying moment, I feel nothing. But then, there it is, faint, fragile, but there. She's alive. *Thank fucking Christ.*

"Sam! Sam!"

My voice cracks as I shout, panic bleeding through every syllable. He stumbles into the doorway, his blood-soaked shirt clinging to his chest, eyes wide and glossy. But he's not frozen, not this time. He sees her, and something inside him snaps. He rushes forward, collapsing to his knees on the floor beside her, gathering her into his arms with a fierce desperation. He cradles her gently, rocking her slightly, whispering her name like a prayer.

"Peyton...Peyton, angel, stay with me. Angel, please. I can't do this! Please! Oh God, angel!"

His voice is raw, thick with grief and unshed tears. I watch as he presses his forehead to hers, his arms wrapped protectively around her, shielding her from the world around them.

"What the fuck happened?"

I demand, my voice sharp, but the accusation dies in my throat when I see the anguish carved into Sam's face. He doesn't look at me; his entire focus is on her.

"I didn't...I fucking wouldn't..."

He chokes out, his voice barely audible.

"She collapsed, I tried...I tried to help her, but there was so much fucking blood. I didn't know what to do. I can't...I can't fucking lose her, Jax. I love her too fucking much!"

I nod, swallowing the lump in my throat, guilt clawing at my insides for ever doubting him. I tear my phone from my pocket and dial an ambulance, my voice a garbled mess as I explain the situation. They promise me help is on the way.

Sam doesn't move; he's still holding her, murmuring soft reassurances, his hands trembling as he strokes her hair. I kneel beside them, watching helplessly as he places a towel beneath her, trying to stem the bleeding. I flash him a questioning look, and he shakes his head, eyes brimming with unshed tears, and then it hits me. She's miscarrying again. *Fuck.* She was almost six months along, with a baby girl. The realisation slams into me like a freight train, and I feel the air leave my lungs. Sam's cradling her like he's trying to hold on to everything they're losing, and I can't breathe.

"Come on, angel."

He whispers, voice cracking.

"Please don't leave me. Don't leave us, I can't do this without you, angel."

His words slice through the room, and I turn away, giving them some privacy in this brutal moment. But I still hear him, his quiet, choked pleas, the way he rocks her gently, refusing to let her go. The paramedics arrive in a blur of motion. One of them gently urges Sam to step back, but he doesn't. I place a hand on his shoulder, grounding him, and he looks up at me with hollow eyes.

"I'll go with her."

He says, voice hoarse.

"I'll take Thea to Brody's."

I reply softly.

"I'll be right behind you."

They lift Peyton onto the stretcher, and Sam climbs in beside her, never releasing her hand. As they wheel her out, he doesn't look back.

The kitchen falls silent, and the blood on the floor is stark against the pale tiles. I stand there, numb, unable to process the devastation that just unfolded. Life is fragile, and far too short to waste on silence and distance.

***

The dull beep of machines anchors me in the sterile hospital room. Peyton lies motionless, her face pale and drawn. Sam sits beside her in the hospital bed, cradling her gently against his chest. His arms are wrapped around her, his chin resting on top of her head, whispering softly into her hair. Her labour had been induced, Oxytocin administered, and their baby girl was stillborn, and it wasn't just their loss; it was ours. We were a family; we had weathered storms together, but this... this was different. This could break Sam; he was already fragile, teetering on the edge of a bipolar episode. But he held her, refusing to let go, because she needed him now more than ever.

I pulled out my phone and typed a message to Zeppelin.

Something's happened.Something so bad it made me realise how precious life is.Life is too short for us to be apart any longer.I need you.J x

My thumb hovered over the send button, then I pressed it. The air in the room was thick with sorrow, so heavy it felt like drowning. Peyton hadn't spoken since the nurse placed the lifeless bundle in her arms. Her tears had dried, leaving her hollow.

Sam hadn't left her side; he held her close, whispering apologies and promises into the silence. His hands trembled every time he touched her, as though afraid she might shatter. Peyton stirred, her eyes fluttered open, and she looked at Sam, then at me. Her voice was barely a whisper.

"It wasn't supposed to be like this, Jax."

Her voice was cracking under the weight of their loss.

"I know, sweetheart."

I said, sitting on the edge of the bed and taking her hand in mine. *What else could I say?* There were no words for this kind of pain. Sam tightened his hold around her, pressing a kiss to her temple. His shoulders shook with silent sobs, and my heart broke for them both. I felt like an intruder in their grief, but I stayed. Because family doesn't walk away, *not now, not ever.*

35

Zeppelin

My phone pinged with a text notification. My stomach flipped at the sight of his name. Jax.

Something's happened

Something so bad that it made me realise that life is precious

Life is too short for us to be apart any longer, Zeppelin

I need you

Jx

I sat frozen, the message burning into me. He sounded so broken, stripped bare. This wasn't the Jax I remembered, the one who always had a comeback, a smirk, a shield. This was someone unravelling, and it shattered something inside me. I typed, erased, typed again, and nothing felt right. I turned the phone over in my hands, like it might offer me the answers I sought. I paced the room, once, twice, then stopped and whispered into the quiet.

"I don't know how to fix this, Jax."

Another message, and I grabbed the phone with trembling fingers.

I'm sorryI didn't know who else to turn toYou're the only one who ever saw all of itAll of meJ x

I read it once, then again. Each time, the words hit harder. No bitterness, no bravado, just raw honesty. I typed back, hands shaking.

You don't have to go through this aloneIf you need me, say whereI'll be thereZ x

I didn't wait for a reply; I haphazardly pulled on my jacket, shoved my feet into my Vans, grabbed my bag and my keys, gave Jericho a quick pat on the head, and slammed the door behind me. The cold air outside hit me, sharp, bracing. I walked fast, nowhere on my mind, just needing to move. The city was alive in that chaotic way, horns, footsteps, laughter spilling from cafés. I pulled out my phone again, thumb hovering.

Talk to meWhere are you?I need to see youZ x

I kept walking, half afraid he wouldn't answer, then a message pinged.

Flying Horse CaféBack cornerI'll waitJ x

That was all I needed, as I turned on my heel and ran.

The streets blurred around me; all I could think about was him. The Flying Horse Café came into view, its striped awning familiar, although I hadn't been there in over a year, the last time was with Rian. I didn't allow myself to think about why, as I pushed through the door, the bell above it jangling, and was met with warmth and the scent of espresso. My eyes scanned the room, couples hunched over laptops, a barista singing along to Benson Boone Beautiful Things. A man in the corner in a black hoodie, a baseball cap pulled low over his eyes, and his head bowed. *My Handsome Jack.*

He hadn't seen me yet, as I took a moment to take him in. One hand wrapped around the cup of coffee, and the other fiddling with the sleeve of his jumper. He looked...wrecked. Beautiful, but wrecked. My heart clenched at the sight of him. I stepped forward, and he looked up, as if he felt me before he saw me. Our eyes met, silver on brown, and the world fell away around us; all I could see was him. Nothing else mattered, just him. He gestured to the seat opposite him, and I sat down hesitantly as he pulled off his baseball cap, setting it down on the table in front of him. He ran his fingers through his hair and let out the breath he didn't realise he was holding. I observed him for a few minutes; he didn't speak right away, and I didn't push. The silence between us wasn't uncomfortable, as the coffee steamed quietly between us, untouched.

"I wasn't sure you'd come."

He said finally, his voice low and hoarse, as the chatter around us became a little louder. His gaze shifted, his eyes fixed on the table.

"I've been at the hospital all night. Peyton and Sam's baby...she was stillborn."

The words hit like a wave, sudden and cold, pulling the air straight from my lungs. I let out an audible gasp, slapping my hands over my mouth.

"Oh God...Jax."

I breathed, the only sound I could manage for a moment.

"She was perfect, in every way."

He said softly.

"Tiny, quiet, they named her Elodie."

The name hung in the air like a prayer, and I swallowed hard, my throat tight, unsure of how to continue, my heart aching for a type of grief I couldn't even begin to comprehend. My heart hurt for all of them. I know from conversations with Peyton that she was excited to finally have a baby girl after giving birth to two boys.

"I'm so sorry."

I said, and I meant it with every part of me.

"For all of you."

He nodded, lips pressed together, eyes distant.

"The paparazzi are camped outside the hospital; they've got no fucking idea."

The anger in his voice is evident as I reach across the table and place my hand on top of his. I expect him to pull his hand away, but he doesn't; he lets me take his hand in mine, as if my touch grounded him somehow and brought him back to the here and now.

"I held her."

He whispers.

"Peyton asked me to, she said I was the only one who could. Sam...he was gone. Just...gone."

He paused, his breath hitching.

"I didn't know what to do. I just held her, told her she was loved, that she was safe, even though she was already..."

His voice cracked, and he didn't finish his sentence.

"Sam found her."

He continued, after a moment.

"Collapsed on the kitchen floor, covered in blood. He's...*Jesus Christ*, he's fucking broken."

I didn't speak; I couldn't. The grief in his voice was too much.

"I sat with him for hours."

Jax said.

"He wouldn't let go of Peyton, not even when she was sedated. Just kept saying her name, repeatedly."

He looked up at me, eyes glossy.

"I'm sorry I sent that message. I just needed someone, something. You."

"Don't be sorry."

I said, squeezing his hand. I'm about to continue when I feel a presence at the table. It's a young girl, with short blonde curly hair, bright green eyes, she is wearing a Rancid Vengeance t-shirt, short denim cut-off shorts, and black and white Converse. She approaches tentatively, as if she knows she's interrupting a private moment.

"Erm...excuse me...are you Flash from Rancid Vengeance?"

She asks in a small voice, and Jax looks up, his expression switching from solemn to a full, beaming smile in a split second.

"The one and only, my love!"

He states, as if a switch had suddenly been switched. A beaming smile spreads across her face, mirroring his. She asks for a selfie, he obliges, and she walks away happy. I stared at him.

"How do you do that?"

He shrugged, the smile fading.

"It's just what you do, fake it, till you make it, I guess. It's what we've been conditioned to do for the past fifteen fucking years! Do you think I like sitting there and pretending everything's hunky dory when my best friend has just lost his daughter?"

He picks up his baseball cap and pulls it on his head so it's low over his eyes. The chatter around us has got louder, as if more people have realised they have a real-life celebrity in their midst.

"I can't be here; can we go back to your place?"

He asks, suddenly unsure of himself, and I nod. He stands, pulling me up with him, and takes my hand in his, tight, like he was afraid I'd vanish.

We walked out together, leaving the noise behind, and for the first time in a long time, he wasn't alone.

36

Zeppelin

We make our way back to my apartment in relative silence, and the air is charged with something I can't quite put my finger on. The streets blur past us, the hum of the city around us. We make it to my apartment, and as we step into the lift, the space feels smaller, heavier. I glance at Jax, catching a brief flicker of something, maybe anticipation, but before he looks away, his gaze is fixed firmly on the doors. I can't tell if he's avoiding me or the truth, maybe both.

When we reach my floor, I take a moment before unlocking the door, suddenly unsure of how to move forward. The door swings open, and I step aside, waiting for him to enter first. Jax's hand brushes the doorframe as he steps in, and for a moment, it feels like a quiet question hanging in the air, asking if we can go back to what we were, or if we're already too far gone.

The doors shut with a click behind us, and suddenly, he pulls off his hat, discarding it on the side table beside the door. He spins me around and presses me against the door, the steady rhythm of his heartbeat grounding me in the present. His scent, a mix of clean linen and faintly of Diesel Only the Brave, envelopes me. I lift my head up, unexpectedly feeling a needy ache between my legs, and I desperately need him to take it away. I need him to remind me what it feels like, and I need him to replace it with only him; I need him more than my next breath, and by the look in his eyes, he knows it.

"Jax."

I mewl softly, my voice not sounding like my own. I pull away from him briefly and take a moment to take every single inch of him in. He's glorious, he's lean but very well built, his shoulders broad and his biceps thick. His jawline makes him look like he has been carved by the most famous of sculptors. His nose was sharp and his cheekbones perfect. His thighs are powerful, and as he shifts backwards to regard me intently.

"Do you need something?"

He asks innocently, flashing me his signature Hollywood smile, and I nod slowly.

"I need you to take it away, Jax. I need you; I need you."

My request sounds like a plea, but I don't care; I just need him to do this one thing for me. We're both naked in record time, as I tackle him to the soft, plush carpeted floor and straddle him, my breasts feel heavy and desperate to have his hands on them. The delicious, sweet ache between my thighs is almost unbearable, and my pussy floods as I grind myself on him. He moves his hands up to cup my breasts, as he grips me with both hands on my waist and flips us, so I'm pinned beneath him.

"Game on, sweetheart."

He flashes me a cocky grin as he leans down and takes my tender nipple between his teeth, alternating between lapping and suckling gently.

"Oh, God! That feels so good!"

I moan softly as he moves down my chest, pressing kisses on my chest, my stomach, and down to the place I want him to touch me the most. I have never been so turned on in my whole life, and I'm needy and desperate to feel him inside me again after all this time. Jax moves down and settles himself between my legs. The sight of him causes slick heat to flood my pussy. He licks a path up my wet centre, and I scream out at the contact, as I writhe beneath him. He sucks my swollen nub between his teeth, as I cup my breasts in my hands. My blood feels like it's on fire, my pulse racing, and every nerve in my body is tuned in to everything Jackson Chase.

"I want you to come for me, Zeppelin."

He commands, as he pushes two fingers inside, and I gasp out loud at the feel of him. It's been so long since I felt this wanton, this needy and desperate to be fucked. He builds up a rhythm, his fingers push deeper, and his thumb circles my engorged nub.

"I want you to come hard for me, sweetheart."

His words are my undoing, and I scream as his skilful fingers bring me to the most delicious orgasm.

"OH, GOD! OH FUCK! YES! YES! JAX! JAX! OH GOD! JAX!"

I writhe as he squeezes every ounce of pleasure from me. I bask in my post-orgasmic haze for a few moments, as he fists his cock with one hand. He reaches up to the set of drawers underneath the sink and takes out a condom. He's about to tear the foil packet open with his teeth, and I stop him with a slow shake of my head.

"I want to feel you with nothing between us, and I want to remember every single moment."

My voice is barely a whisper, and he acknowledges me with a single nod. I bite my lip as I look up at him.

"I need your cock buried inside me, Jax."

I say shamelessly, and he runs the head of his cock through my slickness. He slips into me with ease, my pussy swallowing him whole. He leans down, stroking my cheek with the back of his hand and kissing a burning trail from my neck down to my collarbone and across my shoulder. I moan softly in his ear, and this is the first time we've made love. Heat blossoms through me, and his name leaves my lips on a ragged pant. I cry out with each measured drive of his length, waves of warmth spread through me, as I move my hips upwards, encouraging him to go faster. He shakes his head with a soft smile.

"No, we're doing this my way, slow, unhurried, we're making love, Zeppelin. I want to take my time worshipping every inch of your perfect body. I want to commit every curve, every dimple, every part of you to memory so when we're apart, I'll never forget what you feel like."

His words are my undoing, as he makes slow, lazy love to me on the bathroom floor. His cock feels like velvet with nothing between us, thrusting unhurried in and out of my wet heat. He builds up a steady pace with every drive of his cock. I feel him push deeper inside me, bumping my cervix with the head of his cock, hitting my G-spot in exactly the right place. I feel an intense orgasm cresting to the surface, and I feel like I'm about to explode.

"Oh, God! I think I'm going to come!"

I yell, as he continues his slow pace, but increasing the rhythm ever so slightly.

"That's it, come for me, I'm right behind you, Zeppelin!"

He grunts, and with another deep plunge of his cock, a powerful orgasm surges through me like a tsunami.

"Jax! Oh Jesus! Fuck! Oh! Oh God! Jax! Yes! Jax!"

I scream, and Jax's release is right behind mine, as he growls out, filling me with his hot seed. We both come down from our orgasms, he pulls out of me, and I shiver, bereft at the loss of contact. He stands at his full height and bends down, scooping me up in his strong, muscular arms. He carries me as if I weigh nothing and deposits me gently on the bed, settling himself beside me. He pulls me into his embrace, and I rest my head wordlessly on his chest, just listening to the sound of his heartbeat. In that moment, I've never been surer of anything in my life that I want to marry this man. This imperfectly perfect rock star has imprisoned my heart and claimed it as his own.

37

Zeppelin

In the weeks that followed, I moved back in with Jax permanently and put my apartment in Notting Hill up for sale. I had finally concluded that my apartment, even though it was my sanctuary for five years, was just bricks and mortar. That didn't compare to the memories I held in my head and in my heart; those were much more important to me.

Selling the apartment in Notting Hill was bittersweet for me, as Jericho and I took one last walk down Portobello Road, an area we had become so familiar with over the last five years. We took our usual route past the colourful townhouses and the little bookshop where I had spent countless afternoons getting lost in books and scribbling down ideas. The small coffee shop where I used to sit, watching the world go by and writing on my laptop, a mug of steaming coffee in my hand.

My apartment in Notting Hill was a stark contrast to Jax's mansion in Chislehurst, Kent. It was worlds away from the hustle and bustle of Portobello Road market, the sounds of the street vendors and market traders. Here, there was nothing but peace and relative quiet. It was unnerving at first, but I grew to appreciate the silence it brought. I was in my writing room that Jax had replicated from my apartment, writing my new book and checking my weekly schedule in my diary. I had been feeling off for the past few weeks, the headaches, the nausea, the tiredness, my sleep pattern was erratic, my appetite almost non-existent, but I just put it down to the emotional upheaval. Moving in with Jax and the complete change in pace, the stillness of Chislehurst, compared to the buzz of Notting Hill, was certainly an adjustment, but I had welcomed it. Sitting with my diary open on my desk, unease began to creep in, and my stomach roiled violently. I slapped my hand over my mouth to quell the sick feeling as I flipped through the pages again, cross-checking dates. I checked repeatedly, counting, recounting, but I couldn't find when my last period was. My heart began to race. Jax and I hadn't exactly been careful since we began our relationship all those months ago. It wasn't something we talked about often; we were just caught up in the moment. I had always thought it wasn't something I needed to worry about.

After the yacht accident, the doctors had been clear; the damage to my body caused by my injuries had made pregnancy highly unlikely, if not impossible. I had mourned that quietly years ago; it was just another thing the accident had stolen from me. As I sat there, the glaring absence of dates staring back at me, doubts began to surface. We had a scare in the Maldives, which turned out to be a false alarm, but we hadn't pursued the conversation further. I couldn't shake the feeling that something felt different, and my hand moved instinctively to my stomach, resting there for a few moments. I leaned back in my chair and stared up at the ceiling. *I couldn't be pregnant, could I?* The subtle changes that I refused to dwell on seemed too much of a coincidence to ignore. My fatigue, the sickness that came and went, the tender soreness I felt in places I hadn't noticed before, it wasn't just stress. *It couldn't be.* I knew my body and these changes weren't normal for me. More importantly, what would Jax say? *Would he be open to a brother or a sister for Thea?* After losing Ruby in such tragic circumstances, would he want another child with a woman who isn't her?

Later that afternoon, when Jax was in the studio working on a track for the band's new album, I slipped out and made the journey to the nearest pharmacy. The quaint Village of Chislehurst, which wasn't far from Vengeance Estates, the gated community that housed all four members of Rancid Vengeance and their close-knit entourage. The pharmacy was quiet, the bell above the door jangling softly, as I stepped inside, notifying them of my presence. My heart pounded in my chest as I scanned the shelves, my fingers hesitating over the rows and rows of pregnancy tests. I grabbed one and paid quickly, avoiding eye contact with the cashier. The box felt heavy in my hand, as I decided I needed the support and reassurance of someone familiar. I made the forty-minute journey to Dulwich to see my Nana and Pops. I needed someone to help me make sense of it all. They were the two constants in my life, and I was grateful they had taken care of me after my dad died.

When the Uber pulled up to their house, the familiar sight of Nana's Garden, always meticulously tended, and the green hedgerow outside the house, neatly trimmed, greeted me. It was the kind of place that never changed; no matter how much time had passed, it was like coming home. I knocked on the door, even though I had my own key, my hand trembling slightly as I waited. Nana's voice called out from inside, her usual warmth and energy bubbling through the door.

"Coming, love!"

The door swung open, and there she stood, smiling broadly, her light grey hair perfectly styled, as she stepped forward and pulled me into a tight hug. Her familiar scent of lavender and vanilla filled my nostrils, and I felt like I wanted to burst into tears right there on the doorstep.

"Well, look at you!"

Nana said, stepping back and taking me in. Pops appeared behind her, his newspaper in hand, his eyes soft with understanding. He didn't say anything immediately; he just gave me his usual look, the one that told me he knew there was something wrong, even if I wasn't ready to talk about it yet.

"Come in, darling."

Nana said, a warm smile on her weathered face, as she ushered me inside and closed the door behind her.

"You look like you could use a cup of tea."

I smile at her words; a cup of tea was her answer to everything. I followed her into the kitchen, as she turned the kettle on to boil and motioned for me to sit at the table with a flick of her tea towel. Pops sat across from me, silently observing, waiting for me to speak. Pops was always a stoic man, but he always had a soft spot for his only granddaughter. Jimmy Fraser was an ex-boxer with a heart of gold and a listening ear. He's a few years from retirement as a security guard and works for Rancid Vengeance in one of their many apartment buildings in Camden.

"So, how are you settling in with Jackson?"

He asks, narrowing his eyes at me and regarding me intently. I nod, plastering a smile on my face, and I know it doesn't reach my eyes.

"Really good, thanks, Pops!"

I say brightly, as Pops shakes his head, frowning, but he doesn't say anything. I take the pregnancy test out of my bag and place it on the table in front of me.

"I think I might be pregnant."

Nana turns to glance at the test, shifting her eyes to Pops and then to me, as she wipes her hands on a tea towel. Nana breaks the comfortable silence, her voice soft but steady.

"You know, love, whatever happens, you're not alone."

I look at the test again, my hands trembling slightly and my eyes glossy with unshed tears.

"I thought...after the accident, I thought it was impossible. The doctors said it wouldn't happen...They said because of my injuries..."

I stop myself from continuing, as Pops nods, his world-weary eyes filled with understanding.

"Life has a way of surprising us. But what matters now is that you've got people who love you. Jackson isn't the type of fella who would abandon you. Those boys, all of them, hearts of gold."

He speaks of the members of Rancid Vengeance as if they are family, and, in a way, they are to him. A tear slips down my cheek, but I don't wipe it away, as Nana reaches over, gently taking my hand in hers.

"It's ok to be scared, love."

She says, her voice filled with reassurance.

"I've been feeling off for weeks now, but I just put it down to the stress of the move."

I explain, my voice shaky.

"I'm late, I'm never late, and... I don't know what to do."

I let out a strangled sob.

"You know, these doctors, they don't know everything. These things happen when you least expect them, love."

She picks up the test, holding it in her hands for a moment.

"Go and take the test, it's better to know once and for all."

Nana hands it to me, and I go upstairs to the bathroom. I shut the door behind me, the test in my hand, and follow the instructions carefully. My breath catches as I place it on the counter. Two minutes, that's all it would take for my life to change forever. I perch on the edge of the bath, my pulse thundering in my ears. Every second felt like an eternity, and when I finally glance at the result, my breath hitches. *Two lines.* I stare at them incredulously, my mind refusing to process what's in front of me. *Two lines. Pregnant.* I stand up, my legs feeling like they are about to buckle underneath me. I grip the edge of the sink to steady myself and look up at my reflection in the mirror.

"This can't be fucking happening."

I whisper to myself, as I sink to the floor, a mixture of emotions barrels through me. Disbelief, pure fear, and something else entirely wash over me. Was *it...excitement?* My hand instinctively rests on my stomach.

"Hey, baby."

I smile softly to myself, and for the first time in weeks, I let myself imagine what might come next.

38

Zeppelin

After a long talk from Nana and Pops, I finally plucked up the courage to return home. The weight bearing down on me had somewhat dissipated, but I knew I still had to tell Jax. I could no longer hide from the truth; I was carrying his baby, and he deserved to know. As soon as I step into the opulent marbled hallway and close the door behind me, Thea comes bounding down the stairs wearing a pretty red dress with a huge smile on her face.

"Zeppelin! Zeppelin!"

She can't seem to contain her excitement as I greet her with a beaming grin in return.

"Hey, Thea! Wow! Look at you! Don't you look pretty!"

I compliment her, as she grabs my hand and leads me through the house. I drop my bag onto the kitchen island and follow her.

"Where are we going?"

I chuckle nervously, the tone of my voice more than curious. She makes a zipping motion across her lips, and I regard her with narrow eyes, intrigued as to where she's taking me. She takes me out into the large, expansive garden, and my breath catches in my throat. The whole area is bathed in soft, ethereal light, white twinkling fairy lights adorning the trees and bushes, casting a magical glow over the wide-open space. A trail of red rose petals leads down a stone pathway. I put my hand over my mouth as the strains of Luke Combs' *Forever After All* start playing from the surround sound system. She's already running across the garden, her movements full of purpose. She reaches a wooden frame draped with white silk, the fairy lights twinkling around it. I watch as she picks up a square canvas from the ground, holding it up with both hands, her eyes dancing with excitement. Written in different coloured crayons are the words:

Will you marry my daddy?

And beneath that, two tick boxes, one for yes and one for no. Tears spring to my eyes without warning, as I stare at the canvas for a moment, trying to process what I'm seeing. She's smiling up at me, her face full of hope, and I feel my heart slam violently against my rib cage. I glance up at Jax, standing in the background, observing me quietly. He's nervous, his hands shoved in his pockets, but his eyes are filled with something I can't quite put my finger on. He steps forward, his warm brown gaze locked on mine, his words low but steady.

"I've been thinking about this for a long time. After everything we've been through, but I needed to be sure, I needed to know you'd say yes."

I look back down at the canvas, my hands trembling as I reach for the pen that rests beside it. I don't need to think twice. I know one million per cent I want to spend the rest of my life with this man. Without hesitation, I check the *yes* box, feeling the weight of the moment settle over me. Thea claps her hands, squealing excitedly, as Jax drops down on one knee.

"I can't imagine my life without you in it, Zeppelin Jade Williams. Will you marry me?"

He opens the black box he is holding in his hand; the ring is a platinum band with three diamonds, a large one in the middle and two on either side. I can't speak, as he holds the ring up to me. I'm so overwhelmed, as my eyes fill with tears, and I nod.

"Yes! Yes! I'll marry you!"

I all but squeal at him, and Thea bounces up and down with excitement.

"Yaaaayy! Can I be a bridesmaid? Please! Please!"

We both laugh at her enthusiasm.

"Of course you can be a bridesmaid!"

I tell her as she takes off at a hundred miles an hour and runs over to Marnie, who picks her up and takes her inside the house. I turn back to Jax, aware that it's just us now. He looks particularly delicious tonight; he's wearing an expensive black Armani suit. It looks perfectly tailored to his body size and shape. His hair is perfectly styled, swept to the side, and his beard is neatly trimmed. Jax slips the engagement ring onto my finger, and I can't help but take a moment to admire it. The band glints under the soft garden lights, the central diamond sparkling brightly. It's perfect, elegant, timeless, and impossibly beautiful, just like this moment.

Before I can say anything, Jax gets to his feet, his movements fluid and confident. In one swift motion, he lifts me off the ground, and a surprised laugh escapes me, but it's cut short as his lips crash against mine. The kiss is searing, filled with such passion and intensity that it makes me want to cry. My arms instinctively wrap around his neck, pulling him closer, as his arms hold me securely and tightly against him. He deepens the kiss, stealing the breath from my lungs and leaving me wanting him with a deep longing. I run my fingers through his hair and lose myself in the sensation of his lips against mine. It's a kiss that erases every doubt, every fear, and replaces them with a cast-iron certainty that this man, this moment, is everything I've ever wanted and that happy endings don't just happen in romance novels, they happen in real life too. When he puts me down and sets me on my feet, I'm bereft at the loss of contact, and I open my eyes to find him staring at me.

"You've got no fucking idea what you do to me, Zeppelin."

He murmurs, his voice husky and low, sending shivers through every inch of my body. I wrap my arms around him and move my hands up to play with his hair at the nape of his neck.

"I think I might have an idea!"

I tease playfully, and he laughs, the sound deep and rich. He presses a kiss to my forehead, his eyes locking with mine. He doesn't say anything for long minutes as I'm suddenly hit with the realisation of the secret that I'm keeping. *I'm pregnant with his baby.* How do I tell him? How do I tell him something so life-changing, after an already perfect moment? My fingers tremble slightly as I slide them down his chest, and he notices immediately, his brow furrowing with concern.

"Hey, you've gone quiet."

He says softly, but the words get caught somewhere in my throat, and I can't speak. I shift my gaze away from him, and his hands come up gently to cup my cheek, turning me back to focus on him.

"You're scaring me, love."

He admits, his thumb brushing my bottom lip.

"I-I..."

My voice cracks slightly, and I take a shaky breath. I pull away from him, putting some distance between us, and shake my head vehemently. The hurt flashing in his eyes breaks something inside me.

"I...I'm sorry...I...can't fucking do this."

I rush into the house, and I don't stop until I reach the kitchen, bracing myself against the kitchen counter and gripping the edge as if it's the only thing keeping me upright. I hear the faint sound of his footsteps approaching, but I don't look up.

"Talk to me."

He says softly from the doorway, his voice laced with worry. My hands instinctively move to my stomach, a small protective gesture that makes me sob harder.

"Look, I'm not upset, but whatever this is, whatever you need to tell me, we'll figure it out together."

He moves further into the room, tucking one hand into his pocket as I reach for my bag, which I dropped onto the kitchen island on the way in. I reach inside for the positive pregnancy test and slide it across to him. He looks from the test and back to me.

"I'm pregnant, Jax, I'm pregnant with your baby. Our baby."

The words seem to tumble out, and the silence that follows sets my nerves on edge. His expression shifts, first to shock, then to something I can't quite read. His lip's part, but no words come out, and the uncertainty in his eyes breaks my heart a little more.

"I didn't even think it was possible; they said after the accident...I...I couldn't, and I..."

Before I can finish, he closes the distance between us in an instant, his hands coming up to cup my face. His touch is gentle, his eyes searching mine.

"You're pregnant."

He says, his voice soft, almost disbelieving.

"You're carrying my baby? Our baby?"

I nod, my tears turning to a watery smile. He sinks to his knees in front of me, his hands gently resting on my hips as he leans forward, pressing his cheek to my stomach. For a moment, he's completely still, then he slides his hands from my hips to cradle my stomach, his thumbs brushing over the grey wool of my jumper dress.

"I didn't think this could happen."

I admit, my voice is trembling.

"After everything...the accident...my injuries...I thought it was impossible."

He pulls back just enough to look up at me, his eyes glossy with unshed tears.

"Nothing is impossible."

He says, his voice firm, his hands never leaving my stomach. With those words, we begin our new chapter together.

39

Jax

The weeks that followed, I couldn't wipe the smile off my face, no matter how hard I tried. I was going to be a dad again. We had told Thea together, and she squealed with delight at the prospect of becoming a big sister. My heart felt almost too big for my chest as I watched Zeppelin sleep, her hand protectively resting on her stomach. We had visited a private medical facility a few days earlier, and it had been confirmed that she was nine weeks pregnant. It was subtle, but I could see a slight curve, the beginning of a bump forming in her once flat stomach, a sign of the life we had created together. She had a glow about her, and she couldn't look more beautiful if she tried. I had never considered the prospect of having a baby with someone that wasn't Ruby, but as soon as Zeppelin told me she was pregnant, I was all in. It was as if the world shifted somehow in that moment, and I knew I wanted to approach fatherhood differently from how I did with Thea. This time, our baby would have two parents to raise them, and I was determined not to let either of them down. Our story had barely begun, and we had been through so much together in such a short space of time, but I knew deep down this was it for me. This was the happy ending that we had fought so hard for. I had just asked her to marry me, and now we were expecting a baby too; life couldn't be more perfect. But I couldn't help but think it was a little too perfect and a little too good to be true. I didn't allow myself to dwell on that thought; I couldn't. I didn't want to carry on waiting for the other shoe to drop, and I didn't want to live my life afraid of finding true happiness.

The Rancid Vengeance family was growing, and I couldn't be happier. We had finished recording our latest album, and we were so proud of the music we had made. We experimented with a brand-new sound; it was fresh again after fifteen long years in the rock music industry. I had a feeling this album would be a game-changer for us. Rancid Vengeance was more than just the music; it was about loyalty, family, and leaving a legacy for our loved ones. We were playing an intimate gig this evening in one of our favourite venues, The Roundhouse. The gig was to showcase the first few tracks from our new album, and the tickets sold out in four minutes, a record for us.

There was always something special about The Roundhouse, its history, its energy, and the way the crowd always seemed to connect with us on a deeper level. The Roundhouse's capacity is 1,000 people; it is one of the most architecturally astounding and unique spaces in all of London. The structure reminds me of an old nineteen-thirties dance hall with an up-to-date twist. It has modern brickwork and ultra-trendy strobe lighting. The circular balcony framing the main space below offers a fantastic vantage point overlooking the breathtaking view. The main space is the beating heart of The Roundhouse, and the low stage is situated in the centre of the room. Tonight, it felt like everything was coming full circle, and I couldn't be more excited to perform for the first time in years.

I had told the boys I had proposed to Zeppelin and that we were expecting a baby. They were elated that our unconventional family was growing, but ever since Sam and Peyton had lost their baby girl to stillbirth, he had withdrawn completely. I couldn't open a newspaper without seeing him drunk and falling out of some club. His eyes were vacant, and he was less than his usual put-together self. He was unravelling and imploding in a way that I had never seen before, and I was terrified for my friend, my brother, who was grieving and didn't seem to give a shit about those around him who had suffered a loss too. It hurt to watch him lashing out and so lost in his own darkness that he didn't notice Peyton, who was grieving too. The baby they had lost, it had torn through them both, but while she was still fighting, trying to find a way to keep going. Even though the doctors couldn't save her reproductive organs, she could no longer conceive or give birth to her own child. My heart broke for her, but Sam had completely checked out. It was like he didn't care anymore, not about his own healing, not about the band, and certainly not about the people who were still there for him.

I couldn't even talk to him anymore, none of us could, not even Brody, Marlowe, or Cole, the only people who ever seemed to get through the impenetrable walls that he had built around himself. Every time I reached out, he shut me down or changed the subject. It was as if he was trying to push away everyone who he loved and cared for. I couldn't stand by and watch my best friend destroy himself, but what choice did I have? He was spiralling, and it was like watching a car crash you couldn't tear your eyes away from. I wanted to believe that Sam would come around, that someday soon he would snap out of it and realise he wasn't alone. That the woman he loved was still there for him, and she needed him just as much as he needed her. But with every new story, every new image of him lost in the haze of drugs and alcohol, I couldn't help but wonder if that day would ever come.

I could hear the crowd outside, their voices rising in a chorus of eager anticipation. Adrenaline surged through me as I grabbed my guitar, running my fingers over the strings, feeling its familiar weight in my hands. This was what I lived for. I peeked into the audience, and Peyton wasn't in her usual spot, and I found that strange; she's never missed a show. I turn to Sam with narrowed eyes.

"Where's Peyton? She's not in her usual spot, mate?"

I ask genuinely curious, and he laughs bitterly.

"She doesn't want to be around me right now."

He mocks and rolls his eyes dramatically.

"Can you fucking blame her? Look at the state of you!"

I snap, as he takes a swig from his vodka bottle. His eyes snap up to meet mine, but there's no fire, no fight in them, just emptiness.

"What the fuck do you want me to say, Jax? That I'm a wreck? That I don't even know how to look her in the eye anymore?"

He laughs again bitterly.

"You think I don't know what I'm doing to her? Our boys? What I'm doing to all of you?"

I take a step closer, my hand instinctively reaching for his shoulder, trying to steady him, to make him see that this self-destructive spiral isn't helping anyone.

"She fucking needs you, Sam! She's suffering too! Don't push her away!"

He scrubs his hands down his face and lets out a sigh.

"Don't you think I don't fucking know that! I don't know how to help her! I don't know what to do! She's crying all the time, she's broken, I'm fucking broken!"

He jabs his thumbs into his chest and looks up at the ceiling.

"Jesus fucking Christ!"

He rasps, his voice cracking as if the dam is going to break at any minute.

"I can't do this! Not now!"

He takes a long pull from the bottle and goes over to the dressing table, snorting a few lines of coke. He drums the table with both of his hands and bounces from one foot to another.

"Are we going to fucking perform, or not?"

I look from Brody to Lucas and back to Sam. *Conversation closed for now.*

***

We stepped out onto the stage to deafening cheers, the lights blinding for a moment before they settled, revealing the sea of faces in front of us. They weren't just fans; they were family, the ones who had supported us from the start, who had stuck with us through thick and thin. Tonight, we weren't just playing music; we were sharing a piece of our souls with them. I strum out a familiar riff to 'Corrupted,' and the crowd erupted, singing along to the familiar tunes from our earlier albums, but when the new tracks hit, the energy in the room seemed to shift. There was something raw and intimate about the way the audience responded. This was a celebration of everything we had worked for, everything we had been through, and everything that was to come. Sam had the audience eating out of the palm of his hand as usual; he was the epitome of a bad-boy rock star, his leather trousers looked as if they were spray-painted on, and his denim waistcoat was open to reveal his bare, tattooed chest. But something seemed off about him. As one of our new songs ends, Sam steps to the front of the stage, putting both hands to his ears, and the crowd erupts into wolf-whistling, cheers, and deafening screams.

"*Wow!* How the fuck are you lovely people doing tonight? You're all looking so fucking beautiful out there! We want to say thank you from the bottom of our hearts for coming to share this special fucking moment with us tonight! Rancid Vengeance chapter fifteen!"

He laughs.

"YEEEAAAHHHHH!"

He turns to me and flashes me a wink.

"Give me a riff, Flash! Let's do this!"

He roars and jumps up and down. Sweat pours from his face, and without warning, the colour drains from him. His expression changes, and his eyes roll back in his head, as he unexpectedly collapses to the floor.

40

Jax

Within seconds, the stage is a hive of activity, and a crowd of concerned roadies gathers round. It's a blur of people, a cacophony of noise, screams, and raised voices. I vaguely hear someone calling for an ambulance in the background. Relief washes over me as a loud voice fills the P.A system.

"If you could all remain calm and make your way to the marked exits in an orderly fashion, thank you."

I rush over to Sam's lifeless body, as if my brain has sent a message to my feet to move, to do something, anything. I shake his shoulders; the sight of my best friend's body lying perfectly still, exposed on stage, completely floors me.

"Sam? Talk to me, mate?"

I check for a pulse, and he's stopped breathing. *Fuck me, I'm way out of my depth here.* Totally on autopilot, I start to do chest compressions. I'm banging on his chest, trying not to freak the fuck out and begging him not to die, all at the same time. I can't help the tremor in my voice as I curse him sternly.

"Come on, Sam, breathe, you absolute prick! Don't you dare die on me, *you selfish motherfucker!"*

After a few minutes, he's not responding to my chest compressions. I swallow hard as the harsh reality of what I have to do next sucker punches me right in the gut. He's going to make me give him the kiss of life. *Fuck my life.*

I place one hand on Sam's forehead and two fingers under his chin. I gently tilt his head back and lift his chin. I take another deep, calming breath and place the heel of one hand in the centre of his chest, pressing down on his breastbone to release the pressure. I repeat this around twenty times. *Fuck, he's still not breathing.*

Brody squeezes my shoulder.

"Mate, stop, you've done all you can, he's not breathing."

He says so softly, I barely hear him.

"I'm not fucking giving up on him!"

My voice is trembling as I say those words. I make sure his airway is open, pinch his nose closed, and I take a deep breath, sealing my lips around his. *I can't believe I'm fucking doing this again.* I blow into his mouth until I see his chest rise. I repeat these four or five times until I hear him start to gasp for breath and blindly grab my t-shirt in his fist. I fall backwards on my arse, scrambling backwards, until I'm leaning on Lucas' drum kit. I stare off into space, almost disbelieving at what just happened, and without warning, I vomit all over the stage as the paramedics arrive.

***

I wake up to the headline *"The rise and fall of Samson Newbolt"* splashed across the newspapers. I turn on the TV as I set out on my early-morning run on the treadmill. I usually run around the grounds of our Vengeance compound, but this morning, I don't want to face anyone.

"The future of world-famous rock band Rancid Vengeance has been thrown into doubt. After the bad boy, front man, Samson Newbolt, collapsed on stage in front of an intimate crowd of one thousand die-hard fans at The Roundhouse last night. Last night, saw the band's first gig to showcase their brand-new album before the pending release date. Speculation that Samson's collapse is drug-related, and sources close to the band say, 'This was the final nail in the coffin for Newbolt.' Rancid Vengeance has been in the music industry for fifteen years, with a string of prestigious awards under its belt. More recently, the band has been inducted into Rock's Hall of Fame. Newbolt, thirty-five, previously linked to a string of women, more recently Lyla Hudson, former Hell on Heels front woman..."

I point the remote control at the TV, not wanting to hear any more of the absolute bullshit coming out of the news anchor's mouth, slowing my run to a brisk walk. I turn to the doorway of my home gym to see Zeppelin leaning against the doorjamb, her hand pressed to her stomach and her hair perfectly sleep-mussed.

"Morning, handsome Jack."

She says, her voice still thick with sleep.

"Morning, beautiful."

I flash her a smile, but I know it doesn't reach my eyes.

"Is there any news on Sam?"

She asks. I stop the treadmill and turn to face her as she moves farther into the room, her hand not moving from her small, barely there bump.

"They took him to a private hospital and resumed his bipolar medication to regulate his moods. They diagnosed him with severe exhaustion and sent him to a rehabilitation centre in Arizona for six months."

It's all everyone's talking about, speculating on whether Sam's collapse was drug-related, whether his marriage is on the rocks, and if he's been having an affair with Lyla Hudson. *Fucking journalist scum bags.* As a band, we decided to continue promoting the new album without Sam, doing interviews with radio stations and TV shows. However, with M.J.'s blessing, we cancelled our upcoming tour indefinitely while Sam recovers, and we will take a hiatus from the music industry after the album's release.

"I don't know how much more we can fucking take, Zeppelin. I'm exhausted."

My voice doesn't sound like my own, and her silver eyes soften as she moves closer to me, stepping into me. I envelope her in my arms and the weight of everything, Sam's breakdown, the rumours surrounding the band, the constant pressure to keep it together and put a smile on my face, it's worn me down over the last twenty-four hours, more than I care to admit.

"I know, babe."

She says quietly, as she hugs me tighter to her.

"But you're doing the right thing. You're just doing what's best for Sam, and for the band, that's all that counts. You must know that, right?"

I swallow hard, feeling the tightness in my chest. The media circus surrounding Sam's collapse has been relentless. It's like they have taken his pain and twisted it into something sordid, turning every rumour into a headline, dragging us all into this fucking mess. They don't care about the truth; they just want a scandal to sell. That's what makes me sick, all they care about is the drama, the dirt. They don't see the human being behind the story.

"I just don't know how much longer I can pretend like everything's fine."

I admit, my voice is low.

"They think he's been sleeping with Lyla Hudson behind Peyton's back! How the fuck do they think that feels for her listening to them talk bullshit about her husband when they've just lost their fucking daughter! It's sick!"

I raise my voice a few decibels louder than necessary, the weight of the rumours, the lies, the chaos, it all feels like it's crushing me.

"It feels like everything's falling apart!"

I bury my face into her neck, breathing in the scent of her, as she presses herself closer to me. I can feel her breasts crushed against me, her nipples pebbled into hard, erect buds through her pyjama t-shirt, and I feel oddly turned on. I don't know whether it's a mixture of emotions barrelling through me, or I need something to take my mind off everything that has happened over the last twenty-four hours. But I lift my head up, and our eyes lock. I can feel her heart pounding in her chest and her warm, minty breath gusting against my cheek. Her eyes turn smoky with pure lust, and I can feel the heat radiating from her. We're silent for a few moments, and it's a race as to who can get naked the fastest. She jumps up, wrapping her legs around me and her arms snake around my neck, I stride with purpose across the room with her attached to me and I slam her against the wall. I devour her mouth, as if it's the last thing I'll ever do, the velvet of her tongue teasing and caressing my mouth. She reaches between us to grab my already hard cock and fists me a few times. I gasp at the feel of her stroking me, as I skate my hand down and run my finger through her dampness. She moans softly in my ear and leans in to whisper.

"*Fuck,* I need you inside me, Jax!"

Her voice was breathless and desperate, as I find her entrance and I shove upward, impaling her on my waiting firmness. She whimpers softly as I allow her to adjust to my length; it's deep at this angle. I feel her pussy swallow my cock whole, and I throw my head back, smacking it against the wall, as I cry out with pleasure.

"Oh, God! Jax!"

She yells as she lifts herself up and down, riding my cock. I pick up the pace, moving in and out of her slick heat. She wraps her arms around my neck, burying her face in my neck to stifle her moans of pleasure. She feels almost too good, as my pace quickens. I can feel her orgasm cresting to the surface like a tidal wave waiting to hit. Her pussy ripples around my cock.

"*Fuck!* I need it harder, Jax! I need you to fuck me! Oh God! And don't you dare fucking stop!"

She demands, as I thrust so deep, I can feel my hardness bump her cervix.

"I can feel you throbbing around my cock, sweetheart. You're close."

She hums with pleasure. I piston in and out of her, fucking her hard like she asked, as she explodes around me.

"I'm coming, fuck, Jax, I'm coming! Jax! Oh God! Yes!"

She yells, and my orgasm is right behind hers, as my hot seed spurts inside her, causing a second orgasm to detonate from deep within her. She cries out around my hand, and as we come down from our orgasms, the room is silent. The only sound is our breathless, post-orgasmic pants. I hold her still for a few moments, allowing her breathing to return to normal before slipping out of her and setting her down on wobbly legs. *Well, that was unexpected.*

41

Jax

Every morning for the past month, I had woken up before her, just to watch her sleep for a few moments longer. I cherished those few extra minutes. Her hand instinctively rested on her stomach even in slumber. It was subtle now, just the beginnings of a bump, but it was there, a sign of the life we had created together. I couldn't help but reach out sometimes, my hand brushing gently over her stomach.

She stirs, her sleepy silver eyes turning to meet mine with a smile that mirrors my own.

"I can feel you staring, handsome Jack."

She teases, her voice thick with sleep, as she turns on her side to face me.

"Can you blame me?"

I counter, leaning down to press a chaste kiss to her forehead.

"You're carrying my baby. I'll probably be staring at you like this for the next nine months!"

She laughs softly, the melodic sound filling the room, as she presses her hand to my warm chest and lets out a long, drawn-out sigh.

“I guess I’ll have to get used to it.”

She rolls her eyes dramatically, and I chuckle softly. She stretches out lazily, the morning sunlight filtering through the floor-to-ceiling windows, casting an ethereal glow across her face, and I can’t take my fucking eyes off her. The sunlight dances across her skin as she blinks up at me, and she stretches her arms above her head, her body arching slightly. I’m struck again by how effortlessly beautiful she is. She props herself up on her elbows; I trace my finger across the curve of her shoulder, and she shivers.

“You’re the first thing I see every morning, and it makes the rest of the day easier to get through, knowing you’re here waiting for me.”

She melts at my words and cocks her eyebrow.

“Barefoot and pregnant?”

She says wryly, and I laugh as I shake my head.

“I was going for radiant and irresistible, but sure, if you want to add ‘barefoot and pregnant,’ who am I to argue?”

She rolls her eyes, but she can’t hide the smile tugging at her lips. She leans into me, her cheek brushing against my shoulder.

“You’re impossible, you know that?”

She says with a chuckle.

“So, I’ve been told.”

I admit, as I brush my nose against hers and roll us, so she’s pinned beneath me. Her laughter turns into a soft gasp as I cage her beneath me, my arms braced on either side of her. Her wide eyes search mine, brown on silver, as her hands slide up my arms and settle on my shoulders, her fingers tracing lazily across my skin.

"Is this your idea of proving a point?"

She teases, her hands resting lightly against my chest.

"Pinning me down and having your wicked way with me, like some sort of caveman?"

She states drily, and I cock my eyebrow at her.

"Not a caveman."

I reply, my voice dropping to a murmur, as I dip my head closer to her. Her warm breath gusts out and tickles my cheek.

"More like...a man who can't resist you. A man who is fucking...starved for you."

I punctuate my words with a soft kiss to her lips, slow and unhurried, savouring the way she melts beneath me. Her hands slide up to tangle in my hair, pulling me closer, as she deepens the kiss. When we break apart, she's breathless, her cheeks flushed, and her eyes full of dark promise. I grip both of her wrists in one of my hands, pressing her into the mattress. Her body arches slightly beneath me, and I feel her flex against my grip. She bites down on her bottom lip, trapping it between her teeth.

"You're trouble, Mr. Chase."

She whispers, her voice barely audible.

"I'd much prefer charming, sexy...irresistible."

I counter, as I release her wrists, and her hands immediately find my face, pulling me down for a kiss. It starts off slow, tender, but it quickly deepens, the kind of kiss that steals the breath from your lungs. Our tongues duelling, the kiss growing hungry, as we lose ourselves in the moment. I brace myself on one arm, the other hand sliding down her side, tracing the curve of her waist, the dip of her hip, until I have her leg hooked around me, pulling us even closer. She exhales sharply against my lips, a sound that sends my pulse racing. My mouth moves to the hollow of her throat, pressing soft, lingering kisses there. Her laughter, light and breathless, turns into a quiet gasp as I graze my teeth over her skin.

"Mmm."

She hums as I groan against her mouth, pressing my hard body into her soft one. Her legs shift, wrapping around my waist, pulling me closer to her, making her intentions clear, and I flash her a seductive smile as I slide my hand down, pushing two fingers inside her. She gasps at the intrusion as my fingers move with deliberate intent, curling, exploring, as her body arches into mine, seeking more.

Her hands find my shoulders, nails digging in just enough to make me hiss in a mix of pleasure and pain.

"More."

She breathes, her voice raw, desperate, and demanding. I tilt my head, trailing my mouth down the column of her throat, as her hips buck against my hand, meeting me thrust for thrust, a rhythm building between us. Her breathing comes in sharp pants, and I can feel her pulsing around my fingers. A loud knock on the door unexpectedly interrupts us. She yells out in frustration as I press my forehead to hers.

"To be continued..."

I breathe as I pull my fingers free from her, sucking them clean. She growls in frustration and climbs off the bed. I open the door and head towards the stairs. I shiver as my feet hit the cold marble, and I walk down to the door. I swing it open, and I'm greeted by a set of twelve pink and blue balloons, equal numbers of both colours. I smile to myself at the thoughtfulness and pick up the card. My blood freezes in my veins as I read the words:

Did you think it was over, bitch?

X

The card trembles in my grip. As I scan the words again, I glance around, suddenly aware of my surroundings. My pulse thunders in my ears as I step back into the house, shutting the door firmly behind me, and I press my bare back to it. I leaned my head against it, the card still clutched in my fist, and I was kidding myself if I thought this was over and we could finally have the happy ending that we deserved.

42

Zeppelin

I roll over, the throbbing between my thighs verging on unbearable, and I ached for him to come back to finish me off. Being pregnant was making me constantly horny, and I wanted him with a fierce longing. It didn't matter where I was or what I was doing; I needed to feel his cock inside me. I was starting to think I was a raving nymphomaniac, but my stomach has other ideas, as it roils violently, and I suddenly feel like I'm going to throw up. I leap off the bed and into the en-suite bathroom, dropping to my knees and vomiting into the toilet bowl. I grip the edge of the cold porcelain as wave after wave of nausea crashes over me. My breath comes in ragged gasps between heaves, and when it finally subsides, I collapse back against the cool tiles, wiping my mouth with the back of my hand, and I press a shaky hand to my stomach.

"You're going to be exactly like your daddy, trouble!"

I whisper to the foetus growing inside me, as I reach for the sink and pull myself to my feet, avoiding my reflection in the mirror. Turning the tap on, I grab my toothbrush, apply some toothpaste, and brush my teeth to rid myself of the acrid taste of vomit in my mouth. When I finish, I spit out into the sink and splash cold water onto my face. Turning off the tap, I grab a towel and pat my face dry, finally allowing myself to look in the mirror. Maybe they're right, women in their early stages of pregnancy do have a certain glow. My hair is super short and glossy. My silver eyes are wide as I take in the sight of my boobs. Despite the tenderness, they look amazing!

I pad across the soft carpet and back into the bedroom; I dress quietly, opting for a pair of loose grey jogging bottoms, a black vest top, and a black chunky knit cardigan. I quickly brush my short hair, secure it in a black headband, and walk down the stairs. The silence feels almost eerie. It's almost too quiet. I can't hear the tip-taps of Jericho's paws across the floor and the infectious giggles from Thea.

"Jax?"

I call out softly as I walk across the marbled hallway floor, and I can hear hushed voices as I go into the kitchen. That's when I see him, Jax leaning on the kitchen island, his head in his hands, his shoulders hunched and heaving. The vein in his neck looks like it's about to explode, and his biceps are taut. He's surrounded by Lucas, Brody, Cole, Trey, Kai, and Jace.

"Jax, baby? W...what's going on?"

I ask apprehensively, the tremor in my voice betraying me. He lifts his head, and his eyes find mine, as he shakes his head slowly.

"I...I...I'm so fucking sorry."

He murmurs, pushing a crumpled card across the kitchen island, and I freeze as I open it up and see the words.

Did you think this was over, bitch?

X

The room seems to tilt beneath me as I stare at the card in my hands, and I discard it as if it has burned me. My stomach churns, the nausea returning with full force. I look up at Jax, my throat tight, and my gaze flicks to the other men gathered around him. Lucas, Brody, Cole, Trey, Kai, and Jace, their faces tense, eyes locked on me.

"What the fuck is going on?"

I repeat, my voice harder this time. The weight of their stares, the tension in the room thick and almost suffocating. Jax doesn't meet my eyes at first. His head hangs low, like he's ashamed, like he's already blaming himself. But when he lifts it, I can see the deep frustration in his dark eyes. He steps away from the kitchen island and strides towards me. He stops in front of me, his face inches from mine, as he cups my face in both of his hands, our eyes locking.

"Look at me, Zeppelin. No one is going to hurt you, Thea, or our baby, I fucking promise you."

His voice filled with such conviction, I have no doubt in my mind that he would make good on his promise. A tear slips down my cheek, and he wipes it away with the pad of his thumb. He kisses me tenderly on the forehead and turns to Cole.

"We need to fucking fix this, Cole! We need to find out who the fuck is behind this! Because I'm not losing anyone else, we've lost enough people!"

Jax shouts, his composure hanging on by the thinnest of threads. His fists clench at his sides, the veins in his tattooed forearms bulging with barely restrained fury. Cole's jaw tightens and nods curtly.

"I'm on it, Jax."

Cole's voice is steady as Jax starts to pace the room like a caged animal.

"Whoever's behind this has been fucking playing us all along!"

Jax yells, and Cole takes a seat on the leather barstool at the kitchen island. He opens his laptop and looks over the top of it directly at Jax.

"Mate, you need to let me do my fucking job! I'll find out who's behind this, and I'll nail them to the wall, but you need to trust me, yeah?"

Cole states, and it's not a question; it's more of a demand. Jax stops pacing for a moment as he exhales sharply through his nose. His hand grips the back of his neck as he shifts his gaze to Lucas and then to Brody.

"I can't just sit here and do nothing!"

The frustration in his voice is evident as I move closer to him and wrap my arms around his neck. I play with the hair at the nape of his neck, and I can feel him visibly relax from just my touch. I'm about to speak when Lucas steps forward.

"Why don't we head out for a bit, dude? Get some air? We could go for a run?"

Jax looks at me, concern in his eyes as if asking for my permission, and I nod my agreement.

"Go, I'll be fine here."

I say gently, and he kisses me tenderly on the lips, as he turns to leave with Lucas and Brody.

Cole glances up from his laptop, his sharp, shrewd eyes briefly meeting mine.

"You've got a knack for handling him. Just like the rest of the Rancid Vengeance women."

He says, his tone wry as the faint hint of a smile plays at the corner of his lips.

"Not many people can talk Jax down when he's on the edge."

I shrug, taking a seat at the kitchen island opposite him and rest my chin on my hand.

"Well, someone has to, I suppose."

He looks over the top of his laptop at me and smirks.

“You fit right in, sugar. You’re...tenacious.”

He reaches over to take a sip of his coffee and regards me intently for a few moments.

“You balance him out, like Peyton balances Sam, and Raleigh balances Brody. I wasn’t sure where you fit in at first, but I can tell you’re a force to be reckoned with.”

I smile thoughtfully.

“I’m a writer. I’ve got an extremely vivid imagination, plus when it comes to the people I care about, I don’t fuck around. I’ve lost people too, and now I’ve just got someone else I’m terrified of losing.”

I move my hand subconsciously to my stomach, and I shake my head.

“I can’t allow myself to think about that. I just can’t.”

I swallow past the lump that has formed in my throat, and I can feel the tears threatening, burning behind my eyes. Cole’s gaze softens, and his fingers hover over the keyboard but stay still. He doesn’t say anything right away but chooses his words carefully.

“You’ve been through a lot.”

He finally says, his voice quiet.

“I can see it in the way you handle things. You care, but you don’t let that make you weak.”

I take a long, steady breath and try to process the weight of his words. I’ve spent so much time trying to protect myself, keeping my emotions in check, not letting anyone see just how much I’ve been holding onto. But Cole’s right, caring doesn’t make me weak. It makes me human, and in that moment, I discovered a completely new understanding. I’ll go to the ends of the earth to protect what’s mine. Our family, me, Jax, our baby, and Thea.

43

Jax

Sam entered rehab a month ago. He's driven everyone away, even Peyton, the woman he loves. He sent her away and refused to see her. As a result, she's gone to stay with Ruby's older brother, Remy Logan, in Santa Monica, where she stayed in the year that she was gone. My heart broke for her, and it felt like it wasn't enough that our family was falling apart at the seams. Just this morning, we had received another threatening note, and I started to wonder when this would all fucking end. The cracks were starting to show, but I had to keep it together for Zeppelin, Thea, and our unborn child. The note that sat on the kitchen island seemed to taunt me, and I had to get out of there. The walls felt like they were closing in, and the words burned into my retinas.

Did you think this was over, bitch?

X

I wanted to scream, I wanted to cry, I wanted to punch something. The note rattled me to the core. I thought we were finally working towards our happy ever after, but it seemed fate had other ideas. *Did you think this was over?* No, I fucking didn't, I had desperately hoped and maybe even foolishly dared to believe it was over. My brain was frantically searching for answers as to who was behind this, *was it someone closer, someone I trusted?* The thought of betrayal, of someone in our lives holding this much malice, sent a fresh wave of nausea crashing through me. I stumbled toward the sink, splashing cold water on my face, forcing myself to breathe, to think clearly. Zeppelin deserved more than me falling apart. I couldn't allow her to see me like this, this out-of-control mess. I grip the back of my neck as I shift my gaze to Lucas and then to Brody.

"I can't just sit here and do nothing!"

Frustration was evident in my voice; if I stayed here for one moment longer, I was going to go insane. Lucas steps forward with his one hand tucked casually into his pocket and concern in his eyes.

"Why don't we head out for a bit, dude? Get some air? We could go for a run?"

I look at Zeppelin, and she wordlessly nods her agreement.

"Go, I'll be fine here."

She says gently, the apprehension in her tone betraying her, as I kiss her gently on the lips, and I leave the room with Lucas. I head up the stairs and quickly change into my running gear. When I return, Lucas is waiting outside on the gravelled driveway. As I step outside and close the door behind me, the cold air instantly prickles my skin, causing goosebumps to form on my arms. We set off at an easy pace, the rhythmic crunch of gravel under our feet soon giving way to the muffled thuds of trainers hitting asphalt as we moved around the acre's wide grounds. The tension from earlier still clings to me, the words from the note on an endless loop in my mind. The steady rhythm of my steps, the rush of blood in my ears, it all dulled my thoughts, if only temporarily. Lucas breaks the silence first.

"So, are we gonna' talk about it, or just fucking pretend like nothing's wrong?"

His tone was light, but the sharp edge was there, as I let out a long, laboured sigh.

“I don’t know how many more times we can do this, man. We’re one of the biggest rock bands in the world, yet we can’t protect the ones we love the most. How the fuck does that work? It feels like everything’s falling apart! Sam’s in rehab, Peyton’s gone, now this. How much more can we take, Luke? At what point do we say enough is enough?”

His jaw tightens, the muscle ticking as he absorbs my words.

“You think I don’t feel the same?”

He says, his voice low but strained.

“Every fucking day, I wonder when we’re gonna’ catch a break. When the people we love can just *be* safe. But that’s not the life we signed up for, is it?”

I scoff, shaking my head.

“That’s bullshit. We didn’t sign up for any of this, yeah, we wanted the music, the fame, but no one warned us about the fucking collateral damage.”

My fingers dig into my scalp, a poor attempt at relieving the tension.

“We’re supposed to protect them, Luke. But we keep failing.”

He runs a few steps closer, his expression unreadable.

“Ya really think it’s a failure? Or do you think it’s just the price we pay for living this life?”

I take a few moments to contemplate his question. *Is this really the price of almost two decades in the music industry?* Years of blood, sweat, and sacrifice. Giving up our privacy, our lives splashed all over the front page. It’s like making a deal with the devil, and as I let his question settle at the forefront of my mind, my decision is made.

"If this is the fucking price, then I sure as shit don't want it anymore. I'm done."

He doesn't react to my words, but he doesn't argue, he doesn't try to talk me down, or tell me I'm overreacting. He just nods, like he's been expecting this, like he understands in a way only he could.

The silence stretches between us, thick with the weight of everyone we've lost, everything we've sacrificed over the years. The band, the fame, the money, it all feels meaningless when the people we love keep getting caught in the crossfire. Luke finally exhales, rubbing the back of his neck.

"You really mean that?"

I nod, my throat tight, the weight of my decision hanging between us.

"Yeah, yeah, I do."

My voice was resolute and full of conviction. Everything comes crashing down all at once. The band, the chaos, the pressure, it all feels suffocating now, like a storm that's finally reached its peak.

"How are we supposed to keep doing this?"

He takes a step forward, his eyes softening just the slightest bit.

"I get it."

He says quietly.

"I do. But you know it's not that simple, right? We've worked too hard, sacrificed too much... It's not going to just disappear because you say it's over. In an ideal world, yeah, but there are four of us that need to make that decision, together."

I grit my teeth as I take in his words. We entered this world together, the four of us snot-nosed kids who knew nothing about the music industry. Now, fifteen years down the line, we have countless awards, number-one albums and singles, and the notoriety we earned as one of the world's biggest rock bands. We're rock royalty, and I felt like we had more than paid our dues.

"I don't care."

I finally admit, my voice is barely above a whisper.

"I can't lose everything just to keep up with this bullshit anymore. I've got Thea to think of, Zeppelin, and our unborn child. I've given up enough, I've given everything I could possibly give, and it's still not enough. I can't keep sacrificing my soul for a fucking headline, Luke."

Luke studies me for a long moment, his brows furrowed in thought. He exhales slowly, dragging a hand through his hair.

"I won't argue with you."

He says, eventually, his voice quieter now, and with that, the decision is made. I'm done. Luke doesn't push, doesn't try to convince me otherwise. He just nods again, his expression resigned, and for the first time in a long while, I feel like I can finally breathe again.

44

Jax

As we head back towards the house, the air feels different, lighter somehow. But I know it's a trick, an illusion masking the storm that hasn't passed yet. My decision to walk away should feel like freedom, but instead, it feels like a countdown, like I've set something in motion that I can't take back.

Lucas walks beside me in silence, hands shoved deep into his pockets. There's nothing left to say, not right now. We both know this isn't over, no matter how much I want it to be. We still had to speak to Brody and Sam; we had to present a united front before we let M.J. know our final decision. We step onto the porch, and I roll my shoulders, trying to shake the tension coiling in my muscles, but it's no use. This isn't something we can walk away from without a fight, and I was fucking stupid to even think that.

Lucas exhales sharply beside me, scrubbing a hand roughly down his face.

"You really think Brody's gonna be on board with this?"

He asks, and I let out a humourless chuckle.

"No, he'll fight it, just like he always does. He's got an addictive personality; he's addicted to fame, and he craves attention. But he's not stupid; he can see what's happening. He knows it's inevitable; this is a final nail in the coffin for us."

I breathe.

"And Sam?"

I hesitate, my fingers tightening around the door handle.

"That depends on what version of him we get."

The truth is, I don't know if Sam is even in a place to *care* right now. He's got his own demons to battle, and the last thing I want is to put more on his shoulders. But we can't make this decision without him, not after everything we've been through. Luke doesn't push for anything further; he just nods once, accepting the uncertainty for what it is.

I push the door open, stepping into the dimly lit marbled hallway. Lucas lets me take the lead; this isn't just about the band; it's about the four of us as individuals. Sam's years-long battle with his mental health, Brody's drug addiction, my constant need to keep those around me safe, and Lucas' unhealthy obsession with Nick Slade. As I close the door behind me with a click, the house is quiet, almost too quiet, and for a second, that unease creeps back in. But then I hear the distant hum of voices from the kitchen, and it seems to ground me somehow. We follow the sound, passing the familiar walls lined with years of memories, fifteen years of platinum records, framed tour posters, photos of us before the weight of this life settled on our shoulders.

Brody looks up when we walk in. He's leaning against the kitchen island, a glass of whiskey in his hand. His sharp gaze flickers between Lucas and me like he already knows what's coming.

"*Jesus fucking Christ,* who died?"

He states wryly with a soft chuckle.

"We need to talk, dude."

Lucas' tone clipped, as Brody regards us both with a cock of his eyebrow.

"That's never a good start."

He says, taking a sip of his whiskey. *Come on, Chase, you can do this.*

"I'm done."

I blurt out as I fold my arms across my chest. Brody's expression remains neutral, but there's something in his gaze, something guarded.

"Done?"

He repeats, as if testing the weight of the word, and I nod.

"I can't fucking do this anymore, Brody. We can't. The threats, the pressure, the fame, the way it keeps tearing our lives apart, I'm done. We've given everything to this band, and it's still *not enough.*"

Silence stretches between us. Brody nods.

"And do any of the rest of us get a say in this, or have you made the unanimous decision for all of us? What about Sam? Rancid Vengeance is his lifeline. What do you think that will do to him if you just rip it away from him like it means nothing? Fifteen fucking years, Jax!"

He raises his voice as he gulps down the last of his whiskey and slams the glass down on the counter. I meet his gaze, refusing to back down.

"You think this is a fucking easy decision for me?"

I snap; my voice rougher than I intended.

"You think I *want* to walk away from everything we've built? I *love* this band, Brody, but loving it hasn't stopped it from fucking destroying everything around us! There was a time when it was my life, I lived for it! The music, the fans, the adoration, but my daughter needs me! My fiancée needs me; my unborn child fucking needs me!"

His jaw clenches, his hands gripping the edge of the counter like he needs to physically hold himself back.

"The band, *this*...it isn't saving us anymore. It's fucking killing us!"

Brody shakes his head, still furious, but quieter now.

"We're not just a fucking band, Jax. We're a family, and you don't just get to *walk out* on your fucking family!"

He yells as he starts pacing the floor. Lucas finally speaks up, his voice calm but firm.

"What happens when there's nothing left of us to hold together, Brody? Do you wanna' pretend we can just keep going until we fall apart completely? When we're fifty years old, still performing and desperately clinging on to our youth!"

Brody stops pacing, but he doesn't say anything because he knows we're right.

"Sam needs to know, and we do this our way! One final album, one final world tour, then we're done, we go our separate ways, and then maybe in...say, twenty years, we'll reunite again? If we don't hate each other by then!"

He says with a smirk. Lucas steps forward, rubbing the back of his neck.

"Then I guess we figure out *how* the fuck we walk away from the biggest rock band in the world without burning everything to the ground."

Easier said than done, but then again, we've never done anything the easy way.

45

Jax

I was fully aware that fame wouldn't fix what was inherently broken inside Sam Newbolt. But he used Rancid Vengeance as a lifeline, a crutch when he felt like he was drowning. I had ultimately set the wheels in motion, and the guilt I felt tore me up inside. He was in rehab for six months; his wife had left him, they had lost their unborn child, and he wasn't allowed to see his sons. He was spiraling, and I felt responsible for all of it. Their perfect life together had been turned upside down, and I believed it was all my fault.

I remember the first time I saw him after his initial stint in rehab all those years ago. He was still just a kid, but he looked like a shadow of the man J.D. had first thrown onto a stage and told in no uncertain terms to scream his pain into a microphone. Hollow cheeks, trembling hands, green eyes that seemed almost too bright with the weight of surviving something most people never even talk about. Sam was good at hiding his pain, and the chaos made more sense to him than comfort ever did. I wanted to reach out to him, apologize, and let him know that this decision wasn't just mine to make. Watching him break down so completely on a FaceTime call nearly shattered my resolve, but I knew it was the right choice. After fifteen years, we deserved a break—after everything, the people we lost, and after selling our souls to John fucking Dalton all those years ago.

I don't regret the past fifteen years; yes, there are things I should have done differently, but walking around my mansion and looking at all the platinum discs, the awards we've won, and the records we've made, made it all worth the blood, sweat, and tears we endured to reach this moment. We planned to wait for Sam to finish rehab, release one final album, go on one last world tour, and participate in a documentary about how Rancid Vengeance started up until the final tour. It would've been cathartic, but I was more than ready to say goodbye to this life that had given me so much luxury and privilege over the years. I had been blessed with my daughter, Thea, who is my entire world, and I was fortunate enough to get a second chance with Zeppelin, who was currently pregnant with our baby.

I was sitting on the deck, staring out at the lush greenery before me, sipping my morning coffee. It was a quiet time of day. Thea was still in bed, and Zeppelin was too. I had just finished my morning run and was taking some time to reflect on our decision. I took a sip of my coffee when my phone started ringing, the sound of Ed Sheeran's "Galway Girl" filling the silence. I answered on the first ring, and I was surprised by the voice on the other end of the line.

"You there?"

Sam, his voice raw and trembling. I freeze, coffee halfway to my lips. For a second, I think I must be imagining things. But the silence that follows is thick with waiting, and I know it's him. That voice, husky and distinctive.

"I'm here."

I say quietly, setting the mug down with a soft clink on the glass tabletop in front of me. There's a pause on the line, filled only with the sound of his uneven breathing.

"I think it's about time we talked properly, man to man."

He says, finally.

"How are you?"

I ask, even though I already know the answer. You don't call someone like me at this hour unless you're hanging by a thread.

"Sober, medicated."

He says, then adds, almost like an apology.

"For now, I guess."

Another pause, and I can hear the strain behind it, like he's fighting to keep the pieces of himself together.

"I didn't know who else to call."

He says, his voice soft and even, though the guilt was eating me up inside, I was grateful that I was the person he still seemed to turn to.

"I didn't think you'd pick up to be honest."

He says, eventually, voice rough at the edges.

"I wasn't even sure I wanted you to."

He states.

"You called anyway."

I reply.

"Yeah."

A breath, then a soft, bitter laugh.

"Guess that says something, doesn't it?"

There is a pregnant pause for a little longer than acceptable.

"Do you think I'm beyond redemption?"

His voice wavers, and his question surprises me. Beyond redemption? That alone is a loaded statement.

"Redemption? Is that what you think this is about?"

I ask quietly.

"I don't know."

He finally says.

"It just feels like...I've fucked up too many times. Burned through too many second chances, I can't keep asking people to forgive me for just being me. I'm fucking broken, Jax."

I close my eyes, and his answer hits somewhere deep.

"We're all broken in some way or another."

He laughs bitterly.

"Is that why my wife's disappeared into the arms of another man?"

His words land like a punch to the gut, but he says them with this calmness that sounds almost hollow, like the devastation has already happened and now he's just making his way through the debris. I don't speak right away; I let the silence stretch between us.

"I'm sorry."

I say it finally, and it's all I can manage. After the death of their baby, Elodie Sophia Newbolt, Sam pushed her away in the worst way possible, and after collapsing on stage in front of thousands of Rancid Vengeance fans, Peyton left for Santa Monica to stay with Remy Logan, Ruby's older brother, who she had stayed with after J.D. kidnapped her.

"Don't be."

He mutters.

"It's not like I didn't hand her the gun."

He pauses.

"I just didn't think she would actually pull the trigger."

There's a kind of grief in his voice, and in that moment, my heart breaks for him. They went through so much to finally find their happily ever after, and they became the perfect couple that we all aspired to be.

"I know I can be hard to love sometimes; I thought our vows meant something to her. In sickness and in health, I fucking needed her, Jax!"

The frustration and hurt in his voice are evident.

"She was fucking grieving, Sam! She carried that baby inside of her. I'm not saying your grief isn't valid, it is, but try to see it from her perspective, for fucks sake!"

I hear the hitch in his breath, like I've slapped him. But I don't take it back, I *can't* take it back. He needs to hear it; he needs someone to say the things no one else will, even if it hurts, like ripping a plaster off a gaping wound.

"I *am* fucking trying."

He says, finally, voice trembling.

"Do you think I don't wake up every fucking day wishing I'd done things differently? That I hadn't shut down, hadn't lashed out, hadn't drowned myself in pills and rage while she was falling apart right beside me?"

His voice is cracking now, unravelling thread by thread.

"I wanted to be strong for her. I fucking *tried*, Jax. But it was like...like there was this hole in my chest and no matter how hard I tried, I couldn't fill it, and everything I said came out wrong, or not enough, just empty fucking words that meant nothing."

"You both lost something."

I say, softer now.

"She looked at me like I was a stranger."

He whispers, almost to himself.

"Like she didn't recognise me anymore, and maybe she was right. I didn't recognise *myself*. I wasn't the man she married, or even the man she fell in love with. I was this...fucking stranger, this broken-down version of myself, and I didn't know how to fix myself, let alone know how to fix her too."

"You were hurting."

I say, unable to find the right words

"But she was, too, and when two people are drowning, sometimes they can't save each other."

I hear him sniff; he's sobbing now.

"I fucking miss her. So, fucking much."

He chokes out, as his grief comes through the phone raw, unfiltered, and jagged around the edges.

"I know."

I say quietly.

"I know you do."

There's a rustle, maybe his palm scrubbing across his face.

"I keep thinking if I'd just held it together a little longer...if I'd said the right things, or just been stronger, or gotten help sooner, maybe she'd still be here. Maybe we'd still have a fucking *chance*, ya know?"

He's silent, but I can hear him listening, breathing, barely holding on.

"Whether you choose to believe it or not, she loves you. She's loved you even when you didn't love yourself."

My voice is gentler now, as if I'm talking to Thea.

"But I fucking broke her, Jax! *My fucking wife*! How do I make that up to her? I don't think diamonds or flashy gifts will cut it this time! I don't deserve her forgiveness, not after what I put her through! I'm the world's biggest fucking idiot!"

His voice is shaky, and my heart hurts for him.

"What if she's gone for good? Because right now, that's a very real possibility, and I can't let myself think that I'll never see her again! What if I lose her to Remy fucking Logan?"

Listening to him so broken, so un-Sam-Newbolt-like, makes me feel like his focus on Peyton is deflecting from the real problem. I didn't know how to bring up the end of Rancid Vengeance, but I felt it needed to be said.

"Maybe when Rancid Vengeance is no more, you can focus on being the husband and father she deserves."

I say carefully, and there's a pregnant pause.

"Don't."

He growls out.

"I can't allow myself to think of that, it's like my lifeline has been torn away, and I'm fucking drowning! I thought maybe I could work on some solo stuff, write music for other artists, or...I don't fucking know! I feel so...lost right now, like I don't know which direction I'm going! I wake up, and the silence is deafening, just this hollow ache, and all I have in here is time to fucking think, and I don't want to think! I used to have purpose. Now I just have noise in my head and nothing that sticks. I'm scared, Jax, scared that I've peaked, scared that I've already given the best of me and what's left isn't worth a fucking damn! I feel that Sam Newbolt without Rancid Vengeance is irrelevant...what if I become irrelevant, some washed-up old has-been rock star!"

He lets out a breath that's part frustration, part exhaustion.

"I don't know if I can keep going like this."

I don't know how to follow on from that; I can't find the right words. There's a chink in his armour, and I'm not sure if it can be repaired right now.

46

Zeppelin

As the first pages of my new book unfold, a fresh chapter begins, unwritten and full of promise. After Jax informed me that Rancid Vengeance had decided to retire from the music industry, it felt like a weight had been lifted. It reminded me that our story was ours and ours alone to write, and it was full of possibilities. But a blank page was only exciting if you knew what to write on it. For days, I sat in the quiet confines of my home office, my newfound sanctuary, letting the silence stretch. No deadlines, no expectations, no Jax quietly checking in, just the gentle tippy taps of Jericho's paws across the floor and the comfort of my Spotify playlist as the soundtrack. I hummed along to *I'm the Problem by Morgan Wallen*, as I continued to stare at my blank screen.

"I don't know what the fuck I'm doing!"

I whisper to the empty room, as my fingers hover over the keys again. I click onto a blank document and type *Chapter One* in the header, just to feel like I had started something. It stared back at me, the cursor blinking as if it was taunting me. Unexpectedly, I minimised the document and searched for a book I had started four years ago, right after the accident and just after Abel had died. I had forgotten about it because it felt too honest and too raw in ways I wasn't ready to face back then. But maybe now was the time, maybe what I needed wasn't something new, maybe I just needed to start with something real and honest. I opened the document and idly cradled my stomach with the other hand, as if it was going to offer me comfort in some way. I put my glasses back on and blinked a few times, as my eyes started to skim over the words.

I built a home in the sound of your silence, echoing all around me. You were gone; I couldn't hear you anymore. I couldn't hear the sound of your laughter, the way you hummed a random tune when you were inspired, the way your voice sounded first thing in the morning, and the way you whispered, "I love you."

My eyes brimmed with tears as I read those words back, reminding me of a time I would rather forget. I take off my glasses and press the heels of my hands to my eyes, desperately trying to stop the inevitable tears from falling. The words on the screen began to blur; I hadn't even remembered writing that. Maybe it had spilled out in one of those sleepless nights. I exhaled shakily, a sob threatening to escape, as my hands hovered over the keyboard again. I start to type again, not overthinking it this time.

I'm learning to breathe again in that silence, learning that even in your absence, I'm still here in the wreckage of everything you left behind.

The cursor blinks, but this time it doesn't feel like it's taunting me. I lean back in the chair, my hand still resting on the soft curve of my stomach. I smile softly at the words I had written, feeling hopeful. I move the mouse up to the save button and save it under a new title, 'Echoes of the Past.' There's no deadline, no one asking for pages. This story, this was somehow different from everything else I had written.

This was a story I never thought I'd write; it was the story I was meant to tell. But this time, I wasn't writing it for them—I was writing it for myself.

***

The next evening, I was in my office writing, and I heard tentative footsteps outside the door. Jax had been quiet for the past few days after his conversation with Sam. I know he was feeling guilty and second-guessing the decision to retire Rancid Vengeance after fifteen years. I turned to the side, and he was standing in the doorway, his brown eyes flicking between me and the screen. I had left the document open, Echoes of the Past, not intentionally, but not entirely by accident either.

"You wrote this?"

He asks softly, and I hesitate, then nod.

"Yeah, last night, and this morning...I guess I've been writing it for a while."

He steps closer, his gaze never leaving the screen. His fingers brush the mouse, scrolling down.

"This part..."

He whispers, pointing to the paragraph about breathing again in the silence.

"Is this about...?"

He doesn't finish the sentence; he doesn't have to. I nod again, slower this time.

"It's about all of it. Him, me, you, Thea, what it means to stay behind, what it means to be given a second chance."

I explain, and he nods in understanding, his eyes searching.

"I didn't know I could let anyone see this part of me before. Or maybe I was just fucking terrified of what it meant."

He moves closer until he's standing beside me, reading over my shoulder now.

"It's beautiful."

He says, finally.

"Painful, but beautiful."

I swallow past the lump that has formed in my throat, and he lightly brushes my fingers as if he knows it's what I need right now.

I'm not sure if it's a book yet, a journal, or just... me pouring my unresolved grief onto the page.

I say on a shrug, unable to meet his gaze.

It doesn't have to be anything right now; it just has to be yours. If it helps you deal with your pain, your past, and your grief, then explore it. I had the band and Thea when I was dealing with my own grief. I had support, but you had no one. You didn't deal with it at the time because you had no outlet for it. Yeah, you had your writing, but you lost yourself in fictional worlds; you hid behind your characters' personas. But this, this feels real, raw, and honest. I'm so proud of you.

He kisses me gently on the forehead and places his hand on top of mine on my stomach. Maybe he's right, maybe it doesn't have to be anything right now, but maybe it's the right time for me to finally tell my story.

47

Zeppelin

I had been in the Rancid Vengeance compound for almost six weeks now. Time stretched and seemed to bleed into one endless day like some twisted Disney Princess. After receiving my best friend's severed head in a box, the balloons with a sick message attached, and the intruder in my old apartment. All these incidents were deemed active threats, and security had ramped up tenfold. I wasn't allowed out without a security detail, and for a month, I had been going to the Green Parks because I felt like I was going stir-crazy. I had been accompanied by Jace from Rancid Vengeance's security team. I had a soft spot for Jace; he had a droll sense of humour, he laughed a lot, and I found his Irish accent endearing.

I had started the day making slow, gentle, sensual love with Jax in our bed. He had taken his time caressing every inch of my body, slowly tracing patterns over my stomach with his tongue and making me come repeatedly. I was one lucky lady, and I couldn't help the smile that spread across my face when I relived the moment when I was in the shower. There had been no active threats in the weeks that had passed, and security was slowly being relaxed. I dressed quickly, styling my hair and jamming my feet into my favourite pair of Vans. I pulled on my jacket, admiring my reflection in the mirror. My bump was growing every day, and even though I was just over four months pregnant, I was starting to show. I ran my fingers lightly over my swelling stomach. There was something beautiful about the way my body was changing, making room for someone I hadn't met yet, but already loved with all my heart.

I grabbed my bag, giving Jericho one last pat on his head before leaving the house. Green Parks was one of my favourite places. It used to be my favourite time of the week when Rian and I met for lunch, watching the world go by, and eating homemade chicken and bacon ranch pasta from plastic tubs. We would spend hours people-watching, making up whole life stories for each person who passed. I smiled softly at the memory. The journey to the park was uneventful, with Jace and me idly chatting about everything and nothing all at the same time. When he pulled up at the familiar park gates, the car stopped at the curb, and I got out, closing the door with a click behind me, as Jace stepped out of the driver's seat.

"I gotta' take a piss, darlin', wait there."

He says with a wink, and I nod, as I ignore his instructions and eagerly make my way through to the park's entrance. The Green Parks were tranquil oases in the hectic, bustling city of London. It was almost sunset, with its shaded tree-lined avenues and acres of picturesque grassland; it was the perfect backdrop and just what I needed. I looked forward to this time of the day, and I felt like I had a little piece of heaven here for at least a few hours a night. I had my notebook handy in case inspiration struck while I was here. My feet crunched on the gravelled path. I made my way to our favourite spot, with Jace a few steps behind me now. The wooden bench looked different from how I remembered, and I could picture us laughing together. My heart slammed against my ribcage at the thought, and I sat down, pulling my coat tighter around me. A light breeze rustled through the trees as I sat with my notebook resting in my lap, unopened. I wasn't ready to write just yet. I wanted to take in my surroundings and remember the last time we were here. I wanted to hold on to that memory for just a little while longer because I couldn't look at the empty spot beside me without my heart physically aching. I traced the edges of the notebook with my fingers, trying to ground myself. The quiet should have been calming, but it only made Rian's absence more prominent.

Then something in the air shifted. I screamed as panic surged through me. I turned to run, but he was lightning fast. He was dressed plainly, in a dark hoodie, plain black combat trousers, and black Doc Marten boots. An arm wrapped around my waist, pinning my arms to my sides. I screamed again, but he clamped a gloved hand over my mouth before I could take another breath, as I felt something jab into my neck, cold, sharp. I kicked and thrashed against him, but it was like fighting steel. I turned my head to see Jace lying motionless on the grass, and he lifted me off the ground, as if I weighed nothing. Everything around me seemed to slow somehow, and my vision started to blur, my tongue feeling almost too big for my mouth. My arms felt heavy, and my legs felt like jelly. I was vaguely aware of a distinctly male voice, distorted, distant.

"FUUUUCCKKK!"

He curses low and loud. The last thing I heard before everything went black was the sound of doors slamming shut.

48

Zeppelin

My eyes flutter open, my vision blurred, as I struggle to focus on my surroundings. My head is pounding, and my mouth feels like sandpaper. I tried to move my hands, but they were bound, wrists raw against rope, or tape, I couldn't tell. I blink a few times, as my gaze shifts to the figure sitting in the corner, leaning forward and scratching his head with a glistening blade. My breath catches in my throat; I'd know that face anywhere. It was the face of my ex-boyfriend Abel. *What the fuck.*

"A...A...Abel?"

I manage to stutter out, as he looks up, his gaze locking with mine.

"Wrong, brother."

His tone flat. *Of course, Abel was dead, and there was only one other person in the world who looked like him, and that was his twin, Carston Creed.* It wasn't just familiarity; it was recognition. He was the mirror image of Abel; he was at least six feet one, his dark hair was loose and brushing his shoulders, his blue eyes recognisable to me, yet so different. He was clean-shaven and so much bigger than the last time I saw him. He looked bulkier, solid, with broad shoulders and lean hips. He was built like an MMA fighter, and that sparked an underlying fear in me that he could snap me like a twig if he wanted to.

"Ah, we meet again at last, Zeppelin."

His voice was so similar to Abel's, full of amusement, sending a chill down my spine.

"You? It was you all along?"

I state incredulously, unwilling to believe it's been Carston behind this all along. He quirks his eyebrow with a smirk and spreads his arms out to the side in an over-the-top gesture.

"In the flesh, sweetheart."

He flashes me an Oscar-worthy Hollywood smile and a cheeky wink. My mouth drops open, forming a perfect 'O' shape, and I'm frozen to the spot, unable to move. I can't comprehend the turn of events, but even when I was with Abel, I oddly found a sense of comfort in Carston's presence. I don't know whether it was because he resembled Abel or because his whole persona seemed to calm me in some way. *He was the calm to Abel's chaos.*

"W...what do you want, Carston? It's been years."

I state, trying to sound confident but failing miserably.

"That's no way to talk to the man who was going to be your future brother-in-law. Anyway, I see you've landed on your feet again, you've ensnared another rock star with that platinum-encrusted pussy of yours."

I wrinkle my nose at his distasteful statement, as he gets to his feet, rising to his full height, and approaches me, stopping in front of me. He towers over me, making me feel intimidated and small. He cocks his head to the side, making him look almost rodent-like.

"You're fucking disgusting!"

I spit out angrily. *How fucking dare he?*

"Does Jackson Chase know that you murdered my brother? I'm sure that's a story he'd love to hear."

He says in a sinister tone.

"When are you going to get it into your thick fucking skull that my only crime was falling in love with Abel Creed! I loved him! More than you, or anyone else will ever know, and he broke my fucking heart with his lies and his filthy cheating ways! I'm sorry you didn't get to say goodbye. I'm so sorry for what you and your family went through, but none of that is my fault. Abel Creed was a victim of his own fucking success! He let the fame go to his head, and I got so caught up in that, I lost the person I really was. I've closed that chapter in my life, and it's about time you did too, Carston."

I explain with such conviction, and he seems a little taken aback by my sincere words. He seems to realise, as he straightens and tucks his hands into the pockets of his trousers, leaning in close to me.

"And just how long have you been rehearsing that little speech, Zeppelin? Because it sounded almost believable."

His voice flat and void of all emotion. He removes one of his hands from his pockets, and he cups my chin. His hand is clammy, and his touch repulses me, making my stomach roil.

"Almost, Zeppelin."

He whispers, as I look up into his cold blue eyes, it sends shivers down my spine, and every nerve in my body is on high alert.

"The world will find out the truth; it might not be soon, but they will know, and it will be fucking spectacular. I will get justice for Abel once and for all."

His voice is menacing, and I'm frozen to the spot.

"I don't know what you want from me, Carston."

A tear slips down my cheek, and he reaches over to swipe it away with his thumb. He brings his thumb up to his lips and licks my tears.

"I want you to fucking pay for murdering my brother! I want closure...Revenge, I don't fucking know, alright! But I do know that you owe me and my family, Zeppelin! You owe us for taking Abel from us!"

His name hits me like a sucker punch to the gut, and I swallow the golf ball lump that has formed in my throat.

"I don't fucking owe you anything! I was just as much of a victim as Abel was!"

I spit, my tone filled with vitriol, as his jaw tightens.

"The only difference is you escaped with your life, Zeppelin! My brother wasn't that fucking lucky!"

His face contorts with anger, and I can't stop myself from blurting out.

"You fucking murdered my best friend! What was that? A life for a life? In your eyes, I took your brother away from you, so you took someone who meant everything to me. You're fucking sick!"

I scream, and he's taken aback by my words, as the atmosphere falls into uncomfortable silence, the weight of my accusation lingering in the air. He seems to battle somewhere between rage and disbelief. I can't tell if the surprise on his face is real, or if he's just a better liar than I gave him credit for. I shake my head in disbelief, my throat raw from shouting.

"Don't you fucking dare stand there and deny it!"

I challenge, my voice cracking, and I hate the way it makes me sound, small, broken, and desperate for answers that might never come.

"Zeppelin."

His tone unsteady, as he says my name.

"I swear to you, I didn't touch your friend! Whatever you think happened, whatever you think I did, you're wrong. I'm a lot of things, but a murderer isn't one of them!"

His eyes search mine, but I turn my head away from him.

"You're a fucking liar, Carston!"

The words burst from me before I can stop them, venomous and sharp. I see the sting of my words hit him, his jaw tightening and his expression hardening.

"You think I wanted this?"

He fires back, his voice rising now, defensive and raw.

"You think I don't wake up every fucking day wishing things were different? Wishing my brother wasn't..."

His voice breaks, and for a split second, I see the cracks beneath his rage, the pain he tries so hard to hide.

"Then who?"

I demand, my voice trembling but resolute.

"If it wasn't you, then who the fuck was it?"

I yell, as his gaze flickers, a shadow passing over his face that makes my stomach twist. *He knows something.*

"Zeppelin, I..."

He starts, but then stops, his shoulders sagging like the weight of whatever he's carrying is too much to bear.

"I don't know."

He mutters finally, but it doesn't sound convincing. *Not at all.*

"Stop fucking lying to me!"

I snap.

"You know something. You *know*."

My voice drops to a whisper, shaking with the force of barely contained emotion.

"Tell me."

He doesn't respond right away, as his gaze drops to the floor, and he drags a hand through his hair.

"I don't know, alright? Now just shut the fuck up, or I'll be forced to fucking gag you!"

The harsh tone of his voice made me flinch, and something tells me that's the end of it. *At least for now.*

49

Zeppelin

I struggle to process the events of however much time has passed, and I can't comprehend the enormity of it all. I shift in the cold metal chair, testing my restraints. My wrists are bound so tightly the circulation is already faltering, a dull ache pulsing beneath the surface. I lift my head up and take in my surroundings. The room is empty except for two chairs and a round wooden table in the corner. It looks like someone's living room with a grey curtain closed, a single pendant light hanging down in the centre of the ceiling, and grey wooden floors.

Carston's expression is inscrutable, but there's a tension in his posture, like he's bracing himself for something. My stomach was in knots, and I felt sick. I was terrified of what this man was capable of, but something in his expression told me he didn't want to hurt me.

"What do you *want* from me, Carston?"

I cry, my voice breaking. The words sound pathetic, and I hate myself for being so weak. He doesn't answer right away.

"You'll find out soon enough, you see, I've had five fucking years to think about this, Zeppelin."

His voice was soft but laced with menace. I try desperately to twist my wrists again, testing the bonds, but they're so tight and unyielding. My heartbeat pounds in my ears, the chair rocking slightly as I struggle against the inevitable.

"I was in prison for five fucking years! After Abel died, I was so consumed with grief that I drank myself into oblivion most nights just to forget. One night, I went on a bender and got so drunk that I thought it was a good idea to drive my car, and I fucking hit someone! This is all your fault! You survived, and Abel didn't! How the fuck is that fair, Zeppelin? So, this is me balancing the fucking scales! If Abel hadn't died, I wouldn't have got drunk and driven my car!"

He's completely unhinged now, and his words hit me like a sledgehammer, each syllable ringing with venom. *I have to buy myself some time. Think, Williams. What would one of your book characters do?*

"Do you think this is what Abel would want? Do you think he would want to see you like...like this? Do you think this is going to bring him back?"

I sob, trying and failing miserably to break free of my restraints.

"Don't you dare fucking say his name! You didn't know him, not really! We shared a fucking womb!"

A chilling venom coated his words; my mouth fell open in stunned silence at the harsh tone.

"I didn't know him! We were together for five fucking years, Carston! I knew him better than he knew himself!"

I know I'm goading him, but I can't seem to help myself.

50

Zeppelin

It feels like I've been here for hours, Carston becoming increasingly more agitated and completely unhinged with every minute that ticks by. I struggle hopelessly against my restraints, the restraints biting into my wrists, stinging and pinching my skin. He seems to suck all the air out of the room, as his pacing grows more anxious, his boots scuffing impatiently on the wooden floor. The sound sets my teeth on edge, and I can't help but think that no one is coming to my rescue. *Not this time.*

Carston stops pacing suddenly, his shoulders rising and falling with each ragged breath. His back is to me, but I can see the tension in his broad shoulders like a coil about to snap. He's talking to himself, low and frantic. I can't make out the words, but the tone is enough to make my stomach roil and twist violently. I swallow back a whimper as I shift again, testing my restraints, but it's no use. *Don't show weakness, Williams. Do not fucking cry. Don't cry, don't cry.*

"Did my brother suffer?"

His question caught me off guard, and I contemplated carefully how I'm going to answer him. *Did Abel suffer?*

"Did he suffer?"

He repeats, as I open and close my mouth to answer, but the words don't come. *Because I genuinely don't know the answer.*

"Answer the fucking question!"

He roars, and I flinch at the angry tone in his voice.

"I...I...I don't know, I w...wasn't there."

I admit shamefully. My voice is small as I shift my gaze to the floor. Carston's face contorts, and his cold eyes are unblinking, so very different from Abel's. His nostrils flare, and his chest heaves like he's trying to hold something back, but he's losing the battle.

"You weren't there."

He repeats, his voice barely audible, as he takes a menacing step closer, then another. I feel my body instinctively press back into the chair, desperate to get away from him.

"And I'm supposed to fucking believe that as his girlfriend, the woman who had spent four years with him, you weren't there with him at the end?"

He spits incredulously, and I shake my head.

"I'd just fucking caught him with his pants down! I didn't want to be anywhere near him! He had just screamed at me that he had wasted four years of his life with me, and he wanted nothing more to do with me! How do you think I felt, Carston? I'd just had my heart broken by the man I wanted to spend the rest of my life with!"

I yell at him, reliving that heartbreak all over again, and I curse my hormones to hell as a tear slips down my cheek. Carston's expression hardens at my honest words, as if my pain is fuelling his angry tirade. His eyes bore into me, unrelenting and filled with rage.

“So what? You just fucking *walked away* like he meant nothing to you? What kind of monster does that make you?”

His voice is thick with emotion and disbelief that he’s desperately trying to keep at bay, and I can’t comprehend the hatred that drips from his tone.

“You caught him, you argued, and then what? You just left him to die alone? That doesn’t sound like love to me.”

The words hit me like a slap in the face, as my breath caught in my throat, and for a moment, I couldn’t speak, I couldn’t fucking move. It’s like he’s twisted the knife already buried deep in my chest, and I’m bleeding all over again. I feel the heat rising in my neck, a mixture of shame, anger, and grief threatening to pull me under. The hatred I felt for Abel, myself, and the fucked-up situation concerning the yacht fire resurfaced.

“Don’t you *dare* fucking judge me, Carston!”

I hiss, my voice trembling, as my tears turn to full-on sobs.

“You weren’t there! You don’t know what it was like! You don’t know how it felt to see him with his pants down and another woman tending to his fucking needs! To have him rip me apart with his words and then act like *I* was the one who destroyed everything. I left because I had to! Because if I hadn’t, I would have shattered into a million pieces right in front of him! I hate that he did that to me. I hate that it came to that after four fucking years!”

Carston exhales, squeezing his eyes shut briefly as if to compose himself.

“And look how well that worked out for you, Zeppelin.”

He sneers, his words heavy with sarcasm.

“Now he’s gone, and what? You get to play the grieving girlfriend? You get to pretend you had nothing at all to do with this? Take some fucking responsibility for once in your sorry life!”

He roars, and I let out a bitter laugh.

"I had nothing to do with it! Are you fucking delusional? What happened that day was a terrible accident! I wish I knew what caused that fire. I wish I'd gotten to make peace with Abel! I wish I had the opportunity to take those hurtful words back!"

I sob, as he rolls his eyes dramatically.

"It didn't take you long before you were on your back with your legs open for the next rockstar!"He shouts, and I wince at his crass words.

"You're fucking disgusting, do you know that? It wasn't like that! Not that I must justify myself to you, but Jax found me when I needed him the most!"

He pretends to yawn, stepping closer to me and placing his hands on either side of the chair, trapping me beneath him. He's so close I can feel the warmth of his breath against my cheek.

"So, he found you like some little lost puppy? Drop the act, Zeppelin! Because I see you for what you really are! A gold-digging fucking whore!"

I've had enough of his cruel words, as I lift my chin defiantly and spit in his face. He raises his hand and slaps me hard across my face. The sharp crack of his palm against my cheek echoes through the room, as pain explodes across my face, white-hot and blinding, and my head snaps to the side with the force. For a moment, the world tilts off its axis, my ears ringing and the taste of metallic blood on my tongue where I've bitten the inside of my cheek. I sit frozen to the spot, my chest heaving, my breath coming in short, sharp pants.

"How fucking dare you! You think calling me a whore makes you less fucking pathetic for chasing a ghost? Abel's dead, Carston, and nothing you do or *say* is going to change that or bring him back!"

His jaw clenches, the muscle twitching beneath his skin as his knuckles whiten against the arms of the chair.

"Shut the fuck up, bitch!"

He growls as my pulse pounds in my ears, adrenaline overriding my fear now.

"You want someone to blame? Fine, blame me all you want, blame the whole fucking world if it makes you feel better, whatever helps you sleep at night! But that won't bring Abel back, and it certainly won't fix whatever the hell is broken in you, Carston!"

I spit; I'm trembling with anger now.

"I said shut the fuck up!"

His voice was low and menacing.

"Why? Is it because you can't stand hearing the truth?"

I challenge, lifting my chin again even though my face throbs.

"You think you loved him more than I did? You didn't know him as I did. You didn't know *us!* We were happy once! And where were you, anyway? Where the fuck were you when your twin brother was dying? When he was fucking suffocating because he couldn't breathe due to inhaling so much smoke, his lungs gave out! When he was burning alive somewhere off the Italian fucking coast!"

I goad him as he slams his hands against the arms of the chair, the sound making me flinch despite myself. My heart is pounding so hard, and he leans in close, so close I can see the fury blazing in his eyes, the veins at his temples pulsing. He moves lightning fast across the room and over to the table, grabbing the knife he left there. I press myself back into the chair and grip the arms so tightly my knuckles turn white. The knife is steady in his grip, as his chest heaves, his eyes wild, the blade glistening under the harsh light. My heart slams against my ribs as a scream rips from my throat.

Terror claws its way up my throat, and my blood chills; his breath is slow, steady, rhythmic, and deliberate. The blade catches the light as he lunges forward, and I let out another blood-curdling scream, bracing myself for his next move. But we are interrupted by the bathroom door bursting open and ricocheting off the adjoining wall with a loud thud.

"Did your mother teach you not to play with your food?"

He is half-shrouded in shadow, his face obscured by a black mask that clings to his features like a second skin. Only his eyes are visible; dark, cold, observing, as if he's been waiting for just the right moment to reveal himself. He's taller than Carston by a few inches, with a solid build, broad shoulders, narrow hips, and a posture that radiates control. Carston stares at him, confusion written all over his face. The masked man steps fully into the room with deliberate confidence, his presence commanding instant attention. He's dressed in all black, sleeves rolled up to reveal inked forearms, and a machete is strapped low at his hip. His eyes flick to mine for a moment, sharp, calculating, before shifting back to Carston.

"Who the fuck are you?"

Carston spits out angrily. His gaze stays steady on Carston, unwavering, calm in a way that makes the hairs on the back of my neck stand up. The man doesn't answer, as my gaze flicks between the two men. Carston launches the knife in his hand in the man's general direction; he ducks out of the way, and the knife embeds itself into the opposite wall.

"I asked you a fucking question!"

Carston barks, taking a step forward, his stance ready to attack.

"Now that wasn't nice, was it?"

The masked man's voice dripped with sarcasm.

"Who the fuck are you?"

Carston bellows, as the man in black smiles faintly, like Carston's rage is amusing, maybe even a little pathetic.

"Name's not important right now."

He says matter-of-factly, in a nonchalant tone.

"But I've been watching you both for a while now."

My eyes widen, and he grins at the realisation, clapping his hands, as he turns his attention to me.

"Ta-da! It's so good to finally meet you! I'm somewhat of a super fan! I've read everything you've ever written!"

His voice filled with theatrical glee.

"Hold up, what the fuck is going on?"

Carston says, confusion laced in his tone.

"I like to think of myself as an author too! I love a good murder mystery! The character arcs, the suspense, the reveal! But what I don't like is other people taking credit for my excellent fucking work!"

He grinds out with more than a hint of anger in his voice.

"I wrote the fucking ending, and it was magnificent! But what I didn't take into consideration was you."

He sneers in disgust as he points his finger accusingly at Carston

"Always getting in the way, so I had to get smart. The stalker being stalked! It was quite brilliant!"

He turns to me, and I try desperately to think if I know this man, going over my past interactions, but I come up with nothing. *Who are you?*

"I am sorry for Rian, though. He was...collateral damage."

He says with a shrug. I writhe against my restraints as the realisation washes over me. *This man killed Rian, this man killed my best friend! What the actual fucking fuck?*

"YOU! WHY? WHY THE FUCK DID YOU TAKE HIM AWAY FROM ME?"

I'm sobbing uncontrollably now and trying desperately, like a madwoman, to free myself from my restraints.

"The head in a box was a fucking genius idea! I think I was feeling particularly dramatic that day! And he was so easy to lure into the trap that I had set for him!"

He does a theatrical twirl and kicks his leg out, reminding me of Rian. The tears won't stop falling. *This fucking psychopath killed Rian.*

Carston blinks rapidly, as if trying to process the words, his breath shallow. He takes a step back, his eyes darting around, searching for an escape he knows isn't coming.

"You're..."

Carston stutters.

"You're *fucking mental!*"

The man's grin stretches wider, almost manic.

"You have no idea, my friend. You think you've been playing some grand game? You think you're the one pulling all the strings? The one in control?"

He shakes his head slowly, eyes gleaming with something far too gleeful for this moment.

"You have no fucking idea who you're dealing with."

The man doesn't give him another chance. He reaches down, his hand moving with precision, lightning-fast, unsheathing the machete from his hip in one fluid motion. Carston doesn't even have time to react. The blade is quick, so fast, cutting through the air with a sharp, whistling sound as it slashes across Carston's throat, a clean, brutal strike that silences him in an instant. His eyes widen, shock and disbelief mixing in the last moments of his life. I gasp at the sight of the blood spraying out viscerally from his neck. Carston's body jerks, his eyes going wide in shock, he stumbles, a ragged gasp escaping his lips, as his hands clutch at his neck. For a moment, time seems to freeze, and Carston lets out a gurgling sound as he crumples to the floor with a heavy thud, motionless, the pool of blood slowly seeping across the wooden floor. I sit frozen, my breath trapped in my chest, eyes wide as the scene unfolds in front of me, brutal and horrifying. Dark crimson is pooling fast beneath him, and my stomach roils at the sight of his dead, gazeless eyes. For a moment, it's as if I'm looking into Abel's lifeless eyes, and I let out a gut-wrenching sob from somewhere deep within me, and I can't stop the tears from falling. *For Abel, for Carston, and for Rian.*

51

Zeppelin

I can't tear my eyes away from Carston's motionless body on the floor, dark crimson settling around him. His face pale, his eyes gazeless, and the clean cut across his throat made my stomach roil. I don't flinch when the masked man, who still hasn't given a name, leans against the far wall, arms crossed, and the machete still stained with Carston's blood hanging limply at his side. His expression was hidden beneath his mask.

"He was talking far too fucking much."

He says nonchalantly, with a dismissive wave of his hand, wiping the blood off the blade on his trousers and placing the machete down on the table. The large blade looks foreboding and menacing as the light glistens off the shiny surface. I was truly terrified of this stranger who had orchestrated this whole thing. This stranger had killed my best friend in cold blood and was standing there acting like it was nothing, like Rian's life meant nothing. I wanted to ask him why, I wanted to ask him why Rian, but the words were lodged in my throat and threatened to choke me where I sat. The room is eerily silent, and all I wanted to do was go home to Jax and Thea.

My mind races, heart pounding in my chest as a flood of emotions threatens to overwhelm me. I couldn't help thinking about all the times Rian had been there for me; his laughter and his friendship meant everything to me, and he was the only person who truly knew the real me. But now he was gone, taken so suddenly and brutally. This stranger's indifference, his ice-cold detachment, fuels a fire within me, a fire of anger, fear, and desperation.

"You're a fucking monster."

I manage to choke out, my voice trembling with a mix of pure terror and rage. He doesn't even flinch, as if my words mean nothing, as if he's heard them a hundred times before.

"Name-calling as well, I'm truly flattered."

His voice void of any emotion.

"But know this, everything has a purpose, even Rian's death."

He states cryptically, as he steps a few inches closer to me, and I visibly balk at his presence. If he notices, he doesn't say anything.

"I always dreamt of the day that we would meet again!"

Again? What the fuck is he going on about? He changes the subject swiftly, and his voice is filled with awe, as if he's finally meeting his hero. *His mood swings are giving me major whiplash.*

"Although this isn't quite how I envisioned it."

He gestures to Carston's lifeless body, his nose crinkling slightly, as he shifts his dark gaze back to me. He steps a few inches closer to me, not taking his eyes off me.

"I pictured something...far more elaborate, something with a little je ne sais quoi. A little less blood obviously, maybe an audience, applause, a spotlight!"

His mouth forms a perfect O shape as he dances around me. *This man is a fucking certified lunatic.*

"Not this...tragedy in a council flat...UGGHH!"

He gestures around us as I press myself back into the chair, trying to make myself smaller somehow, but failing miserably.

"You really don't remember me, do you?"

He asks, almost fondly, cocking his head to the side and regarding me intently.

"Of course you don't, but I remember *you.* Every detail."

He reminds me of an insect, and he's making my skin crawl.

"What do you want from me?"

I barely manage to speak.

"Ah ha! Finally, a question worth answering!

He says with a loud clap of his hands, and I flinch at the sudden sound.

"You see, I'm going to tell you a story!"

I look up at him.

"I'm going to tell you a story."

He repeats, as he comes to a stop in front of me and gets down on his haunches.

"Once upon a time...no, no, that's not the right way to start...ahem."

He clears his throat and shakes his head, tapping his temple in quick succession.

"No, no, no, I can't seem to find the right words...the right way to begin our story, Zeppelin!"

I'm truly terrified of this man.

"Let's go back to the beginning...our dark, brooding hero, moi."

He points to himself.

"And our beautifully flawed wallflower."

He points to me as he gets to his feet.

"You see, our dark, brooding hero sees himself as an aspiring writer. After what seemed like a hundred rejections, he decided to give up on his dream, and he settled for a job in a quaint book shop. Enter our beautifully flawed wallflower. She frequented his book shop almost every day, and it became his favourite pastime to watch her wander aimlessly up and down the aisles, her fingers brushing the pages of the books, as if they were the most delicate thing in the world. Soon, she would become his favourite story."

He pauses as his hand reaches up, fingers gripping the edge of the black mask. Before I can brace myself, he tears it off. My breath catches, and I let out an audible gasp. Familiar eyes, familiar face, twisted slightly with satisfaction, with menace. *I know this man.* I take a moment to take in his harsh features. He has a sharp, angular nose, his face is tanned, his dark hair is a mass of messy curls, and a thick, dark beard covers his chin. He is at least six feet tall, if not taller, and could easily overpower me.

The recognition crashes over me, and memories from all those years ago flood my brain. The bookshop, the stranger behind the counter, scribbling in his dog-eared notebook. The meaningful conversations among dusty shelves about books we'd read, books we were currently working on, and the sound of our shared laughter. *I remembered it all.*

52

Jax

I was reeling from the phone call I got from Cole, explaining that Jace had been brutally hit across the back of the head in the Green Parks and was rushed to the hospital with severe head injuries. My fiancée, who he was meant to be protecting, had been kidnapped. My pulse was pounding in my ears, she was pregnant with our baby, and I was terrified that both were going to be hurt. As I pulled up in the driveway, I was met by Cole, leaning heavily on his walking cane.

"So, what's the plan?"

I ask hopefully, and he nods curtly, cocking his head to the side. I follow him into Sam's house and down into the bowels of his surveillance room. Ever since the J.D. incident, he's been overly cautious about security. I head down the stairs, where I'm met by Brody, Lucas, Jace, Trey, and Kai, all gathered around the bank of CCTV monitors. An unfamiliar feeling settles heavily in my gut as I stare blankly at a bank of TV screens. I fold my arms and bite down anxiously on my lip.

"Surely there must be something you can do; can't you track the GPS on her phone?"

I ask hopefully, and Cole shakes his head.

"Sorry, mate, there's nothing I can do. Let me make a few calls."

Cole pulls out his phone and taps the screen a few times.

"Mate, it's Cole."

He steps away from us for a couple of minutes and returns with a grainy screenshot of a license plate and a prison mugshot of Carston Creed.

"Do you know this guy?"

Cole asks as he drops down onto the leather Captain's chair in front of the computer. I shake my head; it was news to me, as it was to everyone else, and it makes me feel uneasy. He leans back in the chair, glancing at the CCTV monitor.

"I'm on it, boys."

Lightning fast, he types in Carston's name, and after a few minutes, he states.

"Got him! He's Abel Creed from The Poison Puppets; it's his twin brother. He's recently been released from prison on probation for good behaviour. He was incarcerated at Our Majesty's pleasure for almost five years for drink driving and a hit and run, sounds like a real upstanding citizen."

Cole says wryly and cocks his eyebrow.

"So, what do the Creeds have to do with Zeppelin?"

Cole leans back in his chair, his fingers drumming against the edge of the desk.

"I know Zeppelin dated Abel for four years. She was one of three survivors from the yacht fire that killed all the Poison Puppets. She was generously compensated after the accident; she suffered third-degree burns."

I volunteer, and Lucas's brows knit together.

"So, this is just me thinking out loud, right? She walks away from the yacht fire with her life and one hell of a payday. That's a motive for someone, depending on how you spin it. What about Carston? Was he around back then?"

He asks, his curiosity piqued, as Cole shakes his head.

"Not that I can find, it looks like Abel was the golden child. Carston just got out of prison after five years; so, he's definitely had some time to think about it."

Cole frowns at the screen, his fingers hesitating over the keys, as I cross my arms.

"But if Carston's only been out of prison a few months, why now? Why wait this long to act?"

My question hangs in the air as Cole leans forward, squinting at the screen.

"That's the million-dollar question, mate. Maybe he just got the means to do something about it. Someone could have fed him information, or misinformation, while he was locked up. Prison is a literal cesspit for conspiracies; I know that firsthand from my time in the Old Bill."

I watch him work, the soft glow of the monitor casting pale blue light across his face, highlighting the furrow in his brow and the tight line of his jaw. The room is quiet except for the occasional click of the mouse and the low hum of his laptop. Cole clears his throat, the sound abrupt in the silence. His voice is low and almost cautious.

"There's something else."

He says, not looking at me.

"I just found an old interview, one of the other survivors from the yacht fire, Jayson Mendoza. He was the Poison Puppets' manager back then."

Cole explains, as I straighten, heart thudding hard in my chest.

"Mendoza?"

I echo, the name ringing a bell in my chaotic mind. Tabloids, rehab stints, a reputation for riding off the coattails of The Poison Puppets, and desperate for fame himself.

"What did he say?"

I ask, as Cole hesitates, fingers hovering over the keyboard. He exhales and clicks a few links on the screen. The screen shifts and a transcript loads.

"He said some...things that didn't make it into the official report."

He murmurs, eyes scanning the lines.

"Things that...change the narrative somewhat."

A chill creeps down my spine as I drop down heavily onto the leather chair next to him in front of the bank of monitors.

"Like what?"

Cole's jaw tightens, and he begins to scroll, then reads aloud, his voice flat but steady.

"Mendoza claimed Abel and Zeppelin had a massive fight the night of the fire. Screaming, broken glass, the whole nine yards. He said she caught him with his pants down, literally. He was cheating on her, and she lost it. He lost it right back, according to Mendoza. Mendoza says he heard Abel threaten her, before storming off to his cabin."

He pauses; his eyes fixed on the screen in front of him.

"A few hours later."

He continues.

"The fire broke out."

I suck in air, sharp and cold, and try to make sense of what I've just heard. *This can't be true.* "That wasn't in the report."

I whisper.

"None of that was in the report."

Cole nods grimly.

"Because it was probably written off as bullshit. Mendoza wasn't exactly a reliable source. He had his own demons, pills, booze, and a tendency to embellish when the cameras were rolling. The investigators probably chalked it up to attention-seeking."

"But if it's true..."

I trail off, the implications crashing over me like a wave.

"If it's true, then everything we thought we knew about that night, about Zeppelin, about Abel, it's all wrong."

I state, my voice filled with disbelief.

"Or someone wants us to think it's wrong."

Cole says quietly.

"Either way, it changes the game."

I sink further into the leather office chair, the cushions sighing under my weight. My mind spins, trying to reconcile the Zeppelin I know with the version painted in Mendoza's account. The fierce loyalty, the haunted look in her silver eyes, the silence she never broke about that night.

If she really was threatened, then maybe she's been hiding more than just trauma. Maybe she's been protecting herself from something darker, or maybe someone's rewriting history to destroy her.

"Do you think this is connected to Rian's murder?"

I ask the question slipping out before I can stop myself. Cole leans back, rubbing a hand over his face.

"Possibly."

He says.

"But I'm not convinced Carston Creed would kill just for revenge. Rage and grief can twist a man, sure. But kidnap and murder? That's a whole different level of crazy."

I nod slowly.

"I don't know,"

I murmur.

"But someone's playing a dangerous game, and Zeppelin's right in the middle of it all."

Cole's eyes meet mine, sharp and resolute.

"Then we need to change the rules."

I blink.

"What do you mean?"

"We bring in the detectives working Rian's case. Tell them what we've found, tell them we think it's all connected, the fire, the fight, the murder. We make them look at it again, with fresh eyes. Potentially re-open the case, because it was declared a cold case after they couldn't find who or what caused the fire."

Cole leans back in his chair, kicking his feet up on the desk.

"And Zeppelin?"

I ask, my voice barely above a whisper.

"We find her."

He says, placing his hands behind his head.

"We get our girl back, and then we find out the fucking truth, no matter what it costs."

I rise to my feet, the weight of the moment settling on my shoulders. Whatever happens next, there's no turning back.

53

Zeppelin

Past

Today had been one of my particularly bad days; sleep seemed to evade me for the fifth night in a row. I think it was the unfamiliarity of being in a new place. I had been in London for three weeks, and I was still adjusting to life in the big city. Everyone was always in such a rush; I was used to a slower-paced way of life, and being here was the exact opposite. I had approximately one friend and an overwhelming amount of time on my hands. I was still recovering from the yacht accident, the cuts and bruises had faded, but the nightmares still plagued me on a nightly basis. I had never felt more alone.

It was raining outside, the grey drizzle matching my mood. I didn't really have a destination in mind; I just needed some fresh air. I had writer's block, and staring at the four walls in my flat wasn't helping. The distant hum of traffic, the sound of people laughing and chattering at the tables outside the café. My feet carried me without direction, as I pulled my coat tighter around me. I found myself in front of a quaint bookstore tucked between the café and a dry cleaner. The warm glow from the windows spilled onto the pavement. It looked inviting and was a good spot to shelter from the rain. I hesitated for a few moments and then ducked inside. The bell chimed as I stepped inside; the warmth was a stark contrast to the biting cold outside. The air smelled of old books and stale coffee, but it was full of possibilities. I could easily get inspired in a place like this. Somewhere, music played softly. I recognised the song as Duffy Syrup and Honey. I hummed along as I walked towards the first set of shelves filled with hundreds upon hundreds of books, some old, some new. Some that were familiar, and some I had never heard of before.

Behind the counter, sat a young man scribbling furiously in a battered notebook, a look of pure concentration on his face, a frown line between his eyebrows, as he pushed his black-rimmed glasses further up the bridge of his nose. He was wearing a black-and-white checkered shirt with the sleeves rolled up, ink staining his slender fingers. He looked up briefly as he registered my presence, dark eyes locking with mine for just a few seconds too long. The dull ache I felt in my chest began to fade as I continued to browse the books, my fingers gliding over them lightly. I could feel his eyes on me, observing every movement, and it wasn't awkward; I actually found it comforting in some way. For the first time in weeks, I had found somewhere I felt like I belonged.

I pulled out a book I had read hundreds of times before, Bared to You by Sylvia Day. It was the first book that introduced me to spicy romance and inspired me to write my own books. I smiled at the memory as my fingers brushed the cover.

"I wouldn't have pegged you as a spicy romance girl."

His amused voice came from just behind me, low, warm, with the slightest rasp. I turned and found him standing there. He was tall, lean, his hair a mass of dark, wild curls, and his square jaw clean-shaven. His notebook was in one hand, and his pen was tucked behind his ear. His smile lit up his harsh features, and I found myself smiling right along with him.

"Well, I guess I'm full of surprises."

I smiled as he leaned against the bookcase, watching me just as intensely as I was watching him.

"That book got me through a particularly...messy break-up."

His answer catches me off guard, and I cock my eyebrow, my curiosity about this man piqued.

"Really? Or are you just fucking with me?"

I asked with an incredulous tone to my voice, as he nodded, eyes drifting to the shelf, then back to me.

"There's something about messy love that feels more honest than the...conventional kind. Like it knows how flawed we are, but it chooses us, anyway."

I blinked, turning the book over in my hands a few times and taking a few moments to consider his words.

"That's...unexpectedly poetic."

I say wistfully, and he shifts his gaze to the floor, as if he didn't expect those words to come out of my mouth.

"I write."

He says, with a nonchalant shrug, as an explanation.

"Not published or anything, not yet anyway."

He states quickly, but hopefully, and I smile at his answer.

"Aren't we all?"

I say, a whimsical tone to my voice, and I was fully aware that I was flirting with him.

He was a world away from Abel; they were total opposites. He seemed smart and witty; we had books in common, and I wanted to explore where this could go. He holds out his ink-stained hand, and I look up at him, our gazes locking.

"Thorne, Thorne Mercer."

I reach out, shaking his hand, his grip warm but firm.

"Zeppelin."

I reply, my hand still in his for a few moments longer than acceptable, but I didn't want to let go, not just yet.

"Of course it is."

He says, almost to himself, and that smile returns. With those words, a spark flared quietly between us, two strangers, both a little broken, both hiding in our unwritten stories.

Zeppelin

Present

I'm jolted back to the present by the sound of his familiar voice. The voice that used to quiet the noise in my head.

"That fucking smile ruined me."

His voice cuts through my thoughts, and I look up at him.

"Thorne."

I whisper his name, slipping from my lips before I can stop it. His smile widens, like he's been waiting years to hear that single word fall from my mouth again.

"There she is."

He breathes, as if he's greeting an old friend. I remember the way he used to watch me, like I was a puzzle he was desperate to solve. Back then, he was just Thorne. Quiet, with a brilliant mind, a little too intense, but he was different around me, lighter, a little less dark. I shake my head in disbelief and look up at him.

"I never forgot you, Thorne."

My voice is soft as I swallow past the lump that's formed in my throat. The man standing in front of me wasn't the Thorne Mercer that I once knew. My heartbeat started to quicken, my mind spinning.

"You stopped coming to the shop after your book got published. I thought it was something I'd done wrong."

The hurt in his voice is evident, and I shake my head.

"It wasn't like that!"

My throat constricted, my breath hitching as icy fear gripped me.

"You broke me, Zeppelin! Everything I wrote after you left seemed...insignificant...fucking meaningless without anyone to share it with! You were my FUCKING MUSE!"

He raises his voice as a tear slips down my cheek.

"I remember the first time we met; you told me about the accident and how everything you wrote after felt shallow...I didn't know how to respond before because I didn't get it, but now...Now I think I do!"

His voice falters as I writhe against my restraints again.

"W...what do you want from me, Thorne?"

I choke out, desperate to quell the sob I can feel trying to escape. *Please don't hurt us, Thorne. Please.*

"I want us to write the ending we were supposed to have! Like Ava and Gideon! Like Ana and Christian! Like Rylee and Colton fucking Donovan!"

His voice cracks, breath hitching on the names as he believes them, as those twisted, passionate love stories had ever resembled real life.

"Do you think this is love, Thorne? This isn't love!"

I rasp, voice raw from the tightness in my throat. My wrists burn where the restraints dig into my skin, but I can't stop pulling against them.

"This isn't a story! This is a fucking nightmare! You killed Carston! You killed my best friend! If you loved me, why would you do this to me?"

I sob. I was desperate for the answers, but I knew he wasn't going to give them to me willingly.

"Because I loved you once, Zeppelin!"

He whispers, sincerity in his voice.

"You were the first person who ever saw me. Not as some broken, struggling writer behind a counter, but as someone who mattered! You made the words mean something for the first time! I was so fucking happy for you when your book got published! My book might have been rejected by the same damn publisher, but I was happy for you! You deserved it! You deserved to be recognised for your work! But you left me behind! All those nights we spent scribbling down our ideas, talking for hours about -"

He starts to pace the room, running his fingers through his mass of curls.

"I gave up waiting for someone to recognise me years ago, Zeppelin! So, I started writing my own stories, in blood! It satisfied the deep-seated need in me to be recognised, to finally be fucking seen for the first time by someone other than you!"

My mouth instantly goes dry, and I look up at him, wondering if this is some sort of sick joke.

"What are you talking about, Thorne?"

My tone was incredulous and barely audible over the pounding in my ears. My throat is dry, my hands clammy. I already know I won't like the answer, but I need to understand what the fuck is going on right now. Thorne doesn't look at me right away; he stares past me, as if I'm not even there. He exhales, slow and methodical. He turns to me now, and there's something unrecognisable in his expression, something raw and unfiltered. His voice drops to a whisper.

"I stopped being invisible when I started taking lives, Zeppelin!"

My stomach drops, the room starts to spin, and I grip the arms of the chair a little too tightly to steady myself.

"It was like flipping a switch."

He continues, like he's been holding this in for years, and now it's pouring out.

"For the first time in my life, I wasn't just drifting, I was in fucking control! I decided who lived and who didn't. It felt..."

He pauses, eyes gleaming, as if he were almost proud to finally be telling someone about it.

"It felt fucking magnificent."

He says it with pride, as if he's describing a masterpiece he painted with blood. My breath catches in my throat.

"What...what are you trying to say?"

My voice cracks, trembling with a fear I can no longer hide. Thorne watches me, and something shifts in his face, a slow, almost regretful smile curling at the corners of his mouth.

"I never meant for you to find out; it was like a hidden part of me, my hidden little secret."

He says softly, as he takes a step forward, and my blood runs cold.

"I kept souvenirs, Zep."

He says, voice almost tender now.

"Names, dates, places, locks of hair, pages torn from their books, my...trophies."

He admits, and I shake my head, unable to process what I'm hearing.

"Why?"

I whisper.

"Why would you do that?"

He shrugs, and for a moment, he looks almost childlike, lost in a world only he understands. "Because I needed to remember, I needed to feel it again, the power, the clarity...the silence after. It was...addictive, it was like a drug to me!"

He closes his eyes and swipes his tongue across his bottom lip, as if savouring the memory.

"I never wanted any of this to touch you. You were too precious, too good for this world."

He says, as he opens his dark eyes, and they're colder than I've ever seen them.

"Now you know."

He sounds almost gleeful as he explains that he's been killing people for years.

"You're lying."

I shake my head vehemently and whisper in disbelief, unable to wrap my head around any of this.

"I'm not."

Thorne shakes his head as he takes a step forward.

"I wanted to tell you; I wanted you to *understand*. They were all writers, some aspiring, some just published! I wanted revenge for them being recognised for their work! It should have been me!"

He yells, frantically jabbing his thumbs into his chest, and he comes to a stop in front of me, regarding me intently. *What kind of person does this? Oh God, did I drive him to do this? Or was he always destined to be a killer?*

"But now you know, I can't let you leave."

He yells, voice cracking with fury, and his dark eyes blaze, wild and unhinged. He storms toward me, closing the distance in a few long strides, my heart hammering in my chest. He stops inches from me, breathing hard, his chest rising and falling, then, with a trembling hand, he reaches out and brushes a lock of hair from my face. The gesture, once tender and reverent, now makes my skin crawl. I flinch at his touch, bile rising in my throat. *That hand, how many lives had it ended? How many final breaths had it stolen?* He's killed people, not in self-defence, not by accident, but fucking deliberately, methodically. All under the guise of petty revenge. I felt sick. What kind of person does that? *Was there something I missed? Some sort of warning sign was buried in the time we spent together. Did I drive him to this?* Or was he always destined to become the Red Quill killer? He smiles, slow, twisted, almost mournful, as he storms toward me, and I brace myself, twisting as far as the ropes will allow. His hand shoots out, grabbing my arm with bruising force. He yanks me sideways, and the chair tips with a sickening thud. I crash into the edge of the desk, the corner slamming into my ribs. Pain explodes through my side, sharp and breath-stealing. I cry out, the sound raw and involuntary. *My baby, please God no, please don't hurt my baby.*

"Stop fighting me!"

He snarls, voice cracking with something between desperation and fury. I don't stop, I kick out blindly, the chair scraping violently across the floor. My foot connects with something, and he stumbles back with a grunt. In that moment, my eyes dart to the desk. A heavy glass paperweight sits just within reach, glinting under the overhead light. I lunge as far as I can, straining against the ropes, and manage to knock it off the edge. It clatters to the floor, he turns just as I hook it with my foot and fling it upward, it hits his shoulder with a dull thud. He roars in pain, staggering back, clutching his arm.

"You fucking bitch!"

I try to use the moment to wriggle free, but the ropes are too tight. My wrists are slick with sweat and blood now, but not enough to slip through. I'm still bound, still vulnerable, still in danger from this fucking psychopath. He recovers quickly, as he lunges again, and this time, I can't move. His elbow clips the side of my head with brutal force. White-hot pain erupts behind my eyes, and the world tilts. My vision blurs, I slump in the chair, dazed, blood trickling warm and slow from a gash above my eyebrow. Not life-threatening, but enough to leave me dizzy and disoriented. He stands over me, panting, chest rising and falling like a man on the edge of something irreversible. His eyes flicker with something I can't quite put my finger on, regret? Rage? Madness? I can't tell; I don't care, because I'm not done fighting, not yet.

54

Zeppelin

The room spins, blood dripping steadily from the gash above my eyebrow, warm and sticky, blurring my vision. My wrists burn, raw from the ropes, and every breath sends a jolt of agony through my ribs where the desk struck me. Thorne paces in front of me; he's muttering to himself now, incoherent words that I can't quite make out. The chair is now upright, and I'm in the same position as I was before.

"They weren't innocent."

He growls, finally.

"None of them, they fucking deserved it! Every single one of them!"

I try to stay still, try not to provoke him further, but the chair creaks beneath me, and his head snaps toward me like a predator.

"You think I'm a monster."

He says, voice trembling, as if my opinion of him means something to him. He steps closer, and I brace myself, heart thundering. His hand shoots out again, this time grabbing my chin, forcing my face upward. His grip is bruising, deft fingers digging into my jaw.

"You of all people were supposed to understand."

He whispers.

"You were supposed to see me."

I twist away, and he lets go, but not before his fingernails rake across my cheek, leaving behind a stinging trail. I cry out, more from shock than pain. Thorne's expression hardens, something cold behind his eyes, causing me a chill to make its way down my spine. His hand darts towards the table beside him, fingers closing around his machete. The metal catches the dim light as he lifts it, looking from the machete to me and back again. Instinct takes over, and I jerk sideways, the chair legs screeching against the floor, and my world tilts as I throw my weight in the opposite direction. Desperate to get out of his reach, the chair tips, and I crash to the ground with a sickening thud that knocks the air temporarily from my lungs. I can't catch my breath, and for a second, everything is still, my eyes flickering shut. I hear him shuffling around the room, and I don't move, I don't speak.

"Zeppelin?"

His voice is barely audible, with something that sounds like panic. *He thinks he's killed me*. I hear a sudden sound, a loud bang, from the front door. Another bang, louder than the previous, urgent now.

"Police!"

A voice shouts.

"Open the door!"

Relief washes over every inch of me, and I start to think that maybe it was Cole or Jax who called them. Maybe a neighbour who heard the crash, or maybe it was simply fate, finally decided to intervene. I hear drawers opening, something metal clattering to the floor. He's looking for a way out, or a weapon, as the front door bursts open.

"Clear left!"

Someone shouts.

"We've got movement!"

Boots thunder through the flat, flashlights slice through the dimness. I scream as loud as I can. A group of armed police officers in full uniforms and bullet-proof vests, and I recognise the two officers who were investigating Rian's murder, Detective Maddox and Detective Fellows.

"She's in here!"

Detective Fellows yells.

"We've got her!"

Two more officers rush in behind him, one crouches down on his haunches and cuts the ropes at my wrists. I start sobbing, clutching my ribs, as another gently lifts my chin, inspecting the bleeding cut on my face.

"You're safe now, sweetheart."

He says softly, almost sympathetically.

"We've got you."

But I'm not safe, not yet, because somewhere in this flat, Thorne is still on the loose, still dangerous. A crash echoes from somewhere in the back of the room, as the officers draw their weapons and fan out, shouting commands. I choke on a sob I didn't feel coming. Detective Maddox and Detective Fellows push through the swarm. One of them calls my name, but it barely registers. My eyes blur, my body shaking violently. I'm not sure I'm even breathing anymore; I can feel hands on me, as the world goes dark.

55

Jax

Cole made a few more calls, and after receiving some information from an old police friend, we headed over to a block of flats in Peckham. The place was already swarming with uniforms and flashing blue lights. My pulse thundered in my ears as we pulled up, the knot in my stomach growing tighter with every step closer to the scene. Relief crashed into me all at once as two paramedics emerged from the building, wheeling a stretcher between them. Zeppelin was lying motionless, strapped down, her face pale and streaked with blood. Her dark hair clung to her forehead, her lips parted slightly, and her wrists. *Jesus fucking Christ*, her wrists were raw, bruised, and covered in blood. She looked so small, so fragile. I shifted to run to her, but Lucas caught my shoulder with a firm grip, holding me back.

"Let them work, man."

He says quietly, his voice tight with emotion. Detective Fellows walks beside the stretcher, his expression grim and unreadable.

"Get her in the ambulance."

He instructs the paramedics.

"She needs to be checked over immediately."

They wheeled her toward the waiting vehicle, and I couldn't hold back any longer. I broke free from Lucas's grip and rushed to her side as they were lifting the stretcher into the back.

"Wait, please."

I said, breathless.

"I need to be with her."

One of the paramedics, a tall red-haired man with a kind face, looked me over quickly and nodded questioningly, but didn't say anything. He steps aside, and I climb in, settling beside her as the doors shut behind us. The inside of the ambulance was bright and sterile, the hum of equipment and the beeping of monitors filling the silence. The paramedic, Regan, began checking her vitals, his movements swift but careful.

"She's stable."

He says, more to himself than to me.

"Pulse is weak, but steady. She's dehydrated, and there's evidence of blunt force trauma to the ribs and head. We'll need to scan for a concussion."

I reached for her hand; her fingers were cold, limp in mine. I swallowed hard, trying to keep it together.

"She's pregnant."

My voice hoarse, desperate to quell the tears I could feel burning behind my eyes.

"Please...please, just make sure our baby's ok."

I plead, Regan's eyes flicking to me, then back to her, nodding curtly. *I can't lose both, please God.*

"We'll do everything we can."

As the ambulance pulled away, I kept my eyes fixed on her face, willing her to wake up. I brush a strand of hair away from her cheek, my hand trembling.

"I've got you,"

I whispered.

"You're safe now, sweetheart. I'm right here."

Outside, the chaos continues. Reporters shouting questions, cameras flashing like lightning, and Trey, Jace, and Kai move in to form a human barrier. I catch a glimpse of Detective Maddox speaking to the press, his tone clipped and dismissive.

"Is this connected to the Rian St. James case?"

Someone catcalls. I see Detective Fellows glance toward the ambulance, his eyes meeting mine through the window. He gives a single, curt nod, a silent promise that justice would follow. Inside, Regan continues his work, checking her pupils, monitoring her breathing, and gently cleaning the blood from her temple.

"Something tells me that she's a tough cookie."

He muses.

"She's been through hell, but she's still hanging on."

I nod, unable to speak, my throat tight and my heart aching. *That's what they said about Ruby, and look how that one turned out.* I push that wayward thought away, but whatever came next, the questions, the investigations, the headlines, none of it mattered right now. All that mattered was her, and I wasn't going to let go. *Not now, not ever.*

***

I'm forced to let go of her hand as they wheel her away down the corridor. I follow, my heart in my throat, barely registering the blur of nurses, the strong scent of antiseptic, and the echo of footsteps. A nurse stops me just outside the hospital room.

"You'll have to wait here, love."

She says gently, blocking my path and shielding Zeppelin from my sight.

"I'm not leaving her."

I say resolutely, but I wanted to scream, 'Do you know who I am?', but I wasn't going to be *that* dickhead.

"She's in good hands; we'll update you as soon as we know anything."

I nod as I sink into the nearest chair, elbows resting on my knees. Every second feels like hours, as I stare at the swinging doors, willing someone to come through with good news. Cole, Brody, and Lucas arrive not long after. Neither of them says anything. They just sit beside me, their presence grounding me somehow.

After what feels like an eternity, a doctor finally steps out. She's in her late forties, with dark hair pulled back into a tight bun, her expression calm but serious.

"Are you here for Miss Zeppelin Williams?"

She asks.

"Yes."

I say, standing as the chair scrapes loudly against the floor.

"Is she going to be okay?"

My voice trembles as I tuck my hand into my pocket.

"She's stable."

The doctor says, and I feel my knees nearly give out with relief.

"She regained consciousness briefly, but she's still very weak. She's dehydrated, suffering from a mild concussion, and has multiple lacerations. We've cleaned and dressed her wounds; she's resting now."

I nod.

"And the baby?"

The doctor hesitates.

"There's some...concern."

She says carefully.

"We detected signs of uterine irritability; it could be a stress response, or it could indicate the early stages of a threatened miscarriage. We're monitoring her closely. Right now, the baby's heartbeat is present, but it's very faint."

My breath catches, and I feel like I've been punched in the chest.

"So, what happens now?"

I manage.

"She needs rest, no stress, no movement. We've administered medication to help stabilise the pregnancy, but the next twenty-four to forty-eight hours are critical. We'll be doing another ultrasound shortly. You can see her, but please keep it brief."

I nod, already moving toward the room before she finishes speaking.

The lights are dimmed, Zeppelin lies curled on her side, a drip in her arm, her face pale against the stark white pillow. Her eyes are closed; lashes dark against her cheeks. I pull a chair up beside her bed and take her hand gently in mine, careful not to disturb the bandages. Her fingers twitch slightly at my touch.

"It's just me, love, I'm here,"

I whisper.

"You're safe."

She stirs, her eyes fluttering open. They're glossy, unfocused at first, but then they find me. Her lips part, and a tear slips down her cheek.

"Is the baby ok?"

She croaks, the panic in her voice evident, as I squeeze her hand.

"The baby's fine, but you need to rest."

I explain, and she nods faintly, her eyes closing again. I stay there, holding her hand like it's a lifeline, because right now, it is. *She is.*

56

Zeppelin

The dull beep of machines and the low murmur of voices outside my door all seem to blend into a distant hum. I blink slowly, my eyes struggle to focus, the fluorescent light almost too bright. Unexpectedly, I feel a dull, low ache in my abdomen, not painful, not sharp, but I instantly know something is very wrong. I shift slightly, and the pain tightens, becoming more intense, and my hand moves instinctively to my stomach, as the door opens quietly. I look up wide-eyed and panicked, and he's there in an instant, moving swiftly to my side. His hand wraps around mine, his eyes red-rimmed, his stubbled jaw tight.

"I'm here."

He murmurs, his voice barely audible.

"I...the baby...?"

My throat is dry, and I can barely string a sentence together. The pain is dulling now, and his expression shifts. He doesn't answer right away. Instead, he brushes the hair from my forehead, his touch gentle.

The same doctor from before steps in behind him, clipboard in hand, her expression solemn.

"Miss Williams."

She says gently.

"I'm so sorry."

The words hit me like a ten-tonne truck.

"We did everything we could."

She continues.

"But the trauma, the stress, your body couldn't sustain the pregnancy. You experienced a miscarriage early this morning."

I don't hear the rest; her voice fades into the background. My chest tightens, and I shake my head slowly.

"No,"

I whisper.

"No, no, no..."

He pulls me into his arms, and I collapse against him, sobbing. A hollow ache wraps around my ribs and squeezes until I can't breathe.

"I'm so sorry, love."

He murmurs, over and over, his voice breaking.

"I'm so sorry."

I clutch at him, my bandaged wrists trembling, my tears soaking into his shirt. I don't know how long we stay like that, minutes, hours, time doesn't matter anymore.

Eventually, the doctor leaves us alone. The machines keep beeping, the world keeps turning, but mine has stopped, and all I can do is hold on.

***

The ache inside me was raw, and I whispered empty apologies to a child I would never get to hold. I would never get to see their first steps, hear their first words, or hear their wailing cries as they entered the world for the first time. Their fingers curling around mine, seeking warmth and protection. I pressed my palm to the curve of my abdomen, desperate to feel movement, something to let me know that all of this was a horrible dream and any minute I would wake up. A hot tear slips down my cheek, and I can't help but think that this is all my fault. I started to think that maybe we were too happy, and that the engagement and the pregnancy were all a little too good to be true. I had lived the past five years resigned to the fact that I would never carry a baby. I thought I would never know the wonder of growing a tiny human inside me, never experience what it was like to feel the tiny kicks, the flutters of movement, to feel Jax's hand caressing my small bump. The elaborate engagement ring on my finger glinted in the harsh light above me as if it was taunting me somehow, then I remembered us light-heartedly arguing in the kitchen over names, Jax pressing his lips to my stomach, swearing blind that the baby was going to be a boy, and how he'd hate the taste of cucumber just like I did.

Zeppelin

Past

The coffee machine whirrs as sunlight streams through the floor-to-ceiling windows of the double patio doors. There are baby name books scattered across the kitchen island and an empty coffee cup discarded next to them. Jax is perched on a leather stool at the breakfast bar, and I'm scrubbing the kitchen worktops as if my life depends on it. I blow a stray strand of hair out of my face and turn to him with one hand on my hip, my small bump protruding in front of me.

"You can't seriously be suggesting Atlas."

Jax says, voice incredulous, as if he can't believe I've had the audacity to suggest it. This had been the topic we disagreed on the most over the past weeks.

"We live in a mansion with acres of land at our disposal, we don't even own a fucking atlas! You rely on Google Maps or the sat nav that you insist on arguing with!

I roll my eyes at him with a mischievous grin.

"Atlas is a strong name. It carries the world, and it also, it sounds like someone who would always remember to put the bins out. Unlike a certain handsome rock star, I happened to know."

He cocks an eyebrow, amused.

"Who is this rock star? I'd love to meet him sometime. Atlas sounds like someone who would trip over the bins whilst running for the bus."

Jax counters.

"I vote for something soft, playful, like Milo. Cute, manageable, won't intimidate the neighbours, could look after your bearded dragon with a moment's notice."

He smiles, awaiting my response.

"Milo?"

I ask him, is he being fucking serious?

"Milo is a dog name, or a cat. I want a name that screams personality. Zephyr, wind, movement, mystery."

Jax snorts.

"You want to name our child after a breeze? Are you being fucking serious? We live in England, love!"

I throw the cloth I was using to scrub the worktop at him; it bounces off his shoulder and lands on the floor.

"How about something timeless? Elliot. It's got charm, it's got...weight, and it pairs well with a cardigan."

I scrunch my nose at him.

"Elliot sounds like he works in finance and someone who will correct your grammar at dinner, and I definitely don't want our child to be the grammar police."

I quip, and he rolls his eyes as he picks up a baby name book. He starts flicking through the pages, and we fall into a comfortable silence.

"What about something...unexpected? Whimsical, mysterious."

I say after a few moments.

"Like Juniper, it's botanical but not pretentious; it could be June for short."

Jax considers, tapping his fingers on the breakfast bar.

"Juniper is nice, I suppose, if you want people to think we've named our child after a bottle of gin."

He says with a disgusted tone to his voice, and I let out an exasperated sigh. For fucks sake.

"Ok, compromise time."

He says, sliding off the stool and moving closer to me. My pussy floods at the sight of him. I bite my lip, and he smirks as if he knows what I'm thinking.

"We pick a name that sounds good, shouted across a playground, that ages well, that pairs well with Thea, and that we can say with love at three in the morning,"

I nod, over this argument already. He continues to flick through the baby name book, stopping on a particular page.

"What about Rory? Short, friendly, cute?"

He suggests and I muse over the name for a second.

"Rory is adorable."

I agree.

"But now I'm picturing a tiny Rory in a superhero cape. Do we want a superhero? Because I can get behind that."

I quip, and he lets out a bark of laughter.

"Only if the cape is machine washable and if we can agree on the colour!"

I reach out and take his hand in mine, lacing our fingers together.

"We'll pick the name together, and whatever we choose, even if it's Atlas, Milo, Juniper, or Rory, they'll be ours."

We grin at each other, the argument dissolving into a soft silence. The baby-name book lying open between us, a map of futures and possibilities.

Zeppelin

P

resent

It was like my body was a story I knew I'd never finish; the scan photo stuck to the corkboard in my home office was a cruel reminder of what could have been. As I lay there staring at the ceiling, the thought that dominated my mind was that you were wanted, you were loved, you were here, even if only for a moment. *Arlo Rian Chase*. The name felt heavy on my heart, but it was a name I couldn't say out loud, not yet. If I said it out loud, it would become real, but saying the name wouldn't bring Arlo back, and it wouldn't erase the ache. But not saying it felt like keeping a secret from Jax. I had written it in the margin of my notebook when I was writing and underlined it twice. The scan on the corkboard caught the last of the daylight, and I pinned a small Post-it note beside it, just the date and a red heart. I stepped back from the corkboard and let the fading light wash over the scan, the grainy shape that had once been a future I could almost touch. I took the scan down carefully, holding it by the edges, and I carried it to the desk. I laid it on top of my closed notebook, and for a moment, I just stood there. Then I opened the drawer and pulled out the small box Jax and I had decorated weeks ago, stars drawn in yellow marker. It had been meant for keepsakes, for firsts, for beginnings, and now it held something else entirely. I lifted the lid, and inside were the tiny rainbow socks we had bought on a whim, the tiny onesie with the rocket ship, the list of names we'd argued over in the kitchen. I placed the scan on top, smoothing it gently, and felt something inside me break all over again. A tear slipped down my cheek as I pressed a kiss on my hand and onto the scan picture. I closed the lid and traced the stars with my thumb.

"Arlo Rian Chase."

I whispered into the quiet, the name barely more than breath, but it became real somehow. I set the box back in the drawer and slid it shut, not to hide it, but to keep it safe. The room felt different, the cork-board looked bare without the scan, but the post-it note remained, the red heart bright against the fading light. I left it there, a marker, a memory, a promise.

57

Zeppelin

Thorne Mercer was a chapter all his own. He was the chapter I never read out loud, the one that I had tried to erase from my memory. We were an unlikely pairing, but bonded over our love for writing. After Abel, I wasn't looking for anything serious or a relationship in general, but we struck up a friendship that I came to cherish. Rian didn't get the whole writing thing; he thought it was an excuse for me to escape the real world and avoid reality, and in a way, he was right. I had retreated into the quiet sanctuary of my own stories, where heartbreak could be rewritten, and endings were mine to control. Writing was pure escapism for me, and I frequently got lost in my fictional worlds. Thorne understood what it was like to be an author, and I would be forever grateful to him for encouraging me to pursue it further. He made me feel seen, not as a person, but as a storyteller. We connected on a deeper level, and I always looked forward to our meetings, often rearranging my schedule to accommodate our daily writing rituals.

We always met in a quaint café called 'Roger's Café' that smelled of fresh espresso, bacon grease, and faintly of bleach. It was tucked between a locksmith and a charity shop. It was the kind of place where the chairs creaked as if they were on the verge of collapsing beneath the weight of whoever sat on them. The light was perfect for writing, dimly lit, but the perfect atmosphere for a break from the screen. Thorne arrived late, always, with ink-stained fingers and a brown leather satchel that looked like it had seen better days. We exchanged notebooks like precious gifts, but there were rules: no commenting on the content unless invited, no edits without permission, and, more importantly, always a fresh notebook when the last page had been filled. It was the kind of intimacy that didn't require touch, just attention. Thorne had a way of listening that made me feel like my words mattered. His praise was rare, but when he complimented my work, I held onto it like it was the most important thing I had ever heard. He was talented; his love for the English language and literature was verging on obsession.

We never discussed our pasts, but whenever Abel's name came up, he would listen intently but never offer any words of comfort, and looking back, he was the only person who saw me. I would always be grateful for the friendship I forged with Thorne; it was never romantic, just two people who shared a passion for fiction. Thorne Mercer was not a chapter I could revise or edit to fit whatever narrative I wanted. I never knew what happened to him, and I was always morbidly curious. After he just disappeared one day without a trace, I used to find myself typing his name into Google, but I always came up with nothing. I made peace with the fact a long time ago that Thorne Mercer was never meant to be rewritten. He was always the chapter I never read out loud or always skipped over because it hurt too much to think about the cruel, cowardly way he rejected me like I meant nothing, like a discarded book with pages missing. But as time went on, Thorne Mercer stayed in the past where he belonged. He was an unfinished sentence that taught me how to write the next paragraph better. I was just grateful I could skip that chapter without skipping the rest of the book.

***

"Authorities remain on high alert, as the elusive figure known as "The Red Quill" continues to evade capture. The Red Quill has now been identified as Thorne Mercer, a thirty-six-year-old who is said to be highly dangerous and extremely volatile. Mercer, in recent weeks, has kidnapped, injured, and detained New York Times Bestselling author Zeppelin Williams. Williams' injuries are not life-threatening, according to sources. Williams, who in recent months has been linked romantically to Jackson 'Flash' Chase from world famous rock band 'Rancid Vengeance'. Despite years of investigation, the serial killer responsible for a string of chilling murders across the country has not yet been apprehended. Chief Inspector Agnes Bekowsky stated, "We are dealing with a highly intelligent and calculating individual. While the investigation is progressing, we urge the public to report any suspicious activity immediately. The Red Quill will be caught." Authorities stress that while fear is understandable, cooperation and vigilance are the most effective tools in aiding the investigation. Anyone with information is encouraged to contact local police."

A chill works its way down my spine as I stare blankly at the TV. The words from the news report echo in my mind '*kidnapped, injured, detained*' I know they're talking about me, but it's as if they're describing someone else. My name, my life, reduced to nothing but a headline, a cautionary tale for strangers sipping coffee in their kitchens. My body still aches from Thorne's grip; bruises purple and angry across my skin, cuts still raw and held together with stitches. Every breath reminded me of the hours I spent bound, as I pressed my hand against my ribs, wincing in pain. The police say my injuries aren't life-threatening, but they don't know the half of it. The wounds aren't just on my body; they're etched into my mind. Every shadow feels like him, every creak of the floorboards, every slam of the door makes me flinch, and I'm terrified. Even though he thought he'd killed me, he has to know I'm alive because how else would the press and newspapers know who he was? *They've signed my death warrant.*

I try to steady my breathing, but it comes in sharp, shallow bursts, each inhale dragging the memory of rope against my wrists to the forefront of my fragile mind. The stitches tug when I shift, a reminder that I survived, but the baby that Jax and I created didn't. I felt a twisted kind of hatred towards Thorne for taking that away from us, and I clutched the blanket tighter around me, as if it could shield me from the harsh reality somehow. But nothing can. Thorne didn't just hurt me; he stole something precious, something irreplaceable, and I'll never forgive him for that. Every time I close my eyes, I see his face. Calm, deliberate, as if every act of cruelty was part of some grand masterplan. He wanted me broken; he wanted me vulnerable and fragile because that was how he could get in my head. I try to remind myself of who I am, Zeppelin Williams, bestselling author, survivor, fighter. But Thorne doesn't care about my name, my success, or who I really am. He cares about control; he wants me to write his story; to make him more than a monster, and that's the part that terrifies me the most. I know stories have power, and if I give him mine, if I let him take my voice, then he wins.

58

Zeppelin

The lunge, the machete, the blood. The lunge, the machete, the blood. The images are on an endless loop in my mind, each replay sharper and more vivid than the last. My breaths come shallow and quick. The machete, the curve of the blade, the way it glinted in his hand, the deadly intent in his cold eyes. The whooshing sound as the blade sailed through the air and across Carston's throat, silencing everything for a split second, and there was the blood. Too much blood, spreading like a crimson pool, tainting and tarnishing everything around it. Thorne Mercer, an old flame, admitted to me that he was a serial killer. I'm lucky to be alive, I'm lucky that I wasn't his final victim. *Yet.*

"Zeppelin, Zeppelin, sweetheart. Focus on my voice, come back to me."

His voice, soft yet firm, brings me back, as I wake up with a sharp gasp and sit bolt upright in bed. My breathing is laboured, and I am covered in a thin sheen of sweat, while my heart thunders in my chest. I gulp in lungfuls of air and look around the room, momentarily disoriented, as I turn to look into the concerned hazel eyes of Jackson Chase. I blink rapidly, my surroundings slowly coming back into focus. *You're fine, you're safe.*

"Just breathe, you're here with me, you're safe. Just breathe."

He soothes, and I inhale sharply, causing my broken ribs to protest. My lungs are burning as the air rushes in, my chest rises and falls unevenly, and the memories are still clawing at the edges of my mind. Jax's presence keeps me grounded to the here and now, his touch calming me. The nightmare still clings to me, and my stomach roils. I leap ungracefully from the bed and rush into the en-suite bathroom, barely making it to the toilet to empty the contents of my stomach and vomit violently into the toilet bowl. I lean heavily against the wall, pressing my cheek to the cold tiles to cool my damp, heated skin. I hear footsteps approaching and stop outside the bathroom door. I can't hold back the sob that escapes, as I hear him hesitate and tap softly on the door.

"Zeppelin, I'm coming in, ok?"

His voice is soft, and moments later, the door creaks open. His lean frame fills the space, his blonde hair perfectly sleep mussed, and his tattooed biceps bulging as he folds his arms across his bare chest. He approaches me slowly and cautiously, kneeling beside me, his presence reassuring. His hand reaches out, brushing against my shoulder, but I don't stop him. I let him pull me against him and cradle me in his lap.

"I've got you, sweetheart."

We sit like this in silence for long moments, his arms wrapped around me. I lean into him, letting my head fall against the curve of his neck. He smells so good of Diesel Only the Brave and something uniquely Jackson Chase. His breath is warm and steady beneath me, as the tension in his shoulders melts away.

"I was fucking terrified I'd lost you."

He says, finally, breaking the silence between us and pressing gentle kisses to the top of my head. I shake my head and press my finger to his lips to quiet him.

"Shhh."

I press my mouth to his, the kiss starting off slow and deliberate. His hands move up to cup my face, and I arch into him, needing more and letting him know exactly what I need. He stops momentarily, staring longingly into my eyes.

"You're hurt."

He whispers, and I shake my head, pressing myself further into him, feeling his erection digging into me. He growls low in his throat and deepens the kiss as he lifts me up and carries me to the bedroom. He deposits me carefully in the middle of the bed and crawls between my legs like a lion snaring its prey. In a split second, he's trapped me beneath him, as his hands roam deliciously over every inch of my body, pausing at my stomach, then lower. I'm fucking burning for him as he continues exploring my body. Every movement, every touch, every caress is slow and unhurried. His palm settles at my hip and glides up slowly until it rests just beneath my ribs. He pauses there, looking at me like I'm fragile and breakable.

"You're so fucking beautiful."

He murmurs, his voice rough with emotion.

"Every inch of you."

His mouth is back on my skin, trailing a path from my collarbone down to my stomach, his breath warm, his touch reverent. I shudder beneath him, every inch of me tuned to him. He takes his time with me; there is no rush, no urgency, just a steady hum of desire building between us.

"Please, Jax, please."

I breathe, almost begging, desperate for him to take me, as he chuckles softly. I arch my back, pressing myself against him, igniting a fire that spreads through me, fierce and consuming. He crushes his mouth to mine into a white-hot, searing kiss, slow and deliberate as if he is savouring the taste of me. My breath catches in my throat at the way his hands frame my face as if I'm something precious.

"Zeppelin."

He murmurs against my skin. The sound of his voice sends a shiver through me, as the fire inside builds. I want him desperately, almost violently, as I thread my fingers through his hair, tugging lightly and pulling him closer. Every brush of his lips feels like a reminder that I'm alive and I'm not defined by the shadows that haunt me.

"Jax, oh fuck, I want you, I want you to fuck me!"

My voice is breathy, filled with need and passionate hunger. He pauses for a few seconds, cupping my face in both of his hands.

"Are you sure this is what you want? We haven't...since..."

He stops himself from continuing, and I shake my head defiantly.

"No! We will not fucking let him do this to us, Jax! I want you to fuck me! I need you to take it away!"

I all but yell at him as I pull my t-shirt off and toss it to the floor. I push him down into the softness of the mattress and climb on top of him so I'm straddling him. He places one hand on my hip to steady me and strokes my erect nipple, causing me to moan out loud at the feel of his hands on me. I reach down to play with my pussy, rubbing in deliberate circles. Heat blossoms through me, and the throbbing between my thighs is almost unbearable. It's been weeks since we had sex, following the ordeal with Thorne.

"Oh God, Jax!"

I throw my head back in pure ecstasy, panting out his name. Wordlessly, I shift backwards and impale myself on his solid erection. He lets me control the pace, as I move up and down, crying out with each measured drive of his length, waves of warmth spread through me. I move my hips upwards, encouraging him to go faster, as his hands roam all over my body. I lift my hips up again.

"I want you to fuck me, Jax!"

He shakes his head.

"No, we're not fucking, sweetheart, we're making love."

He flips us so I'm trapped beneath him now, as he plunges deep inside my slick, aching channel. I scream out at the feel of him within me; he's so deep that I can't tell where he ends and I begin.

"OH JAX! THAT FEELS SO GOOD! SO FUCKING GOOD!"

His pace is slow and unhurried, each thrust bringing new waves of pleasure with it. He looks into my eyes, silver on brown, and the pure love in his intense gaze is my undoing, as I feel those familiar flutters deep within me.

"I want you to come for me, Zeppelin!"

He encourages, and with those words, I feel heated pleasure within my core, and I explode around him, and I swear I see stars. I cry out, throwing my head back and my pussy contracting around his cock, milking every drop with strong, fluttering pulses. My ribs protest, but I don't care.

"OH FUCK! FUCK! FUCK JAX! I'M COMING! OH GOD! JAX!"

He pants, his sweat-slicked chest heaving, as he pumps harder. Every muscle tenses within him, and he finds his release. His breathing hitches as he comes long and hard, murmuring my name. I feel his hot seed spurt inside me, as my body trembles with post-orgasmic aftershocks. He pulls out of me, rolling onto his back and pulling me closer to him. We lie there in silence for a few precious moments, satiated and content after our lovemaking session, my nightmare long forgotten. I fall asleep hopeful that happy ever after isn't too far out of our grasp.

59

Zeppelin

Today was Carston Creed's funeral. I know I had no right to be there, but I never got to say goodbye to Abel, and I felt like I owed it to Carston. Jax thought it was a bad idea and protested my attendance, but I was adamant about going. I slipped in at the back of the chapel, flanked by Kai and Trey, two of Cole's best men. I tried to stay out of sight; I didn't want to draw attention to myself; I wanted a private goodbye. I observed faces I half-remembered from my time with Abel, some familiar and some not so familiar. Looking back on it now, it was like it was a whole other life, and I felt like an intruder.

The chapel smelt of polished wood and freshly cut lilies, the air thick with unspoken grief. I heard the soft sobs of Abel and Carston's mum, Avril Creed. She was an insufferable woman who thought her precious sons could do no wrong. In her eyes, they were perfect. Abel's family, including Carston, all blamed me for his death because they didn't believe the official conclusion. They hired their own private investigator, and they were certain I had something to do with the yacht fire all those years ago. They dragged my name through the mud for months while I was recovering from my life-altering injuries. When the private investigator couldn't prove anything, he reached the same conclusion as the official police investigation. They weren't content with that and continued to harass me with their wicked accusations, which resulted in me getting a restraining order.

When the minister spoke Carston's name, my chest tightened, and the image of Thorne's machete slicing clean across his throat flashed through my mind. I shook that unwanted image away, and Abel's face flashed to the forefront. His laughter, his anger, and the way Carston had always been the one to calm him. I swallowed hard, wishing Abel were here, wishing I could tell him I was sorry for everything. The rest of the service went by in a blur, and as soon as the closing words were spoken, I got up and rushed outside, leaning against the wall to steady myself. I pressed my back against the cold stone and looked up at the sky, as if it would offer me the answers I sought. For a moment, there was only the distant murmur of people leaving the church solemnly and the sound of shoes crunching on gravel. Unexpectedly, a shrill voice cut through the air, startling me from my thoughts.

"You!"

She spits.

"What the fuck are you doing here?"

She was smaller than I remembered, wearing a black trouser suit with a plain white blouse underneath. Her dark hair is pulled up into a neat chignon, and her face contorts as she steps further towards me.

"Weren't you content that you killed one of my sons, you had to take both of them from me!"

She points her index finger at me accusingly, and my mouth opens and closes, wanting to answer her, wanting to tell her that none of it is true. But the words are trapped in my throat, and I am rendered mute. My eyes fill with tears as she continues her venomous tirade.

"You were nothing but a filthy whore! A...a Jezebel who corrupted my beautiful son!"

She screams, attracting the attention of all the mourners who are leaving the chapel. I wanted to tell her everything, that I hadn't been there the night it happened, that I hadn't meant for any of it to go the way it did. But it's nothing I haven't told her before.

"You left him to burn!"

She said, each word a deliberate punch to the gut.

"You left him when he needed you! You walked away and left him to die!"

Her voice broke on the last word and turned into a sound that was almost a sob, as her husband Robert tries to coax her back, but she bats at his hands.

"Do you know what it's like to have all those unanswered questions? Even after the endless police reports? Do you know what it's like to know that your son died alone? You weren't only content to take Abel, but you had to take Carston too! Both of my sons taken by a scarlet woman!"

She walks towards me, her eyes wild and red-rimmed.

"You walked out on him."

She hisses.

"You left him to die alone. Do you know what that does to a mother? Do you know what it does to a family?"

Her voice was raw with emotion.

"You think you can come here with your pale face, your doe eyes, and your empty apologies and make it right? You were a selfish fucking bitch, and you took him away from me!"

She jabbed a finger toward my chest.

"And then you took Carston too!"

A tear slips down my cheek, and that seems to fuel her ire further.

"Don't you fucking dare! They don't deserve your...your crocodile tears! How do you sleep at night with blood on your hands!"

Robert tried again, softer this time.

"Please, love..."

He says softly, but she shoves him gently until he steps back.

"I don't want your pathetic fucking excuses! I want you to know what you did! She has to know what she's done, Robert!"

She turns to her husband, then back to me.

"I want you to carry it with you the way I carry him."

She leans forward, her hand on her heart. She's so close that I can feel her warm breath on my cheek.

"And if you ever think of leaving anyone ever again, remember this moment. Remember the sound of a mother's heart breaking because someone chose themselves over her child!"

She turns away then, as if the words had exhausted her, and Robert gathers her into his arms. They move slowly down the path, leaving me standing on the cold stone steps, wondering what the fuck just happened.

I stand there for long seconds, her words still stinging and echoing in my ears. I start to think that maybe Jax was right, I should never have come here. I swipe away my tears angrily with the sleeve of my jacket and sniff. Kai and Trey emerge from the chapel, acknowledging me with sombre, curt nods. I start to walk ahead to the black Bentley parked across the road, with them following a few steps behind me, shoulders squared and eyes carefully scanning our surroundings. I was more than ready to go home to Jax and Thea.

I was a few feet away from the Bentley when a figure stepped out: Thorne Mercer. He's wearing a black baseball cap pulled down low to shield his eyes, but I'd recognise him anywhere. My blood turns to ice as Thorne's hand is on me before I have a chance to think. It closes around my wrist with a grip so tight I knew it was going to bruise. I twist and try desperately to pull free, as his fingers dig into my skin with a grip so tight it feels like trying to bend steel. Trey moves; he's fast, closing the distance in three long strides. Kai is right behind him, both shifting into that controlled, efficient readiness I've only ever seen in old war movies. Thorne reacts in a panic, driven by adrenaline rather than skill. He shoves me behind him, using my body as a shield, and swings wildly at Trey. Trey blocks the hit with his forearm, the impact thudding, and steps in to trap Thorne's arm. Thorne jerks back, sloppy but strong, and manages to slam his elbow into Trey's ribs. Trey grunts, stumbling into the Bentley's door, but he's already resetting his stance. Kai doesn't wait; he grabs Thorne's shoulder and wrenches him backward, breaking the grip on my wrist. I stumble free, clutching my arm, as Kai pivots, using Thorne's own momentum to drive him toward the pavement. Thorne thrashes, but Kai ducks and dodges with practiced ease. Trey is back in an instant, flanking him.

"Let fucking go."

Trey warns, voice low, controlled.

"You're done, buddy."

Thorne snarls something incoherent and lunges again, but this time Trey catches his wrist mid-swing, twisting just enough to force Thorne off balance without causing real harm. Kai steps in, blocking Thorne's other arm, and together they pin him, not violently, not cruelly, just decisively. Efficient and trained. Thorne fights like someone who's never learned how to lose, wild, predictable. But he's outmatched, and he knows it. His movements get sloppier, breath coming in ragged bursts, until breath coming in ragged bursts, until finally he sags between them, chest heaving. Kai keeps one hand on his shoulder, steady and unyielding. Trey positions himself between Thorne and me, eyes scanning me quickly, checking for injuries, checking that I'm still standing. My wrist throbs, already swelling, but I nod.

"I'm ok."

I manage, my voice shaking, and Trey's jaw tightens.

"He doesn't fucking touch you again, got me?"

Thorne spits a curse, but it's empty now, more frustration than threat. Kai shifts his grip just enough to keep him still, calm but immovable.

The adrenaline drains from my limbs all at once, leaving me shaky, breathless. The bruise on my wrist blooms darker by the second, a stark reminder of how quickly everything had spiralled. Thorne's eyes flick upward, just enough for me to see something shift behind them. Not surrender, cold and calculated. Before Kai can react, Thorne twists sharply, not trying to break free, but to unbalance him. It's messy, desperate, but it works for a split second, just long enough for him to wrench one arm loose. Trey moves instantly, but Thorne doesn't go for him; he goes for me. A hand clamps around my uninjured arm, yanking me forward with a force that steals my breath. I stumble, colliding with Thorne's shoulder, as he drags me toward the car behind him. Trey lunges, but Thorne uses my body as a barrier, pulling me tight against him.

"Don't."

Thorne snaps, voice raw.

"Back off, or she fucking dies!"

Kai freezes mid-step as he hears those words, hands raised. Trey's expression darkens, but he stops too, because Thorne has me pinned between him and the van door, and one wrong move could send us both crashing inside.

"Fucking let her go!"

Trey says, low and controlled. Thorne doesn't listen; he shifts his grip, pulling me closer, edging us backward. My heart slams against my ribs as the cold metal of the car brushes my hip.

"Thorne! Please stop!"

I choke out, trying to twist away, but his hold tightens.

"I didn't want it to be like this."

He mutters, breathing unevenly, as Kai moves, but Thorne jerks me sideways. I was terrified at the thought of what he was capable of. I kicked, scratched, and screamed until my throat was raw. He yanks me towards him forcefully, twisting me until my back is to his front. A hand clamped over my mouth, swallowing my screams, as he launched me into the side of the open van. I hit the floor with a sickening thud, and the force takes my breath away. *Fuck, I think my shoulder is dislocated.* Trey tried again, swinging with everything he had, and Kai reached for the van's handle. His fingers scrabbling, but the side door slammed before anyone could stop it. The van lurched away, tires screeching until the church became small in the distance.

The light in the van was dim, casting everything in shadow as Thorne concentrated on the road ahead. My hands were shaking so hard as I pressed my forehead to the cool metal of the van's wall and let the sob I had been holding in escape. *Please, please, don't hurt me.*

"So, we meet again, Zeppelin."

I caught Thorne's cold, calculating gaze in the van's interior mirror, and I started to think that maybe I wouldn't be so lucky this time.

60

Zeppelin

My head pounded as the van made its way shakily down a rocky path; I could feel every twist and turn. The low thrum of the engine echoed in my ears as I heard the distinct clink of a metal gate and the sudden rush of water. The van came to a sudden halt as he slammed on the brake and pulled up the handbrake. Thorne climbs ungracefully into the back, and I try desperately to scramble away from him like a frightened animal. My shoulder and my ribs protest as he produces a dark strip of cloth from his pocket. His dark eyes blazed with a fierce intensity, a silent, but raging inferno ready to consume anything that dared to cross its path.

"Eyes."

His voice was soft, but his tone was weary. My throat closed, and I shook my head vehemently, but he was already moving towards me like a predator trying to trap its prey.

"This will be so much fucking easier if you just did as you were told for once!"

He snaps as he tackles me to the floor of the van. My back hits the metal floor with a thud, he grabs my head, and I thrash against him. The cloth cools against my skin as he attempts to tie it over my eyes, and I continue to struggle. He curses low in his throat, my head, arms, and legs flailing in vain. The world goes dark in an instant, and I can feel the van turning, as my stomach drops. He doesn't speak again until the engine cuts out completely, and the van door opens with a dull click. I feel his hands on me as they lift me out, and I stumble, disoriented, his arm steadying me at the elbow.

"Easy."

He murmurs, a hint of what sounds like concern in his voice. We move fast, heavy footsteps on gravel, the scrape of a cumbersome metal gate that protests slightly as I feel him shove it with his shoulder. He guides me up a short flight of concrete steps and through a heavy door that shuts noisily behind us, and I flinch at the loud sound. He sits me down in a chair, metal, cold, and unforgiving. I feel the scrape of leather straps across my wrists, tying me tautly to the chair. Fingers move deftly at my shoulders, securing me, and then a hand brushes my cheek.

"Zeppelin."

Thorne says close to my ear.

"My sweet Zeppelin, unfortunately, this is going to be the end of our story. But don't worry, we'll make it a good one, this one doesn't contain cliffhangers though."

He says with a sigh, and I instantly feel sick, my stomach roiling violently at the sudden realisation of his words, clipped and final. *What the actual fuck.* For a long moment, there is only the sound of my own shallow breaths and the distant trickling of water. Panic rises within me, but I force it down as Thorne's footsteps come closer.

Thorne's large hand finds my jaw, tilting my face to his so I can't turn away.

"You always loved the drama, Zeppelin. You lived for it! It's what makes your pretty pussy wet."

I shudder at his crass words, as he murmurs, close enough that I can feel the heat of his breath. The blindfold presses harder against my skin as he tugs it loose. The sudden rush of light makes my eyes sting, and for a second, I can't see anything. I blink a few times, and when my vision clears, I take in my surroundings properly. Concrete walls daubed with the words *"Fiction dies when the truth bleeds into reality"* written in large red letters that look like blood. A single high window barred like a prison, a metal table bolted to the floor, and the bulb overhead hums and swings from side to side. Then I see him, Thorne Mercer in all his fucked-up glory. He's wearing black jogging bottoms and a black hoodie, and he's removed the black baseball cap. His curly hair was pulled up into a neat man bun. I look closer, and the metal table bolted to the floor has a mobile phone set up on a tripod. He pulls a red demon mask that I didn't notice before down to cover his face.

"This is going to be my most elaborate kill yet! Aren't you excited?"

He says gleefully, his voice high-pitched, as he starts skipping around me, the mask somehow distorting his voice. The red recording light on the phone blinks as he continues to dance around me like a predator playing with its food.

"Let's give the audience what they came here for, a show!"

He says in a sing-song voice, as my eyes shift to the mobile phone set up on the tripod. The screen turned towards me, and that's when I realised that the red light isn't just recording, it's broadcasting. A tiny icon in the corner of the screen pulses with a number that keeps climbing, viewers joining, watching, commenting, sending various emojis, and encouragement.

"You see, I've been gathering an audience on the dark web."

He continues, almost proudly.

"They *love* a good reveal. Something authentic, something... raw and real, ya know."

The comments on the screen flicker past too quickly to read, a blur of usernames and symbols, but the tone is unmistakable: anticipation, excitement, curiosity. My throat tightens as he steps aside just enough for me to see myself on the screen. Wide-eyed, frozen, the harsh ring light was dazzling me, causing white spots to form in front of my eyes. The angle is unflattering, almost clinical, like I'm a specimen under examination.

"I told them."

He says, lowering his voice.

"That tonight would be special, that I'd finally introduce them to the person who inspired all of this. My muse, if you will, like you were all those years ago."

He gestures vaguely around the room.

"I mean, look at you."

He adds with a soft chuckle.

"You're perfect for this, real, relatable. People are tired of polished influencers and scripted drama. Come on, don't be shy! Everyone's watching! Waiting with bated breath! Zeppelin Williams is a New York Times Bestseller, but she doesn't deserve that accolade, oh no!"

He leans in, his grin stretched wide.

"Tell them, Zeppelin!"

My pulse hammers in my ears as the ring light flickers. I try to speak, but my throat tightens, and the words get caught in my throat. He circles, and I can feel my whole body trembling with fear now. I had a feeling of pure dread in the pit of my stomach, and I was terrified that I wasn't going to make it out of here alive.

"Zeppelin Williams."

He continues, theatrically.

"You've built a life on other people's stories!"

He says almost mockingly. My wrists are bound to the arms with thick and unforgiving leather straps, and they bite into my skin every time I move. My ankles are tied too, chair legs digging into the backs of my calves, reminding me I'm not going anywhere anytime soon.

"Tell them, Zeppelin!"

My pulse roars in my ears. I open my mouth to speak, but every breath comes out shallow and laboured. He circles me slowly, deliberately, and the chair shifts with each step, wood scraping softly against the floor. The sound sets my teeth on edge, and a wave of nausea washes over me. He stops behind me. I feel his presence before I feel his hands, one gripping the back of the chair, the other brushing my shoulder. I flinch, hard enough that the cold leather straps burn.

"Hold still."

He murmurs.

"You don't want to make this worse."

The chair jerks suddenly, as he shoves it forward. Pain detonates through my spine as the front legs slam down. My teeth clack together; stars burst behind my eyes. I cry out despite myself, the sound raw and humiliating.

"There it is."

He says, pleased with himself, as he tips the chair again, this time too far. For one suspended, weightless moment, I know exactly what's about to happen. Then the floor rushes up, and my head snaps back as we hit the floor. A sharp, wet crack echoes in the room, followed by a pain so intense it steals my breath entirely. The world fractures into noise, light, and screaming nerves. Something warm spills down the side of my face, pooling in my hair. The chair lies twisted beneath me, one leg snapped clean off. I can't feel my left hand properly; my chest won't expand the way it should; every attempt to breathe sends knives through my ribs. He steps into view, looming above me, breathing a little faster now. The phone is angled down, catching my body sprawled awkwardly on the floor, straps still holding me to the ruined chair.

The comments are evil, blood emojis, knife emojis, and the words 'DIE, DIE, DIE.' I try to focus on one thing, anything. The ceiling has a crack running through the plaster. I blink, and the crack doubles, then triples. My vision fades at the edges, sound dulling as if I'm underwater. I taste blood, but I can't tell where it's coming from. He crouches beside me, careful not to block the shot.

"Don't go yet."

He says softly.

"My delightful dark web followers are still watching."

What the fuck? I try to speak, I want to tell them my name again, remind myself who I am. But my body won't listen. The room tilts, and my eyes flutter, and the last thing I register is the ring light flickering back on, flooding everything with white as my consciousness slips away, leaving my body broken and bleeding on the floor, still bound, still on display for all to see.

61

Jax

I hear the whispered words 'dark web' and 'live streaming.' My stomach drops as I watch Cole's fingers fly across the keyboard, his phone on speaker. He listens intently to the person on the other end, an informant he had from his time on the police force, who happened to be a hacker.

"I'm in, there's a stream running on a hidden node, but it looks like it's bouncing through proxies all over Europe. The connection is unstable, but give me a minute, I'll try to trace the origin."

Cole's fingers never stop moving, lines of code and windows flickering across the screens. My heart hammers in my chest when people hear 'dark web' and imagine monsters. Really, it's just another corner of the internet where anonymity is the currency. I can't help but imagine what's being broadcast, what that fucking psychopath wants the world to see. I start to pace, fists clenched, my face a mask of barely contained panic.

"Can you find her? Can you find my girl?"

I demand, my voice raw, my emotions all over the place. I don't know if I want to cry or punch the fucking shit out of something or someone.

"Can you see where she is?"

I ask, and the hacker's voice is calm, almost clinical.

"There's a live chat running alongside the stream, hundreds if not thousands of viewers. They're... commenting, reacting, fucking sick bastards! Wait, there's a watermark in the corner, it looks like a signature, maybe a clue. Hang on, I'll send you a screenshot."

Cole's phone buzzes almost instantly, and he glances down, then drags the image onto the main monitor. A stylised red quill, dripping ink, or is it blood? It curves across the bottom of the frame, and my stomach twists. *The Red Quill, Thorne's calling card.*

"Can you get a trace on the audio?"

Cole asks, voice tight, and there's a slight pause, then a faint, distorted sound fills the room. A woman's voice, cracking with fear, pleading. The sound of a chair scraping, a man's laughter, cold and theatrical, as my face drains of colour.

"That's her, fuck, that's my Zeppelin."

I'm trembling with fear now, she sounds terrified. Cole's hands fly over the keyboard; his eyes fixed on the screens in front of him.

"We're close, mate. If he's streaming, he's got to be somewhere with a stable connection. I'm running a trace on the IP, but he's using a VPN. Still, he's slipped up; there's a timestamp embedded in the metadata. Local time, he's somewhere in London, East side, maybe Docklands? Come on, where are you, you fucking nutter!"

Cole grinds out, as the hacker's voice returns, urgent now.

"Got it, I'm pushing the coordinates to your phone. I've got a partial address. Get the police there, now!"

Cole grabs his phone, already dialling.

"This is Cole Benedict. I'm calling in a favour, former badge number 1476. I need an armed response team to..."

He rattles off the address, his voice steady, authoritative, and firm.

"Suspect is armed and extremely dangerous, hostage situation. Stream is live on the dark web as we speak; we need to move quickly; this is life or death. Ok...good...thank you...I owe you, Phelps...I know, add it to my tab, mate."

Cole says with a smirk, but I'm already at the door, grabbing my jacket.

"I'm coming with you."

Cole doesn't argue; he just nods, his eyes never leaving the screen. The hacker's voice is softer now, almost apologetic.

"I'll keep the feed open. If anything changes at all, I'll call."

As we rush from the room, the red quill symbol burned into my retinas. The chat scrolls by, a blur of usernames and emojis, the world watching as our story unfolds in real time. I'm in one of the world's biggest rock bands, I'm used to the attention, but I've never felt more exposed. I close my eyes, praying to whoever is listening with everything I've got, that this chapter will end with a heroic rescue and not another tragedy.

***

The world narrows to the pounding of my heart and the blur of streetlights as Cole and I tear through the Kent countryside and into the city. Rolling green hills zip past and soon merge into a grey concrete jungle. Every red light is a personal obstacle; every second wasted is a second longer that Zeppelin is in danger. *Hold on, sweetheart, I'm coming*. Cole's knuckles are white on the steering wheel, his jaw set, dark eyes flicking between the sat nav and the phone, where the hacker's voice mutters updates in our ears through the car speakers.

"We're close."

Cole says, voice clipped. His profile was sharp and stoic in the light of the streetlamps.

"The Docklands is just up ahead; armed response is two minutes out."

Cole glances at his watch and taps the steering wheel impatiently, as we hit another fucking red light. *FUUUCCKK!*

"Not fucking fast enough!"

I grit out, my hands shaking, as I drag one hand through my hair. The black Range Rover screeches to a halt outside a derelict warehouse, the kind of place that you see in the final shoot-out in those British gangster movies. Blue lights flicker in the distance, backup, but still too far away. Cole's already out of the car, moving low, fast, and stealthily, and I'm right behind him, pure adrenaline burning away the fear. He pulls a Revolver from his back pocket, and I cock my eyebrow in surprise at him. He flashes me a wink as he loads the bullets into the chamber. He points it and takes off the safety.

"Stay behind me, Jax, and for fucks sake, do what I say, no heroics, got me?"

He states matter-of-factly, and I nod. The warehouse door is ajar. Inside, the glow of light spills across the concrete floor, and the echo of a man's voice, Thorne's voice, carries through the room. I hear Zeppelin's name, the scrape of a chair, a muffled cry.

"Get the fuck away from her!"

Thorne turns; the red demon mask twisted into a grotesque grin. For a heartbeat, he just stands there, the phone still streaming, the world watching. Then he lunges, a machete flashing in his hand. Cole fires first, a warning shot that ricochets off the metal table, sending

Thorne stumbling back. I cross the distance in three strides, my only thought to get between him and Zeppelin. She's on the floor, a pool of crimson surrounding her, blood in her hair, her wrists bound, and she's unconscious.

"FUCK! SHE'S UNCONSCIOUS! SOMEONE CALL A FUCKING AMBULANCE"

I scream as I desperately try to undo her restraints with shaky hands. There's so much blood, and I'm instantly transported back to that fateful day in Las Vegas. Ruby's beautiful, ethereal face flashes to the forefront of my mind, and a tear rolls down my cheek at the memory. Her smile flickers across my mind, soft, a little mischievous, and then it's gone, replaced by the moment everything collapsed. The chaos, the blood, and the sound of incessant gunshots echoed around me. The memory hits me like a sucker punch to the gut. I drag myself back into the present, forcing the air into my lungs. *Come on, Chase, fucking focus! Now is not the time to dwell on the past, Zeppelin needs you, dickhead!*

Thorne swings the machete, wild and desperate. I duck, the blade whistling past my ear, and slam into him with everything I have. We crash to the ground, the machete clattering across the floor, the sound loud and setting my teeth on edge. He's strong, but I'm stronger, fuelled by pure fury that he dared to lay his hands on my Zeppelin. I drive my fist into his jaw, once, twice, three times, and I can't seem to stop myself, until he goes limp beneath me. His face a mess of blood, Cole gets down on his haunches at Zeppelin's side, cutting the straps, murmuring reassurances to her. The police flood in, shouting commands, guns drawn.

"Armed police!"

The voice booms, followed by heavy footsteps pounding across the concrete and into the room. A group of armed police officers in full uniforms and bullet-proof vests, and I recognise the two officers who were investigating Rian's murder, Detective Maddox and Detective Fellows. Someone drags Thorne up off the floor.

"Thorne Mercer, you're under arrest..."

He's cuffed and bleeding, his bloody and battered face twisted with hate and something like regret. I drop to my knees beside Zeppelin, gathering her into my arms. She's still unconscious, but I can feel her steady heartbeat beneath my touch. *Thank God she's breathing.* I let out a sigh of relief as I press my forehead to hers, tears burning in my eyes.

"I've got you."

I whisper, repeatedly, as if saying it enough times will make it believable.

"You're safe, it's over, I've got you, sweetheart. I'm here."

Outside, the world erupts in sirens, shouts, and chaos, but in this moment, there's only us, the two of us, battered but unbroken, the nightmare finally ending. I hold her tight, vowing that no one will ever hurt her again. *Not while I'm still breathing.*Top of FormBottom of Form

62

Jax

The world outside the warehouse is a blur of blue lights, shouting voices, and the constant flash of the paparazzi's lens. I don't even register their presence, and I don't let go of Zeppelin's hand, not even as the paramedics swarm around us, their voices a jumble of urgent instructions. She's barely conscious, her skin cold and clammy, blood matting her hair and streaking her face. Cole stands nearby, jaw clenched, his cane forgotten, as he has a whispered conversation with Detective Maddox and Detective Fellows. The Red Quill, Thorne is dragged away in cuffs, his face twisted with something between rage and satisfaction. I want to go after him, to make him pay for every bruise, every tear, every nightmare he's given Zeppelin. But I can't leave her, she needs me more.

The ambulance doors slam shut behind us. I sit beside her, gripping her hand as the paramedics work, their movements efficient but gentle. One of them, a woman with kind eyes, who introduces herself as Natalie, checks Zeppelin's pulse and flashes me a reassuring look. She pushes her glasses up the bridge of her nose and smiles softly.

"She's going to need you to be strong for her now."

I nod, swallowing the lump in my throat. I brush a strand of hair from Zeppelin's forehead, my thumb lingering on her cheek.

"I'm here, sweetheart. I'm not going anywhere."

The hospital is a blur of stark white corridors, and the stench of antiseptic causes my nostrils to burn. They wheel her away for scans and stitches, and I'm left pacing the waiting room, my hands shaking, my mind replaying every second of the rescue. Cole joins me, his face drawn and tired.

"She's safe now."

He says quietly.

"You did well, Jax."

I shake my head, trying desperately to quell the tears I can feel burning behind my eyes.

"It wasn't good enough, we should have got there sooner, I should have..."

I trail off, and Cole interrupts me from continuing.

"Stop, stop torturing yourself, mate."

Cole interrupts, his voice firm.

"We saved her life; that should be what matters."

I nod, but the guilt lingers, heavy and suffocating.

***

It feels like hours pass, and the doctors finally let me see her. She's pale, heavily bandaged, with a drip in her arm, but her silver eyes flutter open as I sit beside her, and relief floods through me.

"Hey."

I whisper, taking her hand in mine, and she tries to smile, but her lips tremble.

"Is it really over?"

Her voice is barely audible, and I nod, brushing a tear away from her cheek with the pad of my thumb.

"It's over, sweetheart. He can't hurt you anymore, I promise."

She closes her eyes, a single tear slipping down her face.

"I was terrified, Jax. I thought I'd never see you and Thea again."

I lean in, pressing my forehead to hers.

"You're safe, I'm here, we're going to get through this, together. I'll never let anyone lay a fucking finger on you ever again!"

I say through gritted teeth, almost feeling angry at myself that I let this happen again to a woman I loved with everything in me. I would never let someone I loved be swallowed by chaos while I stood there helpless. Her trembling hand finds mine, and the contact almost undoes me. She's shaking, but she's alive. *She's here and that's all that matters.*

63

Zeppelin

I wish I could sleep the way I slept as a child. Soundly, through the night and dreaming of Gods, monsters, Princes and Princesses. Back then, sleep was easy. No lists running through my head, no alarms waiting to drag me back to reality, and no nightmares of being kidnapped by psychopaths. Just dreams that felt real and endless. Where Gods argued over kingdoms, monsters who lurked in the shadows, and Princes riding in on a white horse to save the day. I didn't worry about tomorrow because I barely knew what tomorrow meant back then. I just closed my eyes and drifted like it was the simplest thing in the world.

Now, it feels like I'm carrying the weight of every tomorrow before it even gets here. My mind won't stop, plans, regrets, what ifs, and the threat of danger prowling in the background waiting to pounce when I least expect it. I miss that quiet magic, the way the night used to feel safe, like a secret place where anything was possible, and it was so full of wonder. I would fall asleep without trying and wake up without thinking, ready to chase the day like it was an adventure waiting for me. Sleep used to be a precious gift, and now it feels like a battle. All I want is one night where I can close my eyes and dream as I used to, of Gods, monsters, and kingdoms that only exist when the world goes quiet.

I had been out of the hospital for a week, with a dull throb in my head and the way my ribs protested every time I breathed too deeply. The doctors called it healing and instructed me to rest, as if rest were something I could choose. I moved carefully, each step reminding me of the impact, the ground rushing up to meet me, the maniacal look in Thorne's eyes as if my pain gave him some sort of twisted pleasure, and the moment everything went black.

Jax had been the attentive, gentle, and loving man that he always was, but I could see it in his eyes that he blamed himself. *How could he not?* He watched the woman he was going to marry, the mother of his child, bleeding out on the floor of a wedding chapel in Las Vegas. I was another woman he could lose, and that thought terrified him. I saw it in the way he kissed me on the forehead as he left the house this morning. He had gone with the remaining two members of Rancid Vengeance to do a range of radio and TV interviews to promote the new album. They all poured their hearts and souls into this album; it should have been a celebration, but tragedy always lurked like an invisible spectre.

I lowered myself onto the sofa, wincing as my ribs complained again. I wasn't afraid of the pain. I was afraid of the quiet because in the quiet, the memories crept back in, but I closed my eyes anyway. For a moment, just a moment, I let myself drift. I let myself imagine those old dreams from when I was a child. The ones with impossible landscapes and ancient magic, where I wasn't broken, or haunted by the past and my present. Where I wasn't waking up gasping for air, heart racing, convinced I was still there. But the dream didn't come, it never does. I opened my eyes and forced myself upright, one hand braced against the sofa.

One week out of the hospital, one step back into the world, and whether I was ready or not, the next chapter was waiting, even if it hadn't been written yet. It was full of possibilities, full of hope, and I allowed myself to believe that we could finally have our happy ending, and for the first time in a long time, that didn't terrify me.

***

I had set my laptop up on the comfortable L-shaped sofa in the living room. I felt like I was ready to start writing again. It had been so long since I immersed myself in fiction that I had missed the feeling of plotting characters, new stories, and the possibility of a happy ever after. I push my black rimmed glasses further up the bridge of my nose and shift myself underneath my blanket that was made up of all the covers of my books, which my Nana had lovingly made for me as a celebration of becoming a New York Times bestseller. Ever since Jax had returned home from his interviews, he had started to hover. Not smothering, not overbearing, just *there*, constantly. He sat across from me now, elbows on his knees, fingers laced so tightly his knuckles were white. His brown eyes tracked every shift I made, every wince I tried to hide.

"You don't have to look at me like that."

I finally say, cocking my head to the side, regarding him intently. His jaw tightened, and his eyes narrowed.

"Like what?"

His voice is gruff.

"Like I'm going to disappear if you blink."

I say with a chuckle, trying to make light of the situation, but his expression doesn't change, and he doesn't deny it. He just exhales, slow and shaky, as he scrubs a hand over his three-day-old stubble.

"I left you; I walked out that door and..."

The guilt that mars his features made my stomach twist.

"I told you to, you were doing your job! Living your life just like normal, you didn't cause this. You didn't ask Thorne to kidnap me."

He shudders at the mention of his name, and his gaze shifts to mine, raw and unguarded.

"I should've protected you better."

His eyes glaze over, and I take his hand in mine, stroking his knuckles with my thumb reassuringly.

"You *do* protect me, every day by just being there, by being you."

He swallows hard, eyes dropping to where our hands are connected.

"I just... I can't lose someone else I love; I won't survive it this time. I won't, it would break me the way it broke Sam when he thought he lost Peyton."

The weight of his words hit me with a force that was unexpected, and my chest tightened. I shook my head and reached up to cup his face in my hand.

"Listen to me, you're not going to lose me."

I whisper.

"I'm right here."

I place his hand on my heart, and he moves closer to me, as if somehow feeling my heartbeat under his palm anchored him. He leans forward, resting his forehead against mine, breathing me in like he needed proof I was real. We stayed like that for long moments, the world outside moving on without us.

64

Zeppelin

I had spent the day writing and getting lost in fictional worlds. It distracted me from reality, and for the first time in a week, I had a smile on my face. Jax had ordered my favourite fish, chips and curry sauce. He had put Thea to bed, and we were curled up on the sofa with my feet resting in his lap. He pauses the movie we were watching on the TV and turns to me.

"So, you never did tell me what the deal was with you and Thorne."

He asks, and I flinch violently at the mention of his name. I shake my head and shift my gaze down to the blanket covering us.

"Jax, don't."

He pauses for a moment.

"If we're going to spend the rest of our lives together, we need to tell each other everything, no more secrets, Zeppelin. We need to start being more honest with each other. I feel like I hardly know anything about you, about Thorne, about Abel. You dated a rock star before me, for fucks sake, and I didn't know that part of you existed!"

His words weren't an accusation; they were a plea, a chink in his armour. A man terrified of losing the woman he loved because he didn't know all the ghosts I carried with me daily. My throat tightens. I'd spent so long burying the past that digging it up felt like opening old wounds. But he deserved to know the ugly truth, not the polished version, the real one. I take a deep, slow breath, my ribs protesting.

"You want the full story, then you'll get everything."

My voice is soft but steady, as his eyes soften, but he doesn't speak. He just nods once, steady and patient.

"I didn't tell you about Thorne because...he was the first person who made me feel seen. Not loved, not cherished, just...noticed. At the time, that felt like enough."

I swallow the memory from the day we met in the book shop.

"He wasn't a bad man; he just wasn't my man. He was my friend, but he wanted more than that. I didn't realise that until it was over. He was very intelligent, very observant. He saw things I didn't, for the first time in my life, someone understood who I was and what I was trying to say without having to say it out loud."

Jax's thumb brushes my skin in a reassuring gesture, encouraging me to continue.

"Rian never understood my writing, not really; he just thought it was an escape from reality, and in a way, it was. Thorne and I bonded over our love of the written word. We would sit for hours writing, sometimes in silence, sometimes discussing chapters or particular storylines we were struggling with. It was refreshing to talk to someone about something other than celebrity gossip and my love life, or lack thereof at the time."

I smile.

"We both approached different publishers to try and pitch our books. We wrote very different genres, and I guess I got lucky. He didn't, and he was so disappointed that it was difficult for me to carry on seeing him after that. I felt so guilty that I got picked up when he was so hungry for it, for the recognition, for the chance to have other people read his work. I couldn't bear the way he looked at me, so I distanced myself from him, and I never saw him again, until that night."

I blinked a few times, desperately trying to push the memories of Thorne to the back of my mind. I pause for a few moments and take a few more steadying breaths before continuing.

"Abel was different; he was chaos wrapped in charm. The kind of person who could make you feel like the centre of the universe one minute and completely invisible the next. I stayed way longer than I should have. I thought I could fix him. I thought loving someone meant carrying their storms." My voice wavered.

"I was wrong. The fame swallowed him whole and spat him back out. Somehow, along the way, he became a completely different person. He was charming one minute, and the next minute, he would degrade me, make me feel inferior, and that night on the yacht, when I caught him with his pants around his ankles with some other woman giving him what I should have been. That was the final nail in the coffin for me. I knew that it was over, four years over just like that."

Jax's jaw tightened, but he stayed silent, letting me speak.

"I didn't tell you about any of it because I didn't want you to look at me differently. I didn't want you to think I was carrying baggage that would weigh you down. I didn't want you to see the absolute fucking disaster I used to be."

I lifted his hand from my chest and pressed it to my cheek.

"But you're right, if we're going to build a life together, you deserve the truth. All of it, even the parts that scare me."

His eyes soften.

"I'm not hiding anymore, Jax."

I whisper.

"Not from you, not anymore."

He exhales and pulls me into his arms, holding me like he finally understood the weight of everything I'd been carrying. For the first time, the past didn't feel like a weight; it felt like a story we could finally end together.

65

Jax

After what Zeppelin had endured at the hands of Thorne Mercer, our friends rally around us: Cole, Lucas, Brody, my mum and dad, and my sisters. They bring food, flowers, and quiet support, filling the house with warmth and laughter, trying to chase away the shadows. The scars remain, Zeppelin flinches at sudden noises, her eyes haunted by memories she can't escape even in slumber. I do my best to be strong for her, but some nights, when she finally falls asleep, I sit in the darkness, my own hands shaking, the weight of what almost happened crushing me. We talk frequently, picking through the wreckage of what Thorne did to us. We see a therapist, together and separately, learning how to breathe again, how to trust that the world can be safe. It's not easy; some days are better than others, but we keep going, one step at a time, hand in hand, together always.

Tonight, after everyone leaves, Zeppelin curls into my side on the sofa. Her head rests on my chest, and I run my fingers through her hair, slow and steady, grounding myself in the simple fact that she's here, alive, healing, mine. She tilts her face up toward me, silver eyes tired, but warm. A long silence stretches between us, and suddenly, the words that have been sitting heavy in my chest for months rise to the surface, clear and certain.

"Zeppelin."

I say softly.

"Hmmm."

She hums and looks up, cocking her perfectly plucked eyebrows. I take her hand, threading our fingers together, the sparkle of her engagement ring glinting in the soft light. I place a gentle kiss on her ring.

"If we've learned anything from all of this,"

My voice is low, but steady.

"Is that life is too fucking short to wait for the perfect moment."

Her breath catches, and I shift, turning fully toward her, my thumb brushing over her knuckles.

"We've survived hell together, and I don't want another day to go by without you knowing exactly how I feel."

Her eyes are glossy, and I swallow hard, emotion tightening my throat.

"We should get married, Zeppelin."

The words hang in the air, simple, honest, and raw. Her lips part, a soft gasp escaping, and for the first time in a long time, the future doesn't feel so scary.

"Say something."

A beaming grin spreads across her face, and she leans in, kissing me, slow, sensual, passionately. The kiss felt full of every emotion she couldn't find the words for. I held her close, careful of her healing ribs, but unable to stop myself from pulling her into me, as if I couldn't get close enough to her. She pulls back, eyes locking onto mine, and she whispers.

"Yes."

I swear my fucking heart stops.

"Yes?"

I ask, barely breathing, and she nods, tears rolling down her cheeks.

"Yes, Jax, let's get married."

I let out a shaky laugh and wrap her in my arms, burying my face in her hair, as she clings to me. In that moment, I knew exactly what I wanted: to be her husband. I didn't want to waste any more time. I didn't want to wait. I wanted to make it official. I wanted her to be Mrs. Zeppelin Jade Chase, and I was willing to do whatever it took to make that happen.

66

Zeppelin

Six Months Later

After I agreed to marry Jax, we didn't want to wait a moment longer, but we decided together to delay it until Sam was out of rehab. It didn't feel right to either of us to celebrate without him. He was, and always had been, an integral part of Rancid Vengeance and of our love story. We had decided to get married on the beach in the Maldives, the place where our love story solidified. We are staying in Jax's large eight-bedroom villa, which was literally paradise, and I couldn't think of a more perfect place to marry the man I was going to spend the rest of my life with. The ocean stretched out in endless shades of blue, the kind that made you believe in second chances, the kind that made you believe that forever was within touching distance.

After a week of preparations and putting our six months of wedding planning into practice, we flew our close friends and family on Air Vengeance so they could witness our marriage. They all made the twenty-minute boat journey to where the wedding would take place. We both stood on the villa's private jetty, the sun high and fierce. The water lapped and glistened like blue diamonds. The large boat approaches, and the grip Jax has on my hand tightens. My breath catches when I see Sam, leaner, but still muscular and covered in tattoos, sunglasses covering his eyes. His raven black hair is shorter, and his skin is tanned. He's holding Peyton's hand as if he's afraid she's going to disappear. The boat comes to a stop, and when he steps onto the jetty, he is wearing blue shorts with black palm trees, black flip-flops, and a white V-neck t-shirt that clings to his muscles. Jax doesn't hesitate, as he approaches him and pulls Sam into a fierce hug, arms wrapped tightly around him. It was the kind of embrace that said everything that words couldn't. Sam hugs him back just as fiercely, shoulders shaking, and I feel my own throat tighten. It was a bittersweet reunion, and it made my heart hurt for both. They hug for long moments as the rest of the wedding party steps off the boat. Peyton who is holding Thea in her arms, Freddie, Zachary, Brody, Raleigh, Bowie, Azalea, Lucas, Nick Slade, Noa Vega, Jamie-Leigh, Jude, Shay, Skye, Cole, Amy, Addison, my Nana and Pops, Danny, Gorgeous George, M.J, and the rest of the bands entourage all make their way down the jetty and into the house. Sam pulls away from Jax's embrace and turns to me.

"Zeppelin."

He rasps, and he flashes me his famous dimpled grin. I throw my arms around him, holding him as tightly as I dare, and he lifts me off the ground.

"I'm so fucking happy for you both, sweetheart!"

I giggle girlishly, and he smells like Joop and something new, something hopeful. Jax observes our exchange as Sam sets me down on my feet and lets go of me. Jax places his hand on the small of my back, and when their eyes lock, it is as if two men who had been through the same storm but had different ways of surviving it. Sam swallows hard before he speaks, his emerald eyes blazing with sincerity.

"Thank you for waiting."

His voice is gruff.

"For not leaving me behind."

The emotion in his voice makes my heart hurt for him. He's missed out on six months with his family; I couldn't imagine what that would be like.

"We're family, family doesn't get left behind. We weather the storm, together."

Jax replied.

"Always."

With those words, I felt the knot in my stomach loosen, and our happy ever after could finally begin.

***

After a few short days of catching up and the boys reuniting, today is our wedding day. The sun was blazing through the patio doors of our suite. The gentle breeze makes the sheer curtains billow around us. My Nana Pru is helping me get into my wedding dress in the full-length mirror. Her weathered face was wet from crying. She dabs at her face with her handkerchief.

"I'm sorry, sweetheart, I'm just so, so proud of how far you've come! You look so much like your mother. You're no longer a little girl, you're a woman, and you look radiant! That rockstar doesn't know how lucky he is to have found you!"

Nana dabbed at her cheeks again, smiling through the tears, as she fussed with the last pin at the back of my dress. My dress was a flowy A-line style dress, with a fitted bodice that complemented my curves and flared into a soft, airy skirt. My hair had been stripped back to my original blonde, and my long pixie cut had been styled into soft, beachy waves courtesy of Danny Debonair. The white silk of my dress felt impossibly light against my skin, and the mirror reflected a version of me I hadn't recognised in a long time, soft around the edges, lighter than I had ever been. Nana sniffed, wiped her nose with the corner of her handkerchief, and gave me a little, fierce nod.

"I need you to promise me he'll keep you safe."

She said, voice wobbling but steady with that stubborn pride only grandmothers have.

"He will, Nana."

I whispered with a soft smile as she took my hands in hers.

"Now go and get your rockstar, sweetheart."

The walk down to the beach felt like stepping into a dream. The villa's staff have set up a simple driftwood arch threaded with frangipani and jasmine. My grandad Jimmy, who is wearing cream linen trousers, a matching cream shirt, and taupe moccasins. He smiles softly and offers me his arm.

"You look like a vision, sweetheart."

He says shakily, desperately trying to quell the tears, as I look up at him and smile softly.

"Don't you bloody dare set me off, Pops!"

I chastise playfully, and he offers me a watery grin, saluting me with his other hand. Thea, wearing a pale blue bridesmaid's dress and her dark hair styled into matching tousled waves, walks ahead of us, scattering white petals down the aisle and along the sand. The soft strains of *Forever After All by Luke Combs* play as Pops walks me down the aisle towards my handsome groom. The sight of him renders me speechless, and it takes everything I have not to burst into tears. He looks gorgeous wearing a white shirt with three buttons open, revealing his striking tattoos and white linen shorts. His blonde hair is perfectly styled into soft spikes, as he stands barefoot on the soft white sand.

Our small circle of friends and family, Cole, Lucas, Brody, Peyton, Freddie, Zach, Raleigh, Bowie, and Azalea. Sam is standing at Jax's side, wearing a white shirt open at the collar and white linen shorts. Marlowe Newbolt, who unequivocally agreed to marry us, was ordained online to officiate Sam and Peyton's wedding and Brody and Raleigh's wedding. He is wearing a clerical collar, a short-sleeved black shirt, and sunglasses. He looks ever the rock star and flashes me a wink. Grandad hands me off to Jax, and his brown eyes are fixed on me the way he always looks at me when he thinks I'm not looking. When I reach him, he takes my hands in his, as Sam squeezes my shoulder, a quick, private smile that says everything about second chances and loyalty. Nana Pru found a spot near the front alongside my Pops and dabs at her face again, beaming, as she reaches for grandad's hand. He takes it without hesitation.

"God, could you look any more beautiful?"

Jax leans in to whisper in my ear, and I smile at his words.

"Just for you, rock star."

I reply, offering him a cheeky wink in return. Marlowe clears his throat and begins to speak.

"Friends, family, and everyone in between, we are gathered here today to celebrate the marriage of Jackson and Zeppelin. Can you believe it? This is my third Rancid Vengeance wedding!"

Marlowe looks between the two of us, then out at the guests.

"Does anyone object to this marriage? Speak now or forever hold your peace."

He asks, and he is met with silence for a few agonising moments, as he breaks out into a wry grin.

"Thank God! That's always the awkward part!"

Everyone laughs at his humour as Jax clears his throat.

"I take you, Zeppelin Jade Williams, to be my lawful wedded wife. To have and hold from this day forward. The way we met was unconventional, but I fell in love with your words before I even saw your face. I promise to be your muse, I promise to be there to catch you if you should stumble, carry you over every threshold, and fall in love with you every day. I can't imagine sharing this adventure with anyone else but you. I know now that what we have transcends and is a much deeper soul connection. You taught me how to fight for something real, and I'm truly in awe of your strength. We've faced so many obstacles, but we've come out the other end stronger, and I couldn't love you more. I promise to be your loudest cheerleader and to keep choosing you even on the days when the world feels heavy."

My eyes glaze over at his words, and I swallow back the golf ball-sized lump in my throat. Silently chanting *'I will not cry, I will not cry.'* Thea steps forward with dark, mischievous eyes and an infectious grin, presenting the rings on a pale blue velvet cushion. Jax takes the ring off the cushion and kisses Thea's cheek.

"Daddy!"

She chastises him with a theatrical eye roll, and the audience starts laughing. Jax places the platinum shadow band with three large diamonds in the centre, designed to fit around my engagement ring,

Drawing a deep breath, I steal a few precious moments to centre myself before I begin to speak.

“I take you, Jackson James Chase, to be my lawful wedded husband, to have and to hold from this day forward. I feel overwhelmingly lucky and proud to be standing beside you today. Thank you for accepting me for all that I am, thank you for always supporting and loving me unconditionally. I know I haven't always made it easy. I was drawn to you from the very first day you truly saw me. You understand me, accept me, in a way no one else has, in a way that I believe no one else can. I swear to you that I will continue to dedicate all the days of my life to filling our days with laughter and reverence. I will celebrate your spirit and all your accomplishments, work to inspire you, and be here to remind you of your strength and talent. You are my partner, my muse, my other half, and I will love you until the day I die.”

Tears pooled in my eyes as I finished speaking, my gaze locked on his, brown on silver. His eyes welled up, glistening with unshed tears, as Thea moved closer, holding out Jax's ring. I carefully took the ring from the cushion, offering her a reassuring wink. I shakily place his simple, platinum wedding band on his finger.

"I love you, so, so much.”

Marlowe says with a grin, as Jax wraps me in his arms and crushes his lips to mine in a white-hot, molten kiss, which steals the breath from my lungs. The air filled with ecstatic cheers and applause, yet my gaze was locked onto Jax. He frames my face with his hands, catching my tears as I let them fall freely down my cheeks. For a few precious moments, the world narrows to just us: my *handsome Jack, my husband.*

***

Somewhere behind us, music begins, an acoustic guitar at first, then the low thrum of speakers kicking in. The beat of *One Margarita by Luke Bryan* fills the air. The villa staff begins guiding everyone down the beach toward the reception area, long wooden tables set beneath lanterns and fairy lights strung between palm trees, white and pale blue linen fluttering in the breeze. Barefoot dancing is already starting, and champagne is already flowing. Someone pops a bottle, and it sprays into the air like fireworks; I spin around, still clutching Jax's hand like a lifeline, to see Brody wiggling his split tongue. He approaches me and looks from me to Jax.

"Come on, Mrs. Chase, first dance?"

He asks, and I take his hand, as he spins me around on the sand to the beat of the music.

"You look like you're about shit yourself, babe!"

Brody says, his tone amused, and I laugh at his statement.

"I'm just...overwhelmed, that's all!"

I say on a soft chuckle, my gaze flicking instinctively towards Jax. He's standing exactly where I left him, hands in his pockets, watching me with that unreadable expression that always makes my pulse quicken. When our eyes meet, something in his softens, enough to make my chest tighten. Brody spins me around again, moving his hips from side to side and pulling me back towards him.

"He's going to fucking burst a blood vessel if I don't give you back!"

He laughs, his eyes dancing with mischief.

"You started this!"

I remind him.

"Yeah, well, I didn't expect him to look like he wants to hit you over the head and drag you back to his sex cave!"

My mouth drops open at his words, and I feel heat crawling up my neck.

"Brody!"

I laugh.

"What?"

He laughs, spinning me again, slower this time.

"I'm just saying, dude is pussy whipped!"

Brody jokes.

"He's not the only one."

As I turn to see Raleigh regarding us intently. The song shifts, mellowing into something slower as I hear "Ordinary" *by Alex Warren*. Brody's hands fall away as he steps back with an elaborate bow.

"Go get him, tiger!"

He says with a wink, jerking his chin toward Jax.

"Before he spontaneously fucking combusts!"

He's already moving, closing the distance between us with long, deliberate strides. When he reaches me, he doesn't say a word, his fingers sliding between mine like they were always meant to fit there.

"You having fun?"

Jax murmurs, voice low enough that only I can hear, and my breath catches.

"I am now."

I say, a hint of relief in my voice. His lips curve, not quite a smile, but close. He draws me in, one hand settling at my waist, and the rest of the beach fades away as he begins to sway with me, slow and sure. We were married, yet the future was still unwritten, but for the first time in a long time, it felt like something we could write together. *One imperfect, beautiful line at a time.*

67

Jax

I can't take my eyes off her, my wife. After all she's been through the past few months, she's still smiling, still radiant, still mine. I couldn't wipe the smile off my face as I watched her dancing with Peyton and Raleigh. Her silver eyes dancing with happiness, she looks so carefree and so fucking beautiful. I stand there observing her for a few moments, with one hand tucked in the pocket of my white linen shorts and the other hand clutching a bottle of beer. I don't register his presence until I hear his husky timbre.

"We're all lucky motherfuckers."

He states, standing next to me. He towers over me by a few inches, and six months in rehab looks like it has done him the world of good. His raven black hair is shorter, his jaw is sharper, and his emerald eyes have their old sparkle back. Six months, six fucking months since I last saw him. Six months since the night he collapsed on stage in front of thousands of Rancid Vengeance fans, six months since he stopped breathing, and I gave him CPR. Six months since we thought he was so far gone he was going to die. Six months since he looked at me like he hated me for being right. His skin isn't pale and sallow anymore, and there aren't dark circles under his eyes. He looks like someone scraped six layers of chaos off him, and just like that, six months collapse into six seconds. Every tour bus, every stupid inside joke, every three a.m. takeaway, every fight, every argument, every almost losing him, and my throat burns with unsaid words. He flashes me a dimpled, crooked smile, the one that he reserves for Peyton.

"You look good, man."

After six months, that's all I can manage. I'm overwhelmed, relieved, and so fucking glad to see him. He chuckles softly.

"Seriously, dude, is that all you've got after six months?"

An amused tone to his voice.

"I feel good...better...clearer."

He nods as he takes a long sip of his bottle of beer. There are a few precious moments of silence as I take him in.

"I'm so fucking sorry."

He says, finally, and I shake my head.

"You've got nothing to be sorry for, not really."

I admit, as he exhales a long and shaky breath. We both watch as our wives spin each other around on the sand, their giggles permeating the air and making everything feel lighter somehow.

"You don't get it; I almost ruined everything, and I dragged everyone into the fallout. You were all in the blast zone of Hurricane fucking Sam. I hate myself for putting you all through that, and I'll never be able to apologise enough for it."

His voice isn't angry, just filled with defeat, and he hangs his head in shame.

"You were drowning."

My voice is barely audible, and we stand there, shoulder to shoulder, the music drifting over us. Bruno Mars *I Just Might* booms out of the speakers as his gaze flicks to me.

"You look...lighter."

He speaks.

"Happier."

I follow his line of sight back to her. *My wife, Mrs. Chase.* Her hair catching the late sun, her silver eyes bright, her laugh carrying across the beach like a promise I never deserved but somehow got anyway.

"Yeah,"

I admit.

"I am."

He nods, swallowing hard.

"She looks good, better than the last time I saw her."

"She's getting there,"

I speak.

"We both are, there's a lot to catch up on, but that's a story for another time."

He nudges me with his elbow.

"You know...There were times when I didn't think I'd make it out of rehab. The shit in my head was holding me hostage, the guilt, finally admitting to myself that I was drowning, and I needed help. But standing here with you? Watching all of this? Your fucking wedding, man."

His voice cracks just a little.

"Feels like maybe I've got a second chance...or third, or fourth."

We both laugh, and the song changes into Let's Take a Drive by Christian Kane. My wife turns, searching the crowd, and when her eyes land on me, her whole face lights up like I'm the only thing she sees. Sam chuckles.

"Go on."

He murmurs.

"She's waiting."

I hesitate, glancing at him.

"You sure?"

He lifts his beer in a mock toast and nods.

"I'm exactly where I need to be, man, we'll catch up later."

I clap a hand on his shoulder, and then I walk toward her, toward the life we're rebuilding, step by step.

Epilogue

Zeppelin

The pages of our story are still blank, waiting for us to write the next chapter. We find magic in the moments and courage in the stories yet to be written.

Today is our final day in the Maldives, and the past three weeks have been perfect. I married the love of my life and became Mrs. Zeppelin Jade Chase. I wake to the sound of waves lapping and the sheer curtains billowing in the early morning breeze. Jax's thick, tattooed arm is heavy across my waist. Solid, possessive, safe, my husband. It still doesn't feel real. I keep thinking any moment I'm going to wake up from this dream, or I'm going to be sitting at my desk, and I'm going to be writing a plot for my new book.

I trace the line of his wedding band with my thumb, where his hand rests on my stomach. I slip out of bed carefully, pulling on Jax's discarded t-shirt. It smells of him, of Diesel Only the Brave, and something uniquely Jackson Chase. I pad barefoot across the cool wooden floor and into the kitchen. But when I reach for the coffee, the smell hits me wrong, too strong, too bitter, and my stomach roils violently. I wrinkle my nose. That's strange. A wave of nausea rolls through me so suddenly that I have to grip the counter to steady myself. My heart starts to beat faster, because there's a date in my head. One I've been subconsciously ignoring since we got here. *No, it can't be, don't be fucking stupid. We had our chance, and Thorne took it away from us. There's no chance it could happen again, is there?* But my feet are already moving from the kitchen and into the bathroom, digging through my wash bag. I find the emergency pregnancy test I packed weeks ago and forgot about, just in case, or was it paranoia? The bathroom feels too small suddenly, and I feel a sheen of sweat pool at the base of my spine. I tear the packet and follow the instructions with shaking fingers, my breath held so tight my chest hurts. I set it on the counter, three minutes, that's all it takes for our lives to change forever. I stare at the floor tiles like they might give me the answers I desperately sought, my pulse loud in my ears. A soft knock at the door interrupts my thoughts as I hear Jax's voice.

"Love?"

His voice is thick with sleep.

"Are you ok in there?"

He asks, his tone full of concern.

"Yeah."

I practically squeak. *Come on, you need to be a little more fucking convincing than that.* He notices everything; he always has. He's too observant, too good at reading people, too good at reading me.

"You ok?"

He asks again.

"Fine! Just brushing my teeth! I'll be out in a sec."

There is a slight pause, as my eyes drift back to the counter. My heartbeat pulses in my throat. I steal a look, and my world starts to tilt off its axis. Two lines, not faint, unmistakable. *Pregnant.* For a second, everything goes completely silent. I press my hand to my stomach automatically, as if something might already be there. A tiny, terrified laugh escapes me.

"Oh, my fucking God."

I whisper, a soft knock again.

"Hey."

Jax says, gentler now.

"You're worrying me, sweetheart. Open the door, please."

I open the door; he's standing there barefoot and bare-chested. I swallow at the sight of him, his hair perfectly sleep mussed—my *husband.*

"Hey."

He repeats, scanning my face.

"You look like you've seen a ghost."

He moves closer to me.

"I..."

My voice breaks, and instant panic floods his eyes.

"What's wrong? Are you sick? Do we need to get a doctor..."

I shake my head and hold the test out to him, and he stares at it. A frown line jumped between his eyebrows. He looks at me, back at the test, and back at me.

"Is that? Are we..."

I nod, tears already spilling.

"Yeah."

I slap my hands over my mouth.

"Holy fucking shit!"

He breathes, his hands come up to his face, then into his hair, then he laughs in disbelief.

"Are you serious? Are you serious right now?"

His eyes widen, and he grins a full megawatt grin.

"I think so."

I sob. He presses his forehead to mine, both of us crying now and laughing like idiots.

"We're having a baby."

He whispers, and he sinks to his knees on the cold marble floor and presses his ear to my stomach like he expects to hear something immediately. He wraps his arms around my waist.

"Hey, it's your daddy here. I already love you more than literally anything! Your big sister is going to be so excited!"

I bury my fingers in his hair and cry into the quiet morning while the ocean hums outside and the sun climbs higher. The pages aren't blank anymore, there's ink now, messy, unexpected, but so fucking perfect. The sudden realisation hits me like a ten-tonne truck; there would be no more little white lies or dark truths. Our happy ever after and whatever comes next, we'll write it together.

---

www.ingramcontent.com/pod-product-compliance
Lightning Source LLC
LaVergne TN
LVHW050921080826
845145LV00001B/157